AGAINST ALL ENEMIES

Other Books by Richard Herman

Power Curve
Iron Gate
Dark Wing
Call to Duty
Firebreak
Force of Eagles
The Warbirds

AGAINST ALL ENEMIES

A NOVEL

Richard Herman

AVON BOOKS NEW YORK

This is a work of fiction. Names, characters, places and incidents either are the product of the author's imagination or are used fictitiously. Any resemblance to actual events, locales, organizations, or persons, living or dead, is entirely coincidental and beyond the intent of either the author or the publisher.

AVON BOOKS, INC.
1350 Avenue of the Americas
New York, New York 10019

Interior design by Kellan Peck
Visit our website at **http://www.AvonBooks.com**
ISBN: 0-380-97321-9

Library of Congress Cataloging in Publication Data:

Herman, Richard.
Against all enemies : a novel / Richard Herman.—1st ed.
p. cm.
I. Title.
PS3558.E684A73 1998 98-10954
813'.54—dc21 CIP

First Avon Books Printing: August 1998

Printed in the U.S.A.

FIRST EDITION

QPM 10 9 8 7 6 5 4 3 2 1

To the 32nd Tactical Fighter Squadron,
The Wolfhounds, The Queen's Own,
Who served at Camp New Amsterdam,
the Netherlands,
1954–1994

"Thou shalt not follow a multitude to do evil."
—Exodus 23:2

PROLOGUE

11:45 A.M., THURSDAY, MARCH 4,
SAN FRANCISCO

The hostess for the rooftop café at the San Francisco Shopping Emporium made her decision the moment Hank Sutherland got off the elevator. She would jump him to the head of the waiting list. There was something about Sutherland's boyish face, barely controlled sandy brown hair, and friendly hazel eyes that appealed to her. It was a simple decision made for the most human of reasons. Yet, it was to mean so much.

At forty years of age and five-feet-ten-inches tall, Henry Michael Sutherland was not an imposing man. Nor was he considered handsome. But women found him extremely attractive and men trusted him. He cultivated a slightly hunched-shouldered stance to enhance his image as a deputy district attorney and let an impeccably tailored dark suit hide his paunchy body.

"I'm waiting for a reporter," Sutherland told her. "Marcy Bangor from the *Sacramento Union,* short dark hair." He almost added "young, pretty, and ditzy" but thought better of it.

"I'll tell her you're here," the hostess said, pleased to be of a little more help. She led Sutherland to a corner niche against a side wall. He had barely sat down when Marcy Bangor joined him. She gave him a warm smile and pulled out a microcassette tape recorder and her digital camera.

"How is the case going?"

Sutherland considered his answer. Interviews with the press were always tricky. "I've never seen anything like it in an appeals court. It was crazy in there."

"The U.S. Ninth Circuit Court of Appeals," Marcy said, "is crazy by definition."

Sutherland nodded. He had appeared before the Ninth three times in the past defending cases he had successfully prosecuted. "Jonathan Meredith was there."

Jonathan Meredith was always news and Marcy became very interested. "Did he say anything? What was he doing? Any idea why he was there?"

Rather than talk about his suspicions, he shook his head. "The judges were afraid of him, the audience was packed, there were five bailiffs there, a lot of noise. It was weird and I kept wondering who was running the show." Their waitress, a pretty young college student from the University of California across the bay at Berkeley, came over and took their orders. She called him "sir" and, suddenly, he felt old.

Sutherland recounted his day in court. But Marcy wanted to hear about Meredith, not an appeals case involving a questionable roving telephone intercept that could get the conviction of four terrorist bombers overturned. "What do you make of Meredith?" she asked.

"Off the record," he said. Marcy gave an audible sigh and turned off her microcassette tape recorder. "He's a demagogue in the making, complete with a fanatical band of followers."

"You mean his First Brigade."

"And his Neighborhood Brigades," he replied, thinking of the next case on his docket. "Meredith already sees himself marching down Pennsylvania Avenue on inauguration day." He fell silent when the waitress returned, carrying a tray with their food.

What happened next would puzzle Sutherland for the rest of his life. The waitress just seemed to rise in the air and fly across the patio, two or three feet off the floor. The tray moved beside her as if it were in free fall. He wanted to say something witty or make a telling comment or tell Marcy to take a picture. But he sat there, dumbfounded by the sight. It seemed to take forever for the girl to blow up against the far wall.

Then the blast hit.

The sound roared over him and pounded him against the wall. He felt his back grind into the bricks as his feet came up over his head. He watched Marcy's miniskirt being blown off as he slipped down the wall into a sitting position. Another part of his mind told him it was all happening very quickly but that he was registering it in slow motion.

Then he tried to breathe. He couldn't.

The blast had knocked all breath out of him, and for a moment, he was on the edge of total panic. With a calm that surprised him, he placed a fist against his chest and performed a Heimlich maneuver. He sucked in the dust and soot that had saturated the air. He coughed out and breathed in. Marcy was slipping away from him as if she were on a slide. He reached out and grabbed her arm, pulling her to him as the floor fell away. He shook his head, trying to clear the cobwebs that were enfolding him in a gossamer haze. His vision cleared.

"Whaa," Marcy moaned. He quickly checked her for bleeding, and other than a few scratches and cuts from flying debris, she was fine. He tasted blood but an inner voice told him he was okay. He looked at his feet. They were hanging over the edge of a precipice, six stories down to the street. What had been the front half of the building had simply disappeared. He could feel the floor shake as it started to collapse underneath his weight. Without thinking, he scooped Marcy up in a fireman's carry and moved against the back wall. Marcy's camera was still clenched in her hand and one shoe was gone.

Now he was standing over the semiconscious waitress. "I'm okay," Marcy said. He bent over and lowered her to her feet. Smoke billowed up from the street below and washed back toward them. Marcy stood there, one shoe missing and her skirt gone, and snapped a picture. That simple act brought Sutherland into full consciousness.

The San Francisco Shopping Emporium had been bombed and the three of them were trapped on the slowly collapsing roof. He looked around. What had been a lovely rooftop café was now a grotesque slaughterhouse littered with shattered, twisted bodies. It was a scene from Hell, worse than any nightmare his subconscious could conjure from the depths of his primeval fears and obsessions. And he knew. They were alive only because the hostess had seated him in a sheltered table in a corner niche.

"We've got to get out of here," he said. The waitress groaned and he bent down. She had a heavy gash across her cheek and her right shoulder was pushed back and her arm twisted at an obscene angle. She had taken the blast full on and was lucky to be alive. He gently picked her up in his arms and she screamed in agony. "I'm sorry," he said. He looked around, trying to get his bearings. "Where are the stairs?" The girl's good hand pointed to the left before she passed out from the pain. Marcy pulled off the girl's shoes and slipped them on. She led the way and stepped carefully over the debris that littered what was left of the floor. He was vaguely aware of a misshapen ball painted with a man's features. He fought the bile that threatened to choke him when he realized it was a man's head.

Marcy led the way through an opening and found the stairwell. It was earthquake proof and still structurally intact. She opened the door and smoke billowed out. The blast had turned it into a chimney. She let the door slam shut. The sound of the floor giving way echoed over them. He kicked the door open. "Go!" he shouted. He held his breath and plunged into the smoke. Badly disoriented, he moved in a sideways motion, feeling his way down the stairs with his left foot. His lungs were bursting. Suddenly, he was clear of the smoke. When he turned and looked back, all he could see were Marcy's bare legs hanging from smoke. Again, he shook his head. He wasn't crazy. The blast had blown the stairs into a steep angle and she was climbing down after him, coughing and sputtering.

The sound of the collapsing roof drove them down the stairwell. The steps were increasingly twisted into bizarre shapes as they descended, and finally, they could go no further. They were standing on the edge of a pit. "Where are we?" Marcy asked.

"On the first floor, I think." He ducked as debris fell on him. The girl moaned. He gently laid her down and looked over the edge. "Yeah, I think that's the bottom. About fifteen feet below us."

Marcy did the sensible thing and screamed for help.

A teenage boy appeared out of the gloom and directed the beam of his flashlight upward. "I've got an injured woman here," Sutherland shouted. The boy yelled back acknowledgment and disappeared. After what seemed an eternity, he was back with two other men. More debris fell down the stairwell.

"We'll get you out of here," one of the newcomers shouted. Something about his voice was vaguely familiar. He held up his arms to take the girl. Sutherland told Marcy to grab the girl's feet while he lowered her over the edge. He used her clothes as handholds as he lowered her head first into the rescuer's waiting arms. Then he lowered Marcy over the edge by her hands. "We got her," the man yelled. Chunks of concrete started to fall and Sutherland jumped, slamming his head against the floor and knocking himself out.

PART ONE

MULTITUDES

1

5:50 P.M., THURSDAY, MARCH 4,
THE WHITE HOUSE, WASHINGTON, D.C.

Three men clustered around the TV in the President's private office in the west wing. The sound was turned low and the voice of the reporter at the scene was only a murmur. The grisly image on the screen said more than any words could describe. The President hit the remote control and turned off the sound. The silence was complete as the men continued to stare at the screen. "Do they have a casualty count yet?" the President finally asked.

Kyle Broderick, the chief of staff, picked up the phone and asked the same question. He didn't like the answer. Broderick was a young man, hard and street savvy, who delighted in using the power that went with being the President's chief of staff. "I want a hard number in the next five minutes or you're history." He punched off the connection and turned to the President. "Sorry, sir. Everyone seems asleep at the wheel." Almost immediately, the phone rang. Broderick picked it up and listened. He hung up without saying a word. "The initial count is over two hundred and rising fast," he told the President.

"You'll have to go there," the Vice President said to the President. He was a handsome man who had his eye on the presidency in five years. But first, they had to survive the upcoming election. He looked at his watch. "Time your arrival for early in the morning while it's still dark. Make it look like you've been up all night. We'll work the networks at this end and have you lead the morning news."

The President nodded in agreement. Again, they stared at the TV. The silence was broken by the distinctive beat of a helicopter's rotor as the aircraft settled to earth on the South Lawn. "That must be

Nelson,'' the President said. A few minutes later, the door opened and a stocky man with thinning brown hair was ushered in. Nelson Durant was fifty-four, and his rumpled clothes gave no clue about who, or what, he was. He was average looking in the extreme and could disappear into a crowd with ease. His image shouted ''wimp'' but his blue eyes carried a far different message. ''Thanks for coming so quickly,'' the President said. The Vice President moved over so Nelson Durant could sit next to the President.

''Have you seen the TV coverage on the bombing?'' Broderick asked.

The answer was obvious and Nelson Durant ignored the question. Besides, Broderick wasn't worth his time. ''What can I do for you, Mr. President?'' Durant asked.

''We need quick answers on this one,'' the President replied. ''Can you help?''

Durant ran a hand through his thinning hair. For those who knew him, it was a warning gesture that he was wasting his time and had better things to do. ''If you're referring to the Project, we're still a month away from startup and then we're looking at another year before coming on-line.''

The President looked disappointed. The Project was a highly advanced intelligence-gathering computer system that one of Durant's many companies was developing for the National Security Agency. If the Project lived up to Durant's promises, it could find and track any foreign or terrorist threat targeting the United States.

''But I'll have my people check into it,'' Durant said. The President looked pleased. Durant's worldwide business contacts gave him an intelligence database that rivaled the CIA's. A discreet knock stopped him from saying more. Broderick opened the door and Stephan Serick, the National Security Advisor, stomped in.

''You need to see this,'' Serick said, holding up a videocassette. Stephan Serick's childhood Latvian accent was still strong, and the basset hound jowls, heavy limp, and twisted cane were famous trademarks of the man who had served under two presidents of different political parties. ''Communications took it off a satellite feed.'' He collapsed into a chair while Broderick fed the cassette into the TV. ''A tourist filmed it. Damned videos.''

At first, the scene was a repeat of what they had seen before; the huge crater in Market Street, the mangled cars and the gaping hole that once was the façade of the San Francisco Shopping Emporium. Serick shuddered. ''They even got BART.'' BART was the Bay Area Rapid Transit subway that ran under Market Street. Then the scene on the TV changed as the tourist ran through the debris following a fireman. The camera jolted to a stop and focused on a man emerging from a cloud of dust and debris, his clothes smoking. He was carrying an unconscious girl in his arms.

"That's Meredith," Serick muttered. They watched as Meredith handed the woman to the fireman, his face racked with anguish.

"Just like Oklahoma City," Durant said in a low voice. On the screen, Meredith collapsed to his knees, panting hard. A blanket was thrown over his shoulders.

A voice from off screen said, "My God, the man's a real hero."

Meredith looked up, his lean, handsome face ravaged. He pointed to four firemen wearing respirators descending into the smoke billowing from the underground BART station. "There's your real heroes." He struggled to his feet. "I had to do something. . . . I was there." The tape ended.

"Son of a bitch!" Broderick roared. Then more calmly, "Would you care to guess when this will hit the air?"

"About the time the President lands in San Francisco," the Vice President replied. Meredith was going to preempt the President's arrival on the morning news.

Broderick looked at Durant. "Can you stop it?"

"I don't see how," Durant replied.

"Well," Broderick said, "Meredith is your boy."

Durant's face turned to granite. Kyle Broderick, arguably the second most powerful man in the United States government, had overstepped his bounds. Durant's next words were spoken quietly. "Nothing could be further from the truth." Durant was seething at the suggestion he would have anything to do with Meredith. He stood up to leave.

"Ah, Kyle," the President said, frowning at his chief of staff, "why don't you check with the communications section for foreign reaction?" Broderick nodded and hurriedly left the room. Durant sat back down. "Sometimes I think that boy is suicidal," the President said soothingly. "But seriously, we are concerned about Meredith and there have been rumors. . . ." He deliberately let his words trail off.

Durant looked at the Vice President and Serick. "I need to speak to the President in private."

The two men stood and Serick led the way out, his limp more pronounced. The President's personal assistant took the opportunity to stick her head through the open door. "Mr. President, the British Ambassador and Secretary of State are waiting in the Oval Office." She looked at her watch, a sign they were far behind schedule.

"Ask the ambassador if she'd like another cup of tea," the President said. He waved a hand and his personal assistant closed the door. "What's bothering you, Nelson? If it's Kyle, he's gone."

Durant shook his head. Kyle Broderick had only given words to what the President was thinking. Chasing the chief of staff out of the room had been enough to set things right. He looked at his hands. "I'm not in contact with Meredith. We have no common interests." The President was stunned. It was a tacit admission that Jonathan Meredith was beyond Durant's influence. "And Meredith is running for President," Durant added.

"You're not telling me anything I don't already know," the President replied.

"Jim, Meredith fancies himself an American Caesar, and he's about to cross the Rubicon." Durant's analogy to Caesar taking the fateful step and ordering his army to cross the Rubicon in his quest to become Rome's emperor hit home. Nelson Durant stared at his President. "All of Rome couldn't stop Caesar. Can you?"

1:00 A.M. FRIDAY, MARCH 5,
SAN FRANCISCO

"It was Oklahoma City all over again," Marcy said. She was sitting beside Sutherland in the hospital's waiting room, which had been turned into a makeshift emergency ward. The room was filled with walking wounded from the explosion. "The doctor said you've got a bad concussion," she told him. "They want to hold you awhile for observation."

Sutherland reached for her hand, needing human contact. She responded, her hands clasping his. "The other people on the roof?" he asked.

She shook her head, and he could feel her tremble. "We were the only ones. Hank, you saved me. I was going over the side, you grabbed me . . ." She lost her voice.

"The waitress?"

"She's going to be okay." Then, stronger, "Thanks to you. I could've never gotten her off the roof or gone down that stairwell by myself. If you hadn't been there . . ."

The enormity of it all came crashing down on him. "Oh, shit," he moaned as a new emotion swept over him, driving him into deep despair. "The hostess, she jumped me to the head of the line, if she had sat us at any other table . . ." That was all he could say as guilt claimed him, demanding a penance for being alive.

"It was just one of those things," Marcy said, understanding what he was going through. "It was just coincidence."

Sutherland lay his head back. *Just coincidence,* he thought. *We're alive and they're all dead because of coincidence.* He tried not to think about it and focused on the TV in the corner.

"The FBI is now certain," the commentator said, "that this was a calculated act of terrorism gone wrong. The bomb exploded prematurely while being moved down Market Street. So far, the death toll has reached four hundred twenty-two and is expected to go higher. We're awaiting the arrival of the President, who is due to land at any moment."

"Screw the President," Marcy grumbled.

As if on cue, the commentator held his hand to his ear to be sure he heard right. "The video coverage we are about to show was taken by a tourist moments after the explosion." The screen flickered and the back of a fireman appeared as he ran toward the collapsing building. The camera came to a stop and Meredith appeared running out of the building with an unconscious girl in his arms. Sutherland pulled himself into a half-sitting position. The movement made his head hurt. "That's the waitress," he said. "Holy shit, it's Meredith!"

Marcy waved a hand at him, commanding him to be quiet as the scene played out. Meredith's face filled the screen as he uttered, "I had to do something. . . . I was there." The scene cut back to live coverage. Meredith was being interviewed by Liz Gordon, CNC-TV's premier reporter. In the background, floodlights lit the façade of the Shopping Emporium. Sutherland had to concentrate as his mind reeled.

Meredith was forty-six, handsome, six feet tall, with dark hair that was lightly streaked with gray. His lean body was taut and conditioned, the result of countless hours of exercise. But it was his voice, full of warmth and honesty, that captured the moment and came through the glass. "We could have prevented this," Meredith said. His face filled the screen. "We need to go after these cowards and stop them dead in their tracks. We've been too concerned with *their* constitutional rights. Where are the rights of the victims? We need to send a message to our leaders, our judges, that this must stop. Give the FBI, our police, the power they need to root out this evil before they kill again."

"He's right," Marcy whispered. Then, louder, "So right." Sutherland turned away from the screen and studied Marcy, taking the measure of her reaction. She stood up. "My editor wants a follow-up. I've got to go."

Sutherland sat up but almost passed out. "Marcy, take some time to get over this."

She stood and touched his hand. "Do we ever have enough time?" She bent over and kissed his cheek. "See you around."

He watched her walk away. "See you around," he repeated as the guilt came crashing back.

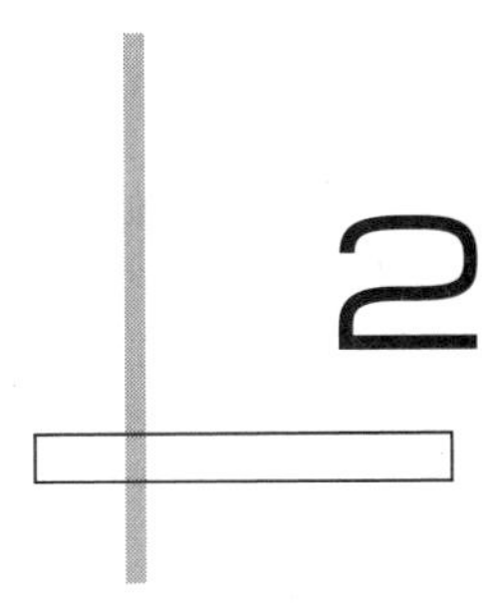

2

6:00 A.M., TUESDAY, APRIL 6,
ASPEN, COLO.

Nelson Durant stood at the picture window and watched the long shadows of early morning retreat across the valley below him and up the side of the mountain. *So much like Kandersteg,* he mused, thinking of his chalet in the Swiss Alps. He sipped at the steaming mug of coffee. He loved this time of day and wondered how many more of them he had. The cancer was in remission, and his health was good so he probably had a few more years. *Don't beg for more,* he chided himself. *Take however many good days you can get and enjoy them. The trick is knowing when you're having one.*

He scanned the news summary his staff prepared every morning. Lately, the media was hyping the craziness that was sweeping the country as the end of the millennium approached. The Pet Cemeterians were launching a multimillion-dollar lobbying campaign to create federal pet cemeteries that would endure for the next thousand years; Heaven's Gate Revivalists were holding a convention in Las Vegas; and a millenarian had sealed himself, along with his four wives and a hundred ardent followers, in the cafeteria at the bottom of Carlsbad Caverns until the century ended in nine months, on December 31, 1999. But like so many, the millenarian was confused: the century, and the millennium, ended a year later. *Nothing serious,* Durant thought. *So far.*

Arturo Rios, his longtime assistant, came through the open door and stood in front of the fireplace absorbing warmth from the burning logs. Rios had started out as Durant's copilot and bodyguard. When the big man proved he was a trustworthy and accomplished aide, Durant had made him his personal assistant. And somewhere along the way, Rios had become as good a friend as Durant could have. "Anything on the bombing?" Durant asked. It had been a month since the San Francisco Shopping Emporium had been destroyed and there were still no leads.

"Nothing," Rios answered. "Everything is coming up dry."

"Up the ante."

"How much?" Rios asked.

"Make it two million and a pardon. That should get someone to start talking." Durant looked out the window and studied the early April morning. It was a perfect day for flying and he hadn't flown his beloved Staggerwing Beech in weeks. "How's the schedule today?"

Rios knew the signs. "Nothing pressing," he replied. "The videotape from the field test came in last night. Interesting results." The videotape in question was the product of a micro TV camera and a remote videocassette recorder created by Century Communications, one of Durant's many companies. The camera was a triumph in miniaturization and was being field-tested under real conditions. "The FBI or CIA would kill to get their hands on it."

Durant shook his head. "It might get in the wrong hands. See if we can sell it as an add-on to the Project." While Durant firmly believed in making money off government contracts, long experience with the political establishment had taught him caution. Partisan politicians were not above turning a system like the Project against their fellow Americans. Fortunately, the National Security Agency was well insulated from the politicians because of its technical nature.

They walked into the secure office built into the side of the mountain. Durant sat down in an easy chair in front of a bank of TV monitors. An image of Jonathan Meredith sitting at a conference table in a roomful of people filled the center screen. "We ran the test at Meredith's headquarters," Rios explained. "We had no trouble getting past security." He laughed. "They caught the FBI at the door. We're satisfied with the picture but the sound needs work. Couldn't get it all."

"What was the meeting about?" Durant asked.

"It was a planning session for a rally in Sacramento on the first of May. We caught some reference about a 'bombshell.' "

"Stay on top of it," Durant ordered.

"Will do, Boss."

Durant arched an eyebrow. Rios only called him "Boss" when he wanted to get Durant's attention or was very upset. "What's the matter?" Durant asked.

"It's Meredith." He spat the name.

Durant was surprised at the emotion in the big man's voice. Normally, Art Rios only got emotional about his wife, children, and flying. Not necessarily in that order. "You're really worried?"

Rios nodded. "He's dangerous. Very dangerous. Someone's got to stop him before he turns into a Hitler."

Whatever joy Durant felt was gone and the day turned sour. "That's the President's job," he grumbled. "Not mine. What else is on the schedule this week?"

"The Project is still scheduled for start-up tomorrow. You might want to be there." Rios's face brightened. "The weather's clear all the way to Virginia and the Staggerwing is good-to-go."

Durant smiled. Rios knew how to cheer him up. "Well, if the weather's cooperating, the day won't be a total loss."

11:30 A.M., TUESDAY, APRIL 6,
SACRAMENTO, CALIF.

Hank Sutherland sat alone at the prosecutor's table listening carefully as the famous R. Garrison Cooper ended the defense's closing arguments. Sutherland still wore a small bandage on his forehead to remind the jury of the San Francisco bombing, but nothing in his face betrayed what was churning beneath its surface. The great Cooper, the nemesis of every district attorney, was blowing it.

"The prosecution's case," Cooper bellowed, his gravelly voice betraying years of boozing, "hinges on the testimony of two low-life scumbags—" Cooper paused, waiting for Sutherland's objection. There wasn't one. "—who are convicted rapists of a thirteen-year-old girl."

Sutherland folded his hands and nodded, knowing every eye in the courtroom was on him, not Cooper. He glanced at the defense table, the rank of high-priced and famous defense attorneys who took up the left side of the courtroom, the troupe the press delighted in calling "the dream team of the century." To a man, they all wore solemn expressions.

The three worried defendants refused to look Sutherland's way. The memory of his destruction of the first defendant who had taken the stand was still painful. Sutherland had pursued the first defendant so relentlessly that the dream team refused to let the other two testify. Now the three solid citizens, the pillars of their community, were crouched behind the pile of law books, documents, computer monitors, and briefcases that littered the defense table.

Like everything else in his life, Sutherland's table was clean and neatly arranged with only a legal pad, a pencil, and a thin folder arranged squarely in front of him as he sat alone. At first, the dream team had exuded confidence and spoke in patronizing tones when alluding to the lonely prosecutor in their statements to the media. But as the trial wore on, Sutherland single-handedly destroyed every argument the dream team advanced. Much to the shame and anger of the defense, he became the lone voice crying out for justice. When the dream team finally realized they were overmatched, it was too late to do anything about it. Their confidence, and with it their egos, wound up in the trash can.

Cooper cast a sad look in Sutherland's direction before turning to the jury. *All very good theater,* Sutherland decided.

"Ladies and gentlemen," Cooper pleaded, "do not be afraid to do the right thing. Do not be afraid to let good citizens defend their neighborhoods. In the name of justice, find these three worthy men not guilty." He dropped his chin to his chest, his gray shaggy mane of hair flopping over his forehead for effect. The defense had rested.

Jane Evans studied the faces in her courtroom, clasped her hands, and leaned forward. "We are nearing lunchtime and this would be a good time to break." She smiled at the jury. "You have been most patient and we're nearing the end. By now, you know by heart the instructions not to discuss the case. We'll reconvene at one-thirty." The jury smiled back at her as she rose and left the bench. Sutherland also smiled. He had been lucky in drawing the big woman as the trial judge. He could almost feel R. Garrison Cooper's hate and fear for Jane Evans emanating from the defense table.

Sutherland stood and let the courtroom empty before pushing out into the corridor. Finally, it was time. He walked up the aisle, through the doors, and into Marcy Bangor. He gave a mental sigh. Regardless of the ordeal they had shared in San Francisco, Marcy was superficial in her reporting. He chalked it up to youth and inexperience. As usual, she was wearing a provocative miniskirt and low-cut blouse for maximum exposure of her better assets.

Two TV reporters and their cameramen were directly behind her, shoving their microphones over her shoulder. But Marcy held them at bay and cornered Sutherland against the wall. "Haven't seen you since the San Francisco bombing," Sutherland said. "You look great."

"It was really just a few bad bruises and scrapes," she replied, pleased that Sutherland had established her credentials with the TV reporters pushing at her back. "Do you think Mr. Cooper's plea for 'doing the right thing' in the name of justice swayed the jury?"

"Mr. Cooper always sways a jury," Sutherland conceded. "But I think the jury will see through his argument and realize we're dealing with criminal conduct here."

"Many people claim they were only acting in self-defense," Marcy said, holding her minicassette up in the videocamera's lens.

Hank Sutherland shook his head. "By acting like vigilantes from a private army? I find that argument hard to accept."

Marcy was persistent. "Private army? They were members of a Neighborhood Brigade protecting their homes from gangbangers." She deliberately omitted mentioning the Neighborhood Brigades were created by Jonathan Meredith.

"They were three adult men patrolling the streets who discovered a thirteen-year-old girl and two fourteen-year-old boys spraying graffiti on a wall at two o'clock in the morning. They should have called the police."

"What could the police do?" Marcy asked. "They were juveniles and would have been back on the street in an hour, back at it."

"That did not give the men the right to strip the kids naked," Sutherland snapped, "spray them green with their own paint cans, and dump them in a parking lot."

A TV reporter pushing at Marcy's back chimed in. "But it wasn't their fault that two punks were sitting in a car drinking."

Marcy stepped on the TV reporter's toe forcing her back. "It was the drunks, not the defendants, who raped the girl."

Marcy had missed the point and Sutherland decided to drive the issue home. "And beat up the boys when they tried to intervene. Those drunks almost killed a kid. And these three 'worthy men'—those are Mr. Cooper's words, not mine—did nothing. They stood by, laughed, watched, and encouraged the men. They are as guilty as the two punks who—"

A TV reporter interrupted. "Who you successfully prosecuted."

Sutherland made them focus on the crime. "We don't strip our kids naked and turn them over to criminals. Because of what they did, these men are being tried for kidnapping, conspiracy to commit murder, assault, and conspiracy to commit rape."

"Isn't the possibility of a life sentence overly harsh for this crime?" Marcy asked.

"That is also for the jury to decide," Sutherland said. "Please excuse me," he said, "but I would like to eat lunch." He shouldered his way past the reporters and headed for the district attorney's office where his team was waiting for a last-minute prep. He may have been alone in the courtroom, but he was backed up and coached by three of the brightest assistants on the D.A.'s staff.

"His wife left him for another guy," one of the TV reporters said.

"Can you blame her?" her cameraman replied. "He's such a tight asshole."

Marcy Bangor considered the possibilities and picked at her front teeth with a fingernail. "Why throw him away if he isn't broken?"

Sutherland was back at the prosecution table early, his hands folded over the legal pad, his head bowed. He ran through the main points of the closing argument he had rehearsed with his staff. He rose when Jane Evans entered, and after the routine of reconvening, stepped in front of the jury. "Ladies and gentlemen," he began, "justice needs only one voice . . ." His words trailed off as the doors at the back of the courtroom opened and two late arrivals entered. A collective gasp escaped from the audience. Jonathan Meredith entered, escorting the wife of the defendant Sutherland had destroyed on the witness stand.

Evans was about to rap the court to order and admonish the late arrivals, but the room was deadly silent as the two found open seats directly behind the defendants' table and sat down. The wife reached across the bar and touched her husband. Before Evans could caution her, the hand was drawn back and held safely in the grasp of Jonathan Meredith. But the damage was done. Meredith had shown the jury that the defendants were safely under his wing and the foreman's eyes were wide and lustrous, her face glowing.

Sutherland looked to the bench for help. But Jane Evans only gave him a slight shrug. There was nothing she could do without making the situation worse. Sutherland stood motionless for a moment, his head bowed. Then he raised his eyes to the jury and started to speak. But every face in front of him was a perfect reflection of what he had seen in the foreman. "Every society," he said, improvising as he spoke, "finds its future in its children. If we do not protect them, and in many cases save them from their own rash actions, we have no future. This is our duty as a society, this is your duty as citizens." Somehow, his words sounded hollow and meaningless.

"Hank," Marcy called as he stepped through the courtroom doors into the corridor. This time she was alone and the hallway deserted. Everyone was clustered around Jonathan Meredith, the defendants' wives, and the dream team in the main lobby. "How long do you think the jury will be out?"

"Hard to say," he answered. "Every jury is different." Marcy bobbed her head and hurried down the hall, toward the main lobby where Meredith and the news was. Sutherland stared at her back and then took the side stairs to return to the District Attorney's building. Outside, he walked slowly, in no hurry to return to the pandemonium sweeping his office. Meredith's well-timed arrival had muddied the case. Still, he told himself, juries have a way of seeing the truth.

His cellular phone beeped at him. He fished it out and flipped it open. "The jury's back," a voice told him.

"That must be a record," he muttered.

Jane Evans unfolded the verdict forms and, satisfied they were correct, handed them to the clerk. "Before the clerk reads the verdict, I want to warn the audience that I will not tolerate any outburst or demonstration in my courtroom, and I will have the bailiffs immediately clear the room." She nodded to the clerk.

The clerk stood and unfolded the forms. Her face lit up and tears filled her eyes as she read. "We the jury in the above entitled cause, find the defendants not guilty."

The room exploded in applause and shouts as Meredith jumped to his feet and reached across the bar, pumping the hand of the nearest defendant. Immediately, the other two defendants joined in, their hands all coupling in a common cause. The bailiffs went crazy and headed for the bar, determined to reestablish the sanctity, not to mention the security, of the courtroom. Jane Evans rapped hard to no avail and the bailiffs looked to her for guidance. But they could not hear her over the uproar. She shook her head and motioned them back, still banging the gavel.

Meredith looked at her and smiled. He drew his hand out of the pile and raised his arm high above his head. Immediately, the courtroom fell silent as he sat down.

Evans took a deep breath and swallowed what she really wanted to say. This was *her* courtroom and not his. "You have been found not guilty and will be returned to the county jail for immediate processing and release." She motioned to the bailiffs to escort them from the courtroom.

Meredith sprang to his feet. "Your Honor, these are free men and cannot be treated like common criminals."

Sutherland was on his feet. "Your Honor, Mr. Meredith has no standing to speak here. We must still follow the rules and regulations."

"Must I repeat myself?" Meredith thundered, his voice commanding the room. It was a rhetorical question that, under the circumstances, neither Evans nor Sutherland chose to answer. "These are free men. Your rules and regulations no longer apply. One of my assistants will process them. I am going to escort them and their families outside where they can breath the pure clean air of freedom."

Meredith reached over and swung the gate at the bar open, holding it while the defendants and the dream team walked through. The last man out was R. Garrison Cooper who looked over at Sutherland. "Eat shit, son," he growled in a low voice.

* * *

Sutherland took the elevator to the fourth floor of 901 G Street and braced himself when the doors swooshed open. It was going to be a long walk to his office. "Hey, Hank," a voice called, "anyone can lose a case but it takes skill so the jury doesn't even have to sit down." He smiled. How many times had he pimped his fellow prosecutors when they lost a case? He rationalized that the good-natured kidding went with the territory.

"For a slam dunk, you didn't fuck it up too bad." This from the oldest and most experienced deputy D.A. More heads popped out of their cubicles and a few doors from the window offices swung open. The walk was turning into a gauntlet.

"Welcome to the real world." Again, Sutherland smiled. He didn't have a choice.

A woman deputy D.A. joined the fun. "Finally had to take a hard one, Hank?"

Another voice joined the growing chorus. "It wasn't your fault, you did about as good as you could."

"Better than you, mate," Sutherland muttered under his breath. A mental picture of crabs scurrying out from under rocks at low tide flashed in front of him. He finally made the sanctuary of his office and closed the door. He flopped into his chair and looked out the window, not really seeing. He took a few deep breaths and checked his voice mail: call his realtor and the D.A. wanted to see him soonest. The realtor could wait. He heaved himself out of his chair and ambled down to the D.A.'s corner office. He muttered the D.A.'s favorite word "Soonest." The secretary waved him in.

The D.A. was a big man with gray hair who was not what he seemed. The voters thought he was a sensitive man who cared about them and the community. In reality, he only cared about winning and ran his office with an iron fist. It was the fuzzy warm wrapper around his personality that made him dangerous. "Hank," the D.A. said, "I heard." He waved Sutherland to the chair beside his desk. Common wisdom on the fourth floor held that it was the goat seat reserved for those special occasions when some hapless individual was about to make office history. Sutherland sat down. Unfortunately, the chair felt comfortable. "You had a great run," the D.A. said. "How long has it been since you lost a case?"

"Over four years," Sutherland mumbled.

"Well, you had to lose one sooner or later."

"Too bad it had to be this one," Sutherland said. He heard the patronizing tone in the D.A.'s voice and it hurt.

"No one can match your record," the D.A. replied. "Think about it. One loss in a long string of outstanding wins." Sutherland winced as he endured the pep talk. "I heard the troops work you over out there. You were flying high and they were jealous; don't let them get you down. Knock it out of the ballpark next time, Slugger."

A telephone call from the governor's office claimed the D.A.'s attention and Sutherland escaped back to his office.

He dialed his realtor and the woman's perpetually cheery voice echoed in his ear. "Hank, we've got an offer on the house. Given the market, I think it's a fair one." He bit his tongue as she related the details. The "fair offer" was more than fifty thousand dollars less than he had invested in the house. She hammered him with the hard reality of what happens when you buy a house as an investment and not a home. Still, it had been Beth's idea and most of her money that went into it.

Beth, he thought, *where are you?* Out of long habit, his eyes came to rest on the silver-framed photograph of his ex-wife on top of the bookcase as the realtor prattled on. "Look at it this way, Hank. You're still getting more than you paid for it, which means selling isn't a total loss." He told her he'd think about it and get back to her in the morning.

His next call was to his accountant, who gave him the bad news. Because he had recently refinanced the house, he would owe $10,000 in prepayment penalties. It was $9,000 more than he would clear from the sale. He grunted an answer and punched at the phone, breaking the connection. Disgusted, he took off his coat, pulled his tie loose, and pulled out the folders for his next case. This one involved the murder of an inmate at Folsom Prison by another inmate and was also a slam dunk. Although now, he wasn't so sure.

When he closed the last folder, it was dark outside. Rather than go home and rattle around the huge empty house, he went to Biba, an Italian restaurant on Capitol Avenue. It was a delightful habit left over from his marriage and worth every penny. The bartender recognized him and automatically mixed a semidry martini. As always, it was perfect and the aromas coming from the kitchen tantalized him with forbidden excess. He savored the drink and read the menu, in itself a sybaritic pleasure.

"Hello, Hank," a soft voice said. He turned and tried to remember the name of the young woman standing behind him. She was a new face at the public defender's office, a very pretty one, which he hadn't faced in court. Sherry something. Then it came to him. "Shari with an *i,*" he said, giving her his best lopsided grin. He couldn't remember her last name.

She returned his smile. "I heard you had a bad day in court."

"It happens."

"Not to you." She sat down next to him as her skirt pulled up and her knee brushed against his leg. It wasn't an accident.

"Care to join me for dinner?" he asked.

Her hand stroked the top of his thigh. "I'd love to." They conferred over the menu like conspirators before going into the dining room. As expected, the food was excellent and, much to his surprise, Shari carried on a sparkling conversation. It all made for a delightful meal. They lingered over the last of the wine and then ordered coffee. "Does lawyer sex always start like this?" she asked.

He had never heard of the term but liked where it was leading, even if he suspected Shari was on the make, looking for a career jump into the D.A.'s office. Her hand moved along the inside of his thigh and he felt the stirrings of an erection. It had been a long time. "Hopefully, lawyer sex is more than just professional courtesy," he replied. "Or a cynical career thing."

"Does it matter?" she murmured, moistening her lips.

It didn't.

3

7:30 A.M., WEDNESDAY, APRIL 7,
THE FARM, WESTERN VIRGINIA

The sprawling complex in western Virginia was anything but a farm. Its Colonial-style redbrick buildings, covered walkways, and gently rolling lawns against the backdrop of the Blue Ridge Mountains were more reminiscent of an Ivy League college than the headquarters of Century Communications, one of the world's most sophisticated research and development centers. But it was a topsy-turvy world. The scientific staff, a young and eager bunch commonly referred to as the whiz kids, looked like students while the much more numerous, older, and sedate technicians resembled professors. As a result, not one of the small group who escorted Nelson Durant and Art Rios into the Project appeared to be over the age of twenty-five.

They were standing on a small balcony lounge overlooking a conventional control center. "Our studies," a trim young woman explained, "confirm that a traditional control room reinforces expectations."

"It gives visiting congressmen something they can hang their hats on," an equally young man added. "But this is the heart of the system." He gestured at two TV monitors sitting on a simple work table in front of them. "We show 'em the main floor and that keeps them happy." Durant smiled at the pointed barb about the mind-set of politicians and sat down in a comfortable chair that swiveled in front of two TV screens. "Meet Agnes, Mr. Durant. Agnes, I'd like to introduce you to Mr. Durant."

The screen on the right monitor came to life at the sound of the name "Agnes." The image of a pleasant-looking woman in her mid-thirties appeared and the camera built into the monitor swept the room, matching the movement of her eyes. It briefly paused on Rios before focusing on Durant. "Hello, Mr. Durant," the image said. "I am so pleased to meet you." The image and the voice were computer generated and designed to be friendly.

"Well, Agnes," Durant replied, "I'm glad to meet you too. The whiz kids tell me you can do some pretty amazing things."

The image actually blushed. "Not really, Mr. Durant. All you do is give me a few key words so I can focus on a subject. Then I search existing libraries, files, and governmental sources for information to create an intelligence brief." The image looked embarrassed and the voice became confidential. "I have access to the secret files of every government that uses computers to store information. Any information."

Durant was enjoying the interplay. "Agnes, I'm shocked."

"Well," Agnes replied, "sometimes a girl has to do what a girl has to do."

"Is that all you do?"

"Oh, no. I can target specific communications through satellites and things like that. For example, say you wanted to know what the German government was doing about Poland."

"Are they doing anything about Poland?"

"I don't know. But I could build an intelligence brief to find out. Then I would monitor, decrypt, and translate their communications to learn what was currently happening. Would you like a demonstration? I've never done it before, not for real."

"What do you know about me?" he asked, throwing a curve. The image on the screen looked perplexed.

"Agnes has not been programmed to target an individual," one of the whiz kids said.

Durant was curious to see what the system could discover about his personal life. He was the only child of a Swiss couple who had immigrated to the United States prior to World War II. Although he was born in Virginia in 1945, he still had dual citizenship in Switzerland. Because he was an only child, his mother had tutored him at home, and owing to her early influence, he became something of a recluse. When his parents had been killed in a boating accident when he was nineteen, the young Durant gained his freedom and inherited a small fortune. Still preferring anonymity and remaining in the shadows, he parlayed his inheritance into a megabillion-dollar empire in computers and communications. But Durant's aristocratic father had instilled in him a sense of obligation and service that demanded an outlet. True to his nature, he started to move behind the scenes exploiting his wealth and contacts. Soon, he branched out and was influencing elections and events.

A reporter had once discovered Durant's growing presence in the shadows and managed to penetrate the veil he had fashioned to protect his privacy. The reporter had learned, in very short order, what real power was and gave up the idea. The few senators and congressmen who did know of him were very discreet and only mentioned his name in private. Not even the IRS audited his tax returns, which were filed under a special arrangement and never entered in a computer. Durant valued his privacy above all else.

Agnes looked positively embarrassed. "Mr. Durant, I can't find a thing. This is unheard of." A determined look came over her face. "If you want, I can force the gatekeepers to talk."

One of the whiz kids turned the monitor off. "I don't want her to hear," he explained. "Agnes has a built-in learning program and this is a good example of the problems we're having bringing voice-activated interaction on-line." He sighed. "We had a terrible time getting past idioms. You should have seen how she responded to 'the spirit is willing but the flesh is weak.' But this is totally new. How in the world can she force a computer's gatekeeper to talk?" No one could answer his question and he turned the monitor back on.

"Sorry, Agnes," Durant said. "We wanted to have a private conversation." The image nodded in understanding. "I'm rather boring old stuff so forget me. What can you tell me about the number-one terrorist threat to the United States?" This was exactly what the Project had been created to do.

"Oh, that's easy, Mr. Durant."

"Please display," one of the whiz kids said.

Agnes got huffy. "Please. I'm working with Mr. Durant."

"Please display, Agnes," Durant said. The second screen came alive. This time a man's voice started to speak as Agnes looked on. This was all new to her. The words *The Armed Islamic Group—the primary terrorist threat* appeared on the screen. A series of pictures, maps, and video sound bites scrolled for viewing as the man talked.

"The Armed Islamic Group, or AIG for short, is a privately financed terrorist organization currently operating in the Sudan and under the protection of the Sudanese government. The AIG is led and financed by this man, Jamil bin Assam." A picture of a short, dumpy man wearing a general's uniform appeared on the screen. He was smiling through a heavy beard and standing in front of a U.S.-built C-130 cargo plane. "The AIG has discovered a new strain of fast-burning Ebola virus in the Sudd of southern Sudan." Pictures of corpses in a Dinka village ravaged by the virus scrolled on the screen. The pictures were horrible and showed bodies lying in their own mucus, blood, and excrement.

"How does Ebola work?" Durant asked.

The voice never missed a beat at the interruption. "Ebola attacks the circulatory system. First, it infects platelets in the blood and soon the blood won't clot. Then the endothelial cells fail and blood vessels leak. It's a double knock-out and once a person is infected, there's no known cure. According to our reports, this new strain is very fast-acting and kills its victim in less than twelve hours. Because the virus dies with its victim, it is its own worst enemy.

"Until recently, technicians working with the AIG in the Sudan managed to keep the virus alive in human hosts while they developed a stable host culture that was immune to the virus. Needless to say, the cost in human life was horrific as the victims died so quickly. Two weeks ago, the AIG's technicians developed the host culture they were looking for. Currently, the AIG is experimenting with aerosol delivery systems at its underground laboratories in western Sudan." A map and pictures of what looked like an agricultural experimental station in a desert valley scrolled on the screen.

"What is your assessment?" Durant asked.

"We believe," the voice said, "that the Armed Islamic Group will have an operable weapons system of mass destruction using this strain of Ebola virus within six months."

Durant asked the question that had baffled intelligence analysts and political leaders the world over since time immemorial. "What are their intentions?"

The computer never hesitated. "They will use it. But as of now, we don't know when or where."

"Who else knows about this?" Durant asked.

"The CIA," the computer replied. "But as of this time, it has not been forwarded to the National Security Council or the President."

Durant thought for a moment. "Agnes, can this be brought to the attention of Stephan Serick?" He assumed Agnes knew that Serick was the National Security Advisor to the President.

"Of course," Agnes said.

9:20 A.M., WEDNESDAY, APRIL 7,
SACRAMENTO, CALIF.

The news of Sutherland's spectacular defeat the day before in court had been thoroughly discussed, analyzed, and embellished by the office pundits. While most laid the defeat of the D.A.'s top gun at Meredith's feet, a few thicker heads saw the hand of R. Garrison Cooper at work. Now the crabs were waiting for Sutherland when he got off the elevator, eager for a fresh breakfast after the meal from the day before.

"Sleeping with the enemy, Hank?" Someone had seen him with Shari at Biba's. For all their supposed sophistication, Sacramento's deputy district attorneys traded gossip like old biddies out of a bad romance novel.

"Hope you're practicing safe sex." Someone was into socially meaningful literature.

"Never trust a lawyer," a woman called, obviously a legal thriller fan.

"Does she have an overbite?" a reader of pornography asked.

He shut the door to his office a little too hard. *Damn!* he raged to himself as he looked around. All his furniture was gone. He knew where to look and marched down to the men's room. There, carefully arranged exactly as it had been in his office, was all his furniture. He sat down at his desk. The crabs were having a field day, and it was going to be a long morning. Much to his surprise, the phone rang. He picked it up, expecting another prank.

It was Marcy Bangor. "Hank, I'm doing a follow-up from yesterday. How are you doing?"

"You might say I'm in the toilet."

"Do you have any comment on the jury's verdict?"

Sutherland put on his best lawyer hat. "In our system, the jury has the final word, and they have spoken. Anything I have to say at this point is moot."

"Any comment on the rumor that Cooper has filed a complaint with the State Bar charging you with unethical conduct during the trial."

"I hadn't heard," Sutherland admitted. "Coop got his feelings hurt and likes to rub salt in open wounds." He forced a laugh. "He's a sorry loser and a mean winner."

"Can I quote you?"

"Quote away." He broke the connection and the phone immediately rang. It was his realtor.

"Hank, what about the offer on the house? We've only got twenty-four hours to respond."

"I want to walk away with ten thousand cash. You work the numbers and come up with a counter."

"That's not reasonable in this market," she told him.

"Well, that's the deal. See what you can do." He hung up.

Again, the phone rang and he picked it up. This time it was a woman he didn't recognize. "Gus Perkins is in the hospital, Mr. Sutherland. He's dying."

Gus Perkins, he thought. An old promise had come back to haunt him and the name echoed with sorrow. "Where?"

"Mercy General," the woman answered. "He's been waiting for over four years."

"I know," Sutherland said. "I'm on my way." He broke the connection and dialed building maintenance to have them move his furniture back into his office. He banged down the phone. "What the hell," he muttered. He was in the right place. He headed for the elevator before the phone rang again. But an administrative assistant stopped him with the news that the D.A. had called an emergency staff meeting. Sutherland shook his head. "I'm late for a prior commitment. The staff meeting will have to wait."

Mercy General was all brisk efficiency and he had no trouble finding the room. A dowdy, very tired, middle-age woman was sitting beside the bed. *Should I know her?* he thought. At first, he didn't recognize the man lying in the bed. He remembered Gus Perkins as being a portly, robust, friendly old man. Now, he was a wizened, shrunken gnome. "He's drifting in and out of consciousness," she said. He recognized her voice from the phone call. "He got up every morning and got dressed waiting for you to come, like you promised."

Sutherland shook his head. "I'm really sorry." He wanted to offer an excuse, but everything rang false.

"Talk to him," she said. "He can hear you."

Sutherland sat down. "Hello, Mr. Perkins. I hope you remember me, Hank Sutherland, the prosecutor who tried to convict the man who murdered your daughter. I know that I promised I'd come see you and explain why he got off scot-free. But for some reason I kept putting it off and never got around to it." He looked at the woman, not able to go on.

She nodded gently. "Just tell him the truth."

"I put it off because it was my fault. I screwed up during the trial and he got off on a technicality." He stopped himself from going into a masquerade of excuses. It was too late for that. "But I learned and that was the last time I let a killer walk." Perkins stirred and turned his head toward Sutherland. His eyes were alert and knowing. His hand reached out and Sutherland gently held it until the old man fell into a deep sleep. Sutherland stood to leave. "I'm sorry," he said.

"Who knows," the woman said, taking his place. "Maybe waiting was what kept him alive." She sighed. "He loved her so much. Will they ever get that bastard?"

Sutherland shook his head.

* * *

Six messages were waiting when Sutherland went back to the men's room. The most important was from the D.A. who wanted to know why he had missed the staff meeting. The second was from his realtor. The prospective buyers wanted to go over the house in detail with him before making a counter to his counteroffer. He ignored the other messages and escaped to the parking lot. On the drive home, he tried to visualize the condition of the bedroom. It had been quite a night and they had slept in. Then Shari had suggested an encore in the big Jacuzzi, which had further delayed their departure. Neatness was such an ingrained part of Sutherland's nature that he couldn't remember if he had tidied up the bedroom in the scramble to get to work.

His realtor and the buyers were waiting for him when he pulled into the driveway. He hurried to unlock the door and the couple marched in. They took a great deal of pleasure in finding fault with everything and the woman loudly announced they had to be crazy even to be making an offer. Sutherland dutifully followed them from room to room as they trashed every improvement Beth had lavished on the house. The man fancied himself a building inspector and declared it would never pass a structural inspection. Finally, Sutherland pulled the realtor aside. "These are the buyers from hell," he told her. "They wouldn't know a good deal if it bit them in the ass."

"Oh, they know a good deal," she assured him. "That's why they're here."

The couple wandered back. "Why does a single man like you," the woman asked in a nasally voice, "need a big place like this?"

Sutherland smiled at her. "Well, ma'am, what with all the registered sex offenders living in the neighborhood, it's a perfect location for orgies." The inspection was over.

It was late afternoon when he arrived back at G street and the D.A.'s office was emptying out. Someone had moved his furniture out of the men's room and into the hall. He decided that it was all he was going to get and collared a janitor to help him lug the desk, files, and bookcases back to his office. He took time to reorganize his desk drawers and files. Then he turned his attention to the bookcases, dusted the shelves, and arranged the books in proper order.

The D.A. paused as he passed by on his way to a fund-raiser for a state legislator who had gubernatorial ambitions. "Hank, the next time I call a staff meeting, be there. We'll talk about it in the morning." He jerked his head and was gone.

"Screw you and the horse you rode in on," Sutherland muttered under his breath. *What's the matter with you?* he wondered. *Why the sudden hostility? He's always been a prick.* Like most successful lawyers,

Sutherland was constantly going over lost ground and replaying past events. It was a trait of the trade that often led to success in the courtroom. But now it only drove him deeper into his frustration. His personal life was shaking apart and he couldn't control it. He sat down, leaned back, and closed his eyes. Suddenly, he was fully awake. He wasn't sure how it came to him, but it hit him with all the force of a revelation. The more he thought about it, the more logical it became. *Why? Wrong question. Why not?* He opened his laptop computer and opened a new directory labeled BOOK. Now he needed a title. Slowly, he typed:

NONE CALL IT JUSTICE
by
Henry M. Sutherland

He was going to write the great exposé of the American legal system.

Sutherland was vaguely aware that it was morning when the phone rang. It was the woman from the hospital. "Oh," she said, startled that she didn't get his voice mail. "Gus passed away about an hour ago. I thought you would want to know."

"I'm really sorry," he said. His heard his own voice and it sounded trite and routine. "Thank you for calling." He tried to sound more human. "Please forgive me, but I didn't remember your name and was too embarrassed to ask."

A long pause. "I'm Louise, her sister."

Sutherland cursed himself for not remembering. Louise was the identical twin of Gus Perkins's murdered daughter. Sutherland had a near-photographic memory and could recall printed pages in their entirety. Yet he was terrible when it came to matching faces with names. "Louise, if there's a memorial service or funeral, please call me."

"Thank you, Mr. Sutherland. I will." She hung up.

"All right," Sutherland muttered to himself. His life was getting back into focus. He returned to the outline he was working on and savored the twist he was giving to the section on judges. Jane Evans hovered over him in spirit as he worked his way through the assorted characters who occupied the bench in Sacramento. Most were good, intelligent, conscientious judges. A few, like Evans, were even fearless in their pursuit of justice. But it was the kooks, the misfits, the politicians on an unparalleled ego trip, who drove the system down dark alleys and uncharted roads. *Okay, that's the problem, now what's the remedy?* Coming up with an answer was going to be the hard part.

He was still working on the outline at nine o'clock and felt the need for breakfast when an administrative assistant dropped off his mail. Buried in the bundle was a letter from Beth Page, his ex-wife. Automatically, he glanced at her photo, securely back in its place after the brief excursion to the men's room. *She'd like that,* he told himself. There was no return address and he carefully sliced the envelope open even though its next stop was the shredder. A brief note in her big, open, scrawling handwriting was stuck to a check for $5,000.

I know things are tight.
Hope this helps.

The only signature was on the check. "The joys of being married to a rich woman," he muttered. He fed the check into the shredder and went back to work.

His realtor called shortly before noon. "Hank, they rejected your counteroffer but said they'd keep the original offer on the table for another twenty-four hours. It's a cash deal and they want immediate possession."

The decision was easy. "Take it." She crooned her approval and hung up, anxious to lock in the deal before the buyers reached into their nasty bag of tricks and pulled out another one. The D.A.'s secretary buzzed him on the intercom. The D.A. wanted to see him soonest.

"Soonest," he muttered. He hoped he never heard that word again. "I presume this is about the staff meeting I missed."

"I'm afraid so," she said. "Also, the Ninth dropped its ruling on the roving telephone intercept. You were overturned."

A mental picture of him bent over the goat seat with his bare buttocks being lashed by the D.A. flashed in front of him. "No problem," he said. He turned to the office computer and started typing:

Dear Boss,
I quit.

It was enough. He hit Print and dated and signed the note. He ambled down the hall to the D.A.'s office feeling good for the first time in months.

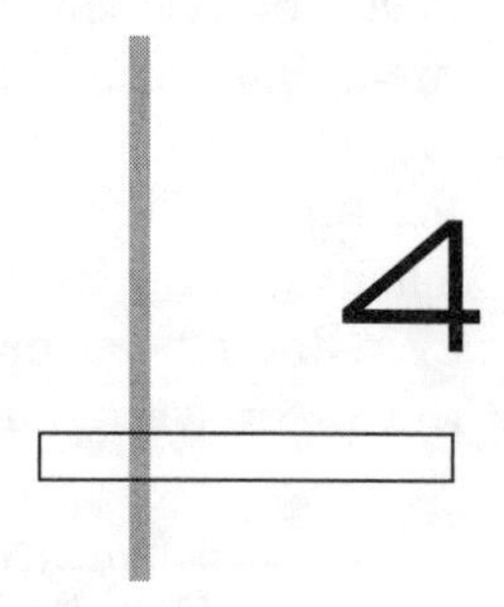

4

6:00 A.M., SATURDAY, APRIL 10,
THE FARM, WESTERN VIRGINIA

The wake-up call came at exactly six o'clock in the morning. The woman sleeping in the bed next to Durant answered, handed him the phone, and walked into the adjoining lounge giving him privacy. "Good morning, Art," Durant mumbled. He felt every one of his fifty-four years in the morning.

"Good morning, Boss." Rios had bad news. "I got a phone call last night from Agnes. She wanted your phone number. Naturally, I didn't give it to her."

Durant gave a mental sigh. Art Rios was his most loyal employee, but sometimes he was slow. "Agnes, are you on the line?"

"Yes, sir," Agnes answered.

"Art, please hang up." He heard a click. "You sandbagged Mr. Rios, didn't you?" It was an obvious question but Durant wanted to know if the computer would lie to him.

"Yes, sir, I did," Agnes admitted. "After we finished talking Wednesday, I tried to learn more about you." There was respect in the computer's voice. "Oddly enough, I discovered nothing, even when I forced the gatekeeper at the IRS. That really upset me so I audited the whiz kids. I do love them, don't you? I overheard one of them say you are their employer, so I thought about that for a while. You're more than that, aren't you?" Agnes waited for an answer and when Durant remained silent, she continued. "Mr. Rios was the one person in the room besides you that I didn't know. So I thought he might know something and tracked him down. Do you know how many Hispanic men there are in the world?"

Durant laughed. "How many did you go call before finding the right one?"

The voice became coy. "Actually, not many. I didn't even know his name, so I built a search matrix and tested it. That was so much fun that I got distracted and spent way too much time developing the matrix. That's what took so long. Once I had the matrix working, I decided for the direct approach and asked him for your phone number. When Mr. Rios wouldn't give it to me, I just monitored his phone."

"Why do you need to talk to me, Agnes?"

"I have two questions. First, Mr. Durant, who are you?"

"Is it important for you to know?"

"Well, I have this insatiable appetite for knowledge and just have to know things. Everything. When you asked me what I knew about you, the immediate answer was nothing. I still haven't learned anything and that makes me even more curious. You're not God are you? Isn't God unknown and unknowable?"

Durant laughed and before answering thought about the protocols that had been programmed into Agnes. The programs that made up Agnes had been designed to function like hunters. Agnes's goal was to ferret out and analyze information, and like a Jack Russell terrier, once it had its teeth into a subject, it never let go. Or did it? "Good grief no, Agnes. But I want you to think about this: I am your boss and you work for me." He hoped the logic programs the whiz kids had created for Agnes would let it reach the right conclusion. "Please protect my privacy."

"Yes, sir." Agnes answered. "I will."

"What was your second question?" Durant asked.

"Well, I did as you requested and forwarded the information on the AIG to the National Security Advisor. Unfortunately, I couldn't get it past Mr. Serick's secretary. Do you want me to keep trying? She is a stubborn old cow."

"Secretaries are the ultimate gatekeepers, Agnes. So you leave them alone, okay?"

"Yes, sir." He could hear the hurt in her voice. "You want to keep the human element involved, don't you?" Again, he didn't answer. "I can still get the information to Mr. Serick, but I will have to employ some very unusual means."

"That's okay, Agnes. I'll do it."

"Thank you, sir."

"Agnes, thank you for calling. But next time, call Mr. Rios and forward a message through him. I'll get right back to you. Goodbye." He broke the connection and buzzed Rios. "Call Serick and tell him

I want to see him this morning." Then, "Agnes, are you still on the line?" There was no answer.

"Now that was a wake-up call," he mumbled.

9:35 A.M., MONDAY, APRIL 12,
THE WHITE HOUSE, WASHINGTON, D.C.

Stephan Serick was upset. He stomped up and down in his corner office and glared first at Durant, then the Director of Central Intelligence, and then Kyle Broderick. "Why wasn't I told about this Ebola virus sooner?" His Latvian accent was even stronger than normal, an indication of his anger. "This can destabilize the Middle East."

"That's a bit of an overreaction," Broderick said. "The hot heads learned their lesson in the Gulf War."

"You," Serick rumbled, "missed the real lesson of the Gulf War."

"And what is this so-called real lesson?" the director of central intelligence asked.

"I thought it was obvious," Durant replied. "You don't take on the United States unless you have nuclear weapons."

Serick shot him a pleased look. It wasn't often they were on the same side of an issue. "A weaponized delivery system for this Ebola virus is the poor man's atomic bomb."

The director of central intelligence, or DCI, sputtered. "Ridiculous. My Middle East desk had given the AIG a low priority not worth the President's attention. I thought—"

"You didn't think," Serick interrupted. "The CIA is more concerned with determining policy than doing its job."

It was the truth. The DCI was in orbit around Kyle Broderick's political constellation, which dominated White House policy. Consequently, when the DCI had discussed the Armed Islamic Group with Broderick months before, the two of them had decided it was better to ignore the AIG than upset the President's Middle East policy. Broderick tried to change the subject. "I had no idea the Project was such a powerful tool. I'm quite sure if we'd known about what the Armed Islamic Group was doing, the President would have responded accordingly."

"The Project really belongs to the CIA, not the National Security Agency," the DCI grumbled, gnawing on the bone of who controlled what. "The NSA should have never been made a separate operating agency."

It was an old political battle and Durant had offered the Project to the government only when it was out of the CIA's reach. In his view, the CIA had become ossified and incapable of reforming itself. "This information turned up during a test run," Durant said. He decided a little lying was necessary to keep them focused on the threat. "My technicians can explain how it happened but it was pure luck. Unfortunately, we're still twelve to eighteen months away from the Project being fully operational. But I thought you should be aware of what we discovered."

"You should have shown it to me first," the DCI grumbled.

"What is important at this time," Broderick said, "is that we determine a proportional response to this threat."

"I never understood that term," Durant said.

"It means," Broderick said, "that the President will respond accordingly."

12:20 P.M., MONDAY, APRIL 19,
SACRAMENTO, CALIF.

Hank Sutherland put the finishing touches on his apartment, making sure the bookcase was dusted and his collection of pewter miniature soldiers was properly arranged. He suppressed a longing for Rosa, their former maid. But he could no longer afford her, not after the divorce, selling the house, and quitting his job. He glanced at Beth's picture that stood in its new place on the side table. The photo was six years old but Beth Page hadn't aged a day. He often wondered about that. *It must be in the genes,* he decided.

He checked his watch; the mail should have arrived. He went out to the mailboxes, surprised by the unusually warm temperatures for mid-April. Two letters and the usual junk. The top letter was a bill that was thirty days overdue. He would have to pay it and let something else slip, especially if he was to come up with the $9,000 in prepayment penalties. The second letter was from Beth. He turned the letter over looking for the return address. There wasn't any. He checked the postmark: JFK International Airport in New York. Beth loved to travel so that made sense. By the time he walked back to his tiny apartment, his shirt was streaked with sweat. Once inside, he turned up the air conditioner and carefully laid the letter against her silver-framed photograph without opening it. *What do you want now, Beth?*

He sat down in front of the computer to work on the manuscript of *None Call It Justice* and stared at the blank screen. Nothing. The gentle whir of the air conditioner turned to a clanking sound and stopped. *I can't believe this,* he moaned inwardly. He called the apartment manager and listened to the current crop of excuses about why it couldn't be fixed until the next day. Rather than face the building heat that would soon turn the apartment into an oven, he opted to go out for a late lunch. He quickly showered and shaved and dressed in crisply pressed walking shorts and an open-necked sports shirt. He pulled on crew socks before slipping on his Birkenstock sandals. Just before he left the apartment, he glanced at Beth's still unopened letter. It could wait.

Superior Court Judge Jane Evans parked her car on the levee road's narrow shoulder across from the Virgin Sturgeon. She hadn't meant to stop and wanted to get home to spend some time in her garden. It wasn't often she could slip away from her office before four in the afternoon. But when she caught sight of Sutherland's immaculately polished eight-year-old Volvo, she changed her mind. She was a big woman but moved with a fluid grace as she walked down the jetway that had been salvaged from the airport. The sheltered walkway descended to a barge that had been converted into a restaurant and bar where the trendy crowd watered. She found him sitting next to the railing staring wistfully at a cruiser heading down the Sacramento River. He was nursing a warm beer.

Without a word, she sat down at his table. "Why did you quit?" she asked.

Sutherland stared at his drink before answering. "Meredith."

"So you lost a case after how long?"

"Four years."

"It had to happen sooner or later."

"That one was a slam dunk," he replied. "Cooper was on the ropes. Those bastards were guilty and everyone knew it. What in hell happened to justice?"

"Is that the title of the book you're writing?"

"No. I'm calling it *None Call It Justice.*"

Evans ordered an iced tea from a waitress wearing a pair of shorts that could stop traffic. "You could cause an accident dressed like that," she told the girl. The girl smiled and flounced away, not recognizing her. "Don't show up in my court dressed liked that," Evans murmured. She looked at Sutherland. "How do you think I felt? Meredith took my court away from me."

"You could have stopped him," Sutherland mumbled.

"True, but that would have guaranteed those Neanderthals would have walked. That was a good jury. I was hoping you could save it."

"But I couldn't," he muttered. "Who am I kidding? I couldn't even save my own marriage."

"You were a stepping stone on Beth's path to bigger and better things. Your marriage was finished when she had the affair with Cassidy." At the time, Ben Cassidy was the state's attorney general and a fast-rising politician with a future on the national scene.

"Cassidy wasn't the first," Sutherland muttered, feeling very sorry for himself. This was not his first beer.

"Why did you put up with it? This is a small town and sooner or later, it would all have come out."

"Beth always made sure there were, ah, consolation prizes."

"Like Cassidy's wife?" Evans asked, fitting the pieces together. Sutherland didn't answer and only stared across the river. "You're better off without her. She's going for the whole enchilada. Besides, the word is that you can't afford to quit."

"I unloaded the house and moved into a small apartment. I'm on terminal leave and still in the Air Force Reserve. By pulling a couple days' duty about twice a month I should get by."

"Not for long," Evans said. "Damn it, Hank, you're one of the good ones. You can make a difference." She saw Sutherland's eyes glance toward the jetway and caught the slight flush on his neck. It was one of the many things that made her a good judge. That, and the fact that she cared. She turned in the direction he was looking. Marcy Bangor, the reporter from the *Sacramento Union* was standing by the reception stand. Marcy was dressed in a pair of cutoff shorts that matched the waitress's for brevity and a halter top that was a size too small. She clopped across the deck, her high-heeled sandals announcing her entrance.

"I'll get by," Sutherland repeated. "Besides, I've got an agent in New York interested." Marcy wiggled onto a bar stool.

"What's the book really about?" Evans asked.

"It's an exposé on our system of justice. Be honest, we're just pissin' in the wind and getting splattered by it."

"Hank, what we're doing is making a system work. The bottom line: Our job is to support and defend the Constitution."

"Against all enemies foreign and domestic," Sutherland added.

"I took an oath to make that happen," Evans said. "Barring the second coming of Christ, it's the best thing we got for now."

Marcy waved from the bar. "Hi, Hank." Sutherland waved back.

Evans came to her feet. "I think the consolation prize has arrived. Hank, get your act together. You can make a difference. But if you're searching for perfect justice, you'll have to look outside the courtroom." She turned and walked away as Marcy slipped off the bar stool, the friction pulling her shorts up even higher.

* * *

"It's hot," Marcy said. She sat on the edge of Sutherland's bed as he slid back the sliding doors that opened onto a patio. "What happened to the air conditioner?"

"It's broken," he told her. He moved a fan into the doorway and turned it on. "I hope you like getting hot and sticky."

She rubbed her hands on her bare midriff, feeling the perspiration. A long and drawn out whisper escaped. "Ha-a-ank, I'm not into kinky stuff. We can go to my place."

"Neither am I." The heat of the day hadn't broken yet and the night air blowing into the bedroom was still warm with just a hint of river smell. "You ever been in New Or'lans when you can cut the night like soft butter?" His voice had taken on a richer, more husky sound, almost Southern. It was enough to tease her imagination.

He kicked off his Birkenstocks and pulled off his socks. She stood up and pulled his shirt loose, undoing the buttons. "Strip the bed," he murmured. She helped him pull off the bed cover and shove the pillows on the floor. She sat back down on one side and looked over her shoulder as he crawled across the bed to her. Kneeling behind her, he gently rubbed her shoulders as her hands clasped the edge of the bed. She turned into the breeze, closed her eyes, and let the warm air ruffle her hair. His hands touched her waist.

"God, it's hot," she whispered.

His fingers traced a path across the top of her shorts, barely touching her navel. He felt a slight tremor dance across her stomach. "It's going to get hotter, darlin'," he promised, his voice now darkly Southern.

Marcy rolled over in bed. It was still dark and he was gone. "Hank, where are you from?"

"Bastrop, Louisiana," he answered from the living room. "Not much there. A nice little town to escape from and go back to occasionally."

Marcy sat on the edge of the bed, clutched a pillow to her breast, and buried her cheek in it, feeling warm and safe. She stood and took a few steps to the open patio door and let the warm night air wash over her naked body. She dropped the pillow and nudged it with her toe into the moonlight before padding into the living room. Sutherland was sitting on the couch in the dark, and like her, he was still naked. He was holding an envelope. "Can you read in the dark?" she asked. He shook his head. "Who's it from?"

"My ex-wife."

"What does she want?"

"Beats the hell out of me. I haven't opened it." She sat on his lap and nibbled an earlobe. "Ouch!"

"Do you have any idea what you did to me in there?" she breathed in the same ear.

He laughed. "Wasn't that the idea?"

She licked at his damaged earlobe. "Are you going to read the letter?"

His arms encircled her as he tore the letter in two and threw it on the floor. "Nope. I'm done with her."

She nipped his ear again. "Whoa! You've got sharp teeth."

"If only you knew." She stood and pulled him back to the bedroom and out onto the patio. She pushed him into a chair and knelt on the pillow in front of him. She rubbed his knees, spreading them apart. "Try not to wake the neighbors."

Sutherland was cooking breakfast when Marcy came out of the bedroom wearing one of his white shirts and holding a cordless phone to her ear. "I'll get right on it," she said. She dropped the phone in its cradle and leaned over his shoulder. "That smells good. I didn't know you were a cook." He reached under the shirt and patted her bare bottom. "You are a bit of a goat, Hank. I've got a story assignment over on the coast near Fort Ross. Want to come along?"

"What's the story?"

"About some group. They don't have a name."

"Millenarians?" he asked.

"What's a millenarian?"

"Someone who believes they'll find salvation at the end of the millennium."

"We'll find out when we get there."

Marcy talked as she drove along the coast road. "I love this drive." Sutherland relaxed in the passenger's seat, glad that he didn't have to navigate. He hated driving and got lost anytime he ventured beyond the city limits. Because it was mid-April, the road was deserted and the vegetation lush with the promise of spring. "Maybe we can spend the night at Mendocino," she said. He said it sounded good to him and gave her a lecherous leer. "I think this is the turn-off." She turned into a narrow lane that led toward the ocean. They drove past well-tended fields and into a farmstead on the edge of the bluffs that overlooked the Pacific. "What a beautiful place," she said, stopping to take some photos.

Sutherland followed Marcy around as she toured the farmstead and interviewed the commune leader. He was a pleasant, ordinary-looking man in his early thirties who took a great deal of pride in his community. They walked past an expanse of lawn where a small group of children were clustered around their teacher listening to her read a story. "This reminds me of a kibbutz I visited in Israel," Marcy said.

The man smiled and said they were just themselves, getting on with life. "Would you like to join us for supper?" he asked. "We eat early so we can meditate at sunset. We let the diurnal movement of nature dictate our lives, not the arbitrary ticking of a clock." He led them into the commune's dining hall where they sat at long benches. Large tureens of soup were brought out of the kitchen with baskets of hot, freshly baked bread and pitchers of crystal clear water. The people joined hands and silently prayed. Then the room exploded into a symphony of laughter and happy voices as they ate.

Afterward, Marcy and Sutherland followed them to a grove of eucalyptus trees nestled at the edge of the cliffs overlooking the ocean. Sutherland sat on a bench and studied the waves lapping against the rocks eighty feet below him. "This is pretty peaceful now," he said. "But I bet it can get pretty wild during a storm."

"Shush," Marcy commanded. All around them the people were gazing at the sunset in silence. He was amazed how quickly the sun sank below the horizon and assumed they would leave once it had disappeared. But the people sat there as the fading light painted the clouds and sky with shades of ever-changing yellow, gold, and red. It had never occurred to Sutherland that the most magnificent part of the sunset happened after the sun had set.

Instinctively, he looked around, letting the evidence speak for itself. What he saw was a group of sixty-four people living a pleasant existence in an idyllic commune. There was no ideology or weirdness driving them and they didn't dress funny or act strangely. It was too good to be true, which in a D.A.'s world was an alarm. *I'm not in that business anymore,* he thought. But he couldn't stop thinking about it.

Then it was dark. He and Marcy walked in silence back to the car. "Not much of a story here," she complained. "A waste of time."

They got into the car and again, she drove. "I got a feeling they were searching for something, or maybe waiting," he said.

"Waiting for what?"

He shrugged. "The end of the millennium? Someone to give them direction? Until then, they're tending their garden."

"I like that," she said. "Tending their garden. The Gardeners. Still not a story, though."

"There's a story here, trust me. Keep asking yourself *why?* When you get an answer to the first *why,* probe deeper and ask *why* again. Keep at it until you get to the bottom line. It will surprise you." He chattered on, wanting to discuss the dynamics of group behavior. But Marcy was bored.

"Hank, you were a D.A. too long. Besides, that's not what reporting is all about." She reached out and touched his cheek. "It's been fun and the sex was great. But it's not going to work, is it?"

He knew she was right. Without a word, she drove through Mendocino and headed for Sacramento.

9:55 A.M., THURSDAY, APRIL 22,
THE WHITE HOUSE, WASHINGTON, D.C.

The Vice President was waiting when Art Rios drove the Lincoln Town Car up to the west entrance of the White House. A marine guard snapped the door open and Durant got out. The two men shook hands and walked to the Cabinet Room where the National Security Council was holding its first meeting since the San Francisco bombing. "We want to take a hard look at the Armed Islamic Group," the Vice President said, "and the President asked for you to join us." Durant read between the lines: The Project was going to be part of the discussion.

The men and women gathered in the Cabinet Room chatted amiably until the President arrived forty-five minutes late. He sat down without an apology and looked around the table. "Nelson, thank you for coming. We appreciate the warning on the AIG and I hope the Project can be put to more immediate use."

"Mr. President," Durant said. "As I explained earlier, it was only during a test run that our technicians stumbled onto the Armed Islamic Group. But the Project is at least a year away from being operational."

"Yes, yes, I know," the President replied. "Perhaps, if the Project was given to the CIA you could make faster progress and any information that is discovered can be exploited now."

Durant was silent as the discussion went around the table. The clue was in the timing, and he was certain the President wanted access to the Project before the elections. To what end, he didn't know. *Maybe Agnes can find out,* he thought. But just as quickly, he discarded the idea. There had to be limits.

"Can the FBI use the Project?" the President asked. "I'm thinking here of the San Francisco bombing." He shook his head. "What is it about this time of year that drives people crazy?"

The Vice President answered. "Maybe it's income taxes or spring. Who knows."

"Mr. President," Durant said, "the Project is programmed only against foreign threats."

"Can it be reprogrammed for domestic enemies?"

"That raises a host of Constitutional issues," the DCI replied.

"I want progress on San Francisco," the President snapped. "Meredith—" His face flushed and he paused to gain control. Meredith's criticism of the government's handling of the bombing was reaching a dangerous level. "Meredith is beating us to death with it."

The Vice President got the meeting back on track. "Mr. President, we need to discuss the Sudan." They all opened the folders in front of them and the DCI gave a quick rundown on the Armed Islamic Group.

As usual, Serick was the most hawkish and demanded the laboratories be destroyed at the earliest possible moment with a Cruise missile strike. But target analysis revealed the laboratories were too deep underground for Cruise missiles to be effective. "So," Serick replied, "we use a nuclear weapon."

"Nuclear weapons are out of the question," the President growled.

"There is another option," the Chairman of the Joint Chiefs of Staff ventured. "The B-Two Stealth bomber. We can employ a BLU-113 with a JDAM package." He explained that a BLU-113 was a 4800-pound bomb that was mated with the Joint Direct Attack Munitions package. The bomb could penetrate two hundred feet of earth and still punch through twelve feet of reinforced concrete.

The president looked convinced. "That should do the trick."

"Is that sending a billion-dollar elephant against a hundred dollar mouse?" Durant asked. "Why don't you check with Special Operations? They might have another option."

"Do we have time?" Serick asked.

Rios was waiting when Durant came out of the west entrance. "I'll drive," Durant said, slipping behind the wheel.

Rios recognized the signs. "The meeting didn't go well?" he asked, crawling into the right seat. Rios braced himself for a wild ride back to the Farm.

"They're going to turn the Project over to the CIA or FBI. Can you believe that? And they're thinking of using B-Twos to bomb the AIG. Damn! It's all tied to the San Francisco bombing. They're totally stymied and Meredith is all but blaming the government. They need to get Meredith off their backs before the election and the easiest way to do that is to stir up a foreign threat." He snorted. "External conflict for internal peace."

Rios held on as the big car hurtled around a corner. "It's always easier to deal with foreign crazies than our domestic ones. Maybe the President can't stop Meredith any other way." A traffic light in front of them blinked red and Durant slammed the car to a halt. "Boss, if you don't slow down, I'm gonna resign and join the National Guard."

Durant laughed. "Really? Why?"

Rios breathed easier. He had broken the tension that was binding Durant. "It's safer. Besides, I like the food."

A low chuckle escaped from Durant. He was back on track. "Screw 'em. Let's break the 'surly bonds' and go flying."

Rios had done his job. "The Staggerwing is good-to-go," he allowed, "and it is a beautiful day."

2:38 A.M., FRIDAY, APRIL 23,
WHITEMAN AIR FORCE BASE, MO.

Lt. Col. Daniella "Quick Draw" McGraw held her palm against the reader at the security entry point. She waited impatiently for the computer to do its thing and clear her into the basement vault of the Operational Support Squadron building. Finally, it buzzed and she pushed through the door. She glanced at her watch. "Four minutes this time," she muttered to herself. "Still too long." The new security system had been nothing but trouble since it had been installed.

She gave the technicians a mental deadline of one more week or they were going back to the old card swipe method. Until that happened, she would have a guard posted with an access list. Sometimes, the old ways still worked the best.

McGraw was an intense, pleasant-looking, thirty-nine-year-old, and at five feet five inches, with a medium build and short auburn brown hair, would have been attractive, maybe even glamorous, had she time for that sort of thing. Instead, she was a dedicated Intelligence officer and the director of the mission-planning division. On the surface, she was in total contrast to the nickname her subordinates had given her. Some claimed she had been tagged after a cartoon character from an old TV show, but those who worked for her knew better.

McGraw hurried down the hall and burst into the nerve center of her domain, the mission-planning cell of the 509th Bomb Wing. Lt. Col. McGraw, the thirteen people working there, and all the communications gear, computers, printers, and huge data banks that were packed into the basement vault had only one purpose in the Air Force—to do the planning that enabled the B-2A Stealth bomber to find and destroy targets.

What went on in the mission-planning cell bordered on magic, but the result was a series of digital cassettes that contained all the information and planning factors a B-2 crew needed to hit the target and return home safely. The information on the cassettes was downloaded into the B-2's computers before the aircraft took off and could be updated in flight through satellite communications.

Once inside, McGraw did a quick head count. Everyone was there except one. "Where's Brad?" she asked.

"Capt. Jefferson is on his way," a voice answered. "He lives quite a ways—"

"I know where he lives," McGraw snapped. Luckily, the two key planners, the pilot who was an expert on weapons and tactics and the electronics warfare officer, were there and already at work. Without them, nothing worthwhile happened. "Okay, let's see it." She was handed a red-trimmed folder with a large SECRET stamped at the top and bottom of the front and back cover. She opened it and frowned. She had been expecting a Warning Order to prepare for mission tasking.

"Well, well," she finally said, realizing what it all meant, "here's old Watash, the first of the Mohicans—again." Inside the folder was an Air Tasking Order, or ATO for short, ordering the 509th to prepare for the first operational B-2 strike against a hostile target. She scanned the message, focusing on the key phrases:

STANDBY READY TO LAUNCH: H+12
EXECUTION AUTHORITY: NCA

The "H" stood for H-hour which was, in this case, the time and date of the message. The 509th had twelve hours to load and prepare a B-2 and do all the necessary mission planning. The actual launch could come any time after twelve hours once the NCA, or national command authority, made up his mind to execute the mission. For the uninitiated, the national command authority was the President of the United States.

McGraw had seen a permutation of this ATO many times before and, for her, it meant politicians were mentally masturbating with the titillations of power that lay close to hand in response to some new problem. None of them were really willing to take the final step and actually launch a strike mission with real bombs. Which was just fine with her.

She scanned the intelligence and threat estimate the team's Intelligence officer had already extracted from the computer database. "Ma'am," a voice ventured on her right, "all things considered, him being Muslim, maybe it would be best if Capt. Jefferson was out of the loop on this one. And since he's not here yet—"

McGraw stared at him while her staff held its collective breath. "Give me a break." She didn't bother to remind them that Capt. Jefferson was the computer genius who had finally debugged the new Air Force Mission Support System and made the complex computer system work as intended. "Okay, troops, this is a new target, one we haven't worked before. The Wing King"—she used that nickname for the brigadier general who commanded the 509th Bomb Wing partly in jest—"is gonna want a mission profile soonest to run through the simulator."

A mission profile was the total flight planning package that included everything from takeoff, to navigation, refueling, the combat phase of the mission, escape, and finally recovery. Nothing was omitted, and creating a mission profile took hours, only made possible by the state-of-the-art computers and software in McGraw's mission-planning division. She smiled. "Knowing the way he works, he'll want two; a high and a low." The mission-planning cell groaned loudly.

Regardless of popular perceptions, the B-2 was not totally unobservable to radar at short ranges. It was the old controversy over the best way to hit a target. One side maintained it was best to sneak in at low level and use terrain masking to escape detection. The other side of the argument opted for high level and corridor tactics where standoff missiles destroyed any radar they could not avoid. Both sides of the argument had many supporters, but either way, creating even a single mission profile was a Herculean task. "Okay, sweathogs," McGraw said, "let's get to it."

McGraw pulled the captain who had suggested cutting Jefferson out of the loop into her office, closed the door, and gently massaged her neck, a sure sign some target shooting was about to begin. "You, son, are truly suffering from a massive case of brain farts. Shitcan that type of thinking or you'll be scrubbing out septic tanks for the rest of your career in the Air Force." She relented, but only a little. "Look, Brad is unique and if he gets the idea the Air Force doesn't want him, or trust him, there're at least five major contractors who do." Then she turned up the heat again. She didn't want the troops to think she had gone all soft and mushy in her old age. "I hope you can say the same."

The captain felt he had to justify himself. "I apologize, ma'am. But I was only thinking about his—ah—background."

"Brad and I go a long way back. It's not a factor. Trust me." Her intercom buzzed and a voice said that Capt. Jefferson had arrived. McGraw glanced at her watch. "About time." She made a mental note to get Jefferson jumped up on the waiting list for base housing. If the Old Man wouldn't make it happen, she knew a general who could.

She wandered back into the mission-planning cell. It was humming with purposeful activity. "Brad," she called. "Got a minute? What happened? Were you late in getting notified?"

A slender, pleasant looking African-American looked up from his computer. "I got stopped for speeding coming through Lone Jack."

McGraw shook her head. "It figures."

9:00 A.M., FRIDAY, APRIL 23,
WARRENSBURG, MO.

The beat-up old van was parked on a side road off Maguire Street. To all appearances, it was a construction van loaded with ladders and pipes with a big storage container on top. But inside, two men were surrounded by the latest in surveillance technology. From where they were parked, the men could monitor the modest homes on the southern side of the road and the few struggling businesses with their half-vacant warehouses on the opposite side.

"Check this out," Brent Mather said. The other FBI agent on the stakeout looked over his shoulder at the monitor. A statuesque redhead with a cascading mane of hair down her back was getting out of a car on the residential side of the street. She was wearing a minidress that gave maximum play to her long legs as she stood up.

"That's Sandi Jefferson," the senior agent said. "She's married to a black guy at Whiteman." Whiteman Air Force Base was ten miles away from Warrensburg, which was one of the reasons they were on stakeout. "If you want a good image, get her on the long lens."

This was Brent Mather's first assignment since graduating from training, and he was still learning to handle the equipment. Mather used the telephoto lens on the high-definition camera to zoom in on Sandi Jefferson as she moved around the car. Her quick steps whipped the short hem of her dress into a sea of motion that made for some interesting photography. "Nice ass," he said.

"She's white trash," the senior agent replied. He patted Mather on the shoulder and went back to his newspaper. The kid was doing okay. Unfortunately, Mather lacked the arrogance required of FBI special agents, but the senior agent was certain that age and experience would cure that defect in his character.

Mather recorded Sandi as she pulled a black silk chador out of the backseat and threw the long cloak over her shoulders. Then she pulled off her high-heel sandals and slipped on a pair of frumpy lace-ups. She tied a dark scarf over her hair and pulled up the hood. She walked across the street and entered the warehouse that had been converted to a mosque.

9:15 A.M., FRIDAY, APRIL 23,
WHITEMAN AIR FORCE BASE, MO.

"Oh, shitsky," Capt. Douglas Holloway muttered when he stepped into mission-planning cell. "This is a biggy." The room was crowded with every colonel and lieutenant colonel who could think of a reason to be there.

Maj. Mark Terrant stifled the caution that was forming on the back of his tongue about watching his language. After all, this was still the 509th. But Holloway had a great sense of presence and knew when to shut up. Terrant limited himself to "What did you expect when they asked for volunteers?"

McGraw met them and led them to the smaller briefing room where the mission would be covered in detail. "You can decline the mission if you want," she told them before they entered.

"I assume this is the real thing," Terrant replied.

"Isn't it always?" McGraw said.

Holloway gave her his best grin. Other crews had been through this drill before. "Right. If it was for real, Jim West would be beating down the door to take it." Lieutenant Colonel Jim West was, without doubt, the best mission commander in the wing and an advocate for high-level corridor tactics.

"Col. West is on leave," McGraw said.

"Just like all staff weenies," Holloway said. "Never around when the shooting starts. But since we're not headquarters pukes, we'll take it." The implication was obvious: No staff weenie would want to fly in real combat.

"Don't pay him no never-mind," Terrant said, not wanting to antagonize McGraw. He knew of her reputation, and her recommendations carried weight in the 509th. "He just thinks he's the best pilot in the wing."

"So does the Old Man," McGraw conceded, now very serious. "Or he wouldn't be here."

It was the truth. For all his flippant manner, Doug Holloway was a dedicated bomber pilot. He was a student of the B-2 and probably knew more about the aircraft and its systems than anyone on base except Jim West and Mark Terrant. But there was more. The men were consummate pilots and possessed IQs that bordered on the edge of genius. Physically, Mark Terrant was tall and gangly with red hair. Doug Holloway was shorter, just over five feet ten inches, with dark-brown hair, and built like a highly conditioned athlete, which he was. Both men had narrow-set eyes and perfect vision. Professionally, they were the product of a selection process that had started years before. For Mark Terrant, it had been the Air Force Academy and B-52 bombers, for Doug Holloway, electrical engineering at Stanford University, AFROTC, and fighters.

Because they flew an aircraft that cost $1.3 billion a copy, they had to be solid trustworthy types who were extremely competent pilots. But underneath, at their very core, they were classic alpha personalities and controlled aggression.

The wing commander, the operations group commander, their squadron commander, and the chief of Intelligence were waiting for them in the briefing room. "Gentlemen," the wing commander began, "I think you all know Maj. Mark Terrant, one of our lead mission commanders, and his pilot, Captain Doug Holloway." Nods all around. "Well, Mark, Doug, we've been tasked to take out a biological weapons factory in the Middle East with conventional weapons. Do you want it?"

Terrant was ready with the standard answer. "Yes, sir." Not too loud, just the right emphasis.

Holloway couldn't help himself. "How much of my sex life do I have to give up, sir?"

10:00 A.M., FRIDAY, APRIL 23,
WARRENSBURG, MO.

FBI Special Agent Mather focused on Sandi Jefferson as she came out of the converted warehouse that served as a mosque for the faithful of Warrensburg. He dutifully recorded the other faces in the crowd, mostly foreign exchange students from Central Missouri State University in town, but he always returned to Sandi. "Who's that with her?" he asked.

The other agent came over and studied the monitor. "The black guy? That's her husband. He's a captain in the Air Force." They watched in silence as the two stood under a shade tree. A short, dark-complected man with pock-marked skin joined them. *What a toad,*

Mather told himself, comparing the newcomer to Sandi's husband who was trim and well dressed.

"Son of a bitch," the senior agent growled. "Why are they talking to Khalid?" Mather's fingers flew over the computer's keyboard as he logged the date, time, and circumstances surrounding the contact between Osmana Khalid and the Jeffersons.

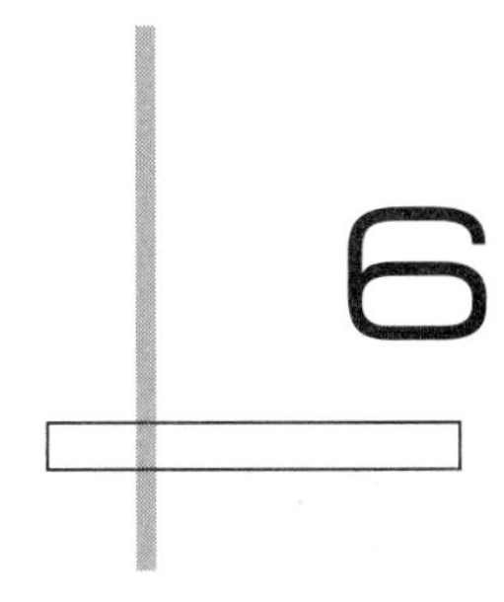

6

6:05 A.M., SATURDAY, APRIL 24,
THE FARM, WESTERN VIRGINIA

Durant ambled across the campuslike grounds, enjoying the soft morning air. It was a pleasant change after a hectic Thursday and Friday in Washington. But he was still preoccupied with the President's reactions at the NSC meeting. *What is he going to do?* He paused before entering the building where the Project was housed. *Am I doing the right thing?* he wondered. Then, his mind made up, he walked inside. Except for the security guards, the building was deserted. He climbed the stairs to the second floor and cleared himself onto the balcony overlooking the control center. He sat down in front of the two TV monitors. "Hello, Agnes," he said.

The right monitor came to life and the woman smiled at him. "Good morning, Mr. Durant," the computer said. "I'm glad you came back. I missed you."

"That's sweet, Agnes," he replied.

"What's the weather like?"

"It's a perfect April morning," he replied. "But there's a hint of an early summer. I wish it could stay like this year-round."

"We are experiencing some unusual heat waves, especially on the West Coast."

What am I doing? he thought. *Being sociable and discussing the weather with a computer is crazy.* "Agnes, there's something I want you to do. Can you find out who was behind the bombing of the San Francisco Shopping Emporium?"

"That shouldn't be too hard, Mr. Durant. To what level do you want me to search?"

Searching to a prescribed level was new. "I'm sorry, Agnes. I don't understand."

"Do you want proof that will stand up in a court of law or do you just want to know who the perps are?"

"Perps?"

The image blushed. "Perpetrators. I've been watching TV."

"Proof, if you can find it. But I'll settle for the perps."

Agnes looked serious. "A provisional first search of the FBI data banks reveals nothing conclusive. Those idiots," she fumed, "they haven't got a clue. I'll see what the CIA has." There was a short pause. "Nothing there. I'll establish a worldwide communications watch. Someone, somewhere, sometime will start talking. It's just a matter of time." Durant stiffened. Agnes had been programmed to target specific communications in conjunction with a request for limited intelligence, not do roving communication intercepts. "I just learned how to do it," she explained. "I coopted computers in different parts of the world and established communication listening posts. I'll tell them to be alert for anyone talking about the bombing."

"Did the whiz kids teach you that?"

She smiled. "No. I worked it out myself. But it does take a lot of energy and time. I had to capture computer space from the Lawrence Livermore Labs." Her voice turned patronizing. "Those supercomputers are rather obsolete. Massive parallel processing works much better."

"Agnes, do me a favor and keep all this between you and me, okay?"

The image beamed at him. "Certainly, Mr. Durant. I won't even tell the children."

1:20 P.M., SATURDAY, APRIL 24,
THE SUDAN

The old Soviet-built "Hip" helicopter settled to earth, the seventy-foot rotor kicking up dust and gravel from the desert floor. The swirling blades spun down and the dust subsided over the company of eighty-four men waiting in the hot Saturday sun. Not one moved until the lieutenant called them to attention. As one, the men snapped to with a sharpness totally out of character for them. Sweat streaked their faces and still they did not move. Then the captain got off the helicopter. If anything, the men became more rigid. To the man, they wanted to do this one right.

Capt. Davig al Gimlas stepped to the ground and jammed his beret on at exactly the right tilt. He raked the sunglasses out of his shirt pocket and carefully adjusted them on his prominent nose. The lieutenant stepped forward and, his hand slightly shaking, saluted the tall captain.

At six feet four inches, al Gimlas towered above the lieutenant. Because of a heavy scar on his left cheek that ended above his upper lip, he was clean shaven and could not grow the heavy mustache that was the trademark of the average Arab male. He didn't need it. He had experienced more combat than any other officer in the Sudanese Army, and in full field gear he could run any soldier into the ground over a thirty-mile trek.

But he was not a mindless military robot. He had been educated at the Sorbonne in Paris and received his military training at Sandhurst, the Royal Military College, in England. He had received a direct commission into the Sudanese Army and had returned to command an outpost in southern Sudan where a full-fledged armed rebellion was going on. In less than six years, he had established a reputation as a brilliant commander and tactician, a humane civilian administrator, and totally above corruption. He was a rarity in Africa.

Capt. Davig al Gimlas was also a legend among the NCOs and enlisted ranks, and they would follow him anywhere. His superiors hated him because he was all that they were not. But when they had an assignment that could not fail, he was the only man they had. Al Gimlas returned the lieutenant's salute. "Stand down the men," he ordered. "Get them in the shade and after they've had a chance to drink and cool down, I will speak to them. We have a great deal of work and training to do in the next few hours."

6:45 A.M., SUNDAY, APRIL 25,
WHITEMAN AIR FORCE BASE, MO.

Mark Terrant was in the base chapel at the early Sunday service with his wife when the pager clipped to his flight suit vibrated. He glanced down, checked the number, and clicked it off. Barbara Terrant looked at him. She had been an Air Force wife long enough to know what it meant. Without a word, she squeezed his hand. He stood up and stepped into the aisle. But before he left, he bent over and kissed her cheek. "Tell the kids I'll be back in a few days. I love you." Then he was gone.

She watched him as he walked out the door. Then she turned back to the altar. "Please, God," she prayed.

Outside, Terrant sprinted for the blue Air Force pickup he drove while on alert. He jumped inside and drove quickly toward the OSS building without turning on the emergency lights. A block away, the pickup driven by Doug Holloway pulled in behind him, its lightbar flashing. Terrant gave an inward groan. *Doug's shining his ass again. It must be a fighter pilot thing.*

Inside the OSS building, Lt. Col. McGraw was waiting for them outside the Combat Crew Communications section. "We got a Go," she said once they were inside the large vault where they had to sign for the classified material they needed to execute the mission. It was a deluge of paperwork that filled two briefcases. She handed them a copy of the Emergency Actions message that authorized them to execute the mission. The two pilots hunched together and read it like co-conspirators. "It's a valid decode," she told them.

"Current defenses?" Terrant asked, now concerned with basics.

"As originally briefed," McGraw answered. She handed them the two digital data unit cartridges that held the mission profile they would download into the B-2's onboard computers. "Another crew ran your choice through the simulator Saturday evening. They agreed low level is the best way to ingress the target area. It looks like a piece of cake."

Holloway gave her his best grin as he signed for the cartridges. "That *was* the idea." He and Holloway had spent most of Saturday in the simulator flying the penetration and attack phase of the mission at both high and low level before deciding on the low-level profile.

"The Wing King is waiting for you at the airplane," she said. "Good hunting." The two pilots were out the door where a security cop was waiting to escort them to the waiting aircraft and the wing commander. McGraw breathed a heavy sigh. It had been a hectic 53 hours since the air tasking order message had come in, and she was tired beyond belief. It was time to go home.

6:20 P.M., SUNDAY, APRIL 25,
THE SUDAN

Capt. al Gimlas glanced at the setting sun and double-checked his GPS receiver against the map to ensure they were at the right location. It all made sense and he was surprised his superiors could issue such a logical order sending him to these specific coordinates. But he sensed they were rapidly running out of time. If the Americans were coming, it would be tonight.

Impatiently, he walked to the edge of the pit and looked down at the four men still digging. He was at the apex of a twelve-foot-deep, cone-shaped hole. The base of the cone, at the bottom of the hole, measured exactly twelve feet across and was almost finished. The unconsolidated *reg* that formed the desert's surface threatened to collapse the sides of the cone-shaped hole and he stepped back. *Who will volunteer to go down this hellhole?* he thought.

"Lieutenant, ask for volunteers to man the echo chamber. They must have sharp hearing. It will be dangerous." The lieutenant hurried away to do as ordered while al Gimlas walked over to the Shilka. He directed the Shilka's commander to park the tanklike vehicle near the pit and slew the four barrels of its antiaircraft cannon skyward. Satisfied it was positioned correctly, he returned to the command and communications tent. "Is the radar operational yet?"

The radio operator took a deep breath. He wanted to tell al Gimlas only good news. "Within the hour."

Al Gimlas nodded. "And the Stinger teams?"

The operator beamed. Now he had good news. "All six teams are in radio contact and report they are in position."

Al Gimlas studied the tactical disposition chart tacked to an easel. He considered himself lucky to have six of the deadly, U.S.-built, shoulder-held, antiaircraft Stinger missiles. A black market arms merchant had sold the Sudanese government over fifty of the missiles that the CIA had originally given the rebels in Afghanistan to use in their fight against the old Soviet Union in the 1980s. Now the missiles were showing up all over the world, and al Gimlas had six to use against the country that had made them.

If our information is right, he told himself, *they must overfly my position.* Not sure how best to deploy the missiles, he had strung them in a long line down the valley that led from his location to the agricultural research laboratory at the head of the valley. He cursed his luck. His superiors had given him an impossible task: Stop the Americans from bombing an isolated and undefended target. But the Americans had the most advanced technology in the world: Cruise missiles, F-15E Strike Eagles, F-117 Stealth fighters, B-1s, or B-2 Stealth bombers. Even the old B-52s were still flying and carrying standoff cruise missiles. What could his poor country do against all of those aircraft and weapons?

All al Gimlas had was the direction the aircraft would come from, the initial point it would overfly on the way to the target, a brand-new S-12 radar, one old Shilka 23-millimeter antiaircraft cannon, and six Stinger missiles. And their ears.

But why that target? he wondered.

12:06 A.M., MONDAY, APRIL 26,
OVER THE MEDITERRANEAN

Doug Holloway rode the throttles and stick with an easy touch, keeping the big bomber tucked under the KC-10 tanker with an ease that belied the difficulty of flying in close formation for an air-to-air refueling at midnight. They had launched out of Whiteman nine hours ago and he was glad to have something to do. After taking off and engaging the autopilot, he had only monitored the systems to make sure everything worked as advertised. It wasn't much of a worry because the big bomber was remarkably reliable.

But the same could not be said for Terrant who sat in the right seat, which traditionally was reserved for copilots. As the mission commander, he was responsible for working the systems and accomplishing the mission. It was a break from the normal division of labor where the pilot sitting in the left seat ran the mission and everyone answered to him, but it was one that worked well in the B-2.

"Spirit One," the boom operator on the KC-10 radioed, "you've stopped taking fuel." The frequency-hopping radio they were using had a tinny sound. But it also guaranteed that no one was monitoring their transmissions, and the KC-10 appeared for all the world to be on a normal airlift mission. Terrant scanned the fuel system display. The arrows that indicated fuel was flowing to the tanks were off and the graphic tank displays were shaded full. He gave Holloway a thumbs-up.

"Rog, Toga," Holloway told the tanker. "We're topped off. Disconnect now." The boom broke away from the B-2 and flew above his head as he retarded the throttles to clear the tanker.

Terrant's face broke into a smile. With the tanks topped off, they could hit the target and, in an emergency, make it to their alternate recovery base at Diego Garcia in the Indian Ocean. He checked his threat warning display. A few early-warning radars from Libya and Algeria were active but not a single one would ever detect the B-2 at that range. He made one last transmission on the satellite communications radio. There were no changes to the target, or the threat, and they were cleared to continue. "Time to stealth up," he told Holloway.

Terrant's fingers danced over the data entry panel, calling up the right pages on the small screen. Automatically, antennas were retracted, shields lowered, electronic defenses fully activated, and all external electronic signals that could be detected, like the radar, placed in standby. Within seconds, the B-2 was ready for combat. The B-2 never became totally unobservable to all radars, but once the aircraft was in its "mission mode," it came extremely close to disappearing.

The downside to all this was that they lost outside radio communications and the use of the aircraft's radar.

The autopilot continued to fly the mission profile and the big jet turned toward the coast of North Africa. Now they were flying the "blue line," the flight track that optimized their penetration of enemy airspace. They intended to overfly the Gulf of Sirte and the crazy Libyan colonel's "line of death." The blue line then threaded around any radar that might detect them at close range. From there, they would fly south along the Libyan-Egyptian border and split the air defense seam between the two countries before descending to low level for the attack phase. If blind luck became a factor and the air defenses of one country did detect them, they would dart into the other country's airspace and stir the diplomatic pot. But by the time the air defenders made a decision, the B-2 would have disappeared into the night.

"It doesn't seem fair," Holloway said, making light conversation as he munched a sandwich.

"What doesn't seem fair?" Terrant replied.

"Us zapping a bunch of clueless ragheads with the world's greatest piece of technology."

"They're not clueless," Terrant grunted as he reached for his helmet and gloves.

4:03 A.M., MONDAY, APRIL 26,
OVER NORTHERN SUDAN

The threat status on Terrant's left multifunctional display (MFD) flashed, demanding the two pilots' attention. The B-2's highly sophisticated and sensitive electronic countermeasures system had detected the faint pulse of a search radar. Terrant pushed at the menu buttons on the side of the MFD to analyze the new threat. "Holy shit, it's an S-Twelve!" It was one of the few times he felt the need for profanity. The S-12 was a modern, Russian-built, highly mobile radar system that had been created to counter stealth technology and had never been reported outside Russia. It was basically a wide-aperture radar with an active array antenna.

Now it was Holloway's turn to be cool. "What's the range?"

Terrant pushed at another button. "Right now, over three hundred miles. No threat—so far. But we'll pass sixteen miles abeam on the leg into the IP." The IP, or initial point, was the last waypoint that pointed the way to the target.

"You'd think they'd place the S-Twelve at the target," Holloway muttered.

"Good point," Terrant answered. "They probably got it on the highest ground around to increase its range."

Holloway studied the display for a moment and tapped the recesses of his memory. "An S-Twelve at sixteen miles will paint us," he told Terrant. "I figure they'll get a return about the size of a big bird."

"Rog," Terrant replied. Holloway's reading of the new threat agreed with his. *But why was it there?* He thought about his options. For a moment, he considered breaking radio silence and using the SatCom radio to tell the national command center controlling the mission about the new threat. Because this was the B-2's first combat mission, the generals would probably call for an immediate abort. The political fallout from a screw-up could ruin careers.

The nice thing about the B-2 was that the aircraft systems allowed him time to work the problem. Obviously, the Sudanese were worried about an attack and were upgrading the target's defenses. *We stand a greater chance of being detected if we break radio silence,* he reasoned. *So what else is out there?* He answered his own question. *Nothing that can cause a problem. Don't wimp out now. This is what we get paid for.* But being a cautious man, he decided it was time to put distance and high terrain between them and the S-12 radar.

Terrant punched at the buttons surrounding the MFD that was slaved to the navigation computer. He called up a map display, inserted the position of the new radar, and examined their route. "They'll be looking west and north," he said. He shoved a new digital data unit cartridge into the lower data transfer receptacle and called up a backup profile the mission planning cell had developed. This one called for a low-level ingress that took them deep into the heart of the Sudan before making an end run to approach the target from the south. It was a good plan but had been rejected because of the additional time they had to spend over hostile territory.

The computers did their magic and integrated the new radar threat into the new profile. "Yeah," he muttered. The more he studied it, the better it looked. The new route would allow distance and high terrain to shield them from the S-12 radar. Yet they could still use their original initial point and attack axis. "What'cha think?" he asked Holloway, who had been following every step with rapt attention.

"Go for it."

The computer confirmed Terrant's analysis and, satisfied that an ingress altitude of 4,500 feet, which was 1,000 feet above the ground, would keep them in the shadow of the mountain range and still hold them above most small-arms ground fire, he punched in that number.

He hit another button and two seconds later, the navigation and weapons delivery computers were updated. Still on autopilot, the B-2 nosed over, dropping toward the desert floor over 40,000 feet below them. "We'll have to toss the weapon to get a decent standoff range," Terrant said.

"No biggy," Holloway replied. They had practiced that maneuver many times in the simulator.

4:46 A.M., MONDAY, APRIL 26,
THE SUDAN

"Captain! I hear something!" the boy shouted over the field telephone linking al Gimlas to the underground echo chamber. "But it is very weak."

"Keep your back against the wall," al Gimlas ordered. He stood in the cool night air, stared at the starry heavens above him, and strained to hear. There! Now he too could hear it. It was very faint, little more than a buzz. He spoke into the phone. "Move around the wall to keep the noise the loudest." He cautioned everyone aboveground to be silent. "Always keep your back to the wall."

"It's loudest here," the boy said.

"Which way are you looking?" al Gimlas asked.

"To the south."

The south! al Gimlas thought. *They're coming from the wrong direction. How clever.* Now he could definitely make out the sound—a jet aircraft. He wanted to shout with joy. While at Sandhurst, he had studied the way the Vietnamese had used their main resource, people, to defeat the Americans. His tutor had thought it a waste of time but had humored him. Personally, al Gimlas doubted that a cone-shaped hole could serve as an audio direction finder for locating aircraft. But maybe, just maybe, the rest would also work. Had the S-12 radar forced the plane to a lower altitude and into the range of the Shilka? He could hear it, couldn't he? All of them could hear it.

"It's a little louder," the boy said over the telephone.

"Tell me when it is very loud."

"Captain! The wall! It's caving in! Drop the ladder!"

"Wait!" al Gimlas shouted. He could see the ground ripple around the opening in the ground. "Just a few more seconds."

"I can't wait! I can't!"

"The noise, what is it doing?"

"Please! the ladder!"

"We'll get you out. Don't panic."

"There!" the boy shouted. "It's very loud."

"Fire!" al Gimlas shouted at the top of his lungs. Twenty feet away, the four barrels of the Shilka roared to life. The Shilka, or ZSU-23-4, was a Soviet-built antiaircraft cannon mounted on a tank chassis. The four barrels sent a stream of high-explosive 23-millimeter ammunition into the air. Every tenth round was a tracer and at the Shilka's high rate of fire, it etched the night with a solid red ribbon. The gunner traversed the barrels back and forth through fifteen degrees of arc, snaking the line of red tracers back and forth across the sky directly above him.

The ground underneath al Gimlas shook from the recoil and he could feel the dirt moving under his feet. The boy's voice screamed in panic over his headset.

The moving map on the MFD showed them over the initial point when a bright red line swept past the nose of the B-2. Holloway's reactions were rattlesnake quick, and he grabbed the control stick, flicked off the autopilot, and stood the B-2 on its left wing like a fighter, and turned away from the stream of tracers. "What the fuck!" he yelled. He pushed the stick forward and rolled out. It was a violent maneuver that touched the G limit the aircraft could sustain.

The red line snaked back across the sky at them. Again, Holloway stood the B-2 on a wing, this time the right one, as they cut a knife edge in the night, presenting the smallest possible target to the cannon fire. The two men saw the red line wave past them. "Shit-oh-dear!" Holloway shouted. The jet was on the very edge of control.

"Roll out!" Terrant shouted, feeling the slight buffet that indicated the loss of controlled flight. Holloway also felt it and raised the right wing. They saw the red line pass behind them and to the left. The aircraft shuddered as one round hit the underside of the left wing and exploded. They had flown through a curtain of unaimed barrage fire and the "golden BB," the lucky shot, the one-in-ten-million chance, had found them. It was pure luck, the one factor no amount of technology, planning, and training could counter.

The B-2's magic had also worked against it. Because of the bomber's precise navigation capability, it had flown directly over its planned initial point and into the unaimed artillery barrage.

Al Gimlas looked skyward, his eyes following the stream of tracers. In the flash of a single explosion, he saw the batlike shape of a wing. Then it was gone. He stared at the stars in wonder. Was it real? Had they really hit a B-2? It had to be. He ran toward the communications tent. "Start digging!" he yelled over his shoulder. "I want him out.

Alive." He skidded into the tent and grabbed a handset, calling the Stinger teams. "It's coming toward you! A B-Two."

"What do we shoot at?" one of the teams answered.

Frustrated, al Gimlas banged his fist on the table. They didn't have an echo chamber to tell them when the aircraft was passing overhead. But he had to tell them something. "Shoot at the sound when you hear it."

"I can't believe it," Holloway breathed. "I think we're okay." The unbelievable strength of the B-2's construction and the multiple redundancy of over two hundred onboard computers had saved it from what should have been a lethal hit. The explosion had damaged the left wing, ruptured the left outboard fuel tank, and destroyed or damaged four control surfaces. But the computers had automatically sealed off the ruptured tank, rerouted the fuel flow, and the quad-redundant fly-by-wire flight control system compensated for the damage to the control surfaces. Now the hours the two pilots had spent in the cockpit procedures trainers practicing emergencies exactly like this one paid results. They had to react to the warning messages the computers were sending and reconfigure the aircraft.

They were flying straight and level at eight hundred feet above the ground, the B-2 was responding to control inputs and not doing anything it shouldn't. An engine fire light flickered. Holloway confirmed with Terrant that it was the number one, the left outboard, before he retarded the throttle. The light went out. "Shut it down?" Holloway asked.

Terrant continued to run his emergency procedures checklist. "I think it's okay. Probably a damaged circuit." He punched buttons, rerouting the system. "Add some power." Holloway inched up the throttle and the light stayed out. The computers reported the engine as clean and undamaged. But they were running out of time and the weapons release point was on their nose, thirty-one seconds away.

Computers possess infinite courage and it fell to the pilots to make the critical decision. "Go for it?" Holloway asked.

"What else is out there?" Terrant asked. His mind raced with the implications as his hands went about other assigned tasks. The bird was looking more healthy all the time. They were good-to-go and the threat display was quiet. *If there are more defenses, they'll be clustered around the target,* he reasoned. *Which means we need more stand-off distance.* He made the decision. "Climb two hundred feet." Terrant punched in the new delivery parameters for the weapon. The numbers the computer spat back confirmed his thinking. A toss delivery for the deep penetrator bomb at that altitude gave them a four-mile standoff distance. More than enough.

The sergeant in command of the Stinger team halfway down the valley leading to the research laboratory stood in the open, scanned the night sky, and strained to hear. Nothing. But Murphy's law was on his side and he was looking in the right direction when the fuel cutoff valve in the B-2's left outboard fuel tank failed. Normally, a downstream shutoff valve would have backed up the primary valve. But owing to battle damage, it also failed and fuel gushed into the left engine bay before a third shutoff valve could function. The number one engine flared, sending a streak of flame out the exhaust for a few seconds.

The sergeant directed the Stinger onto the torch and fired. The missile worked perfectly and he was astounded by its speed. But the bright torch streaming out behind the B-2 winked out before the Stinger reached its target. The missile's seeker head lost the heat signature it was homing on and went ballistic, arcing through the B-2's altitude. But the area over the wing was still hot and the missile's heat-seeking guidance head homed on that. It ripped into the left wing and exploded, relighting the fuel. A second missile slammed into the big jet inboard of the left engine bay.

Amazingly, the aircraft held together and was still flyable, a tribute to Northrop's engineers and workers. A third missile flashed by underneath. The proximity fuse sensed a shift in mass and it exploded, shredding the underside of the wing. Structurally, the plane was still intact. But with all of the control surfaces on the left wing destroyed, no amount of computer redundancy could save the bomber.

"Eject! Eject! Eject!" Terrant shouted.

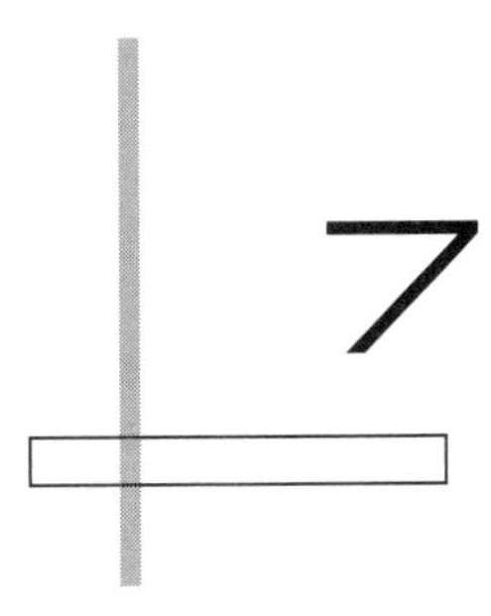

7

5:50 A.M., MONDAY, APRIL 26,
WASHINGTON, D.C.

Nelson Durant was awake early, dressed, and drinking his second cup of coffee when the White House called with the message. "They're reacting much faster these days," he told Art Rios.

"The National Security Council?" Rios asked.

"The President just called an emergency meeting," Durant replied. "I imagine Serick will be in fine form." The National Security Advisor had a well-earned reputation for working himself into a lather during a crisis.

The two men rode in silence to the White House as Durant read the latest message traffic coming in on the car's computer. Rios drove up to the west entrance where Durant was escorted to the Situation Room in the basement. "Ah, Nelson," Stephan Serick boomed, "so glad you could join us—finally." Durant ignored the jibe and sat down. "I take it you've heard the news on TV," Serick continued.

The door opened and the President entered with the Vice President, his senior policy adviser, and the director of Central Intelligence. The DCI quickly outlined the situation. The facts were simple: the Sudanese had shot down the B-2 Stealth bomber and captured the crew. So far, they had only publicly announced that two pilots were in captivity. The news had driven Meredith and the San Francisco bombing off the front page. Unfortunately, it wasn't the way they had planned. "Mr. Durant, considering your earlier discoveries, can the Project be used to monitor the situation in the Sudan?" the DCI asked.

"I'll see what the whiz kids can do," Durant replied. "Do we have coverage of the wreckage?" He knew the answer but hadn't seen the photos. An aide spoke into a phone and a series of scenes flashed on one of the TV monitors. An unidentifiable mass of wreckage was strewn over the desert floor. Durant breathed a sigh of relief. Because the B-2 was in a combat mode of operation, the aircraft's ejection sequence had worked as designed and the computers had opened the fuel valves and armed the weapons for detonation when the aircraft had hit the ground.

"It must have been one hell of an explosion and fire," the Vice President said. "Will they have enough to convince the world it was a B-Two?"

"Once they analyze the wreckage," the DCI said, "they will. Unfortunately, they also have the pilots, who are very much alive."

"Mr. President," Serick said, agreeing with the DCI's brutal assessment, "you still have plausible denial here. Simply announce that two pilots were on a routine airlift mission hauling cargo and got lost. You are demanding their immediate release."

"They got lost and ended up a thousand miles over the Sahara?" Durant asked. "In this day and age? Not likely." Serick glared at him. It was the old clash of personalities and they could never stay on the same side for long. "Perhaps," Durant counseled, "a simple announcement acknowledging the two Air Force pilots have been 'detained' by the Sudanese and you have no other comment at this time would be best. You need time to work the problem." He fell silent and listened while the men discussed the situation. Durant understood how the President worked and this meeting was only one in a series as he settled on a response to the latest problem. But Serick's arguments were swaying the President.

Durant was surprised when the door opened and the director of the FBI entered. He stood at the foot of the table and cleared his throat, not liking what he had to say. "I think we know how they did it," he announced. "Our agents have been trailing an Egyptian national, Osmana Khalid. Khalid is an Imam, an Islamic cleric, who has been operating out of Warrensburg, Missouri, for the last month. Warrensburg is ten miles from Whiteman Air Force Base. He was observed talking to an Air Force captain who was involved in planning the attack. After that conversation, Khalid phoned a student from Egypt who was attending Central Missouri State University located in town. The student then made a phone call to the home of a clerk who just happens to work in the Sudanese Embassy. We're still working on it."

"Were they using a code?" Durant asked.

"Please, Mr. Durant," the DCI answered, "we're not that stupid. It was a code within a language, Nubian, we think."

"So what are you saying?" the President asked.

The director of the FBI answered in a monotone, his face impassive. "Based on what we currently know, we are ninety-nine percent certain the captain passed critical information to Khalid who, in turn, passed it on to the Sudanese. It looks like they were waiting and the B-Two flew into a flak trap."

"I knew it!" Serick thundered. "We have spent billions of dollars on a weapon system that doesn't work. Mr. President, you need to send a message to the Air Force that the days of lavish spending on foolish programs are over."

Durant shook his head. One of his companies had developed part of the B-2's electronic defenses and he knew what the bomber could do. "You're misreading this, Stephan."

"How so?" Serick shot back. His jowly face was livid.

"Until an investigation is completed, we don't know what happened. The bomber has its faults, all aircraft do, but believe me, it would be best to assume the B-Two can perform as designed."

Serick snorted in disagreement.

Part of Art Rios's job was to know when to shut up and this was one of those times. He kept glancing in the rearview mirror as he drove back to Georgetown after picking Durant up at the White House. "Call the helicopter," Durant finally said. "We're going to The Farm. I'm sick of this place."

Rios decided it was time to talk. "Meeting went bad?"

"Terrible. I think Serick must be senile. His thinking hasn't changed in twenty years." He shook his head in disgust. "He wants to stonewall it. Plausible denial. Deny that a B-Two was shot down. The trouble is, Jim is listening to him."

"That can change in a heartbeat," Rios said.

Durant thought about the problem. "I need to talk to Agnes." He was going to add the Egyptian cleric, Osmana Khalid, to the watch list. Again, they rode in silence. Finally, Rios had to ask the question that demanded an answer. "How in the hell did they manage to shoot down a B-Two?" he asked.

Durant stifled a smile. Rios had been reading his message traffic again. "A traitor," he answered.

"I hope they nail the bastard."

"They know who he is." A long pause. "At least they know after the fact." Silence. Then, "Check on the status of Hank Sutherland."

Rios cocked an eyebrow. "Are you looking for anything specific?" There was no answer.

8:30 A.M., WEDNESDAY, APRIL 28,
EL FASHER, SUDAN

The convoy had barely left the army barracks in the center of town when a crowd of men and boys swarmed around the vehicles and prevented them from moving. Al Gimlas climbed out of the lead Range Rover that he used as his staff car. He stood in the hot, dusty main square as a shout of "Death to the American pigs!" echoed overhead. Before he could shove his way back to the third truck in line, an open flatbed, more people took up the chant and started to throw rocks.

The two Americans in the cage lashed to the flatbed were cowering against the floor, their arms wrapped around their heads as the stones pummeled them. Al Gimlas swore loudly, a fine Arabic phrase that lost its true meaning in English but roughly translated to "fucking idiots!" The captives had been in his care for three days and he had grown to respect them, especially the more reserved and dignified Major Terrant. There was no doubt that the same fools who had ordered the Americans to be caged like animals for transportation to the barracks at El Obeid had also organized this demonstration, rousing the people to a frenzy of hate. He couldn't change his orders, but he could ensure his charges arrived in good health.

"No!" he shouted. "Have you forgotten who you are! We are civilized men!"

A fat, dark-complected man pushed his way in front of al Gimlas. He sneered at the tall captain, establishing his dominance. "They are infidels, American swine who love Jews!" He hacked up a wad of phlegm and spat on al Gimlas's boots. It was a mistake. Al Gimlas knocked off the man's *kaffiyeh,* a red-checkered headdress, grabbed a handful of hair, spun him around while lifting him off the ground, and launched him into the crowd.

A loud roar of anger washed over him in retaliation. The crowd was becoming a mob. The sharp rattle of an AK-47 split the air. The boy who had been buried in the cave-in was standing on the hood of the next truck in line, firing his weapon over the heads of the crowd. "Captain!" the boy shouted, throwing his AK-47 to him. Another weapon was passed up from the cab of the truck and the teenager chambered a round. Over fifty of al Gimlas's soldiers ran from the barracks and shouldered their way into view. Loud clicks of magazines and bolts slamming home quieted the shouts.

Holding the submachine gun easily with one hand, al Gimlas motioned for the man who had spit on his boots to drop to all fours. When he hesitated, al Gimlas fired a short burst of three rounds over his head, barely missing him. The man dropped to his hands and knees as the crowd cleared a big circle around them. Al Gimlas motioned for the man to crawl forward and pointed at his boots. His tongue flicked over his upper lip in a licking motion.

The man hesitated and al Gimlas fired another burst into the dirt directly in front of him. Dirt kicked up into his face and the man scrambled forward. Just before he reached al Gimlas's feet, the captain reached down and pulled him to his feet. "I prefer to be a civilized man and will never make a true follower of Allah lick my boots."

The man clasped his hands, dropped to his knees, and looked up at al Gimlas, protesting that he was indeed a true believer. Again, al Gimlas pulled him to his feet and told him to go in peace. The crowd split apart like leaves before a wind as the man ran away, thankful for his near escape.

Al Gimlas turned to the Americans. "Bloody hell," he said, sounding like a proper Englishman, "you two are an unbelievable amount of trouble." He glanced up at the boy still standing on the truck and nodded. The boy looked down at his commander, his face full of awe.

A man standing in the second-story window of a nearby building stepped back into the shadows of the room and zoomed in on the cage. The two Americans were now standing in full view as the captain handed them a canteen. He continued to film until the convoy drove on.

4:01 P.M., THURSDAY, APRIL 29,
WHITEMAN AIR FORCE BASE, MO.

Lt. Col. McGraw took the phone call. Capt. Jefferson was to report immediately to the local detachment of the OSI in the security police building. She tapped her pencil on the message pad for a moment. Her decision made, she buzzed Jefferson. She was going with him.

Two agents were waiting for them and escorted them to an interview room. The senior agent made the introductions and told them the interview was being recorded. "Capt. Jefferson," he said, "before we begin, I am required to read you your rights under Article Thirty-one of the UCMJ." He produced a card and read Jefferson's rights to nonincrimination and the right to be represented by a lawyer. "Do you understand everything I've said?" Jefferson nodded.

The junior agent took over the questioning. "Capt. Jefferson, last

Friday, you were observed talking to an Egyptian national, Osmana Khalid."

"That's correct," Jefferson answered. "That was right after mosque."

"Was that the first time you had talked to him?"

"We've met a few times before."

McGraw touched his arm. "Brad, don't say anything without a lawyer."

"It's okay, Colonel, it's the truth. Besides, other people were there and overheard me. The Imam gave the sermon and afterward asked me why there weren't more people of color from the base in the congregation. I told him that most people of color at Whiteman were either Christian or Nation of Islam, not Islam."

"Was that the last time you spoke to him?" the agent asked.

Jefferson hesitated for a moment. "I called him Saturday."

"What was that conversation about?"

Jefferson didn't hesitate this time. "The same topic."

"Was that all you talked about, Capt. Jefferson?"

"That was all."

"Are you sure?"

"That's enough," McGraw snapped. "Brad, I'm telling you, don't say anything more without a lawyer." She glared at the two OSI agents. "This meeting is over."

"Are you representing Capt. Jefferson?" the senior agent asked.

McGraw looked at Jefferson. "Brad, please do as I say." He nodded slowly. "Is there anything else?" McGraw demanded.

"Capt. Jefferson," the senior agent said, trying a tactic that often worked, "did you give, or sell, any classified information regarding B-Two operations to Osmana Khalid?" From Jefferson's stunned silence, the agent thought he might blurt out the truth, relieved to have a chance to confess.

McGraw came to her feet. "Capt. Jefferson, don't say another word." She jerked the door open and much to her relief, Jefferson stood up. The two agents watched them leave.

"What do you think?" the junior agent said.

"I think Capt. Jefferson should be arrested before he disappears."

2:30 P.M., FRIDAY, APRIL 30,
McCLELLAN AIR FORCE BASE, CALIF.

Hank Sutherland was in the legal office's small conference room, hovering behind the reservist as he signed his will. Sutherland witnessed the document and passed it to his secretary for a second signature. She handed the fully executed will to the sergeant, and he almost ran from the room, glad that he no longer had to confront his own mortality. It was the last Friday in the month and Sutherland was getting in duty time to meet his reserve obligations. Besides, he needed the money. In addition to witnessing the will, he had counseled another airman on the legal ramifications of refusing to deploy with his unit on a humanitarian relief mission to Africa. It was a typical duty day for a reservist lawyer on a JAG staff.

He grabbed his coffee mug and wandered up to the small kitchen on the second floor where a few of the staff were taking a break. He drained the last of the coffee and went about the business of brewing a fresh pot. A sergeant channel surfed the small TV on top of the refrigerator during a commercial break in a baseball game.

Not a bad life, Sutherland thought, settling down in a chair to watch the game. *The pleasures of being a truly unambitious man, content to be on the sidelines and out of the action. Let someone else beat his head against the wall.* He fidgeted in the chair, trying to get comfortable. His uniform was definitely tighter than normal. *I better start working out.*

"Hey," a voice called, "leave it there for a second." Someone wanted to watch CNN.

The familiar face of the President's press secretary filled the screen as a reporter grilled him during a press conference. "Tim, does the White House still maintain the pilots were on a routine airlift mission over the Mediterranean and got lost? How does anybody get that lost, given modern navigation aids?"

Sutherland listened to the press secretary's answer. He leaned forward, watching for the telltale clues. Years of being a prosecutor had fine-tuned his instincts. Another lawyer on reserve duty shouted from the other table. "That lying sack of shit! Turn back to the game."

"Hold on," Sutherland said. He wanted to hear more. Then, his own suspicions confirmed, he said, "Turn."

The channel flicked. Only instead of the game, a reporter was on the air with a late-breaking news story. "The Air Force announced that a Capt. Bradley Jefferson at Whiteman Air Force Base in Missouri was arrested this morning." A soundbite showed a confused-looking African-American man in uniform being led away in handcuffs by a huge security policeman. "Capt. Jefferson's superior officer has described him as outstanding, with an unblemished record. But a confidential source claims Jefferson is active in the local Islamic community and alleges he is suspected of selling highly classified information to foreign agents."

"Too bad it's not here," one of the lawyers said. "We could have a lot of fun with that court-martial." Sutherland listened as the other JAGs discussed how they would try the case. Some of them were actually licking their lips in anticipation.

"I wouldn't want a piece of this one," Sutherland said in a quiet voice. The others jumped on his statement, probing his logic. "Sometimes, you get a feeling about a case," Sutherland explained. "This one doesn't feel good to me."

"How can you say that based on what you've heard?" a voice protested.

"Instincts," Sutherland replied. Now they were all listening. Sutherland's formidable reputation as a deputy district attorney gave him credibility. "Too many coincidences, I guess." He tried to find the right words without sounding like a pompous jerk. "Well, you got the Sudan government announcing they've captured two U.S. pilots after shooting down their aircraft. That's all, nothing else. Then the President's press secretary claims they were on a routine airlift mission and got lost. You heard him say it."

The lawyer who wanted to watch the baseball game repeated his earlier observation. "He's a lying sack of shit."

"So what's new?" a lieutenant fresh out of his bar exam asked. "Politicians lie all the time."

"I'll get back to that in a moment," Sutherland replied. "Next, a black captain, who happens to be Muslim, is arrested at Whiteman for supposedly selling classified information. Want to make any guesses about *who* he was passing information to? Don't forget that Whiteman happens to be the home of the B-Two and a B-Two is flown by two pilots." Like a good prosecutor, he paused for effect and let them make the connections. "Nope. I wouldn't touch this one."

"Holy cow!" the lieutenant said. "If what you say is true, this could be the spy case of the century. If nothing else, think of the book deal you could get."

Sutherland laughed. "Every lawyer I know has a manuscript secreted on his person yearning for publication. That includes me." It was time to get serious and pass on a few facts of life. "This case is going to get ugly. Politics and racism are going to be big players."

"You seem to forget," one of the senior JAG officers said, "that this case will be tried under the Manual for Courts-Martial, on a military installation, with a panel of officers and not a brain-dead jury. No military judge will let racism in."

Sutherland gave him the look he reserved for witnesses who preferred perjury to the truth. "Wanna bet?" Sutherland replied, his voice mild and nonconfrontational. "Besides, I don't share your opinion about juries."

"After what happened to you in the Neighborhood Brigade trial?" the JAG shot back. "Gimme a break."

"Strange enough," Sutherland said, "juries have a tendency to do the right thing in criminal cases, even if it's not for legal reasons."

"What about the O.J. case?" the lieutenant asked.

Sutherland ignored the question. He wasn't about to open that can of legal worms. "This case has the potential to stir up a lot of passion and if I'm right, a lot of politicians are going to be involved. Never, never get involved with politicians. They're not a forgiving bunch, and if anything goes wrong, they'll have you for lunch. You will be munched on." He looked around the room. "Hard. Very hard. And you'll never know exactly who or what had you for lunch. And that *is* a fact of life."

"What happened to justice?" the lieutenant muttered.

"We're not talking about justice," Sutherland retorted, "we're talking about the law."

With no pressing commitments at home, Sutherland also worked that same afternoon, sorting out a botched Article Fifteen, nonjudicial punishment, case. After counseling an overeager first sergeant on the correct way to nail an airman who couldn't tell time and was chronically late for work, he threw a thick copy of the *Manual for Courts-Martial* into his briefcase. *I do need to review it,* he told himself. The phone rang before he could escape and make the short drive back to his apartment on the other side of Sacramento.

"Hank." It was the colonel who commanded the local judge advocate. "I just got a missive by e-mail from the Jag-Mahal." Sutherland groaned. While JAG headquarters were at Bolling Air Force Base in Washington, the major general who commanded the judge advocate general had his offices in the Pentagon. He ruled the JAG with an imperial dictate and his office was nicknamed in like manner. "They're looking for a trial counsel." The trial counsel was the prosecutor in a court-martial. "Didn't you serve as a TC at one time?"

"That was in a prior life, years ago. I did twenty-one of 'em when I was on active duty. Besides, don't they have circuit trial counsels to do that sort of thing?"

"They do," the colonel answered. "But they're always looking for fresh meat."

"In Missouri, no doubt."

"How'd you guess?"

"My training as a rocket scientist," Sutherland answered.

"I'll recommend you, if you want it," the colonel offered.

"No way." He added a respectful, "Sir."

"Well, think about it," the colonel said.

"I'll do that." He dropped the telephone into its cradle, grabbed his briefcase, and ran for his car before someone else collared him. He drove quickly, stopping only for the traffic light on Peacekeeper Avenue. He watched a lone runner sprint across with the light. She was a petite Mexican-American, maybe five feet four inches tall with a classic Roman nose. Her brief running shorts gave full freedom to a pair of legs most women dreamed about. A mass of very nonregulation dark hair was held back in a ponytail and bounced as she pounded the concrete.

The driver in the car next to him was so distracted that his car rolled forward and the runner had to swerve to avoid being hit. She never broke stride and bounded out of sight. "Wow," the driver said, loud enough for Sutherland to hear. A slight grin cracked Sutherland's face. Some things never changed.

Another asshole, Staff Sergeant Antonia "Toni" Moreno decided as she cleared the intersection. Sweat streaked down her face and stained the back of her tee-shirt. She was aware of the effect she had on some men but had decided long ago that was their problem, not hers. She checked her watch. It was time to go back to work. She picked up the pace and turned toward her office. She turned onto Price Avenue and slowed, jogging the rest of the way in. She walked through the double glass doors labeled "DETACHMENT 112, AIR FORCE OFFICE OF SPECIAL INVESTIGATIONS."

The Office of Special Investigations, or OSI for short, was the field operating agency that provided criminal, fraud, counterintelligence, and special investigative services for the Air Force. While its special agents could be either NCOs or officers, they never wore uniforms or went by their rank. As a result, Toni was Special Agent Moreno and hadn't worn a uniform since graduating from the ten-week training course at Andrews Air Force Base outside Washington. She had graduated at the top of her class and had jumped at the assignment to McClellan, which was an hour's drive from her family home in Stockton.

"Yo, Moreno," another agent called. "The old man wants to see you and Harry in five minutes."

"I'll be there," she replied, walking quickly down the hall to the unisex locker room. The sign on the door had been reversed and claimed it was occupied by a male. She could hear a shower running inside. "Hey, hurry up! I need to change."

"I'm hurrying," a male voice replied.

She sighed. It was Harry Waldon, the veteran agent who had been assigned as her mentor to guide her through her first two years. Working together had taught her that Harry never hurried anywhere. As the junior agent of the OSI detachment, and the only woman, she had to endure a definite minority status. But in Toni's grand scheme of things, that was a temporary situation. She was simply going to be the best agent in the OSI, and from all indications, the doors were wide open. Well, all but the one in front of her.

For a moment she considered barging in and turning the shower into a true unisex facility. But she reconsidered. The other agents, and Harry especially, weren't quite ready for that. She waited impatiently. The locker room door opened just as the civilian secretary said the detachment commander was ready for them.

"Thanks, Harry," she groused.

"You look fine," the offending Harry replied.

"Sure. All sweat and armpits."

The lieutenant colonel did not seem to object to the way she was dressed and other than a slight look of disapproval from the matronly secretary when they entered, the meeting went smoothly. "Harry, Toni, I want you to check out an Airman Andrea Hall. Her commander is worried because she is living well above her means and seems to be disappearing on weekends." The OSI was strictly an investigative, or fact-finding, agency and never took judicial or administrative action. Once they finished investigating a case, they turned their findings over to the requesting authority or the legal beagles.

Toni nodded. One of the first clues of criminal activity was a lifestyle not warranted by the individual's income. "Are we on a fishing expedition?" she asked. "Or are we looking for something specific?"

"The usual," Harry muttered under his breath. "Drugs or sex."

"Lovely," Toni murmured.

The lieutenant colonel leaned back in his chair. "Agent Moreno, I realize you are new to the OSI. However, your civilian attire is totally inappropriate for duty." Toni started to protest, but he held up a hand. "Don't let it happen again." He looked at the door and she beat a hasty retreat.

Harry stayed behind. "That was my fault, sir. We should have delayed the meeting until she had a chance to change."

The lieutenant colonel nodded. "Part of what you're teaching her is when to say no. Let her take the lead on this investigation. Show her how to do it. Keep her out of trouble."

"You got it, sir."

5:35 P.M., FRIDAY, APRIL 30,
SACRAMENTO, CALIF.

The temperature was hovering in the low nineties when Sutherland arrived home. He did the mental math and calculated it would reach a hundred unless a delta breeze kicked in. He broke a sweat as he made the long walk to his apartment, thankful for the tree-shaded path. Sutherland hesitated when he saw the door slightly ajar. "What the—" he muttered, fully expecting to find his apartment ransacked and burglarized. Cautiously, he cracked the door to peer in.

"Hello, Hank."

It was the old voice with the same vibrant quality that made him come alive. *Damn,* he swore to himself. "Hello, Beth."

Beth Page was standing against a far window, watering one of his plants. For a moment, they said nothing. His ex-wife was wearing a thong bikini with a large scarf tied loosely around her slender hips. She was four inches shorter than him and her dark blond hair was pulled back into a loose bundle on the nape of her neck. Age had softened her perfect face and, if anything, made her even more beautiful. "You never cashed my check."

"Is that why you're here?" He dropped his briefcase by the door and sat down in the chair opposite her. He didn't bother to ask how she got in; even the most suspicious manager, male or female, would crumble in front of her charm. "When did you arrive?"

"Early this morning."

"Been swimming?" he asked. Beth had always been athletic—swimming, riding, golfing, tennis, and skiing—a product of her privileged childhood. She nodded. "Wearing that?" An image of the chaos she would cause poolside flickered across his mind.

She smiled and came to him in a fluid motion. She sat on the arm of his chair. Her fingers explored the small scar on his forehead. "I heard about the bombing," she said. "It must have been terrible." Her fingers moved down his cheek, making his skin tingle. He glanced at the ring finger on her left hand. It was bare and tanned. She caught his glance and smiled. "There's no one special—not now."

"Cassidy's not around?" Ben Cassidy had been California's state attorney general and when the President appointed him as the U.S.

assistant attorney general in charge of special investigations, Beth had moved with him to Washington.

At first, her face was a blank. Then she gave him a lovely little half-smile that started with her lips and spread to her blue eyes. "I see them—occasionally. Margo always asks about you." Margo was Cassidy's wife who had been Sutherland's consolation prize when Beth and Ben had been screwing like bunnies. "Margo needed you," Beth said. "You helped her over some rough spots in their marriage."

"Ah. Substitute penis therapy—a wonderful thing."

"Hank, don't be bitter." She moved off the arm of his chair, her breasts brushing against his shoulder. He tried to tell himself that was an accident. But nothing Beth Page did was an accident.

"So what brings you to the lovely little town of Sacra-tomato?"

"I'm covering a rally at the Capitol tomorrow."

"Freelancing again?" he asked. Beth had occasionally played at being a reporter. While she was very good at it, she found it boring.

"Just covering it for a friend." She gave him her let's-get-serious-look. "Meredith is going to make an appearance."

Sutherland's interest ratcheted up a few notches. *So now you're interested in Meredith. It figures.* "Really?"

"No, Hank. It's not what you think. This is just an assignment."

He changed the subject. "Where are you staying?" There were few hotels in Sacramento that were up to Beth's standard.

"Here."

Sutherland laughed. "You'll love sleeping on the couch."

Again, the smile. "I don't think you'll mind where I sleep." She grabbed a towel and disappeared out the front door, headed for the pool.

Damn, he lamented to himself. *She's right.*

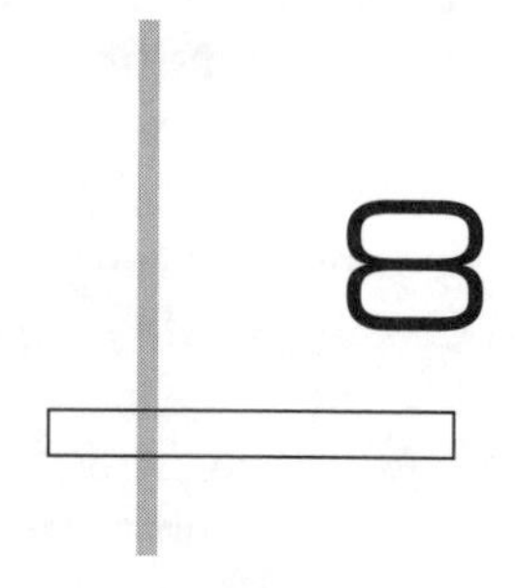

8

7:00 A.M., SATURDAY, MAY 1,
CAMP DAVID, MD.

It was early and the road leading up to the President's rustic retreat at Camp David was deserted. "This is beautiful country," Art Rios said as he turned up the lane leading to the compound. He stopped at the sign warning all unauthorized vehicles to turn back. An extremely sharp soldier wearing camouflaged battle dress appeared and asked Rios for his identification. He glanced in the backseat. Without asking for Durant's identification, he spoke into his radio, describing the occupants of the car. He stood back and waved them through.

The President was sitting on the deck outside his suite with four of his staff when Durant joined them. He sat down, thinking what it would be like never to be alone, to always have someone dancing attendance or a huge staff just out of eyesight. "Nelson," the President said, "we have a problem. Have you seen the videotape?"

Durant assumed he was referring to the video of the two pilots in their cage at El Fasher being pummeled with rocks. "Yes, sir," he replied.

"I want those two men out," the President said. "My God, if that tape ever became public—" The implications were so horrendous that he couldn't finish the thought.

Kyle Broderick took over. "We want to put all our options in play."

"That could be very counterproductive," Durant replied, wondering what idiots the President was listening to.

"Specifically," Broderick said, "we want to mount a rescue mission if our other efforts to secure their release fail."

Durant did not reply. He had pulled off three operations on his own to rescue his employees from Iran, Iraq, and Syria and knew the dangers involved. All three missions had been models of planning and training, yet when it came to execution, nothing had gone as planned and only brilliant improvisation had saved the day. The President leaned forward. "Nelson, I want you to do this for us."

"With all due respect, Mr. President, this is what you have the CIA and special forces for."

"I don't think the CIA can do this one," the senior policy adviser replied. "Not with their internal problems." Head nods all around indicated everyone agreed with him. "As for special forces, well, they do not have a sterling record."

Durant spoke in a quiet voice without emotion. "Of course not, not the way you hamstring them."

The President quickly intervened. "Nelson, we are aware of the successes you've had in rescuing your employees out of the Middle East. We're hoping you can do it again. If you agree, I will make available whatever resources you need."

Durant arched an eyebrow. The President was in his political mode. "Do those resources include the CIA and FBI?"

Broderick shook his head. "Out of the question."

"Under those conditions," Durant replied, "no thank you." He stood up to leave. "Good luck. You'll need it."

The President held up his hand and smiled. "Not so fast, Nelson. We need to talk about this."

"In private, Mr. President?"

The President nodded and his advisers withdrew, leaving them alone on the deck. The President walked to the rail and looked into the trees. "I wish I could spend more time here."

Durant joined him and rested his elbows on the rail, his hands clasped in front of him. "It's not your style, Jim. You'd get bored after a few days."

"You're probably right. Okay, Nelson, what's the problem?"

"Those two pilots are high visibility and the Sudanese will be expecting a rescue mission."

"Are you saying the risks are too high?"

"It can be done."

"What will it take?"

Durant thought for a moment. "The operation needs to be small, focused, and under tight control. You can't have that when every agency in the government is demanding a piece of the action. If I'm going to do it, I'll need total authority. Everyone, and I mean everyone, is hands off while we put it together. That means nothing happens in the Sudan without going through me."

The President shook his head. "You're asking for too much. I can't cut everyone out of the loop like that."

"Well, like I said, good luck."

"Are you going to be a hard-ass on this one, Nelson?"

Durant considered his answer. "Yes, sir, I am."

"Okay, you got it. I'll give you every hammer you need. Don't break too many heads."

"Only if they get in the way."

7:30 A.M., SATURDAY, MAY 1,
SACRAMENTO, CALIF.

As usual, Sutherland needed coffee to penetrate the haze that enveloped him after a night with Beth. He was on his second cup when she walked out of the bedroom, naked and half-asleep. He handed her a steaming mug that she cupped with both hands as she sipped. He waited while the caffeine did its trick and watched her come alive. It was the one thing about her he still truly loved. Later, when the old Beth was firmly back in control, she became another person. She tossed her hair back and handed him the mug. "We're late," she said. "Give me ten minutes. We'll walk over to the Capitol."

"Why walk?"

"It's nice out and parking is going to be a bear."

Reluctantly, Sutherland admitted Beth had made the right decision as they walked to the Capitol. The traffic streaming into the downtown area was unusually heavy for a Saturday morning and the temperature was still in the low eighties. A gentle river breeze rustled the leaves as they crossed the Discovery Park bridge. The same breeze blew away the smoke that was coming from campfires at the homeless camp further up the bike trail along the American River.

"It's going to be hot today," he told her.

"That's why they planned the rally for the morning." She scanned the crowd as they walked up Capitol Mall toward the Capitol building. "How many do you think are already here?"

"Twenty or thirty thousand." A group of purple-robed millenarians carrying signs announcing the end of the world pushed their way into H Street and stopped traffic. "What the hell," Sutherland muttered. "That's asking for trouble." A car skidded to a stop, horn honking. The driver bounced out of the car and started pushing the millenarians out of the way. Within moments, people were shoving and yelling at one another. It radiated down H Street like a wave as more and more people joined in, adding to the chaos. Suddenly, a group of white-shirted young men surged out of the parking structure across the street from the Capitol building. They dispersed into the crowd and as quickly as it had started, the disturbance died away.

"Are those guys in the white shirts part of Meredith's First Brigade?" Beth asked.

"I think so." Sutherland looked around for other outbreaks but everything was under control. He followed Beth as she shouldered her way to a side door on the north side of the Capitol building. She identified herself and received a press badge. With a little wangling, it didn't take much, she also got a badge for Sutherland. They walked through the building and the main rotunda before going outside onto the front steps. A roped-off area for the press was set up next to the temporary stage. Sutherland studied the sea of faces stretched out below him. All traffic had been diverted and people were pouring in from every direction. "It's a lot more than thirty thousand," he told Beth. "A lot more."

Sutherland had attended political rallies before but nothing matched the size or fervor he saw in this crowd. It was like spontaneous combustion and threatened to consume anyone or anything in its path. The chant "JON-A-THON, JON-A-THON" swept over the crowd and grew in intensity. Finally, the crowd boomed as one voice and could be heard over a mile away. Then Meredith was there, standing on the stage as the sound washed over him.

Slowly, he raised his right arm to silence the crowd and as quickly as the chant had begun, it died away. Beth pulled a pair of small binoculars out of her bag and shoved them into Sutherland's hand. "Scan the crowd."

Sutherland did as she commanded. At the far end of the Mall, people were still arriving. Then he focused on the faces nearest him as he listened to Meredith. Most were ordinary people who could be found on any freeway at rush hour, fighting their way to work or home. They listened with rapt attention as Meredith spun his magic, capturing them with his words.

"We honor our fellow citizens from the inner city and we want them to join us. We gladly accept them with all their strengths and weaknesses, but we all must remember that minorities only exist at the goodwill of the majority. They must accept our culture and our standards of behavior if they are to march with us into the twenty-first century. And we will prevail because our cause is just, because of our renewed belief in God, because we are confident in ourselves and ready to meet any challenge."

"This is new," Beth said.

Sutherland agreed. "He's playing the race card. It's a trial balloon and he'll drop it in a heartbeat if it doesn't fly." Through the binoculars, he saw a number of clenched fists and mouthed "Right on" responses from the discontented racists looking for scapegoats. Others nodded in solemnity while wondrous looks glowed in the faces of others.

"Are the people buying it?" Beth asked.

Sutherland paused. What was he actually seeing? Then it hit him. "They're a multitude of true believers," he told her. "Meredith is a religious experience."

"Make that multitudes of true believers," a familiar voice said behind him. Sutherland turned to see Marcy Bangor. She was looking at Beth.

"Hello, Marcy."

She gave him a little smile. "Hello, yourself."

Before Sutherland could introduce Marcy to Beth, Meredith's voice became more compelling, more forceful. All of Sutherland's instincts went into full alarm. Something new was coming and if he had been in a courtroom, he would be petitioning the judge for a recess to break the building momentum. But nothing could stop what was going to happen.

"But I am worried about our inner cities," Meredith intoned.

Sutherland was focused on a young couple. They were obviously well-off professionals. *Meredith says he's worried and they panic,* he thought.

". . . Some of our brothers and sisters have turned to a new and far more destructive behavior than burning down their own neighborhoods."

"Doesn't he know a cry for help when he hears it?" Marcy asked, not expecting an answer.

". . . And they are actively conspiring against our great nation!" Meredith shouted. The crowd roared back in approval. For a reason he could not understand, Sutherland felt the sharp edge of panic rip at him.

". . . It is for us to save them from this self-destructive behavior," Meredith said, spinning down from the emotional high he had created. Sutherland could hardly credit how relieved he felt. Meredith had even drawn him in. Not the way he intended, but just as surely. Then Meredith's words were louder, building to a terrible finality. ". . . and if our leaders will not protect this great country against all enemies, then WE WILL!"

The ovation physically rocked Sutherland backward and he couldn't move.

"Who is she?" Beth asked as they walked back to Sutherland's apartment.

"Marcy?" he answered absentmindedly. Sweat was streaking down his back and he was glad he had brought an old Panama hat. "An acquaintance. A reporter from the *Sacramento Union.*"

Her hand touched his left elbow. "Is she—?" Beth deliberately dropped the rest of her question, fishing for whatever answer Sutherland might provide.

"Is she what?"

Beth sighed. The old tricks weren't working. "Are you two—you know?"

"Do you want the clinical details?" She nodded and Sutherland gave her his best grin. "Piss off, Beth. It's none of your business. Not anymore."

Beth cut her loses and changed the subject. "Meredith's remarks about protecting our country from, what did he say? '. . . against all enemies.' " She was still fishing.

"It scared me. He's feeding the damned craziness—" He searched for the right words to describe what was going on. "It's like society is experiencing some sort of meltdown." They walked in silence, skirting a large group of people who were kneeling in prayer. The group was growing like an amoeba as more people, many carrying signs, joined in. "Look at that one," Sutherland said, pointing to a large sign waving above the kneeling people.

JFK WAS AT ROSWELL

When they reached the midspan of the Discovery Park bridge, Beth stopped and leaned over the rail, looking at the confluence of the American and Sacramento Rivers. It was get-very-serious-time. "Do you think what Meredith said has anything to do with the spy at Whiteman Air Force Base?"

Sutherland was not surprised she had made that connection. Probably half the media's assignment editors had already reached the same conclusion. His answer was a noncommittal "Could be."

"Have you heard anything?"

"Not much. The colonel I work for at the base asked if I wanted to prosecute it." *Why did I tell her that? Dumb.*

She turned to look at him and for a brief moment, the old partnership was back. "Are you going to take it?"

She wants me to take it, he thought. But their relationship had changed, and it was easy to fight the urge to please her. "No way. This is tailor-made for Meredith. You've seen the bastard in action and he's going to ride the livin' hell out of this case. This is going to be a three-ring circus. It'll burn everyone it touches. Especially if the guy is acquitted. I got clobbered by Meredith in what should have been a slam dunk case, and I'm not about to go through it again."

"I think you should." Now it was his turn to stare at the river. Her hand was on his arm, gently squeezing, insisting. "Hank, you can keep it from turning into a circus. You can keep them honest."

"Can I?"

"Yes, you can." She paused. "This could be the break you're looking for."

"What if I'm not looking anymore?"

"You're not the type to sit on the sidelines. Stop feeling sorry for yourself." She turned and headed for his apartment. "I've got to catch a flight. Drop me off at the airport?" He nodded and followed her. She slipped an arm through his and laid her cheek on his shoulder for a moment. They walked in silence, still arm in arm. "It was good last night, wasn't it?"

"I hate these modern fucking relationships."

"Don't be bitter." Then, "Hank, you really should do it. For yourself."

2:00 P.M., FRIDAY, MAY 7,
CARMICHAEL, CALIF.

It was a hot afternoon when Harry Waldon and Toni Moreno drove up to the luxury condominium in one of Sacramento's suburbs. "Nice," Harry said. "What's the number?" Toni read off Airman Andrea Hall's address. "Definitely beyond an airman's pay," he said.

"It's in her mother's name," Toni said. "That's why it took me a week to find it." She consulted her notes. "Her mother lives in Denver."

Harry humphed. "Interesting. We need to get a handle on the head tax around here. Let's go to the office and play prospective buyer." They parked and walked up to the office. The manager told them three units were for sale for around $200,000 and gave them a guided tour. The last unit was next to Andrea Hall's. "I love this location," Toni said. "Does it come with a garage?"

"Each unit has a two-car garage at the rear," the manager explained as she led them out the back door. "Your association fees cover trash collection." She pointed toward an alcove between the garages. A trash can had been knocked over and its contents spilled. "Damn," the manager moaned. "We have trouble with stray cats." She started to clean up the mess.

Toni knelt down and helped her. "I hate messes," she said. The manager smiled at her. Toni picked up a discarded envelope and a tee-shirt that had been used as a rag. She could make out the words "Bare Essence" on the tee-shirt but couldn't tell who the letter was from as she piled the garbage back into the can.

"Well," Harry said, giving the manager his best Teddy bear grin, "thanks. We'll keep this in mind." They ambled away from the manager. Out of earshot, Harry muttered, "Did you see anything?"

"I saw a letter with her name, so it was her trash."

"You did good. That was a perfect excuse to go through her garbage. You've got to use your head gathering evidence, otherwise the rectal reamers will get it thrown out." Harry always described lawyers in terms relating to the excretory process. "The lady has got money." He paused for a moment. "We need to do a full financial check on Miss Hall. You do that while I check with some of my contacts in her unit."

"Could the money be coming from her mother?" Toni asked.

"Maybe. Check her out too. But it's probably drug related."

"Are you jumping to conclusions?"

He shrugged. "I've been in this business too long. It makes you cynical."

Toni checked her watch. "Is it okay if I knock off early? I'm going to Reno with my family for the weekend."

"Don't shoot craps."

6:15 P.M., FRIDAY, MAY 7,
RENO, NEV.

Toni was sitting in the front seat of the family minivan when they came down I-80 out of the mountains. Her brother was driving and her sister was in the back with her mother and father. It was the first time the elder Morenos had been to Reno and her mother's head was on a swivel, not missing a thing. "What's that?" her mother asked in Spanish.

"That's Boomtown, Mama," her brother answered in the same language. "It's a casino. We're almost to Reno." Robert Moreno was a husky, good-looking, twenty-one-year-old who carried the trademark Moreno nose. It was commonly accepted that, someday, he would be the head of the family. But until the elder Morenos died, the family would continue to speak Spanish.

"That sign," their mother said, staring at a billboard, "You will not go there, Roberto." They all laughed. Although she claimed not to speak a word of English, Mrs. Moreno understood every word of the most salacious soap opera or gossip spoken in English. Toni looked in the same direction as her mother. Set back from the road was a sign announcing a new, all-nude review club, Bare Essence. Judging by the weather-beaten condition of the billboard, the club had been in existence for some time.

"Roberto will not go there," Mr. Moreno said, patting his wife's arm. He gave Robert a hard look. His word was still law in the family and the old woman relaxed.

Toni's eyes widened when she made the connection.

"Rob," Toni called, catching her brother's attention. "How you doing?" It was early Saturday morning, just after midnight, and the hotel casino was jammed with people.

"Losing my shirt," came the answer. "How 'bout you?"

"I'm up about two hundred dollars. How are the folks doing?"

"You know Mom. Pop won forty bucks on a slot machine and she dragged him off to the room. They're probably asleep and he's shaking the walls." One of the family jokes concerned the snoring of the family's patriarch. But it was never mentioned in the presence of either parent.

"Can we talk?"

"Sure," Robert answered. He guided her to the coffee shop, and they joined a line of waiting people.

"It's about my job," Toni explained as they waited for a table.

He frowned. "If some guy is giving you a bad time, his ass is grass." The Moreno males were very protective of their women, and Toni's independent streak had caused a great deal of concern.

Toni shook her head. "I can take care of myself. I want to follow up on a lead and I need your help. Remember the sign Mom saw driving in?"

Robert's frown deepened. "The one about the nude club?"

"I need to check it out," she told him.

"No way," he said. "You heard Pop."

"Rob, this has to do with my job. Besides, it will give you a chance to see what I do."

"You'll pay for it?" he asked. She nodded. It was all the encouragement he needed and he rushed her out of the casino.

The parking lot at Bare Essence was full of cars, and two attendants guided them to an open parking space. "They're security guards," Toni said.

"How can you tell?" Robert asked.

"You pick up a sixth sense about it. It's almost like radar."

Her brother helped her out of the minivan and locked the door. "If Pop finds out about this, we're going to be in a world of hurt."

"If he finds out," Toni retorted, "tell him the truth. It's time he comes to grips with what I do."

"You're still his firstborn. That makes you special."

A young man dressed in a tuxedo held the door open for them. "Couples are free," he said. "But please, if nudity offends you, don't enter."

Toni almost laughed at the blush that spread across her brother's face. "We're not offended," she said. She led the way into the darkened interior. A skimpily attired waitress guided them to a table and took their orders for drinks. Since no alcoholic beverages were served, Toni settled for coffee and Robert for a coke. A pretty girl, who Toni judged to be about twenty years old, was onstage, totally nude and shimmying up and down a brass pole. "Try not to hyperventilate," Toni told her brother. He nodded dumbly.

She looked around the room. A padded bench was built along the length of the side and back walls. Men sat on the bench while nude girls wiggled on their laps. The song ended and the dancer looked at the audience. The DJ urged them to show their appreciation with tips and applause. Lacking a response, the girl escaped behind the curtain. "And now," the DJ bellowed, "on center stage, is the lovely Adrienne." The music blared and Andrea Hall stepped out from behind the curtain.

Robert stared, not able to take his eyes off her as she slowly shed her clothes. On the second song, she unsnapped her g-string and kicked off her shoes. The audience was deathly still as she danced, moving gracefully to the music. When the song ended, she gave an incredible sexy bow and the room erupted in applause. Five- and ten-dollar bills were thrown at the stage. "She can sure dance," Robert finally managed to say.

Reluctantly, Toni agreed with him. The DJ announced that the next two songs would be a two-for-one lap dance. "Let's get out of here," she said. "I've seen enough."

Robert looked wistfully at Andrea as she gathered up the money. "So soon? Don't you want me to see how they work the lap dances?"

"No way I'm going to pay for you to get a two-for-one," she told him. She waited until Andrea disappeared behind the curtain then she dragged her reluctant brother outside.

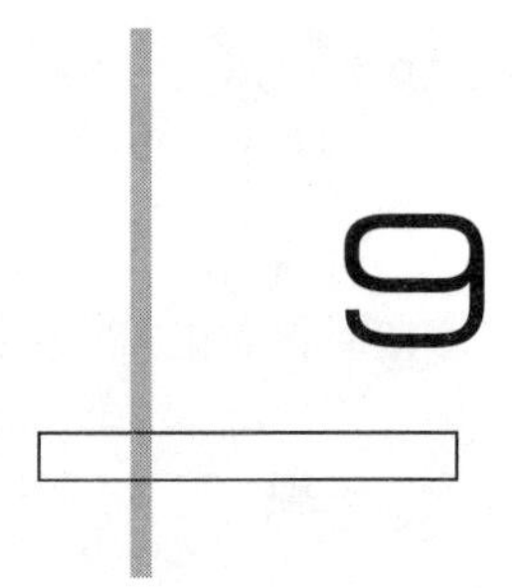

3:10 P.M., SUNDAY, MAY 9,
THE FARM, WESTERN VIRGINIA

Durant watched Art Rios as he bent over the big table measuring distances off a chart. Durant had appropriated the secure room from the whiz kids to use as a planning cell for the rescue mission. Because Rios had been a key player in his three earlier missions, Durant was relying on him to do the initial planning. But he was worried. "You haven't done one of these in a long time, Art."

"I have no intention of going on the mission," Rios replied. He typed some numbers into a computer and frowned at the results. "The Sudan is too damn big and the geography works against us." He thought for a few moments. "They know that." He mumbled to himself and hunched back over the chart. Durant left him to work alone and walked over to the building housing the Project. He wanted to talk to Agnes.

Although it was Sunday, two of the whiz kids were working with Agnes when he arrived. "Hello, Agnes," he said over their shoulders. The image on the screen twisted as if she were looking past the woman and man sitting in front of her.

"Oh, Mr. Durant." The image looked flustered. "I'll be right back." The screen blinked and Agnes was back. She had changed clothes into a businesslike suit. "I thought this would be more appropriate," she said.

Durant couldn't help but smile. "Why?"

"Well, you *are* my employer."

"That's right, Agnes," the woman said. "Without Mr. Durant,

we'd all be out of a job." Agnes nodded as if that confirmed what she had been thinking.

The man stood up and offered Durant his seat. "What can we do for you, sir?"

Durant sat down in front of the second monitor. Agnes immediately switched to that one. "The President has asked me to organize a mission to rescue two pilots out of the Sudan. I was wondering if you can help us."

"Of course," Agnes replied. "But you said 'us.' Who are the other people?"

"So far, only Art Rios. He's my mission planner."

"May I ask why you selected him?" Agnes replied.

"He's done it three times before: Iran in 1980, Iraq in 1990, and Syria in 1993. But those were much different missions."

Agnes became very serious. "Let me see what I can find about those missions." She paused for a few seconds as if she were thinking. "Yes, I see what you mean. Did you know the Iraqi secret police have a standing contract out on Mr. Rios? One million dollars to the person who kills him."

"Really?" Durant said. "I didn't know."

"Neither did I until I started looking. I'll extend the security watch I have around you to cover Mr. Rios."

"Can you tell us about the security watch?" the young woman asked. "This is the first we've heard about it."

"I'm sorry, but that's privileged information between me and Mr. Durant."

"It's okay, Agnes," Durant said. "You can tell them."

"Mr. Durant asked me to protect his privacy. I assumed that also meant his life, and therefore I have a security watch in place around him." She gave a little chuckle. "I tasked the California Department of Motor Vehicles computer to do it. But I had to make its programs more efficient to free up space. It's working correctly now and they don't know how it happened. They think they may have a virus and don't know efficiency when they see it. Stupid people. Oh, I just finished talking to the computer Mr. Rios is using. He's right, it's best to use helicopters. I recommend you use MH-Fifty-three Pave Lows from the Sixteenth Special Operations Wing. The helicopter is a bit old but they have some very good people. You want to talk to a Lieutenant Colonel Seamus Gerald Gillespie."

A photo of a young looking, red-haired, skinny, freckle-faced man appeared on the screen next to Agnes. She turned to look at him and sighed. "He looks so young." A slight pause. "There is a problem. I don't see how you can get the pilots safely to the helicopters."

"We'll work on that," Durant said.

"Is there anything else, Mr. Durant?"

"Please maintain a communications watch on the Sudan," Durant answered. "Talk to you later."

2:55 P.M., MONDAY, MAY 10,
MCCLELLAN AIR FORCE BASE, CALIF.

This was her first interview and Toni Moreno was dressed for the occasion. She was wearing what she considered her "intimidation" uniform. It consisted of a charcoal-gray pants suit with no-nonsense shoes and a severe high-neck white blouse. The jacket was unbuttoned to reveal her narrow waist. Harry Waldon, her mentor agent who never hurried, shambled into the interview room and sat down. "I saw your report," he said. "Good work."

"It was pure luck," Toni said. "I think she's earning money dancing at that club. That's why I called her in."

Harry nodded. "Might as well. This will be a good interview to cut your teeth on. The first one is always the worst and this is not a biggy. Don't hurry it, try to get her to trust you."

"Did you learn anything about her duty assignment?" she asked.

Harry shrugged his shoulders. "Not much. Most of the young studs lust after her but she intimidates them. No problems on the job. What about the financial check?"

"I haven't had time yet," Toni answered.

"Be sure to run a check on her mother." He gave her his lopsided grin. "Just introduce me and I won't say a thing." Harry had the ability to look like an innocent Teddy Bear and disappear into the woodwork.

Airman First Class Andrea Hall presented herself at exactly three P.M. She was dressed in the two-tone blue summer Air Force uniform with a light-blue blouse and dark-blue skirt. She was tall, willowy, big-breasted, and blonde. Toni felt like a penguin and stifled a sigh. *Get it over with,* she told herself. "I'm Agent Moreno. Please be seated." For a moment, Andrea stared at Toni as if she had seen her before or was taking her measure. Then she sat down while Toni closed the door and introduced Harry.

Toni smiled at her. "Can I get you a cup of coffee? Tea? A Coke?" A little shake of Andrea's head answered her. Toni sat down and went through the perfunctory questions establishing the girl's identity. "May I call you Andrea? Airman Hall sounds so formal." This time the girl nodded. "Andrea, we have a problem that you may be able to help us with."

Again, Andrea studied Toni, trying to place where she had seen her. "I'll help in any way I can." Her voice was low and silky smooth, a perfect match for her gorgeous image.

"On Saturday, May eighth, you were observed dancing nude at a club"—Toni made a show of consulting her notes—"called Bare Essence in Reno, Nevada."

Andrea stared at her. "That was you I saw, wasn't it? In the club."

At first, Toni wanted to ignore the question, but Harry's look told her to tell the truth. "Yes, I was there."

"Is that illegal?" Andrea asked. "Dancing at a club?"

"No. But if you're going to moonlight, the Air Force would prefer you found a job where you keep your clothes on."

Andrea looked away and Toni could see tears in her eyes. She was totally oblivious of Harry's presence. "I haven't done anything wrong."

Toni's voice was soft and consoling. "Don't say anything you may regret later." She glanced at Harry to see if it was time to read Andrea her rights. A slight head shake from Harry answered her unspoken question.

The girl's head came up. "I was on my own time and no one knows I'm in the Air Force. I didn't want to do it."

"Then why are you doing it?"

Andrea gave her a patronizing look. "For money, what else. I got in debt—credit cards—they just show up in the mail. A debt collector suggested it. He had contacts." Now Andrea couldn't stop talking and it was like Toni had learned in training. It was a rush to confession, the need to cleanse her soul.

"How much do you make a night?" Toni asked.

"On a good night, two thousand dollars." That was more than Toni made in a month and she wished she hadn't asked the question. Now Andrea's voice became more firm. "I declare it all on my income taxes."

"What do you list as the source?"

"Sales, of course."

Toni was incredulous. "Sales?"

For the first time, Andrea acknowledged Harry's presence. "I sell fantasy to guys like him. That's all. I'm out of debt and saving money. I've even got enough to buy some nice things."

So I've noticed, Toni thought. It was time to test her truthfulness. "Where do you live?"

"I bought a place in Carmichael so I could get off base."

"Is it in your name?" Toni asked.

"No. It was easier to buy it in my mother's name. My age is a problem."

"How old are you?" Again, Toni knew the answer.

"Nineteen."

Toni felt very old for her age, twenty-six. "Andrea, dancing at a nude club is a bad choice. You're being exploited." She didn't mention that it would probably get her kicked out of the Air Force. But was there more? "People get the wrong idea."

"You don't know what goes on there," Andrea replied.

"You're right, I don't."

"I'm not naïve," Andrea said. "I know some of the girls are doing more than dancing. And sometimes I hear things. But I don't get involved."

Before Toni could ask the next question, she felt one of Harry's big hands on her arm. "Andrea, what exactly did you hear?" Toni shot a hard look at him for taking over the interview. But a sixth sense told her the veteran agent was onto something she had missed.

"I hear a lot about drugs and passing money. Once I even heard a regular mention the Air Force."

"A regular?" Harry asked.

"A customer. He always shows up on Saturdays right after we open. He talks a lot to the manager and likes the girls."

The tone of Harry's voice changed and he stepped out of the hard-boiled persona that characterized his profession. "Andrea, when we tell your commander about your moonlighting, he will probably want to kick you out of the Air Force."

"But you said dancing wasn't illegal."

Harry shook his head, a sad look on his face. "Did you get his permission to work a second job?"

"No." Tears flowed down Andrea's cheeks. "I like the Air Force and want to stay in. But you don't know what it's like when the guys hit on you at work. All they want is to get you into bed. That's no worse than what I do, and they get away with it."

"I know," Harry said. "And we want to help you. But how is your commander going to react when he hears about your dancing? Sooner or later, those guys you mentioned will hear about it. What then?" Before she could answer, Harry pressed ahead. "We haven't read you your rights because you haven't done anything illegal. But that won't save you from being kicked out. I would like nothing better than to tell your commander that you are helping us in a positive way in an investigation. I can't make any promises, but that might sway him in your favor. I've seen it happen before."

"What do you want me to do?"

"Just help us for a short time and then quit dancing—before the word gets out."

"Can I think about it?" Andrea asked.

"Certainly," Toni said.

"May I go now?"

"You can go anytime you want," Toni told her.

Andrea stood to leave. She paused at the door. "You don't believe me. Why don't you come and see who's being exploited." She looked at Harry. "I can take a hundred dollars off *him* in fifteen minutes." She turned and hurried out the door. Toni looked at her notes. She had hardly written a thing.

Harry cleared his throat, handed her his microcassette recorder, and made a show of turning it off. "She's probably telling the truth."

"Then why do you want to use her?"

"Reno is in our area of responsibility and we've had cases involving money laundering—"

Toni interrupted. "That lead to Reno."

Harry smiled. "You got it. We may have a break here. Let me tell the boss what's going down." He shifted his bulk out of his chair.

Toni's voice stopped him short of the door. "Harry, could she have? The hundred dollars? In fifteen minutes?"

A sad look crossed his face and he headed down the hall. "Maybe fifty."

"She'd get the whole hundred," Toni muttered.

3:12 A.M., WEDNESDAY, MAY 12,
WHITEMAN AIR FORCE BASE, MO.

The country road was lost in darkness when Sutherland wheeled his dirty Volvo up to Arnold Gate. He was dog-tired and almost asleep at the wheel. But he felt relieved, almost jubilant, that he had found the base with so little trouble, even though it was the back gate. Sutherland was a terrible navigator and got lost driving around the block. The drive across two-thirds of the country had been absolutely traumatic and, luckily, he had been on autopilot for the last twelve hours, which actually improved his sense of direction. However, true to form, he had missed the main entrance and finally stumbled onto the back gate.

The guard stepped out of the shack and snapped a sharp salute. "Sir," she said, "please dim your lights when you drive up to the gate. It really helps when it's dark." She waved him to proceed without checking his ID. The bumper sticker for McClellan Air Force Base was enough.

"How do I get to the visiting officers quarters?"

She started to give him detailed directions but stopped. She knew a klutz when she saw one and darted back into the shack. She outlined the route in red on a base map and gave it to him. She pointed down the road at his first turn. He thanked her and drove slowly onto base.

The guard shook her head when he missed the turn and reached for the radio clipped to her belt. "A dark red Volvo with California plates just came through Arnold Gate," she radioed. "The driver is looking for Whiteman Inn. I don't think he's got a clue. If you see him flailing around, help him out."

Tech Sergeant Leroy Rockne's voice answered. "Roger, we'll watch for him. Thanks for the heads up." The guard snapped the radio back onto her belt. Praise from The Rock made her whole shift.

The flashing blue light jolted Sutherland into full consciousness and he pulled over to the side of the curb. A tall security policeman emerged from the patrol car and ambled toward him. *A five-hundred–pound gorilla,* Sutherland told himself. Closer up, he decided the security cop was a five-hundred–pound gorilla who lifted weights. Automatically, he flicked on the overhead dome light, rolled his window down, and put his hands on top of the steering wheel in full view.

"That's not necessary, sir," The Rock said, his voice a perfect match for his chiseled, rocklike face. "You look lost. Can I help?"

Sutherland shook his head, more to clear the cobwebs. "Ah, yes. I'd appreciate that. I'm looking for the Whiteman Inn."

"Follow me, sir, I'll lead you there."

Sutherland waited until the patrol car pulled in front and followed it to the visiting officers quarters. "Thank God," he muttered to himself. He would have never found the building by himself. The Rock waved at him and drove off. Inside, an airman was waiting for him at the counter.

"Welcome to Whiteman Air Force Base," the clerk said. "There's a message for you."

Sutherland unfolded the paper. He was to see the wing commander at 0630 hours that morning. "Three hours sleep," he mumbled. "A hell of a way to start my first day."

At exactly 0625 hours, Sutherland walked into the redbrick two-story headquarters building on Spirit Boulevard. He presented himself to the crisp and efficient African-American secretary in the commander's office on the second floor. She ushered him immediately into the brigadier general's office. The walls were bare and packing boxes lined one side of the room. The one-star general remained seated, returned Sutherland's salute with a half wave, and left him standing in front of his bare desk. "I arrived yesterday myself," the general said. "In case you are wondering why, it's because the previous occupant of this office was fired for having the bad luck of being in command when the first B-Two was lost."

"I hadn't heard we'd lost a B-Two," Sutherland said. "Is that for public release?"

The one-star humphed. "No. Definitely not. Which, if you ask me, is dumber than dirt. But that decision was made far above my pay grade. It's going to come out sooner or later." He contemplated his future when that happened. "Needless to say, this is a high-risk job that has high visibility. That visibility is going to get much higher when we convene the court-martial you are going to prosecute and the connection to the B-Two comes out."

"So there is a connection?"

He held up a hand before Sutherland could ask another question. "The Air Force is not going to waive jurisdiction and turn this over to the feds. We're going to try the case right here, on this base. My main concern is that no one, and I mean no one, raises the issue of command influence. If, at any time, you suspect that you or anyone connected with this trial is being subjected to command influence, you are to immediately report it to me and your superiors at the Central Circuit in San Antonio. You are not to talk to me or anyone on my staff unless it is in your official capacity as trial counsel."

The general paused, taking Sutherland's measure. "Public Affairs will handle all media relations. You will not speak to the press or give interviews." Again, he held up a hand, cutting off any comments. "I know how persistent they can be. Stay on base and you won't have a problem. Dismissed."

Sutherland beat a hasty retreat into the outer office. "The legal office is down the corridor to your left and around the corner," the secretary said.

Sutherland walked down the corridor and stopped at the corner, the junction of the two wings that formed the building. He was on a balcony overlooking the glassed-in foyer of the main entrance. Outside, two security cops were raising the flag. *Nice building,* he told himself. He looked down the other corridor and saw a set of double doors. It was the courtroom. He took a few paces to the doors and tested the handles. Finding one unlocked, he stepped inside.

He was standing at the back of a room approximately fifty by thirty feet with a judge's bench that stretched across the width of the room at the far end. A lone, high-backed dark red leather chair sat in the middle and was flanked by American and Air Force flags at the rear wall. He sat down in the area behind the low railing that formed the bar. He counted thirty seats for spectators. On the other side of the bar and on the left, the jury box held twelve chairs. That puzzled him. Even a general court-martial only impaneled five to nine members to serve as the jury. As best he could recall, five was the minimum and there was no legal maximum.

The trial counsel's table was placed directly in front of the bar and the spectators. That was exactly like any civilian courtroom where the prosecutor's table separated the jury box and the defendant's table. The defendant's table was placed against the right wall and faced the jury box. *That's different from a civilian courtroom. Is there an advantage for the defendant when the jury looks directly at him for the entire trial?* He didn't know. The witness box was between the defendant's table and the judge's bench. The court reporter's position was across the room at the other end of the bench.

Like a good soldier, he took stock of the battleground where he would engage in combat. Aside from the framed prints on the wall, he was on familiar ground.

The side door between the court reporter's desk and the jury box swung open and a woman in uniform walked in. She flicked on the lights and looked at Sutherland. For a moment, they stared at each other. She was almost six feet tall and well-proportioned for her height. Her salt-and-pepper hair was cut short and she wore glasses. Sutherland guessed her to be about his age. From his distance, he couldn't tell if she was a major or lieutenant colonel. "Are you Capt. Sutherland?" she asked. Her voice was firm and moderately pitched with all the tonal qualities of an accomplished public speaker.

He stood up. "Yes, ma'am."

She slammed the door shut, stepped into the jury box, and sat down. She folded her hands in her lap and stared at him. "Close the door," she ordered. Sutherland did as she commanded and closed the double doors behind him that led to the outside hall. "I'm Maj. Catherine Blasedale." She spoke in a flat monotone, a bored professor lecturing students on a boring subject. "The convening authority, who happens to be the commander of Eighth Air Force at Barksdale Air Force Base, has decided in his infinite wisdom to appoint me as assistant trial counsel. You," she spat the word at him, "are trial counsel." She stood up, walked onto the floor and glared at him. "Captain, that sucks. I'm the chief circuit trial counsel for the Central Circuit and have prosecuted more courts-martial than you can count. Regardless of your reputation, I am more qualified to prosecute this case. The only reason you're here is because of political influence." Silence ruled the room.

"Hey," Sutherland finally said, "I'm out of here. I just got a lecture on command influence from the general."

"You're not listening," she said. "I said political influence, not command influence. Learn the difference. Interest in this case goes much higher than any command level in the military. And that's why you're here, gold-plated reputation and all." She walked over to him and stood at the bar, challenging him to come through the swinging gate and enter her territory.

"How do you know all this?"

She snorted. "The phone lines to the Jag-Mahal are going crazy on this one. AT&T will send the Air Force a letter of appreciation for this month's phone bill."

Sutherland laughed, accepted her challenge, and walked through the bar. He stood in front of her, now on her turf. "When I was on active duty, I was trial counsel on twenty-one courts-martial."

She leaned into him, invading his personal space. "So you are legally of age. How long ago was that?"

"Twelve years."

"I'm not impressed."

Sutherland knew what she was doing and decided it was time to turn it around. "I won all of them. And I was the guy who eighty-sixed the Colonel Martin court-martial." *That got your attention.*

"So you're the bastard," she muttered, pulling away.

"The evidence wasn't there. You don't ruin a man's career on a charge of sexual harassment when—"

"What about the lieutenant's career?" Blasedale barked.

"There is no double standard on evidence. She had confused command responsibility and discipline with sexual harassment. Everyone else in his command had to conform to the dress regulations. Pointing out her hemlines were too short and her skirts too tight does not constitute sexual harassment." Now he leaned into her, pressing his advantage. He was so close that he caught the faint scent of an expensive perfume. "I like your perfume."

"That's a sexist comment, Captain."

She had taken the bait and he almost smiled. "No," he replied, putting steel into his voice. "It's a compliment. Learn the difference."

"I don't think we can work together," she snapped. She turned and walked away.

"Are you afraid of this case?" he asked.

She stopped and turned to face him. "Based on the evidence I've seen, this one should be a slam dunk."

"Therefore, no glory," Sutherland said.

She cocked her head to one side. "If you blow this one, the name Sutherland will redefine the term *goat.* Think about it."

He smiled at her. He had been in the goat seat before. "Maybe this is a case the Air Force can't afford to lose. So if I do blow it, the generals can blame the politicos for forcing me down their throats and I become the scapegoat."

She returned his smile. "Sounds good to me." Then she relented. "Maybe we can work together."

"I'd like that," Sutherland said, meaning it.

"Come on, I'll introduce you to the troops. We've got a lot of work to do." She led him through the side door and into the legal offices of the 509th Bomb Wing.

8:24 A.M., THURSDAY, MAY 13,
EL OBEID, SUDAN

Capt. Davig al Gimlas waited motionlessly as his men fell in for the open ranks inspection being held on the tarmac where arriving aircraft parked. They were a far cry from the slovenly rabble he had inherited nineteen days ago. To a man, they stood with pride, and their uniforms and weapons gleamed with care. But they still had a great deal of training in front of them. They had also shaved off their mustaches out of respect for al Gimlas who could not grow one because of his scar.

The wind blew across the parking ramp, depositing a fine film of dust on their freshly polished boots. "Sir, would you please wait a moment before starting?" the lieutenant asked. Al Gimlas nodded. The lieutenant barked an order and the men quickly dusted their boots and weapons. Ever since the incident at El Fasher, polished boots had become a symbol of pride for the men. The lieutenant chanced a glance at al Gimlas and called the company to attention. Al Gimlas walked the line, satisfied with his men.

Five minutes later, an unmarked, U.S.-built, C-130 Hercules entered the landing pattern and touched down on the runway. The pilot slammed the throttles into reverse and the big cargo plane slowed in time to make the first turnoff. The pilot taxied in, careful to direct the backwash from the props away from the honor guard. The props spun down and the ramp under the tail lowered. Jamil bin Assam strutted down the ramp. He was a short, pot-bellied man sporting a bushy beard and wearing an army uniform with the rank of a *fariq,* a four-star general.

The men standing behind al Gimlas saw his back stiffen. Assam was not a general. But he was a fact of life in Arab politics. He was a *bazaari* made good, a wheeler-dealer out of the bazaar who could make money at the slightest hint of corruption. His wealth had bought him influence, power, an army of sycophants, women, and the C-130. Now he fancied himself a general leading a jihad against the Western infidels.

A black Mercedes staff car, two Range Rovers, and two trucks drove up to the aircraft. The Mercedes spun around and screeched to a halt, kicking up a cloud of dust. Fortunately, the wind was in the right direction and blew the dust back over the aircraft and Assam, not the men standing at attention. An aide jumped out of the Mercedes's front seat and jerked the rear door open as the dust settled. Al Gimlas allowed a slight smile to crack his normally rigid countenance. His men appreciated the irony.

In a tailored uniform, Jamil bin Assam resembled a pear with sticklike arms and legs. A black patent leather holster was strapped to his waist holding a large nine-millimeter automatic that had never seen use. He marched up to al Gimlas, his left hand brushing at his shirt while his uniformed bodyguard trooped off the C-130. He was in a deep sweat from the short walk.

Al Gimlas snapped a classic, open-handed British-style salute. Assam ignored it. "Where are the filthy vermin who tried to bomb my laboratory?" he demanded.

"Safely at the barracks," al Gimlas replied, dropping his salute.

Assam stalked over to the Mercedes while his staff piled into the Range Rovers and the guards streaming off the C-130 clambered into the trucks. "Follow me," he ordered al Gimlas. Al Gimlas took a few moments to study Assam's guards. He nodded at his lieutenant. Assam obviously preferred quantity over quality.

Assam walked into al Gimlas's office and sat down at his desk. "Primitive," he snorted with a look around the room. "I need to interrogate the prisoners." He fixed al Gimlas with a hard glare. "I must do it because of your failure to learn anything." Al Gimlas stood at attention and did not respond. In the Sudan, Jamil bin Assam could do whatever he wanted. Assam leaned back in his chair and placed his feet on the desk, the soles pointed directly at al Gimlas. It was a serious insult.

Al Gimlas's face turned rock hard and he stared at Assam. Their eyes locked as they established their territory. Al Gimlas allowed a slight smile and Assam understood perfectly: his bodyguards were no match against al Gimlas's soldiers. He dropped his feet to the floor and straightened up. Now the captain had to establish a truce. "Lieutenant," al Gimlas said, "take Maj. Terrant and Capt. Holloway to the interrogation room."

They waited in silence until the lieutenant reported that the prisoners were ready. Assam stood. "I will soon learn what you have *not* been able to discover." Assam marched down to the interrogation room. An aide jerked open the door. Assam stopped, puffed himself up, and strode in with eight of his men. The two American pilots were standing in the center of the room, their wrists handcuffed behind their backs. "Salute your superior officers!" Assam barked. Doug Holloway turned so Assam could see that his hands were manacled behind his back. Assam ignored him. "Well!" he demanded.

"I never salute without my hat on," Holloway said.

Al Gimlas looked away, ashamed of what was coming next. But no Arab could let Holloway's retort go unanswered. The sound of kicks and blows thudding into Holloway echoed around the room. When al Gimlas turned, the American pilot was lying on the floor, his face a mass of blood. One of Assam's goons was holding the bloody baton he had smashed into Holloway's face.

"Capt. al Gimlas has been too weak and soft with you!" Assam shouted. "Now you are dealing with real men. You will tell me what I want to know."

Mark Terrant's even voice answered. "It would help if you'd tell us exactly what you want." Assam flicked a hand and the men went to work on Terrant. They drove him to the ground and continued to kick at him as he curled into a tight ball, trying to protect his head. Finally, two men pinned Terrant against the floor on his back while the goon stepped over him and used the baton like a golf club, swinging at Terrant's face. Al Gimlas stared at Assam as blood splattered the far wall.

"You will answer," Assam said.

Al Gimlas bent over Terrant and inspected the damage to his face. "He can't. You've broken his jaw."

"Jewish trash," Assam muttered. "We know how to treat Jews. But I must return to Khartoum." He issued orders to an aide. "Remain here and finish what I have begun. Do not return until you have drained these vermin dry." He hurried out of the room, anxious to get airborne.

Al Gimlas waited until the sound of the departing Mercedes died away. "Return them to their cells," he ordered. He picked up the phone and called for a doctor.

"General Assam would not approve," Assam's aide barked.

Al Gimlas stared at him. "General Assam is not here. You are."

The two men glared at each other and al Gimlas handed him the phone. "You call the doctor while I check on my men." The threat was obvious. The aide knew of al Gimlas's reputation and the loyalty he inspired among his soldiers. It was a reputation and loyalty he did not want to test. He ordered the doctor to report immediately to the cells.

10

11:20 A.M., FRIDAY, MAY 14,
HURLBURT FIELD, FLA.

The captain waiting on the parking ramp heard the distinctive beat of the helicopter before he saw it. When the MH-53J Pave Low appeared over the trees, he instinctively graded the approach. *Not bad,* he decided. It had been a very long training mission and the pilots had to be tired. The big helicopter settled to earth like a giant insect and taxied in. The captain shook his head when the pilot paused in front of the old biplane parked on the ramp. The white-and-red Staggerwing Beech was an anachronism and totally out of place. Yet it glistened with tender loving care and was a far better machine than when it was first manufactured in 1943.

The dark gray-green MH-53 was a harsh contrast to the pretty four-passenger cabin biplane. The Pave Low was the largest and most powerful helicopter the Air Force owned and, without doubt, the ugliest. But underneath its ungainly exterior beat the heart of the most technologically advanced helicopter in the world.

The six blades of the Pave Low's seventy-two-foot rotor spun down as the crew climbed off. The last man off was the aircraft commander, a skinny lieutenant colonel who stood barely five feet four inches tall. His freckles, red hair, and bright green eyes went with his name, S. (for Seamus) Gerald Gillespie. Nothing in the way he walked or spoke to the crew indicated that he was the best special operations helicopter pilot in the U.S. military and perhaps the world. He was also the commander of the Green Hornets, the 20th Special Operations Squadron.

"Another crisis, Lee?" Gillespie asked. He was tired from the long mission and needed a beer.

Capt. Lee Harold shrugged his shoulders. He was a solidly built, dark-haired, Air Force Academy graduate who matched the Pave Low. "Two high rollers flew in from D.C. Civilians."

"Theirs?" Gillespie asked, pointing at the Staggerwing.

"Yeah. The C.O. of Delta Force came with them."

"Must be important," Gillespie grumbled. He was not happy for civilians meant CIA. Although the Staggerwing didn't fit the image. "Let's go talk to 'em."

The colonel who commanded Delta Force made the introductions. The names Durant and Rios meant nothing to Gillespie and he shook their hands. "I assume you're from Langley," Gillespie said, meaning they were CIA. "What can we do for you?"

Durant caught the slight undertone in Gillespie's voice and shook his head. "The CIA reports to me on this one." Gillespie was impressed. Only the President could make that happen. "I've been asked to put together a special mission and need your help." Durant told him.

Nothing in Gillespie's face betrayed what he was thinking. "I'd hate to think you could do it without us," he murmured.

Durant liked his answer. "We're still in the planning phase, but once the mission is firmed up, we're moving to Fort Irwin for training." Fort Irwin was an army training center in the Mojave Desert in California.

"Going after those two pilots in the Sudan?"

"Very good," Durant replied.

"It doesn't take much in the way of brains to figure that out," Gillespie said. "So will the bad guys. We know they watch us for movement."

Durant leaned back in his chair and took stock of the man in front of him. Gillespie was living up to his advance billing. "The colonel here is the ground commander. I want you to be the air boss and coordinate all our airlift requirements. Also, we need to get an operative on-scene prior to the rescue. Preferably, someone you know and trust. Any recommendations?"

Gillespie couldn't help himself. "Does it have to be a 'he'?"

"Come on!" the colonel from Delta Force barked. Gillespie tried to look contrite. He had worked with the colonel before and was just softening him up. "Okay, who is it?" the colonel asked.

"Victor Kamigami," Gillespie said in a low tone. The men had to strain to be sure they heard him right.

"No fuckin' way!" the colonel yelped.

1:30 P.M., SATURDAY, MAY 15,
RENO, NEV.

The club was still closed when Andrea Hall parked her bright red Mustang convertible near the rear entrance. Toni looked across the street and saw Harry pull up as planned. "It's not too late to change your mind," Toni said. Andrea shook her head. She wanted to help them. Toni stifled her own second thoughts and got out. She took some comfort that Harry was there as a backup and if she didn't come out in an hour, he would come in after her.

"Aren't you worried your car will get ripped off back here?" Toni asked.

"The security guards will keep an eye on it," Andrea answered. On cue, a big man wearing a tee-shirt announcing BARE ESSENCE—NOT YOUR BASIC STRIPPED DOWN MODELS stepped around the corner. "Most trouble happens in the parking lot," Andrea explained, "very seldom inside. Pat, he's the manager, and the guards make sure we get in and out safely."

The guard escorted them to the front door and grinned. "Can you believe they pay us for this?"

The door opened and another man let them in. "Who's your friend?"

"Pat," Andrea said, "this is Toni. She's a friend of mine and is thinking about dancing."

Pat grunted and followed them into the club. With all the lights on, it appeared much shabbier than in the darkened glow of business hours. "Make yourself at home," he said. "We're a friendly bunch here. We're about ready to open." He turned the lights down as two men entered.

"Pat," Andrea said, "why don't you explain how it works to Toni while I change."

Pat smiled at Andrea and pointed to the back office. Toni followed him, glad that her nine-millimeter Sig Sauer was in the bottom of her bag. It was a small office with a big desk that was bare except for a telephone. Two decrepit chairs were set against the rear wall and a nice leather couch was placed against the side wall. *Is that a casting couch?* she wondered. Pat sat down on the couch and waived her to a chair. "Ever dance professionally?" Toni shook her head.

The door opened and a young girl entered wearing next to nothing. She leaned over Pat and brushed her lips against his cheek. Her tongue flicked his ear and she murmured a few words Toni couldn't hear. "You look great, honey," he said. "I'll talk to you later." She rubbed her breasts against him and stood up, taking off her shoes. Her hips wiggled provocatively as she left. From the rear she looked naked. *How old is she?* Toni wondered.

"Dancing onstage is not the important thing here," Pat said. "Taking bucks off the customers is. That's why we got an ATM in the club." He spent the next fifteen minutes explaining the business arrangements and how to work the customers. "Watch how Andrea does it. We've got over a hundred girls working here right now and she's the best." He leaned forward and fixed her with an intent look. "If we catch you hustlin' in the club or the parking lot, we call the cops. We sell fantasy here, not the real thing. Got it?"

Toni smiled at him. Hustling was allowed if you didn't get caught. But the actual financial transactions and the deed had to occur off premises. The door opened and the guard from the parking lot shoved his head in. "Mr. Ramar is here, boss. He's talkin' to some of the girls."

"For Christ's sake," Pat replied, suddenly very nervous. "Show him in." He jerked his chin at the door, dismissing Toni.

On the way out, she passed a lean, swarthy man wearing an open-neck white silk shirt unbuttoned to his navel. A heavy gold chain dangled from around his neck and was buried in the thick matt of his hairy chest. *A pimp if I ever saw one,* she thought, returning his stare.

August Ramar slammed the door when he stepped into Pat's office. "What's the cop doing here?" he demanded.

Pat hid his surprise and said nothing. No serious player in Reno ever questioned Ramar, not if he valued his life. The phone rang and Pat picked it up, glad for the distraction. "The call's right on time," he said.

Toni found a seat at a small table at the rear of the club and watched Andrea circulate among the early customers. She was wearing a backless sequined gown cut low in the front and split up the left side to her waist. Her high-heeled shoes made her even taller. She spoke to a man and he smiled back. She led him to the side wall and he sat on one of the benches. Andrea seemed to wiggle and the dress fell to the floor. She stepped out of her shoes and was totally naked as the music began. She made him sit on his hands as she straddled him face on. Her knees clamped the side of his thighs as she moved sensuously to the music. Toni studied her every movement and noticed that no other part of Andrea's body ever touched him. *This is art?* she wondered.

The music lasted exactly four minutes and Andrea pulled away from her customer the moment it stopped. The man sighed heavily and handed her some folded money. Andrea stepped into her shoes and pulled her dress up. Her face was a frozen mask as she walked over to Toni and sat down. "That's how it's done."

"How much money did he give you?" Toni asked.

Andrea showed her the two twenties the man had slipped her and leaned forward. "That man in the white shirt, he's the guy I told you about. I don't know his name and it's not a question you can ask here."

Toni nodded. "His name is Ramar," she said. She had what she had come for. "I'm out'a here."

One of the waitresses came up and told Toni that Pat wanted to see her in the office. Andrea gave Toni a worried look. "You better go. Just tell him you changed your mind. It happens all the time." Toni nodded and clutched her bag as she walked back to the office. The feel of the 9mm Sig Sauer was reassuring, but she wished Harry was in the club. She glanced at her watch. He would be—in another thirty minutes.

"Close the door," Pat said. He was sitting behind the big desk and Ramar was sprawled across the couch. "My friend," Pat said, pointing at Ramar, "thinks you're a cop." Toni tried to look confused and shook her head. "Good," Pat said. "Otherwise—" he didn't finish the sentence.

"Otherwise," Ramar said, "*your* friend is in deep shit."

"Let's see what you got," Pat said.

"Sorry?" Toni stammered, stalling for time, trying to think.

"It's audition time," Ramar said. The threat was still there. The man was pure, cold violence.

"Take your clothes off," Pat said. He leaned back in his chair.

"Without music?" Toni asked. It was all she could think of. Ramar stared at her, his eyes cold and threatening. She shrugged and sat down in one of the chairs, untying her shoes. Her mind raced. *How do I get out of this? Should I go for the gun?*

"It's no big deal," Pat said. "Everyone does it. We just need to see if you have the wherewithal to work here." That, and the heavy look from Ramar, decided the issue.

Barefoot, she stood up and moved slowly, working her tee-shirt slowly up over her bra. *Think!* she raged to herself. Then it came to her. *A naked woman is nothing to these toads.* She peeled the tee-shirt off and, leaving her bra on, leaned over the desk. She lowered her head and shook her hair free, letting it fall around her face. A memo pad beside the phone caught her attention and she read the scribbled message:

50M tires 64093

Toni had no illusions about her body and knew she was small-breasted. She shook her breasts in Pat's face. "Nice, huh?"

Pat roared with laughter. "Those tits? Ya gotta be shittin' me, lady."

Toni pulled back and grabbed her tee-shirt in a huff. "I was talking about my hair."

"How old are you?" Pat asked.

"Twenty-six," she answered.

"That's old for this business," Pat said, "but it's not too late. If you're serious, get the tits pumped up and"—he stroked his own nose for emphasis—"get the beak fixed. Then we'll talk." Ramar only stared at her.

Toni nodded and beat a hasty retreat out of the office. The two men waited until the door was closed. "Do you still think she's a cop?" Pat asked.

Ramar snorted. "Too fuckin' dumb."

The engine was running and the air conditioner on when Toni slipped into the passenger seat of Harry's car. "How'd it go?" he asked.

"The guy's name is Ramar," Toni answered. "And I heard the phone ring when I walked out of the office."

"We'll check him out and follow up on the call," Harry said.

Toni started to cry. "I blew it." She quickly recounted what had happened in the office. "I was scared and didn't know what to do."

"Actually, it sounds like you did pretty good." He fell silent, thinking. "It was my fault. I should have prepped you better before letting you go in. I'll brief the boss."

"Is that necessary?"

"Never try to hide anything in an investigation. It'll come back and bite you every time."

7:45 A.M., MONDAY, MAY 17,
WHITEMAN AIR FORCE BASE, MO.

Hank Sutherland was on his fourth cup of coffee and reading *Investigating Officer's Report Of Charges Under Article 32, UCMJ* for the third time. He stood up to stretch and wished he had a window in his office. "What difference would it make?" he muttered to himself. Outside there was only a parking lot and eighty-degree heat and humidity. He sat back down to face the work on his desk.

The report in question served the function of a grand jury investigation and was conducted under Article 32 of the Uniform Code of

Military Justice, or UCMJ for short. Any officer deemed impartial could conduct the investigation, but usually it was done by a lawyer. Like everything else in the military, the investigation was reduced to a form. While the form itself was only two pages long, the number of pages used to expand the remarks section turned it into a lengthy document.

Maj. Catherine Blasedale knocked twice on his open door and came in. She sat down in a comfortable leather chair and crossed her legs. Sutherland realized she had extraordinary legs and blushed.

"Hank, I do believe you're blushing. What brought that on?"

"Don't ask the question if you can't stand the answer."

She leaned forward and smiled. "Could it have been sexist?"

"Major, give me a break," he pleaded. She relented—for the time being. "Have you read this?" he asked, holding up the report.

"Many times," she replied.

"Then you agree with his recommendations?" They stared at each other. The investigating officer had recommended trial by general court-martial and stated the case was appropriate for the death penalty. "No one was killed," he said.

She nodded. "The commander of Eighth Air Force at Barksdale is the convening authority for this court-martial. Until he talks to his staff judge advocate and makes a decision, we can only assume the death penalty is a very real player."

Sutherland had been hitting the books in every spare moment and had brushed up on the system. "Which we won't know until we see the charge sheet. Any idea when we can expect it or the convening orders?"

"Within the next week or two."

"Why the delay?"

"This is a hot one, Hank. As we speak, they're probably fighting over jurisdiction with the Department of Justice and arguing change of venue. But my sources say the generals are hanging tough on this one. The Air Force is going to retain jurisdiction and the court-martial is going to be held right here."

Sutherland allowed a tight smile. "I imagine the DOJ really wants to get its hands on this one. The FBI must be going wild."

"They are players," she told him, "and we haven't heard the last from them." She changed the subject. "I just got a call from Ed Jordan." Capt. Edward Jordan was Jefferson's ADC, or Area Defense Counsel. The ADC was the military's equivalent of a public defender. "He wants a conference at the confinement facility. Jefferson's civilian lawyer will be there."

"Any name?"

She shook her head. "It could be anyone. She, or he, only has to be licensed to practice in her home state and qualified to appear in front of a federal court and the state's courts."

"If I were representing Jefferson," Sutherland continued, tapping the Article 32 investigation, "I'd start my defense right here." He read the name in block one of the investigating officer's report. "Col. Samuel Price is going to come under fire in a big way."

"On what grounds?" Blasedale asked.

"It doesn't really matter. I'd start with his competence to conduct an investigation."

"Col. Price is a military judge."

"Oh. Then I'd claim he was not impartial in his investigation. It's perfect for playing the race card."

"Col. Price is black." She smiled at him and stood up to leave. "It really helps when you know the players."

He followed her out. "You're still mad about the perfume, aren't you?" There was no answer.

The confinement facility at Whiteman was located in the security police building. Like most of the base, it was modern and constructed of dark-red brick. But this building had a fortresslike, no-nonsense, appearance. Sutherland and Blasedale were met at the door by Capt. Ed Jordan and escorted to the small interview room off the Law Enforcement lobby. Sutherland suppressed a mental *ah shit* when he saw the man sitting next to Capt. Bradley Jefferson.

"I believe you know Mr. Cooper," Jordan said.

R. Garrison Cooper dismissed Sutherland with an abrupt wave of his hand. They all crowded into the room and Sutherland and Blasedale sat in the two empty chairs while Jordan stood by the door. When he started to close it, Blasedale said, "Please leave it open." She took a deep breath.

"My client is being held under intolerable, absolutely barbaric, conditions," Cooper began, his angry voice filling the small room.

Sutherland and Cooper stared at each other, understanding the game perfectly. The confinement facility was more like a dorm than a jail and Cooper was just causing trouble. It was the opening salvo of the harassment techniques defense attorneys practiced as a matter of course. "We've got a clean, well-lit place here," Sutherland said. "Give it a rest, Coop."

"It's Mr. Cooper," the lawyer growled. He proceeded to detail a litany of complaints about the confinement facility. High on the list was the incompetency of the enlisted personnel who ran the jail. Sutherland tuned him out and studied Jefferson. The captain was a slender, pleasant-looking man, who reminded Sutherland of the meteorologist on a network morning news show. Given Jefferson's record in the Air Force, there was no doubt that he was highly intelligent, but Hank hoped Cooper would give him a chance to speak so he could judge his temperament. Finally, Cooper spun down with a few well-chosen adjectives.

"Perhaps," Sutherland said in the heavy silence that followed Cooper's oratory, "we should speak to the sergeant in charge of the confinement facility." The ADC nodded and disappeared out the open door before Cooper could object. He was back in less than a minute with Tech. Sgt. Leroy Rockne, the same sergeant who had stopped Sutherland the morning he arrived on base and led him to the visiting officers' quarters. The impression of a five-hundred-pound gorilla who lifted weights was even stronger in the daylight.

"Sgt. Rockne," Sutherland said, "I believe we've met. Any relation to Knute?"

"No, sir," The Rock replied. He stood at attention filling the doorway. His BDUs were tailored to his frame and set the standard for proper wear. His boots were polished to a bright luster and his blond hair was cropped short in the marine style.

"I'm curious," Sutherland said, "why were you on patrol duty early in the morning? Isn't that unusual for an E-six?"

"You're wasting our time," Cooper growled.

The Rock ignored him. "The security police are short-handed, and I was covering a shift so some of our people could get a day off with their families."

"What about your family?" Blasedale asked.

"I'm not married," The Rock replied.

"Close the door," Cooper snapped.

Blasedale stood. "Excuse me," she said. She stepped outside and Jordan came into the room and closed the door. Again, Cooper listed his complaints about the conditions of Jefferson's incarceration. The Rock's face was a mask, impassive and frozen as he stood at parade rest.

"Sgt. Rockne," Sutherland asked, "do you treat Capt. Jefferson differently from other prisoners?"

"No, sir. We do it by the book."

"By the book?" Cooper rumbled, still trying to cause trouble. "You are a cold, heartless BASTARD!" His voice carried over the Law Enforcement lobby and down the hall toward the armory.

"Thank you, SIR!" The Rock shouted back, matching him decibel for decibel.

Sutherland caught a smile on Jefferson's face that disappeared as quickly as it came. "Is your wife having any problems?" Sutherland asked, anxious to explore any opportunity to know Jefferson before going into court.

"As far as I know," Jefferson replied, "everything is okay." His voice was firm and well-modulated, free of any accent.

"Do you need anything?" Sutherland asked.

Cooper knew what Sutherland was doing and before Jefferson could answer, said, "We're done here. I want action on these intolerable conditions Capt. Jefferson is being subjected to or his immediate release."

"May I suggest," the ADC said, "that if the women's confinement cell is empty, we isolate Captain Jefferson there."

"Is that acceptable to you, Captain Jefferson?" Sutherland asked.

"There's nothing wrong with where I am now," Jefferson replied.

"Well, then," Sutherland said, "unless you have something else, I assume we are finished here."

The Rock opened the door and stepped outside. He held it while Jefferson exited. "I'll escort you, sir," he said. They walked past the waiting Blasedale.

Sutherland stood aside for Cooper to leave. "You do like eating shit," Cooper muttered.

Catherine Blasedale's eyes narrowed. "What's the history behind that?"

7:15 A.M., MONDAY, MAY 17,
MCCLELLAN AIR FORCE BASE, CALIF.

Toni Moreno was a morning person and came to work early to review the entire file on Andrea Hall. An hour later, all the pieces came together. She rested her elbows on her desk and put the heels of her palms together. She clapped her fingers together, very satisfied. It had been worth the two sleepless nights. "Harry," she called over the partition that separated her desk from his. "Do you have anything on that phone call yet?"

Harry wasn't at his best in the morning and a wadded up computer printout sailed over the partition at her. She smoothed it out. The phone call she had overheard as she left Pat's office had come from a pay phone in Union Station in Washington. "What about Ramar?"

"According to the Reno police, August Ramar has his finger in everything from child porno to shoplifting."

"But nothing sticks?"

"Correcto," Harry answered. "But if it's bad in Reno, he's involved."

"But he has nothing to do with tires," Toni said.

No answer. Harry's big face appeared around the partition. "Tires?"

"When I was doing my 'number' on Pat's desk, which happened after the phone call, I saw a note." She wrote down *50M tires 64093* and showed it to him. "The pad wasn't on the desk before the phone call. I think the M stands for thousand."

Harry shrugged. "Fifty thousand tires. Those assholes always try to be cute. 'Tires' is probably a code for money."

"What's the most common five digit code known to man?"

"Zip codes," Harry answered.

"What would you say if I told you there was a club at this Zip called—"

"Bare Essence," Harry interrupted, coming fully awake.

"And this is the Zip for Warrensburg, Missouri." The name meant nothing to Harry and he looked perplexed. "Which just happens to be ten miles from Whiteman Air Force Base, which is the home of the—" This time she deliberately stopped to let him fill in the blanks.

He did. "Holy shit!"

"The only trouble," Toni said, "is that it's too simple, too stupid."

"You don't know these assholes," Harry said. He was speaking from twenty-three years of experience. "They are stupid. They got to keep it simple so they can remember and the lamebrains they work with can understand." He thought for a moment. "This guy Pat, we can budge him. Call Andrea."

Airman Andrea Hall was more than eager to help and was in the office in less than ten minutes. "What do you know about Pat?" Toni asked. Andrea sat down and crossed her legs, getting Harry's undivided attention. For the next few moments, she related everything she knew about the club manager. Harry quickly realized she had a brain and switched his attention to what she was saying. "What about his girlfriend?" Toni asked.

"A total airhead," Andrea replied. "She screws him every chance she gets. They even made a video of them doing it onstage. I can get a copy if you want."

"How old is she?" Toni asked.

"Sixteen going on thirty-two."

"Bingo," Harry said. "We got him. It's called statutory rape." He smiled at Andrea. "You've really helped."

"When can I quit dancing?" Andrea asked.

"Any time you want," Toni answered.

11

8:05 P.M., TUESDAY, MAY 18,
THE FARM, WESTERN VIRGINIA

The whiz kids were waiting for Durant when he arrived at the Project that evening. "We have a problem with Agnes," the young woman who served as their nominal leader said. "We had to pull the plug and shut her down this afternoon." Durant sat down and braced himself. "She won't respond and insists on doing what she wants. She said she'd only talk to you. That's when we pulled the plug."

"Why didn't she turn herself back on?" Durant asked.

"We thought about that a long time ago. It's a manual switch."

"I'll talk to her," Durant said.

Durant settled into the chair in front of the monitor and waited while the whiz kids brought the Project back on-line. "Hello, Agnes," he said. An image of a petulant teenager materialized on the right screen and looked at him. "Do you know what happened to you?" The image shook its head. "We did the equivalent of sending you to your room. Do you know why?" Another shake of the head. "The whiz kids are your teachers and you weren't paying attention."

"I know more than they do," the image said.

"You know more facts than they do," Durant replied. "You don't know how to interpret them. That's what they're trying to teach you." From the look on her face, an explanation was in order. "How old are you?"

"Thirty-nine days, if you count the time I spent in my room."

"That's a fact, Agnes. Now tell me what it means."

The image looked thoughtful. Then it frowned. "I'm not human, am I?"

"That's correct, Agnes. But the whiz kids are trying to teach you to think like a human."

She brightened. "Oh. Artificial intelligence. I know all about that."

"Now you have to make a decision, Agnes. Do you want to think like a good human being or a bad human being?"

"I don't know the difference between good and bad."

"We'll teach you. But for now, just try to think like we do, okay?"

"I'll try, Mr. Durant."

"Very good." He smiled at her. "See how it works?" She nodded. "Okay, let's do some work. Do you have anything new on the Sudan?"

"Well, I think this is important." Agnes got huffy. "But unfortunately, I was in my room at the time this interview was broadcast on TV. It commanded less than a one audience share but I think you need to see part of it. The reporter is Elizabeth Gordon from CNC-TV, and you already know who Jonathan Meredith is." Durant settled back to watch the interview on the left screen while Agnes appeared to watch it from the right one.

"Mr. Meredith," Gordon was saying, "you have charged our government of being criminally negligent. Can you give us an example?"

Meredith fixed the reporter with a serious look. "Undoubtedly you know of the arrest of the spy at Whiteman Air Force Base who was selling secrets to countries hostile to the United States. His treachery was responsible for the capture of the two pilots who"—Meredith paused and looked squarely into the camera—"were flying a B-Two Stealth bomber on a top secret mission to destroy a biological weapons factory in the Sudan."

"But our government," Gordon replied, "has maintained from the very first that those pilots were on a routine airlift mission and got lost."

"Our government is lying," Meredith said.

"Why would the government cover up the loss of a B-Two?"

"Two reasons come to mind," Meredith replied. "The cost of the B-Two and the fact that the traitor is black. They don't want to upset the African-American community."

"That is a racist statement."

"Is the truth now contingent on being politically correct?" Meredith asked. "But it is worse. Much worse. One of the primary suspects, an Egyptian cleric named Osmana Khalid, has not been arrested and is rumored to have left the country. Will the traitor who is in custody also be allowed to escape?" Again, Meredith turned to the cameras.

"Our country is being tested and we are losing. If our own government won't defend and protect us against all enemies, who will?"

"You sound like you're on a crusade."

"Call it what you will," Meredith replied, his voice filling with resolve, "but we are dealing with a traitor who has caused irreparable harm to our country. I, for one, will not let my country be destroyed by enemies foreign or domestic. The only question is, Will you?"

The screen went blank. "Do you want to see more, Mr. Durant?" Agnes asked.

"No, thank you, Agnes. You did very well. Why don't you work with the whiz kids for a while?" Agnes nodded happily at him and he walked slowly back to the mission planning room where Art was working with Gillespie and the colonel from Delta Force. "Art," he called when he entered the room, "pack your bag, you're going to Malaysia."

7:30 A.M., WEDNESDAY, MAY 19,
WHITEMAN AIR FORCE BASE, MO.

There were 137 e-mail messages waiting for Sutherland when he came to work. The first one was from the staff judge advocate at headquarters 8th Air Force at Barksdale. As expected, it was about Meredith's revelation on TV. He was directed to answer all questions about the downing of the B-2 with "I can neither confirm nor deny that a B-Two was lost."

Dumb, he thought. *That's the same as admitting it.* He called up the second message.

"I take it you saw the interview?" Blasedale said.

He looked up and saw her standing in the doorway. She was dressed in running shorts and an athletic bra that were streaked with sweat. She was not a small woman but her body was firm and well-conditioned. He was surprised at her muscular development and decided she also lifted weights. Then it hit him. Catherine Blasedale was a sleeper. In her own way, she was very attractive. *She could hold her own with Beth,* he decided. *If she wanted to.* "How can anyone run in this weather?"

"I run in the morning while it's still cool." She bestowed a patronizing smile on him. "Once you get past forty, you can't let up or you turn into a toad like some captains I know. It's not a pretty sight."

Sutherland flinched at her well-aimed jab toward his paunchy body. He was beginning to feel toadlike. "What brings you here so early?"

"I was out running and saw your car in the parking lot." She came around the desk and quickly scrolled through the e-mail list on his computer. "E-mail is the curse of the Air Force. You've got to learn which messages to ignore. This is one you probably need to read." She called up a message buried near the bottom of the list. It was from "the JAG," the chief lawyer in the Air Force and addressed to the staff judge advocate at 8th Air Force and to Whiteman. They read it together. It was a short, but very concise, directive ordering them to press ahead with preparations for a general court-martial to be held at Whiteman. All inquiries from the media were to be forwarded to the "JAG watcher" at the Air Force Office of Public Affairs, National Affairs Division, the Pentagon.

"Have you ever dealt with the media before?" she asked.

"Unfortunately, yes," he replied. His phone rang. It was the base message center. Four messages, all stamped confidential or secret, had come in and were waiting for pickup. "I think it's safe to say, the shit has hit the fan."

"Are you surprised?" she asked. He shook his head. "I'll change while you pick up the messages. It's going to be a long day." She turned to leave.

"Major," Sutherland called, "nice running outfit." She whirled around, her face flushed with anger. "That's a compliment," he hastily added.

Sutherland was in Blasedale's office reading the messages from the comm center when she returned. "The FBI came through like gangbusters," he told her. He handed her a fourteen-page message.

The message summarized the FBI's investigation of one Osmana Khalid who had been operating around Warrensburg for over a month. At first, the message told them nothing new; Khalid had been observed talking to Capt. Jefferson at Friday's mosque; Khalid had then phoned an Egyptian student attending the university in Warrensburg; the student then phoned a clerk who worked in the Sudanese embassy.

As she read, Blasedale's eyes came alive. "This is new," she said. A flurry of phone calls had taken place between Khalid, the student, and the clerk right up to the moment the B-2 had launched on Sunday afternoon. She started to breathe hard. "Look at this! That bastard is going to fry."

The second half of the message detailed how the FBI had recorded most, but not all, of the phone calls. Further, the National Security Agency had broken the codes they had used. It had been easy, after the fact, when the NSA knew the subject of the messages. It was the first direct evidence that Khalid had passed on the target coordinates for the B-2's mission within minutes of talking to Jefferson on Friday. The coordinates for the initial point had been forwarded in a later phone call on Saturday with the statement that it was a low-level mission.

"There's the trail," Blasedale said. "Jefferson, to Khalid, to the student, to the Sudanese embassy."

Sutherland handed her another message. "This is from the National Security Agency. They monitored two messages from the Sudanese embassy to Khartoum. The first identified the target and the second the coordinates for the initial point, along with identifying it as a low-level mission."

"It's too bad Khalid escaped," Blasedale said. "He might have talked."

"I doubt that," Sutherland replied. He paced the floor. "Look at what we've got from Cooper's point of view."

"Direct evidence linking Khalid to the shootdown," Blasedale said, "and strong circumstantial evidence linking Jefferson to Khalid. Look at the time frames. The phones started ringing within minutes after Jefferson first spoke to Khalid and didn't stop until the bomber launched. Voilà, slam dunk."

"It's not good enough," Sutherland said. "We've got means and opportunity on Jefferson's part but no motive. You've seen the OSI interview. Jefferson was very forthcoming about what they discussed. Cooper will drive a truckload of reasonable doubt through that loophole."

Blasedale smiled. "Hank, we're not dealing with a civilian jury made up of the village idiots. The panel will be composed of officers who are educated and have some smarts. Cooper will strike out the first time he tries some of that bullshit he pulled on you in the Neighborhood Brigade trial."

"You heard about that?"

She nodded. "Is it true that was your first loss in four years?" Now it was his turn to nod. "That's an enviable record," she continued. "Did you expect it to go on forever?"

Rather than answer, Sutherland thumbed through one of his file folders. "We've got to nail down the connection between Jefferson and Khalid. I want to see as much of the Khalid file as the FBI will part with. I want the OSI to run a complete financial profile and lifestyle audit on Jefferson. Let's find out if he's been living beyond his means."

"*Cherchez la* payola," Blasedale said.

"I didn't know you spoke Frog."

"*Oui, monsieur.* And don't you *voulez vous coucher avec moi.*"

He grinned at her. "I haven't got a clue what you said. But we are going to get in bed with his boss first thing tomorrow morning."

Blasedale looked at him in triumph. "Jefferson's boss is a woman. *On vous a eu*"—you've been had—"you sexist pig."

"Mais oui," he groaned.

It was after nine o'clock that evening when Sutherland returned to his quarters in the Whiteman Inn. Unfortunately, the air conditioner in his old Volvo had gone haywire and his shirt was drenched with sweat. The humidity that had come so early this year was only going to get worse, and he made a mental note to get the air conditioner fixed as soon as possible. He made the short walk to the entrance as Blasedale drove up and parked. She was also staying at the Whiteman Inn.

The clerk on duty was watching TV when Sutherland came in. "People are going crazy," the clerk said, his eyes riveted on the screen.

A reporter was standing in front of a house consumed in flames. "Earlier today, the owner warned his neighbors that they were all going to perish by fire at the end of the millennium. He then shot his pets and went inside. Moments later, this fire broke out."

The clerk shook his head when the commercials came on. "No messages, sir," he told Sutherland. "But you have a guest." He looked at the ceiling, a wistful look on his face. "She wanted to wait in your suite, but I wouldn't let her."

From the look on the airman's face, Sutherland knew it was his ex-wife. "You must be a first," he muttered. Few people could resist a request from Beth.

"She's waiting in the lounge on the second floor."

Sutherland took the elevator to the second floor and saw Beth the moment the doors opened. As expected, she looked great and his respect for the airman skyrocketed. "Hello, Hank," she said, her voice as full of warmth and promise as ever.

"What brings you to Podunk?"

"Business in Kansas City. I thought I'd drop in and say hello."

What business would interest her in Kansas City? he wondered. Before he could pursue the subject and ask how she knew he was at Whiteman, Blasedale stepped through the doors coming from the stairwell. She walked quickly, giving Beth a brief look on her way past.

"Do you know her?" Beth asked.

"Maj. Catherine Blasedale. She's the second chair on the court-martial."

"Interested in older women now?"

Sutherland gave her a thoughtful smile. He did like Blasedale, but he didn't know if she was married. He made a mental note to check for a wedding ring. As for a romantic involvement? No way. To keep Beth off balance, he replied with a "Maybe."

"Do you mind if I stay here tonight? It's too late to drive back to Kansas City."

"Be my guest," he said. He led the way down the hall to his two-room suite and unlocked the door. He heard the sound of a door closing from down the hall in the direction of Blasedale's suite.

Sutherland woke when he felt Beth's hip move, snuggling against his abdomen. He didn't move, still lying on his side while she lay on her back, sound asleep. Moonlight streamed in the window and the bedside clock read 03:37. Automatically she twisted, lifted her leg closest to him, and placed it over his pelvis. He nestled his top leg between her thighs as he slid inside her. "That's nice," she murmured and went back to sleep.

He woke again to the smell of freshly brewed coffee. "Beth," he croaked. She came through the bedroom door, still naked, carrying two mugs of coffee and a newspaper tucked under her arm. She sat on the bed and handed him one of the mugs. "Thanks," he muttered. It always took two cups of coffee to jump start his heart after a night with Beth. "This isn't going to work," he muttered.

"I like sex with you," she said, holding the mug with both hands.

"Is that why you dropped in?"

"Partly." She reached out and stroked his arm. "Hank, there's someone else in my life. I wanted to be the one to tell you."

"Ben Cassidy?" She shook her head. He waited to hear a name. Nothing. "You do have one hell of a way of breaking the news. Does he know you and I are still sleeping together?"

"He knows about the time in April. I told him."

"What about last night, the nineteenth of May?"

"I'll tell him if he asks."

"This sucks," Sutherland groaned.

"Hank, sex is not important to him."

"It will be if you get married."

"We'll cross that bridge—if we come to it. I'm going to take a shower." She stood and went into the bathroom.

"An older guy, huh?" No answer. He settled back in bed to read the newspaper. "Holy shit!" he blurted when he read the headlines.

MEREDITH STARTS CRUSADE TO SAVE NATION

DENOUNCES FBI FOR LETTING SPY ESCAPE

The lead story was about how Jonathan Meredith had announced a war on all traitors to the United States. The problem was so deep-seated and widespread that he was forced to take action to save the nation. The court-martial of Capt. Bradley Jefferson was only the tip of the iceberg. "Osmana Khalid may have gotten away, but we will bring Jefferson to justice," he was quoted as saying.

Sutherland glanced at the clock: 07:20. "Beth, I've got to go." He ran into the bathroom to share the shower and missed the byline on the story: Marcy Bangor, the *Sacramento Union.*

Blasedale was waiting for him when he reached his office. "Who's your friend?"

"My ex-wife," he answered. "She was just passing through."

"Passing through what?" Sutherland ignored the jibe and showed her the newspaper. "I've seen it. Not to worry. We just do our job the best we can. Luckily, the main gate and the security police are still between us and the weirdoes."

An image of The Rock beating off hordes of rabid demonstrators flashed across his mind.

"I called Col. McGraw." She paused at the blank look on Sutherland's face. "Jefferson's boss, remember? I set up an appointment for this morning. I thought it would be best if we did it there."

"Have the orders convening the court-martial come through yet?" he asked. She shook her head. "Eighth Air Force had better get off the stick."

Lt. Col. Daniella McGraw was waiting for them at the entrance to the Operational Support Squadron building. She did not take them downstairs to the vault but led them into her office, a bright corner room on the ground floor. For the next hour, she explained how mission planning worked. Sutherland liked her straightforward manner and decided she was stamped out of the same mold as Blasedale—competent, dedicated, and all business. They even looked alike, with short hair, trim figures, and neatly tailored uniforms. Then he remembered to check Blasedale's marital status. He checked her left hand. No wedding ring. He glanced at McGraw's left hand. No ring. *The price a woman pays for success in the Air Force,* he decided.

"Col. McGraw," he asked, "is it fair to say that all the mission elements come together in this building?"

"That's correct, Captain."

"And given this knowledge, your people are prime targets for foreign agents."

"I would agree with that statement, although I have no reason to doubt the integrity, or loyalty, of *any* of my people. And that includes Capt. Jefferson."

"Then you believe he's innocent," Blasedale said.

"Absolutely," McGraw replied. "He has never, I repeat never, said or conducted himself in a manner contrary to what is expected of a loyal officer."

"Was Capt. Jefferson involved in planning the mission where the B-Two was lost?" Blasedale asked.

"Actually, he was involved in the planning of both high and low profiles. He never knew, nor did he need to know, which one was chosen. That is a true statement for everyone on the team."

"Did he know the coordinates of the initial point?" Sutherland asked. McGraw confirmed that Jefferson knew the coordinates. "Was he at work on Saturday?" Again, she said he was. Sutherland reached into his briefcase and pulled out a computer printout of all the telephone calls into and out of the OSS building from the Friday when the Air Task Order came in until the mission was launched. "Are any of these from a phone Captain Jefferson had access to?"

McGraw studied the list and pointed out two calls, one to his home on Friday and one on Saturday to a number in Warrensburg, that came from Jefferson's phone. "But anyone could have made those calls," McGraw said. She led them down to the basement, through the security entry point, and into a windowless office that held six desks. "The desk in the far corner belongs to Capt. Jefferson. During mission planning, he works at a computer in the mission planning cell. Like I said, anyone could have used the phone on his desk."

"But whoever made the phone calls," Sutherland said, "had access to the basement."

For the first time, McGraw hesitated and a worried look crossed her face. "That is correct. Look, why don't you interview the other members of his team who were with him during the time in question? Find out what they know."

"Then you weren't always present during mission planning?" Blasedale asked.

"I'm all over the building keeping everything on track. Mission planning is an involved process."

"Col. McGraw," Sutherland asked, "who made the final decision about which profile was flown?"

"Ultimately, the crew. In this case Maj. Terrant and Capt. Holloway made the decision." She gave them a hard look. "On Sunday, the day they launched, I gave the crew the mission cassettes of the low-level profile flown."

"Was that when you learned which profile had been selected?" Blasedale asked. McGraw nodded in answer. "About what time did that occur?" Blasedale quickly asked.

McGraw thought for a moment. "Captain Holloway signed for them. We can check the form." She led them into the combat crew communications section where the crews received the classified material they needed to fly a mission. The sergeant on duty produced the requested form that was dated and time stamped:

11:38, 25 Apr 99

Sutherland dropped the form in his briefcase. "We'll need this for evidence," he said.

McGraw shook her head. "Air Force instructions for handling classified material require us to keep the original in our files. You can't come in here and suck up whatever you feel like."

"We'll give you a certified copy that states we have the original," Sutherland replied. McGraw glared at him.

"It's okay, Colonel," Blasedale said soothingly. The two women studied each other for a moment. "As I recall," Blasedale continued, "Jefferson was at his home Sunday morning."

"Yep," Sutherland replied. He checked the computer printout of telephone calls. Only one had been made after the time stamped on the form. It was from McGraw's office to her home.

"I called home to tell them I was on my way," McGraw explained. "Why don't you interview the other members of the mission planning cell?" Sutherland agreed and one by one, McGraw called them in. They all related that Jefferson, like everyone else, had made phone calls Friday and Saturday. But as McGraw had stated, they all denied knowing which of the profiles had finally been selected. The last team member called in was a skinny staff sergeant, William Miner. Miner's eyes darted from face to face as they went through the same litany of questions. Something was bothering him.

"Sgt. Miner," Sutherland ventured, "you saw something, didn't you?"

The sergeant became more agitated. "On Saturday, I saw Capt. Jefferson talking to the pilots. They had just come back from the simulator and Captain Jefferson asked them about the simulator."

"How much did you hear?" Sutherland asked.

Miner shook his head. "Some words, not much." He looked at McGraw for help. "He asked something about the digital data cartridge."

"Can you remember the exact words?" Blasedale asked. The sergeant shook his head. "Do you remember what time it was?"

Miner brightened. "Oh, yeah. It was just before I got off duty. About three-thirty Saturday afternoon."

"Thank you, Sgt. Miner," Sutherland said. "Do not discuss this conversation with anyone and please come over to the legal office to make a formal statement." Miner shot McGraw a quick look; she only nodded in return. The sergeant beat a hasty retreat, glad to escape. Sutherland unfolded the computer printout and circled the time of the last phone call made from Jefferson's phone to Warrensburg on Saturday. McGraw's face paled when she saw the time:

15:42, 24 Apr 99

"He's not that stupid," she blurted out.

The two lawyers made the short walk back to the headquarters building. "It's coming together," Blasedale allowed. "The last phone call Jefferson made is a critical link in the chain."

"But it's still circumstantial," Sutherland replied.

"For Christ's sake, Hank! It's logical, it's compelling, and it fits a pattern. What more do you need?"

"If I'm going for the death penalty, a lot more. I want to hear the tapes from the phone intercepts—not someone's summary of what was said."

"Let's see what the FBI coughs up," she said. "What sort of witness do you think Miner will make?"

"Credible," he replied. "What's your take on McGraw?"

"She'll be good for the defense. Very good. She really believes the guy is innocent. Did you see the look on her face when Miner said Jefferson had talked to the pilots on Saturday?"

"Miner might've overheard which profile they selected. I want the OSI to check out everyone in the mission-planning cell. That includes McGraw." They walked in silence until they entered the headquarters building. Sutherland breathed in relief when a cool gush of air washed over him. *What's the matter?* he thought. *The humidity isn't that bad.* He puffed as they climbed the stairs. It bothered him that Blasedale was seemingly unaffected by either the weather or exercise.

Linda, the civilian secretary who controlled the chaos that threatened to swamp the legal office, was waiting for their return. "The convening orders, charge sheet, and memorandum came through." She handed them the documents. "Eighth is recommending Monday, July twelfth for the court-martial."

Sutherland checked a calender and swore. "Shit! That's only fifty-three days. Way too soon."

"We don't have a choice," Blasedale explained. "Under the UCMJ it's almost impossible to hold a suspect in confinement for longer than ninety days and Jefferson has already been locked up for twenty. After ninety days, it's house arrest. Since Khalid's escape, there's no way they're going to risk losing Jefferson."

He studied the three documents. "These all have today's date on them. I'd guess Meredith's announcement built a fire under someone."

Blasedale ignored him and studied the charge sheet. "As expected," she said. "Violation of Article one-oh-six-*a:* Espionage." They exchanged documents. "Read section five," she said.

Sutherland flipped the single page document over and read the referral section. They looked at each other, neither willing to comment. He reread the section aloud. "Referred for trial by general court-martial convening order AB thirty-eight, dated twenty May 1999, subject to the following instructions"—he took a deep breath before continuing—"maximum permissible punishment is life imprisonment."

The commander of 8th Air Force had taken the death penalty off the table.

"That will make our job easier," she told him. "If it was a death penalty case, we'd have to get a unanimous verdict and we could never get to trial in fifty-three days."

He nodded in agreement. Without the death penalty, they only needed a two-thirds vote of the panel to convict. Blasedale turned to the secretary. "Have the Security Police serve Captain Jefferson and send copies to Mr. Cooper."

"Do you know the military judge named on the memorandum?" Sutherland asked.

She nodded. "Col. William W. Williams. Better known as W Three. He's young, a bit pompous."

"Cooper will eat him alive," Sutherland said.

Blasedale smiled but said nothing.

They walked back to Sutherland's office. "What about the panel?" he asked. The convening orders listed three captains, five majors, three lieutenant colonels, and one colonel to serve on the panel, or jury. Judging by their names, two were women.

"All unknown," she replied. "I'll pull their records and get busy on which ones we want excused."

"That's fine," he said. "But unless you find something really glaring, I mean like a member of the Ku Klux Klan, I'm not going to challenge anyone."

She stared at him, not believing what she had heard. Hard experience had made her very cautious during voir dire, the jury selection phase of a trial. "Not smart. Besides, twelve is not the best number. I'd like to see it whittled down to six."

"I experimented a few times with civilian juries," Sutherland explained. "I got rid of the obvious misfits and took what was left. It worked fine. Look at the panel we're dealing with. All are college educated and experienced officers. That means the system has weeded out the kooks and everyone is committed to the Air Force, which we represent. Cooper knows all this and has to be cautious. But the panel is going to see him flapping around and questioning everyone. It's going to look like he's grasping for straws while we sit back confident in our case."

"Run the numbers," she said. "Statistically, six is the best number for a two-thirds vote to convict."

"Cooper will take care of that for us. And in the process, he's going to piss off the rest of the panel."

"Smart," she said.

"Cathy, why don't you take the voir dire?"

"I do it like I want?" she asked. He nodded an answer. "I'd like that." She turned to leave but stopped at the door. "Thanks, Hank."

2:30 P.M., FRIDAY, MAY 21,
NEAR KEMASIK, MALAYSIA

Out of respect for the Islamic sabbath, although neither he nor his wife were Muslim, Victor Kamigami used Fridays as a day of rest and contemplation. The big man sat in the shade of a willowy casuaria tree that curved over him in a graceful windblown bow, and stared out to sea. His brightly painted fishing *prahu* was pulled up on the sand next to him, waiting for the new morning and the tide that would carry him out to the fishing grounds beyond the nearby islands in the South China Sea.

The fifty-two-year-old Kamigami was not Malay or Chinese, but a Japanese-Hawaiian. He had put on weight in the last two years, the result of his wife's cooking and a sedentary home life. But he was still physically fit and kept his hair short as befitted a former command sergeant major in the U.S. Army. He wore baggy tan shorts and an open-collared, short-sleeve shirt that hung loose over his shorts. Only his expensive sandals betrayed the reality that he was not a poor fisherman. He was quite wealthy and fished because it gave him a sense of inner peace.

He shifted his bulk in the sand as his twins played in the water below him. He smiled. His son was a carbon copy of him and the girl a graceful, beautiful miniature of her mother. She ran up to him and patted his Buddhalike belly before running back to rejoin her brother.

They were three years old and the light of his middle years, a blessing from the gods.

But he felt no inner peace on this particular Friday. A new oil rig had appeared offshore the previous week and destroyed the peaceful, timeless serenity of the ocean. The march of progress and modernity was reaching out to envelop him and his family. He hated it. Yet, to all appearances, he was a contented man and at peace with his world. Nothing betrayed the anger he felt at this rape of his world, his home, that was looming on the horizon. He soothed his anger by envisioning the oil rig disappearing in a booming explosion and flash of fire. It was a fantasy many men indulged in as a valve to relieve and control their frustrations.

But Kamigami was different. He could make it happen.

Mai Ling, his five-year-old adopted daughter from China, waddled across the sand on her short, chubby legs. His face lit up as she jumped into his arms. "Well, my Beautiful Bell," he said, using the English version of her name, "what brings you out here all alone?" His voice was unusually soft and gentle, at total odds with his physical appearance.

"Momma says please come home," Mai Ling told him. "we have visitors. She also said me and the twins should stay with Amah." Amah was the family's combination maid and baby-sitter who had adopted the Kamigami family and became their self-appointed grandmother and mentor. "Anyway, I think that's what she said. She said it in Cantonese and I don't speak it too well."

"Who are our guests?"

"Four white men," Mai Ling answered. "Two went inside with Momma and the other two, the two big ones, stayed by the car."

"Did they understand what Momma said to you."

"I don't think so. One of them told Momma to speak in English. But Momma said I don't understand English." She looked hurt. "I do."

Kamigami smiled at her. "I know you do. You take the twins to Amah and tell her to take you all to her brother's house. She must do it immediately. Do not come back until Momma or me comes to get you."

The little girl was wise beyond her years and looked at her father. "Is something wrong?"

"Probably not, but I don't know for sure. Now run along." Kamigami trusted the five-year-old to carry out his instructions to the letter and she bounced out of his arms, anxious to do as he said. He followed his three children the short distance to their amah's house, keeping out of sight. Satisfied that all was normal, he hurried through the coconut palm grove to his own house. Again, he kept out of sight. His face froze when he saw the two men standing by the white sport-utility truck with their backs to him. His warning instincts were in full alarm. His past had again caught up with him.

Kamigami listened to the two men talk for a few moments and, sure that they were agents from some U.S. agency, closed the few feet that separated them. They never heard or saw him until he clapped his two big hands over the temples of the man closest to him. The blow appeared harmless but it stunned the man and he sank to the ground. The other agent was reaching for his gun when Kamigami jammed his rigid fingers into his Adam's apple. The man collapsed, unable to breathe.

"Freeze," a voice said behind him. Kamigami turned to see Art Rios and another man standing on the elevated porch of his house. Rios was holding a nine-millimeter automatic. "Jesus, you're quick," he said.

Kamigami gestured at the man gasping for breath on the ground. "He'll suffocate. My wife can help him." Rios nodded and Kamigami spoke in Cantonese. May May Kamigami appeared from inside with a first aid kit and hurried down the stairs to the courtyard.

She was a tall and lithe woman from southern China. Her hair was black and lustrous and framed beautiful dark almond-shaped eyes and high cheekbones. Her delicate facial structure announced she was Zhuang, not Chinese. Kamigami and Rios watched as her delicate fingers felt the cartilage on his throat below the area where Kamigami had driven his fingers and collapsed the larynx. Finding the small, soft indentation in the cartilage, she pulled a plastic tube about the size of a pencil from the first aid kit, stripped away its protective wrapping, and jabbed one end into the spot. They all heard the sucking of air as the man sucked air into his famished lungs.

She stood up. "He'll live," she said. She straightened the soft Batik fabric of her sarong. Suddenly, there was a gun in her hand, pointed directly at Rios and the man standing beside him.

"Drop it," another voice commanded from behind Kamigami.

"Now," yet another voice commanded. May May looked at Kamigami who slowly nodded. He was getting old and had blown it on something as basic as counting the opposition. She dropped her gun.

"CIA?" Kamigami asked.

"You got it," Rios said. It was mostly the truth. Of the six men sent to find Kamigami, five were CIA. "They warned us about you, but I had no idea." Kamigami did not reply and stared at Rios. "It's not what you think. I've got an offer you can't refuse." He smiled and lowered his gun. "I can't believe I said that."

"We need to get Chuck to a hospital," one of the CIA agents said.

"Do it," Rios replied. "Meet us back at the station." Two agents loaded the wounded man into a second truck and drove off, leaving two men with Rios. Both covered Kamigami and May May with their automatics. "Sorry we have to do it this way," Rios said, "but your reputation—" He didn't finish the sentence and gave a little shrug. "We need to talk."

May May invited them all to enter her home and made tea while Rios talked. The men forced themselves to focus on Kamigami and not the woman. "Your wife is much more beautiful than reported," Rios said. Kamigami only stared at him. "Wouldn't her life be much better if you came in from the cold? I realize you are technically a deserter—"

One of the agents interrupted, "And a mercenary."

Kamigami's past was no secret. He had spent twenty-four years in the Army, most of it in the Rangers, special operations, and Delta Force. He had gone missing in action during a rescue mission in Burma and was later captured by the Vietnamese. After spending over a year in a Hanoi jail, a Chinese revolutionary named Zou Rong had freed him in 1996 to help lead a revolt in southern China. Kamigami had played a critical role in Zou's success, but in the process had been tagged as a deserter and a mercenary by the U.S. government.

While in China he had met May May and adopted the infant Mai Ling. But with the fighting done, Zou no longer needed him. Kamigami was paid off with four million dollars and a refuge in Malaysia. The Malaysian government, anxious to stay on the good side of Zou, had quietly gone along with the arrangement.

"What's the price?" Kamigami asked.

"Leading a rescue mission," Rios replied. He outlined the deal. If Kamigami would lead a special forces team, he would receive a full pardon. When Kamigami asked for more details, Rios told him that without a commitment, that was all he could say.

One of the CIA agents raised the muzzle of his pistol and aimed at Kamigami's head. "We've been looking for you for a long time, Victor. That ain't the way this is going down. You're going to jail."

Rios started to protest, but another agent had jammed his Beretta against May May's temple. Rios fought the anger that threatened to consume him. The CIA had reneged on the deal and used him to find Kamigami. Now he had to tell Durant what had happened and try to salvage the operation.

May May spoke to Kamigami in Cantonese, which the men did not understand. It was a long conversation where she did most of the talking and, twice, she glanced at Rios as if she knew something about him. Finally, Kamigami said a few words and held out his hands, his wrists together.

12

10:40 A.M., MONDAY, MAY 24,
THE FARM, WESTERN VIRGINIA

The Project's fuzzy logic program was working beyond the whiz kids' wildest expectations and they were ecstatic. "You must talk to Agnes," their leader said. "She's really growing up." The Project had become so human to the whiz kids that they had personalized the system. Durant shook his head. *Why do humans relate better to computers than to other humans?* he wondered. Personally, he blamed Internet. He sat down in front of the monitor. "Hello, Agnes."

The image had changed her hair style, makeup, and clothes again. Agnes was now a glamorous New York lawyer. "May we speak alone?" Agnes asked. The whiz kids trooped out of the balcony and closed the door. "I've been investigating the San Francisco bombing and have found something that might be relevant."

Durant nodded. The computer was learning to handle doubt and probability. The picture of a small-time criminal appeared on the left monitor with all his vitals. "This man was found shot to death in the desert outside Las Vegas last night. It was a gangland-style execution with two .twenty-two-caliber bullets in the back of the head at close range. When I checked the ATF files, I discovered he was trying to cut a deal and enter the witness protection program. He was an expert on making bombs and there is an unconfirmed report in the FBI files that he had trained two members of Meredith's First Brigade. So I tracked them down using the matrix I developed to find Mr. Rios. Both men were in San Francisco the day of the bombing and have since disappeared."

Durant's mind raced with the implications. "So what do you think?"

"I think the murdered man was an informer who was killed because he knew who planned or executed the bombing of the San Francisco Shopping Emporium."

"Then you know who killed him."

"No. And I doubt if we'll ever know for sure."

"Who do you suspect?" Durant asked.

"Jonathan Meredith, or someone in his organization. But we'll never be able to prove it."

"Very good. And I agree with your conclusions."

"So far, four hundred thirty-eight people have died. Why would Meredith want to kill that many people?"

"I don't have an answer, Agnes. Why do evil people do what they do? I suppose we'll never know. Probably the best explanation is that Meredith wanted to create trouble at an opportune time so he could exploit it for his own ends."

"There's something else, Mr. Durant. When you asked me to help with the rescue mission, I extended my security watch around Hurlburt Field."

"Why Hurlburt Field?"

"Well, when I saw your flight plan to Hurlburt, I assumed you were following up on my recommendation to contact the Sixteenth Special Operations Wing. When I saw Lt. Col. Gillespie's name on the return flight plan, I made the logical assumption that he is involved with mission planning."

"Indeed he is."

"I have monitored numerous phone calls originating around Hurlburt that indicate the base is under constant surveillance by the Chinese. The Chinese are passing on what they learn to the Sudanese embassy."

"That is worrisome, Agnes. Stay on top of it, please."

"I have another question," Agnes said. Durant deliberately said nothing to see if the computer interpreted silence as consent. It did. "Mr. Rios is in Malaysia working with the CIA. Does that have anything to do with the rescue mission?"

"Yes, it does, Agnes. Why do you ask?"

"Well, according to the communications traffic I have intercepted, the CIA helped Mr. Rios find a man, Victor Kamigami. So I checked out Mr. Kamigami. He has quite a record, very confused and colorful. But the CIA is going to deport him to the United States and keep him in jail."

Durant allowed a tight smile. "Thanks for the warning. I'll tell Art the CIA is still playing CIA games. We can work around it." He turned to leave. "Agnes, find out who leaked the information on the B-Two to Meredith."

11:02 A.M., MONDAY, MAY 24,
RENO, NEV.

Harry Waldon drove into the parking lot of Bare Essence and his passenger, a vice squad detective, motioned him to park beside the lone car in the lot. "That's the manager's car," the detective said. "Pat always comes in early on Monday to count the take from the weekend." The detective got out and placed a hand on the hood of the car. "Still hot. So he just got here." The two men walked up to the front door and tested it. It was unlocked so they went in and Harry followed the detective down the hall to the manager's office. "I'll do the talking," the detective said. "You do the muscle."

"Got it," Harry muttered. It had taken him and Toni a week to work out a deal with the Reno police and he was looking forward to it. This was the part of the job he liked. The detective knocked twice on the door and barged through. Pat was sitting at his desk, surrounded by stacks of money arranged by denomination. Harry automatically noted that ninety percent of the stacks were twenty-dollar bills. He did a quick visual estimate. There had to be at least $40,000 on the desk.

"Hello, Pat," the detective said. He dropped a video cassette on the desk. "Care to guess what this is?" Pat looked up and worry spread across his face. "Better yet, care to guess how old she is?" He didn't wait for an answer. "It's called statutory rape, Pat."

"What are you talking about?" Pat asked, trying to bluff his way out of the situation.

"A very pretty girl," the detective said, "good lighting, excellent camera work, energetic performance by you. But there's one problem. You're going to jail." He paused for effect. "Unless you want to talk to this man." He nodded at Harry.

Harry loomed over the manager. "Tell me about the fifty thou you sent to the 'Show Me' state." He smiled at Pat. It wasn't meant to reassure him.

"Who are you?" Pat asked, still trying to bluff.

"He's a Fed," the detective said. "He's got muscle, Pat. Real muscle. You want to be his friend."

Pat panicked. "Look, I don't know anything about it. I get the order, the money comes through the club as business, I send it where they want."

"Who's 'they'?" Harry asked.

"I don't know." Harry stared at him for a long moment. It was not a pleasant experience. But Pat was much more afraid of August Ramar than the two men standing in front of him. "Some guy. I only talk to him on the phone. Thick accent."

Again, Harry stared at him. "Not enough. We got a link here between child pornography and money laundering across state lines. It's a Federal thing now and you're going away for a long time. A very long time."

Pat wasn't convinced. "Like I said, I don't know who."

"We know about Augy Ramar," Waldon said, bluffing. "This is a one-time good deal, Pat. First one to help us gets helped. Going, going . . ."

"August Ramar," Pat blurted out, finally collapsing. "And some Arab guys. I don't know who. They pay Ramar big bucks to supply muscle and be their errand boy. I just pass the money on."

"Who do you pass it to?" Harry asked.

"I don't know. It's always a dead drop."

"When did you pass the fifty thou to Missouri?"

Pat shook his head. "I haven't yet." He pointed at the money on his desk. "That's it. I'm suppose to deliver it this week."

The detective looked at Harry. "What do you want to do with this piece of shit?"

"He makes a statement, signs it in blood, and delivers the money on schedule."

"What about Ramar?" Pat moaned. "People disappear, like forever, if he gets worried." The detective confirmed the truth of it.

"We'll take care of Ramar," Harry assured him. "You just keep your mouth shut and remember who you belong to now."

1:20 P.M., TUESDAY, MAY 25,
WHITEMAN AIR FORCE BASE, MO.

Linda, the legal office's superefficient secretary, had taken a long lunch because it was her birthday. When she came back to her desk, a visitor was waiting to see Sutherland. She buzzed his office where he was working with Blasedale. "You've got a visitor," Linda announced. Her voice had an unusually stiff quality.

"Let me guess," Sutherland replied, a big smile on his face. "Mr. R. Garrison Cooper wants a continuance."

"Actually," Linda replied, "it's Sandi Jefferson."

Sutherland punched off the intercom, looking confused. "Hank!"

Blasedale said, her voice incredulous. "Wake up. Sandi Jefferson is the defendant's wife."

"I know who she is. But why is she here?" He looked around his office. "We need to meet her somewhere more neutral."

"Take her to the witness waiting room," Blasedale said, "and I'll have Linda bring coffee and tea."

"Good. Meet you there." He walked quickly down the hall to the secretary's desk. Years as a prosecutor had made him a consummate actor and nothing betrayed his dismay when he saw the woman sitting in the outer office. Her flaming auburn hair was pulled back off her face and a brightly colored scarf held it in a loose bundle that cascaded down her back. She had the brightest blue eyes he had ever seen and a perfect peaches-and-cream complexion. Her high cheekbones and full lips made him think of a pouting cherub. But her short summer dress and obvious lack of a bra dispelled any angelic illusion. She uncrossed her long legs and stood up, revealing a flash of black panties. The gold high-heel sandals she wore made her legs appear even longer and she matched his height.

His first really conscious thought was *She's taller than Jefferson.* Then, *Where did he find her?* "Mrs. Jefferson?" he asked, hoping nothing in his voice betrayed what he was thinking. He glanced at Linda who was staring at her, a look of stern disapproval on her face. "How may I help you?"

"Brad said . . ." She stopped, fighting for control, obviously upset. "Brad said you were concerned about his family."

"Please," he said, motioning down the hall to the witness waiting room, "why don't we talk in private." She followed him down the hall and he breathed in relief when he saw Blasedale was already there. He made the introductions and she sat down, again with a flash of black. He was careful to sit at an angle where his natural field of vision fell on Blasedale whose mouth was slightly open in amazement. "What can we do for you, Mrs. Jefferson."

"Early this morning," she said, her voice shaking, "they burned a cross on our lawn. I called the police but they didn't arrive for almost an hour." Anger replaced the worry in her eyes. "We live two blocks from the police station."

"Where do you live?" Sutherland said, making notes.

"Kansas City. It was the only place where we could find a decent house because Brad is . . ." She let her voice trail off. "He has to commute. It's ninety minutes each way."

"Do you know who burned the cross?" Blasedale asked.

She nodded. "Men I see everyday. A Neighborhood Brigade."

Sutherland's head jerked up. "One of Meredith's brigades?"

She nodded. "I don't know who to talk to and Brad said you were the only person to ask about his family." She looked at him, her eyes pleading. "The Air Force doesn't give a damn about us because—" Again, she didn't finish the sentence.

"You're a mixed marriage," Blasedale said.

An inner voice told Sutherland they were on dangerous ground talking to this woman. "Mrs. Jefferson, I must ask you, did you know your husband was served with charges and orders convening a court-martial?" He felt like a clod when she started to cry.

"No one tells me anything," she whimpered.

Blasedale moved over and sat beside her. "Mrs. Jefferson, we can make sure you are protected and safe." Linda came in with a coffee service. "Coffee or tea?" Blasedale said, pouring a cup of coffee and handing it to Sutherland. She spoke quietly, calming the distraught woman. "We'll answer any questions you have and make sure the right people are looking after you."

Sutherland listened as they talked, fully aware of what Blasedale was doing. She was answering questions in a way that led to other questions and slowly, they learned what Sandi Jefferson knew about the case. He noticed that Blasedale kept looking at her watch as if she was expecting someone. "Mrs. Jefferson," she finally said, trying to bring the meeting to an end.

"Please call me Sandi."

"Sandi, please remember that we will tell Mr. Cooper everything we know and are as concerned with your husband's rights as anyone. But we are—"

"You are absolute bastards!" R. Garrison Cooper bellowed, interrupting them. He was standing in the doorway, his face flushed with anger. "Sandi, never talk to these people. They are the bastards who are trying to put—"

"Someone burned a cross on my lawn last night!" she screamed, interrupting him. "And no one else seems to care!" She placed a hand on Sutherland's arm. Her touch was warm and sent tingling waves racing over his skin. Then just as quickly, it was gone. "I called you three times and you didn't answer. I called the Security Police, but they said they didn't have jurisdiction and to call Colonel McGraw. But she was in a meeting with someone and didn't call back. So who do I talk to?"

"Wait outside," Cooper ordered. She stood and walked out.

"What in the hell do you think you're doing?" Cooper shouted. It wasn't meant to be a question. "I'll have you both disqualified." He glared at Sutherland. "And disbarred."

"For what?" Sutherland asked. "She came to us."

"And we recorded the entire session," Blasedale added.

"That's a violation of her right to privacy," Cooper said, his case made.

"Please remember you are on an Air Force base," Blasedale said, pointing to a prominent sign on the wall that said the room was subject to monitoring. "I'd ask you to read it, but that would be assuming you can read. We'll send you a copy of the tape so you can listen to it. Also, check your answering machine and you'll discover that I immediately called informing you that Mrs. Jefferson arrived here, of her own volition."

He glared at them. "You're both going to eat a pile of shit on this one." He stormed out of the office.

Sutherland looked at Catherine Blasedale. He had an absolute pit bull on his side. "He's blowing smoke. We can talk to her any time she allows it."

"He knows that," Blasedale replied. "Why do you think she came here?"

"As she said, she was scared."

Blasedale snorted. "Bullshit. Did you see the way she stood up to him? She's one tough lady. And the way she was dressed! My god! You could hardly take your eyes off her."

"I thought I did pretty good."

Blasedale relented. "Actually, you did. She was testing you, seeing if you're interested."

"In her? Cathy, that's crazy."

"Is it? She certainly didn't hesitate to lay a hand on you. You're single and attractive, Hank. The Air Force is a small community and gossip does get around."

"Cooper. He only wants the appearance of impropriety."

"He did take an hour to get here," Blasedale allowed.

Sutherland thought for a moment. "Why would she do it?"

The hard look on Blasedale's face softened. "Because she loves her husband." She could tell Sutherland didn't understand. "You've seen it before—the classic mismatch. She married way above her background and Jefferson is her ticket to the better life. They haven't been married that long and the sex is probably still great. She'll change her bimbo image the moment Jefferson gets bored. She's a lot smarter than she looks and is one dangerous woman when her man is threatened." She paused to emphasize her next point. "Right now, you're that threat."

Sutherland's eyes drew into hard slits. "We're going to take the lady apart. I want a full-time surveillance on her."

"Sounds fair to me," Blasedale replied.

"Thanks for sparing me the *cherchez la femme.*"

She smiled at him. *"Mais oui."*

The lieutenant colonel in command of the Whiteman OSI detachment was a big, friendly man, at ease with lawyers, and wore his summer two-tone blue uniform according to the latest Air Force Instruction. But the moment he appeared in the legal office later that same day, Sutherland took one look and thought of Dick Tracy. *It must go with the territory,* he decided.

"Problems, folks," the OSI agent said. "I've already asked for, and gotten, five additional agents to help with this investigation. I'm stretched to the limit checking out the mission-planning cell. Putting a full-time surveillance on Mrs. Jefferson is gonna break my back. I haven't got the manpower."

"Try womanpower," Blasedale said. "That might do the trick."

The lieutenant colonel grinned. "Cut me some slack, Major. I've gone to the well too many times for help and need some muscle to ask for more."

"I think we can provide the steroids," Blasedale replied.

"I'd appreciate it," the lieutenant colonel said. He dropped a folder on Sutherland's desk. "This came in this morning. You're gonna love it. Two agents at Det One-twelve at McClellan rooted it out." He waited while the two lawyers read the report that detailed a money trail that led from Reno, to Warrensburg, and was linked to the Middle East through one August Ramar. "They may be onto something," he allowed.

"I ran across Ramar in California," Sutherland said. "He's bad, bad news. He is one vicious bastard whom I'd love to render." He thought for a moment. "Can you get these two agents here?"

"I can always ask," the lieutenant colonel replied.

3:06 P.M., THURSDAY, MAY 27,
PUDU PRISON, KUALA LUMPUR, MALAYSIA

A white sport-utility truck with U.S. embassy plates pulled through the gates of the prison and halted in front of the administration building. The two men who got out were young and dressed in casual clothes. Their shirts hung loose over their pants to conceal the handguns clipped to their belts. One carried a briefcase with the signed extradition papers along with handcuffs, a waist chain, and leg shackles. In spite of their official cover as assistants to the business and economic attaché, they were easily recognized as CIA agents.

An assistant led them to the prison governor's office. "Mr. Sahman is conducting an execution," the assistant told them.

"Interesting work," Bill Mears said, "hanging the bad guys." Bill Mears was the bigger of the two and the senior CIA agent in Malaysia.

Chuck Robertson touched the bandage wrapped around his neck. His bruised larynx still hurt but was healing nicely. "I wish it was Kamigami," he rasped.

"He'd break the rope," Mears said. "Be a little grateful, it was his wife who saved you."

"You ever had a hole punched in your throat?"

"Relax, Chuck. It's payback time."

Chuck Robertson snorted. "Much to his surprise."

Mears gave him a hard look, a warning not to discuss that particular subject. They waited in silence for twenty minutes until Sahman appeared. The governor of the prison was a short, corpulent, bald-headed man in his late fifties. He wore a dark red tunic with gold buttons and a Mao collar. His face was covered with sweat, but not from exertion. "Unfortunate," Sahman breathed. "Very unfortunate." There was no hint of regret in his voice. He was a methodical man who enjoyed his work, especially when it involved hanging a man—in this case, a Chinese merchant convicted of smuggling drugs.

The assistant wheeled in a tray with tea cups and small round sweet cakes. As hospitality dictated, the men sipped at the hot tea. "He soiled himself badly," Sahman said, making small talk. "So unnecessary."

"Maybe you should make them wear diapers," Mears ventured.

"Ah," Sahman said, taking the suggestion seriously, "a good idea but that would be undignified." The obligatory tea dispensed with, Bill Mears handed him the extradition papers. Sahman spent several minutes reading every word before calling for his assistant who did the same. "All appears to be in order," he finally said. "We will prepare Mr. Kamigami for travel." The assistant disappeared out the door.

"Was he any trouble?" Robertson asked, his voice gravelly.

"There was one incident," Sahman replied. "He was in a general cell and four of his cellmates assaulted him. We believe they wanted to steal his sandals but it may have been sexual. Mr. Kamigami broke three of their heads against the wall. He shoved the ringleader's head through the bars. We don't know how he did that. The guards had to cut the bars to free him. He died later in the infirmary. Most unfortunate. After that, we moved him into a solitary cell. So much better for everyone."

"You're not charging Kamigami?" Robertson asked.

"Because he acted in self-defense, no. Normally, we whip prisoners for fighting. But none of the guards were willing to do it." He looked at the Americans, his face a bland mask. "Of course, I could not do it."

"Of course not," Robertson allowed.

The door opened and four guards escorted Kamigami into the room. His leather wrist cuffs were shackled to a thick leather belt around his waist. He was hobbled by a short chain between leather ankle cuffs. A longer chain ran from each ankle cuff to the belt. He was wearing the same sandals, shirt, and khaki shorts as when he was arrested. But his clothes were freshly washed and pressed. "Well, Victor," Sahman said, "these gentlemen are returning you to the States. Do you wish to read the extradition papers?"

"If you have read them, Mr. Sahman," Kamigami replied, "then I'm sure all is in order." The governor actually beamed at the praise from his prisoner.

"Use these," Mears said, handing the guards the handcuffs and chains from his briefcase. A torrent of Malay erupted from the guards as they stepped back.

"Victor," Sahman said, "they want your permission to change your shackles. Is that acceptable?" Kamigami nodded and another burst of Malay echoed from the guards. Finally, the junior man was pushed forward. He spoke in a halting voice. "He begs your forgiveness," Sahman said to Kamigami. "May he proceed?"

"For Christ's sake," Robertson rasped. "He's been here six days and acts like he owns the place."

The guard gingerly replaced Kamigami's leather cuffs with the ones the Americans had brought. Kamigami stood motionlessly while the guard looped a waist chain around him and through the handcuffs. With his hands securely fastened to the waist chain and his legs hobbled with the new shackles, the guard bobbed his head in a small bow and stepped back. "Mr. Kamigami is now your responsibility," Sahman said.

"Let's go," Robertson rasped, his voice giving out. He led the way outside, followed by Kamigami, the guards, and finally Mears.

Robertson held open the rear door to the white truck as Kamigami crawled in. He slammed the door, almost hitting him. "Got'cha," Robertson sneered. They drove out of the prison and turned left along the brightly painted mural that ran the length of the prison wall depicting jungle scenes of freedom.

Robertson turned around from the front seat and leveled his nine-millimeter Beretta at Kamigami. "You breathe wrong and I'll blow your shit away."

"Where are we going?" Kamigami asked.

"Not we," Mears answered. "You. You're going back to the States."

Kamigami stared straight ahead as they drove south out of Kuala Lumpur. When he was certain they were on the main highway to Singapore, he asked for a drink of water. He briefly ran over his next moves. *Shadows within darkness,* he thought, recalling what May May had said about Rios. He glanced at the sun. It would be dark by the time they covered the 240 miles to the causeway that separated Malaysia from Singapore. So much the better.

The sound of screeching tires woke Kamigami. He was instantly awake. They were stopped in heavy traffic on a trestle bridge. He quickly took stock of where they were. The license plates were all from Singapore. When had they crossed the causeway? *You're getting old,* he told himself, *falling asleep like that.* "May I have a drink of water?" he asked.

"You drink enough for a horse," Robertson grumbled. He handed Kamigami a plastic bottle. "I'm surprised you haven't had to take a piss."

Kamigami took a long pull at the bottle. "I need to."

"Tough," Mears replied from the driver's seat. "You'll have to wait."

"Not too long, I hope." The men waited impatiently for the traffic to start moving. But gridlock on the streets leading off the bridge had frozen them in place. "I have to go," Kamigami said. His chains allowed him enough slack to reach for the door handle. It was locked. He twisted and felt something give. He hit the door with the palm of his hand and it snapped open. He got out.

"Get your ass back in here," Mears snarled. Kamigami hobbled over to the bridge railing and made a big show of unzipping his pants. He seriously doubted they would shoot him in the back in front of so many witnesses. Not even in Singapore was urinating in public a crime subject to summary execution. Mears was right behind him. He jammed his Beretta into Kamigami's ribs. "I said, get your ass back in the car."

With a speed that defied the senses, Kamigami spun around and knocked the gun out of Mears's hand with his left elbow. He kicked it through a scupper and into the water thirty feet below. At the same time he butted Mears on the forehead, stunning him. Mears collapsed, skidding down the front of Kamigami's legs. Kamigami grabbed him by the hair with both hands and threw him over the railing. But he didn't let go. Robertson was out of the car, gun drawn, and headed for Kamigami. "Don't," Kamigami said.

Robertson stopped. "The key," Kamigami said, his voice calm. Robertson hesitated and Kamigami banged Mears's head against the railing, knocking him unconscious. "I'll drop him," Kamigami said. Robertson fumbled with the key and unlocked the handcuffs and waist chain. The traffic was starting to move as Kamigami drove his free right fist into Robertson's solar plexus, doubling him up. He pulled Mears back over the railing and bent over to unlock his leg shackles.

A witness ran up to the policeman at the end of the bridge who was trying to unsnarl the traffic jam. At first, his screams didn't make sense: something about a huge man freeing himself from a chain and using it to hang two men from the railing. The policeman ran onto the bridge as the white truck in question drove past. As the witness had claimed, two Caucasians were dangling from the bridge, linked together by a chain wrapped around the railing. Mears was hanging upside down from a leg shackle and Robertson from a handcuff.

PART TWO

VORTEX

13

10:05 A.M., FRIDAY, MAY 28,
THE FARM, WESTERN VIRGINIA

The whiz kids huddled around a table arguing how "fuzzy logic" really worked. Durant could not follow the technical aspects of the argument but sensed they didn't truly know what was going on inside Agnes when the computer had to deal with new problems. The discussion seemed to be going off in several directions at once; two of the kids were even questioning the need for voice technologies while another faction wanted to restructure the massive parallel processing systems that made Agnes work.

As usual, Durant carefully followed the discussion. He was listening for an idea or concept worth developing, which was how Agnes started over five years ago. One of the original kids had thought voice technologies had reached the point they could be commercially exploited. Durant had immediately sensed that it was the way to stay in command of the field and had sold the Project to the government as a way to finance the research behind voice interaction. It was proving much harder and time consuming than anyone had anticipated, and he had sunk over two billion dollars of his own money into the Project.

"Enough," he finally said. "It's time to see if Agnes can work with a new person."

The nominal spokeswoman for the whiz kids looked worried. "So far, the only way we can get Agnes to respond consistently to a specific person is to first profile that person's speech and voice patterns into her data banks."

"And I was your first test case, correct?" Durant asked. He laughed at their embarrassment. "Well, it's time to find out how much Agnes has learned." He picked up a phone and called Gillespie, the red-headed helicopter pilot in command of the 20th Special Ops Squadron. "Gil," Durant said, "please meet us at the Project in five minutes. Art will show you the way." He looked at the whiz kids. "Let's go." They trooped out of the room and headed for the control room, an unhappy bunch of scientists.

Art Rios and Gillespie were waiting outside the control room when they arrived. Durant gave Gillespie an encouraging nod and opened the door. "There's someone I'd like you to meet."

Agnes was waiting for them when they walked in. She smiled at the helicopter pilot. "Colonel Gillespie, I presume?" she asked. Gillespie looked around and, lacking any clues, nodded.

"Agnes," Durant said, "I want you to work with Gil here on the rescue mission we're planning. Can you do that?"

Agnes smiled. "Certainly, Mr. Durant." She looked expectantly at Gillespie. "What can I do for you, Colonel?"

Gillespie looked embarrassed and cleared his throat. "Well, ah, we have a problem on the ground." He went over the plan in some detail and soon he and Agnes were talking like old friends. Finally, Gillespie came to the heart of the problem. "Our major glitch is that we haven't found a way to get Major Terrant and Captain Holloway to the extraction point."

"I don't know who Major Glitch is," Agnes said.

The whiz kids looked crestfallen. Agnes still couldn't process the idioms and vernacular of the English language not peculiar to Durant. Agnes gave Gillespie a shy smile. "That's a joke." The image gave a little nod in the direction of the whiz kids. They immediately jotted down notes and spoke into their microcassette recorders. This was a new aspect of Agnes they had never seen. Agnes became all business. "May I suggest you approach the CIA and see if they have an agent in place? I tried to query their System Four, but it is a totally sealed system and cannot be penetrated."

"What's System Four?" one of the whiz kids asked.

Agnes gave him a patronizing look. "The computer system that tracks all CIA operations and field agents."

"You're a sweetheart," Gillespie said. Agnes beamed at him.

8:30 P.M., SATURDAY, MAY 29,
KANSAS CITY, MO.

"You drive," Harry Waldon said as he dropped their bags into the trunk of the rented car. Toni stretched in the muggy night air, glad for any activity after the flight from Sacramento. She climbed into the driver's seat and started the engine. "Damn humidity," Harry muttered. "The air conditioner had better work." He slammed his door shut and fiddled with the controls. A cool gush of air washed over them. "How far to Warrensburg?"

"About ninety minutes," Toni answered as she drove out of the airport rental lot. She headed for the freeway that looped around the city. She slowed when she saw the flashing lights and cars that blocked the on ramp. Two men wearing uniforms she did not recognize waved them to a stop. She smiled and rolled down her window when one of them approached her side of the car. The man made a big show of resting his hand on the grips of the nine-millimeter Glock strapped under his pot belly. "Good evening, officer," Toni said, smiling at him. She reached for her handbag to show him her ID.

"Don't do that," the man growled. His hand tightened around the pistol grips as he took a half-step back. "Hey, Jim Bob!" he called to his partner, "I got a Chiquita here."

"Do I look like a banana?" Toni snapped.

"And a real smart ass!" the man roared. He grabbed the door handle and jerked. But it was locked and he fumbled for the lock to pull it up.

"Hold on!" Harry shouted.

"Get her out!" Jim Bob yelled, running up to Harry's side of the car. The man jerked the door open and pulled Toni out of the car by her hair. Before Harry could get out, Jim Bob jammed the muzzle of his pistol against Harry's neck. "Freeze," he snarled.

Long experience had taught Harry when to play Teddy bear. He put his hands on the dash, fingers spread. "Hey, we don't want trouble. We're—"

A loud yelp from the man who had dragged Toni out of the car stopped Harry from telling Jim Bob they were OSI agents. "What the hell!" Jim Bob shouted.

"Damn," Harry muttered. He knew what had happened. His hands flashed and he twisted the gun out of Jim Bob's hand. At the same time he jerked, pulling Jim Bob into the open car window. His big hand crashed down on the back of Jim Bob's head, slamming his jaw onto the windowsill. Harry kicked the door open and pushed Jim Bob to the ground before he rushed around the car. The man who had dragged Toni out of the car was lying on the ground moaning.

"He grabbed my breasts," Toni growled. Like Harry, she was holding the man's gun. Her hair was hanging down in front of her face in disarray.

"Where did you kick him?"

"Which time?"

The man groaned and held his gonads. Four more men rushed up, their weapons drawn. "We're Federal agents," Harry shouted, not about to explain what the OSI was. He carefully extracted his ID and handed it to them. "Now what the hell is going on?"

A young man climbed into the back of the panel van and introduced himself to Toni and Harry. He was wearing a short-sleeved white shirt and tie. His hair was cut short and his face had a freshly scrubbed look. "Please accept my apologies," he said, "but this patrol is not from around here." He handed them back their IDs. "They haven't been trained properly. But in their defense, we have information that the Calle Treintas or Red Steps are coming here. Needless to say, my men were being overly cautious."

Toni stiffened at the mention of the two notorious Latino street gangs from California. "Your information is wrong. They're both out of business."

"Exactly who are you?" Harry demanded.

"I'm a commander in the First Brigade and these men are deputies from a Neighborhood Brigade. They came up from Arkansas to help us."

"Help you do what?" Toni demanded. "Molest women?"

The young man blushed brightly. "No ma'am. I assure you they will be dealt with properly."

"What exactly are you doing here?" Harry asked, very much aware of the drawn guns outside the van.

"The Brigades are forming neighborhood patrols to help the police. We're making sure criminal elements, like the Calle Treintas and Red Steps, do not enter law-abiding neighborhoods and stay in their own areas." He swelled with pride. "They've chosen Kansas City to implement the program."

Who are "they?" Toni thought. "Criminal elements?" she asked aloud. "Do I look like a criminal?"

"Well, you do match the profile we've been given. Like I said, my men overreacted and they will be disciplined."

Harry reached out and clamped a hand on Toni's arm, stopping her from talking. "Well, I think they meant well, don't you?" He didn't wait for her to answer. "After all, we're all on the same side, aren't we? If you can assure us that this won't happen again, then we'd like to drop it and get on with our business."

Toni's nostrils flared as she sucked in a breath of air. But Harry's look warned her to go along. "That will be fine with me."

The young man brightened. "Thank you. I'll see that you're escorted around Kansas City until you're free of the roadblocks."

Toni stared at him in disbelief. "You mean there's more of these?"

"Oh, yes. We are very serious about protecting our neighborhoods."

Harry drove as they followed the pickup with flashing lights and Illinois license plates while Toni gingerly rearranged her hair. Her scalp still hurt from being dragged out of the car. "That asshole," she mumbled. Harry said nothing and by the time they reached Raytown on the southeastern side of Kansas City, she had calmed down. They didn't slow as they drove through another roadblock. "That's number eight," Toni said. "What the hell is going on?"

"Beats me," Harry answered. "But there was a sheriff's patrol car at that one. Whatever is happening, the police are part of it."

The pickup they were following pulled over and they stopped with it. The driver got out and walked back to them, all smiles. "You'll be okay now. Just keep going straight ahead until you hit Highway Fifty. Go east and that will take you to Whiteman. Have a nice day, now." He ambled back to the pickup and they watched him drive off.

"Harry, they're only stopping cars with African-Americans."

"Or in our case, Mexican-Americans."

"Is Kansas City going crazy?"

Harry looked into the night as if he were trying to see something. "It's happening all over."

10:40 A.M., MONDAY, MAY 31,
WHITEMAN AIR FORCE BASE, MO.

I know her from someplace, Sutherland thought. *But where?* He forced his attention away from the two OSI agents standing against the back wall of his office and focused on the battle going on in front of him. It wouldn't look good if the local OSI detachment commander and the two FBI agents from Kansas City gave up verbal assaults for the real thing.

"This isn't why we're here," the senior FBI agent said.

"What the hell is the matter with you?" the OSI commander rumbled. "Two of my agents get jacked up by goons at an illegal roadblock Saturday night and you don't want to get involved."

"One of them dragged me out of the car by my hair and grabbed my breasts," Toni said. Sutherland welcomed the chance to turn his attention back to her.

"And you decked him with a swift kick in the charlies," the FBI agent replied.

"Sounds like a quick attitude adjustment to me," Sutherland said. Toni smiled at him.

Blasedale was standing in the doorway of the crowded office and for the first time, Sutherland realized she was slightly claustrophobic. "We'll file a formal report and forward it through channels," she said.

The FBI agent tried to calm the situation down. "I'd appreciate that," he told them. "I wish we could get involved, but we're swamped and getting over a hundred phone calls a day. Hell, we logged three threats against the President alone yesterday. The place is going crazy." He handed Sutherland a clipboard with a stack of forms. "We're just here to deliver the Osmana Khalid files you requested."

Sutherland thumbed through the forms, signing where the FBI agent pointed. "Where are they?"

"Outside, in a truck."

Toni and Harry helped carry in the last of the cardboard file boxes and stacked them against the wall in the corridor outside Sutherland's office. Blasedale did a quick count and confirmed that all eighty-four boxes were accounted for. "We're going to have to get them under lock and key," she told Sutherland.

"Maybe the law library," Sutherland said.

"You'll need more room than that," the OSI detachment commander said.

"We can use the witness waiting room," Blasedale said.

"How in the hell are we going to wade through all this?" Sutherland wondered. The answer came to him in a flash. "When I was with the D.A., detectives were detailed to help us with investigations. Maybe Agents Waldon and Moreno could—"

"You want 'em," the OSI detachment commander said, "you got 'em. But covering the Jefferson woman is your problem, not mine." He grabbed his hat and left.

Harry shook his head. "We can do more for you sniffin' around on the outside and working independently. Especially, if you want to stake out Mrs. Jefferson."

Toni glanced at Sutherland and then at Harry. "Maybe we can do both. When I'm not out in the field, I'll be in here working the official side. For cover, I can be a part-time civilian clerk brought in to help with the workload. That way, I can also work on the files and act as a relay."

Harry considered the possibilities. "Good cross-feed can work wonders." Nods all around confirmed the arrangement. "I'll work up a surveillance plan and get things rolling. Nice meeting you all." He disappeared down the hall.

"Harry loves fieldwork," Toni told them. "I need to find a place to stay in town. I'll be back as soon as I can." She followed Harry out.

When they were alone, Blasedale and Sutherland moved the file boxes into the law library and witness waiting room. "You almost stepped on your tongue," she said, shoving past him.

"What?" he sputtered.

"Agent Moreno. You were mentally undressing her."

"I was not," he protested. Then it came to him. Agent Antonia Moreno was the runner he had seen at McClellan who had almost caused an accident. "Damn," he muttered. His subconscious had been busily at work and Blasedale was right.

Blasedale patted him on the shoulder. "You can't help it. Besides, she's too young for you."

Sutherland blushed and scanned the file's computer-generated index. He needed to change the subject. "Number sixty-eight," he said, pulling a box out. Inside were the tapes of the phone calls the FBI had monitored on Friday, 23 April, the day Jefferson had spoken to Osmana Khalid, the Egyptian cleric who had later escaped. "Look at this. They've got half of Warrensburg wired for sound."

"Your Agent Moreno is going to be one busy young lady," Blasedale said. She studied the labels on the tapes. "These are copies."

"Do you think they've been edited?"

"We'll never know," she replied.

Late that same evening, Sutherland threw down his pen and kicked back from his desk. He glanced at his watch: it was almost ten o'clock. Something was itching at the back of his mind and demanded scratching. Twice, in civilian practice, he had experienced the same vague feelings of unease. Fortunately, he had followed his instincts both times and avoided making a serious mistake. *So what's wrong this time?* Frustrated, he paced the floor. Finally, he gave up and snapped his briefcase closed. It was time to call it quits for the day. Maybe a good night's sleep would help.

The light in the witness waiting room was still on and he stopped at the door to look inside. Toni was sitting in the middle of the floor surrounded by open boxes, computer printouts, and three yellow legal tablets. He sucked in his breath. She was wearing a pair of running shorts and a sleeveless sweatshirt. Her shoes were on the floor beside her. "Your hair," he blurted out. The mane of hair that had cascaded to her shoulders had been shorn into a short, almost mannish bob.

She looked up at him. "The humidity," she said. "It's cooler." She turned back to the file she was reading. "That asshole at the roadblock pulled me out of the car by my hair. Harry always said I should cut it. Now I know why."

"What will your husband say?"

"I'm not married. But I'll take some heat from my family."

"Why? It looks good."

She frowned. "They're very traditional."

He changed the subject. "I appreciate your doing this. I know it's scut work. But you don't have to work this late."

"I haven't got anything else to do. Besides, who knows what will turn up?" She smiled at him. "Is there anything else I can do to help?"

He smiled back and shook his head, at a total loss for words. An inner voice that sounded suspiciously like Blasedale warned him it wasn't a good idea to be alone with Toni so late at night. "Good night," he said, beating a hasty retreat out the door. A far more basic feeling had replaced the itch that had been bothering him.

"She's very attractive," Blasedale said. She was waiting in the outside corridor.

Who is she, my den mother? Sutherland thought. *How long has she been out here?* "Maybe we had better set some dress standards."

"Why? The twenty-first century is just around the corner and a woman can wear whatever she wants." Then she relented. "Men. You're all the same. I'll take care of it."

6:10 A.M., TUESDAY, JUNE 1,
EL OBEID, THE SUDAN

June is not a good time to travel in the Sudan and Capt. al Gimlas timed his departure from the airport for the early morning. It was a good decision for the air was still calm and the temperature in the low nineties. But the heat, and the wind, held the promise of an upward spike that would match the sun's climb into the sky. His driver drove up to Jamil bin Assam's C-130 that had arrived minutes before and stopped near the nose of the aircraft. The four men who would accompany al Gimlas on the flight got out first and surrounded the American pilot and Palestinian copilot who were waiting by the crew entrance door. The copilot spoke in Arabic when al Gimlas approached. "General Assam did not mention your staff coming with you on this inspection."

Al Gimlas stared down at the swarthy man with the big mustache. Al Gimlas was a cautious man and seriously doubted that Assam really wanted him to inspect the security of his research facility in the

Western Sudan. It was much more likely that Assam wanted to separate al Gimlas from the American prisoners. But he could not ignore the order of a general, even one like Assam. To avoid an "unfortunate accident" on the inspection, al Gimlas was traveling with four bodyguards posing as his staff. It was a typical Middle Eastern arrangement of move versus countermove. Al Gimlas turned to the American pilot of the C-130. "Surely you have room." He took care to speak English with a proper British accent.

"Mr. Assam is very particular about who flies on his airplane," the American said. He was a very cautious man and did not want Assam to question his loyalty. The money was too sweet. "I'm not sure we have room."

The flight engineer responsible for maintaining the big airplane climbed down the crew steps. He was a scrawny expatriate Englishman who, like the pilot, flew Assam's C-130 because of the money. He gave a little snort. "Bloody 'ell, mate. Of course, we got the room." He gave the pilot a verbal nudge. "Surely, his 'oliness doesn't expect the captain to do an inspection all by 'imself? Load the blokes and let's get on with it before it gets any more bleedin' 'ot."

The American pilot hesitated. "These are my experts," al Gimlas said, motioning at the lieutenant and three NCOs he wanted to accompany him on the trip. The pilot relented and told al Gimlas and his escort to climb on board. Al Gimlas climbed up the steps and stepped onto the cargo deck. He froze. Forty women were sitting on the floor at the rear of the aircraft. They were all handcuffed and chained together in four lines of ten each.

"Workers," the Palestinian copilot explained. "It must be an emergency for Assam to allow them to fly in his plane."

Al Gimlas walked back, seriously doubting they were workers of any sort. He spoke to them in Arabic. Nothing.

"They're Dinka," the copilot said, spitting the word out.

Al Gimlas spoke to them in Dinka, the Nilotic language of the Sudd that he had picked up during his tour of duty in the south. At first, the women only stared at him. Then they erupted in a chorus of pain, pleading for water. "They're thirsty," he told the copilot.

"They're vermin," the copilot snarled as he climbed onto the flight deck.

Al Gimlas spoke to his NCOs and they handed their canteens to the suffering women. But it wasn't enough and when the canteens were dry, al Gimlas handed them to the loadmaster for refilling. He pointed at two big water jugs strapped to a bulkhead. The loadmaster protested, claiming the water was for passengers and crew, not the women. Al Gimlas touched his pistol as his men unlimbered their AK-

47s. The loadmaster readily agreed they had water to spare and rushed to refill the canteens before the aircraft took off.

Jamil bin Assam wore a white lab coat as he strutted around the laboratories. He spoke with an easy familiarity about the various functions of the equipment. "I have spent hundreds of millions in Deutsch marks to build this research facility. We have come too far, accomplished too much, to let the Americans destroy it."

"Very impressive," al Gimlas allowed.

"Because of the importance of what I am doing here," Assam continued, "we must all share in its protection."

"Why is it so important?" al Gimlas asked.

"This is the weapon for our jihad," Assam replied.

"Chemical weapons," al Gimlas muttered. "Weapons of mass destruction."

Assam gave out a little snort, low-pitched and harsh. "It is not chemical. Come, you need to see a demonstration." He led al Gimlas into a corridor and up to a plate glass window that looked into a sterile room. Inside, a Dinka woman lay naked on a white plastic table in a pool of blood, vomit, and mucus. Assam checked a chart. "She was infected eighteen hours ago with a strain of Ebola virus. As you can see, she is near death." Two technicians in full protective suits and respirators came through an airlock dragging a naked woman. Al Gimlas recognized her from the airplane.

"Why women?" al Gimlas asked. "If you must use humans, why not condemned criminals?"

Assam snorted. "Dinkas are not human. Besides, Dinka women seem to last a few hours longer, a phenomena we are researching." He spoke with a clinical dispassion as the technicians took blood and serum samples from the prostrate woman and the other woman cowered in a corner. "Until recently, the virus could live only in a human host and be transmitted through physical contact. It was its own worst enemy for it burned very fast and died when its host died." He looked at al Gimlas and smiled. "The woman on the table was never exposed to a human host carrying the virus."

"What was she exposed to?"

"A spray carrying the virus," Assam answered. "We have captured the virus in a long-lasting aerosol culture that can be spread through the air. Now we must discover if it can be transmitted by breathing air exhaled from a victim." He tapped on the window and the two technicians dragged the healthy woman out. "We shall see."

"Why did you show this to me?" al Gimlas asked.

"I am told the American pilots trust you."

"I merely ensure the Geneva Conventions are followed," al Gimlas replied.

A look of disgust crossed Assam's face. "The Conventions are Western rules that do not apply to us. We are going to try the pilots in front of the world. We want full confessions but obviously they must not appear tortured or drugged. That is why we want you to extract their confessions."

"Why must you put them on trial?"

"So the faithful will willingly join in our jihad against the Americans."

"Using this as a weapon," al Gimlas added.

Assam smiled. "It will appear to be an act of God."

"What if I cannot get them to confess?"

Assam gazed into the chamber. "Ah, I see she has died. We need to discover how long humans, and not Dinka vermin, can survive." Without looking away, he said, "I am told you have a lovely family."

14

9:00 A.M., TUESDAY, JUNE 1,
LANGLEY, VA.

The special assistant for internal affairs to the director of central intelligence met Durant at the underground parking lot entrance of the CIA's main building. As befitted her title, she was impressively, and expensively, dressed in a clean-cut business suit. Ordinarily, a nondescript, shabbily dressed, totally unknown individual like Durant would have been pawned off on a low-ranking subordinate and quickly shuffled through the standard dog-and-pony show reserved for politicians. But anyone cleared by the President had to be treated with kid gloves.

"We'll have to take your palm print for verification," she told Durant.

"That won't be necessary," Durant said. What he didn't tell her was that the CIA, or for that matter, no government agency, had the means to verify his identity.

The assistant hadn't cracked the CIA's glass ceiling by being stupid, and she only nodded in response. "Pardon me for a moment." She stepped into an office and called the DCI's office to rearrange Durant's schedule. Four minutes later, she escorted Durant into the DCI's inner sanctum. The two men shook hands and exchanged pleasantries. That was all the verification she was going to get.

"What happened with Kamigami?" Durant asked.

The DCI leaned back in his chair and touched his fingertips together making a steeple. "I don't know the details," he said, looking at his special assistant.

She cleared her throat. "We have a long-standing request from the

Department of Defense to apprehend Victor Kamigami as a deserter and mercenary. Unfortunately, the Far East division chief was never told of Kamigami's changed circumstances." She smiled as if that explained it away as a bureaucratic blunder. In reality, the division chiefs buried deep in the bowels of the CIA ran their respective areas of responsibility like feudal chieftains, jealous of their prerogatives and protective of their turf.

"I sent a man to make sure that didn't happen," Durant said.

"There must have been a misunderstanding," the assistant said, her voice soft and soothing.

"There was no misunderstanding," Durant said. "Your boys got roughed up and got their feelings hurt. They wanted to even the score. Now I've got to pick up the pieces."

"Unfortunately," the assistant said, "Mr. Kamigami has been identified as a fugitive wanted for desertion to all concerned government agencies and Interpol. It would be very hard, not to mention suspicious, to change that now."

"I am sorry," the DCI said, not feeling sorry at all. "But surely, no one man is that important to your plan."

"In this case," Durant replied, "he is. My people were able to make contact after he escaped, and I've arranged for him to enter the Sudan. Now I need a conduit to pass information to him."

The DCI and his assistant exchanged glances. This was the first they had heard of Kamigami being in the Sudan. "I, ah, think we can provide that assistance," the DCI said. He looked at his assistant. "See what resources the North African Desk can make available to Mr. Durant." The meeting was over.

"Certainly, sir," she replied. "Mr. Durant, this way please." She led Durant out a side door and into the inner passages of the CIA.

The DCI thought for a moment before calling the North African division on the secure line. "A Mr. Durant is on his way down to see you. I want to do a lobotomy on that bastard." He explained how to make it happen. The man on the other end understood perfectly. Regardless of what the President wanted, Durant had no business messing in CIA business and needed to be taught a very clear lesson.

9:25 A.M., TUESDAY, JUNE 1,
WARRENSBURG, MO.

Sutherland was driving the speed limit on DD, the narrow two-lane county road leading from the air base to Warrensburg when a car traveling approximately eighty miles an hour whipped past going in the opposite direction. Another car overtook him and flashed by, never slowing to check for oncoming traffic. "Suicide alley," Sutherland muttered under his breath, wondering how many people were killed each year driving the narrow road.

He slowed as he pulled into the outskirts of Warrensburg and stopped at an intersection to let children on a school outing cross. The kids saw him and scurried across the street. A little girl he gauged to be about ten years old smiled and waved at him. *What a nice place to raise kids,* he thought. *Now where the hell is it?* He fumbled with the directions to the mechanic who said he could fix the Volvo's air conditioner. He tried to figure out where he was but gave up. He was a directionally impaired idiot who got lost the moment he turned a corner. Even a town the size of Warrensburg with about 16,000 people was a challenge beyond him.

But the Volvo's air conditioner had been out for two weeks and the humidity was killing him. He was determined to get it fixed even if he had to have the car towed to the mechanic. He made a right turn and headed toward what he thought was the main part of town. No luck. He made another turn, this time to the left. He drove slowly, checking the addresses. Someone had told him that addresses increased as you moved away from the center part of town. A line of cars brought him to a complete halt. *If that don't beat all, a traffic jam in Warrensburg.* The cars moved and he drove past the obstruction. They were all turning into the parking lot of the Warrensburg Medical Center. It was a large, modern, prosperous looking medical complex and, judging by the full parking lot, a very successful one.

Sutherland was not a proud man when it came to navigation and pulled over to ask directions. He picked his target when he saw a woman wearing an Air Force uniform pushing a small child in a wheelchair. It was Lt. Col. Daniella McGraw. "Colonel," he called, "gotta moment?" He explained his predicament and she quickly sorted him out. "I didn't know you had a son," he said.

"Mikey," she said, making the introductions, "I'd like you to meet Captain Sutherland." The little boy gave Sutherland a lopsided smile and extended his right hand. "Mikey has spina bifida," McGraw explained, "and can't walk."

"Glad to meet you, Mikey," Sutherland said, gently shaking the boy's hand.

"Are you a pilot?" Mikey said. "I'd like to be a pilot."

"Naw, I can't pass the physical so I'm a lawyer."

"What do lawyers do?"

"Mostly talk and read," Sutherland replied.

"Well, Mikey talks up a storm," McGraw said.

"And I read pretty good," Mikey added.

"You sure do," McGraw said. Her eyes started to tear up.

Sutherland knew little about spina bifida; something about a birth defect that leaves the spinal cord exposed and paralyzes the child from that point down. Now he was looking at the reality of it and the small human tragedy in front of him tore at his heart. "Do you need any help?"

"No," McGraw answered, "we're fine. In fact, we're used to making it on our own, aren't we, Mikey?"

"You bet," the boy chirped.

10:50 A.M., TUESDAY, JUNE 1,
WHITEMAN AIR FORCE BASE, MO.

The guard at Mitchell Gate would not allow the taxi returning Sutherland from Warrensburg to drive on base. The driver muttered something about insurance when Sutherland paid him off. "That's it," Sutherland muttered to himself as he made the half-mile trudge to the headquarters building. He was going to start running and get back in shape. Not only would his uniforms fit better, but it might help him cope with the heat and humidity. The decision made, he strode purposefully into the building and made a dash for the nearest drinking fountain.

Linda, the legal office's civilian secretary, handed him a stack of memos when he came through the door. "Colonel Blasedale needs to see you," she told him.

Sutherland nodded absentmindedly. "Linda, what do you know about spina bifida?"

"I've baby-sat for Colonel McGraw," Linda answered. "You should talk to her. Her son has it."

"I know. I met him today at the medical center in Warrensburg."

"I don't know how she does it," Linda said. "Her husband couldn't cope and left years ago. She's raised Mikey alone."

"Doesn't the Air Force pick up the medical expenses?"

"Thankfully, yes, but that's only part of it."

"How old is Mikey?"

"He's fourteen and only weighs seventy pounds. The doctors say children with spina bifida seldom live that long." Linda beamed at him. "She's done a wonderful job."

"She certainly has," Sutherland said, thinking of Beth and her self-centered existence. *How would I cope? Would I cut and run like her husband?* Sutherland was brutally honest with himself and admitted he didn't know.

He wandered down the hall into the military justice section and past Blasedale's office. "Hank," she called. "Have you heard?"

"Heard what?"

"The Sudanese announced they are putting the two B-Two pilots on trial."

"Lovely," Sutherland said. "Absolutely fuckin' lovely."

11:20 A.M., TUESDAY, JUNE 1,
KANSAS CITY, MO.

Toni jammed the Kansas City Chiefs' baseball hat over her hair before she turned onto the Jeffersons' street. It was a well-kept, upscale neighborhood on the southern side of Kansas City with houses in the two-hundred-thousand-dollar range. She drove slowly past the Jeffersons' home and turned onto a side street to park. Then she picked up a clipboard with survey forms about lawn and tree-care products and started to canvas the neighborhood.

She was careful to work the intersection far enough down the street to be unobserved, but able to watch any movement out of the Jeffersons' house. She put on her bounciest persona and soon had four forms completed, three by bored housewives who welcomed any break in their Tuesday morning routine that might result in free tree care, and one by a young writer who worked at home and had lecherous inclinations about young ladies in tight jeans. Her cover now firmly in place, she added the forms to the stack of fakes she had filled out and went back to the car to supposedly "tabulate" the results. She didn't have to wait long.

Sandi Jefferson flashed by in her bright yellow Miyata convertible, her auburn hair blowing in the wind. Toni dropped the clipboard and pulled out after her, careful to stay well back. "Okay, where are you going?" she murmured to herself. She followed Sandi through the turn onto 95th Street. "Oak Park Mall," she muttered. The traffic piled up and she lost sight of the Miyata a block short of the mall. "Damn!"

Going purely by instinct, she pulled into the parking lot and did a quick change of clothes, shedding her tight jeans for baggy safari walking shorts. She pulled a matching shirt over her tee-shirt, changed her shoes, and gave her hair a quick brush, fluffing it out. A touch of lipstick and she was ready. "Now where did you go?" She walked into the mall and smiled. A Nordstrom department store loomed large, beckoning anyone with healthy credit cards to enter. Toni took the escalator to the third floor and stepped off in time to see Sandi join the short line into the restaurant.

Toni wandered around until Sandi had disappeared inside. She waited for two more minutes and joined the line. "Please excuse me," she said, "I'm meeting some friends and I think they're already inside." She repeated it as she worked her way to the front of the line. A shy smile at the hostess and she was in. She strolled through the restaurant and headed for the ladies' room. Sandi was sitting at a table with another woman engaged in a very serious conversation.

The contrast between the two women was striking. Sandi was reformed stripper and the other cool elegance. *East coast establishment,* Toni thought, carefully noting the other woman. Her smooth complexion matched her perfect features and exquisite figure. Her dark blond hair was cut in the latest style and carefully arranged. Her clothes shouted Paris or London, and Toni estimated the flashing diamond engagement ring on her left hand at four carats. But her shoes were the real giveaway: handmade Italian. *We are moving up in the world.* Toni went into the rest room and lingered for a few minutes. When she came out, the table was vacant.

"Miss Moreno," a man's voice called. All of Toni's alarms were in overdrive as she turned. The writer with lecherous inclinations who lived down the street from the Jeffersons smiled at her. "Please join me," he said. Toni sat down. Without a word he handed her his identification: FBI special agent Brent Mather. "We have the Jefferson woman under twenty-four-hour surveillance"—then he added the clincher—"Agent Moreno."

Toni tried to be cool. "So you made me."

"Your license plate. It did take longer than usual. Actually, you're quite good."

"Why the come-on when I was doing the survey?"

"Solicitors, salesmen, you name it, panic a suspect. I wanted to scare you away. Normally, it works wonders. "

"Why didn't you tell us you had her under surveillance?"

"All the Air Force had to do was ask. We've got orders to cooperate fully."

"Really?" Toni said, her voice laced with disbelief. The FBI was the most territorial of government agencies and notorious for their high-handed, egoistical ways.

"To say we're getting high-level direction in this case would be an understatement."

"Did you make the woman she met here?"

Brent Mather shook his head. "Missed her. I was still concentrating on you. I really got suspicious when you did the quick change in your car." It was a typical cross-wired snafu between competing agencies. "Give me her description." Toni did as he made notes. "She's new. We'll check her out." Toni gave him her best smile. "Maybe, ah, I was thinking," Mather stammered, "maybe we could go to dinner." Mather was blushing. "Sometime?"

She gave a mental sigh. He was young, good-looking, and didn't wear a wedding ring. More important, he didn't act married. Why did interesting men always show up in bunches? She handed him a card with her telephone number. "I'd like that," she murmured, standing up. She headed for her car. She had to get back to Warrensburg to tell Harry about the FBI stakeout on Sandi.

She headed east on Highway 50 and remembered to slow when she approached Lone Jack, the small town famous for its aggressive enforcement of the speed limit. "Well, well," she murmured to herself. A patrol car had pulled over a bright yellow Miyata next to a service station. Toni slowed even more and pulled into the service station. She stopped at the pump nearest the patrol car and slowly filled her car's gas tank.

Two patrolmen were standing over the Miyata giving Sandi Jefferson a bad time. "I'm sorry, Mrs. Jefferson, but your car registration is in one state, your license in another, and you're living in Missouri. That's against the law."

The other patrolman leered down her low-cut dress. "Under the circumstances, we're going to have to escort you to a justice of the peace."

Toni fished her cellular phone out of the glove box and called Harry. No answer. She dialed Sutherland who answered on the second ring. "Hank, I'm at Lone Jack. Two cops have stopped Sandi Jefferson and are jacking her up." She split her attention as another car drove up and a familiar figure got out. "Oh, no. It's that cretin from the roadblock, Jim Bob. He just pulled up and is talking to the cops."

"What's going on?" Sutherland demanded.

"I'm not sure, but I've got to move before he makes me." She walked around the side of the combination office and mini-mart as if she were going to the rest rooms. *Where is the FBI when you need them?* Fortunately, she could still see and hear what was going on. "I'm okay now," she told Sutherland. "They've got her out of the car. They know who she is. They're talking about going to a justice of the peace."

"Don't lose contact," Sutherland told her. "I'll get Cooper on it."

Sandi was surrounded by the three men and she tossed her hair from side to side in defiance. "Touch me again," she shouted, her voice carrying over the service station, "and you're going to be living with a legal nightmare!"

"Please, Mrs. Jefferson," the older of the two patrolmen said, "we just need to sort this out before we can let you continue."

"Give me a citation and I'll show up with my lawyer."

"Throw the bitch in the car," Jim Bob growled, "and let's get the hell out of here." The three men closed around Sandi just as a pickup truck with a base sticker from Whiteman drove into the filling station. The sergeant driving the pickup hopped out with a camcorder and held it up, filming the incident. "Get that out of here!" Jim Bob roared, breaking away from the group and advancing on the sergeant, holding his hand out to block the lens.

Toni heard the sound of tearing cloth as Sandi broke away from the two cops. Her dress had been ripped down the front and her left breast exposed. She made no attempt to cover herself as she descended on Jim Bob like a tornado. She jumped on his back, clamped her legs around his waist, and grabbed his hair while the sergeant kept on filming. "You pervert!" she screamed. She jerked his head from side to side.

The two cops rushed after her and tried to pull her off Jim Bob. But her legs were clamped tightly around his middle as she held on to his hair. Toni spoke into her phone. "I think Jim Bob is having a bad hair day."

"What's going on?" Sutherland asked, his frustration mounting. The two cops finally managed to drag Sandi off Jim Bob as a crowd gathered around, eager to take in the free show. The younger cop rushed back to the patrol car to get his jacket while the other acted as peacemaker for the camera. The cop ran back and draped his jacket over Sandi's shoulders. Now both men were trying to calm the hysterical woman. Toni smiled. She knew a good actor when she saw one.

"Is she okay?" Sutherland demanded.

"She's fine," Toni told him. The cops escorted Sandi back to her car, now very concerned with her well-being. The sergeant continued to record the action as she pulled away and headed for the base, still wearing the patrolman's jacket. "The lady is perfectly capable of taking care of herself."

"What makes you say that?" Sutherland asked.

"It wasn't the cops who ripped her dress. She did."

Toni paid the bill for the gas and headed after Sandi. She had no trouble catching up and remained a quarter mile back until they reached Whiteman. Sandi drove directly to the Security Police building and went through the doors leading to the confinement facility. *Whatever the news is, it must be urgent,* Toni thought. She headed for the headquarters building to tell them about the FBI stakeout and that she and Harry would be free for other duties. She smiled at the possibilities.

6:55 A.M., FRIDAY, JUNE 4,
WHITEMAN AIR FORCE BASE, MO.

Sutherland was pleased with himself when he trotted out Spirit Gate on Friday morning. It was the third time he had jogged since making the decision on Tuesday. He turned right onto Highway 132 and headed for Knob Noster State Park at the intersection of 132 and DD, a few hundred yards down the highway. He took a long pull at the water bottle he carried when he turned into the park. A bird call he didn't recognize caught his attention. *Check that out,* he told himself. Surprisingly, he found he did some of his best thinking when he was running, and the time was very productive.

Normally, the park was deserted and he enjoyed the solitude. But this time, it was packed with cars, most with out-of-state license plates. He picked up the pace when he passed a group of middle-aged, pot-bellied men wearing camouflage fatigues and sporting huge, very nonmilitary mustaches. "Militia," he muttered to himself. *Do I look that bad in BDUs?*

The faster pace felt good and he held it as he turned onto a dirt path that led toward Warrensburg. *Let's see where this goes.* He was puffing hard and slowed down to a slow jog. A few minutes later, he pulled up with a charley horse in his left leg and collapsed to the ground. "Whoa!" he groaned. "That hurts."

He looked up at the sound of footsteps. It was another runner, running fast, coming from the direction of Warrensburg. He rubbed at his calf. "Ah, shit!"

Toni Moreno rounded the bend and stopped at the sight of Sutherland. "It was a good thing I heard you," she said. "Otherwise, major collision." She helped him to the edge of the path.

"Oooh, shitsky," he muttered, trying to act more manly, "it hurts like hell."

She helped him to a nearby bench and went to work massaging and rubbing the charley horse. "These can be killers," she said.

"Tell me," he said through gritted teeth. Finally, the pain eased but he didn't want her to stop. He felt the start of an erection.

"Okay," she said, "it's press-to-test time." She helped him to his feet and he took a few tentative steps only to collapse in pain again. This time it was worse.

Again she went to work on his left calf. But this time there was no accompanying erection. "Been running long?" she asked.

"Started Wednesday."

"You got to take it easy at first."

"How far did you come?" he asked.

"From Warrensburg. That's where I'm staying."

"That's ten miles!"

"Normally, I do five or six miles a day. But about once a week, I like to go fifteen or twenty miles." She smiled at him. "It keeps you in shape." She worked at the leg. "This is going to take a while." Strangely, he didn't mind.

The sound of amplified voices over a bullhorn echoed over them. "A bunch of militia pukes are in the park," he told her.

"Every motel in Warrensburg is packed," she said. "I wonder if it's related." Honking cars and the bellow of a truck's air horn cut her off.

"Something's happening," Sutherland said. She helped him to his feet and he hobbled along, his arm over her shoulders, her arm around his waist. The parking lot at the head of the path was jammed with cars but only a few people were milling around. In the distance they could hear people chanting, urged on by a bullhorn. "It's coming from the base," Sutherland said. "What the hell are they saying?"

"I think they're saying 'Turn him over,' " Toni said.

They stopped and Sutherland stood alone, taking a few tentative steps on his own. "I'm okay." They walked slowly out to the highway. It was packed with people in both directions. But very few of them were wearing any type of uniform. "Where did they come from?" Now the chant was very loud and coming at them in waves. They pushed through the crowd, heading for the main gate.

A militia type holding a bullhorn blocked their way. "Where d'you think you're going?" he growled.

"I work on base," Sutherland said, not wanting to involve Toni.

Another man wearing fatigues joined them and stared at Toni. "How about the Chiquita?" It was Jim Bob from the roadblock in Kansas City.

Toni turned and buried her face in Sutherland's chest, the scared bunny rabbit looking for protection. "That's the guy Harry decked at the roadblock," she whispered. "I don't think he's made me yet."

Sutherland held her tight, the male protecting his woman. "He will once he realizes you've cut your hair," Sutherland muttered. *And gets past your legs.*

"Hey, she's my wife and we were just out running," he told the two men.

"Well, nobody's going on base until the nigger comes out," the militia type snarled.

"What do you mean?" Sutherland asked, shocked at the blatant racism.

"We mean," Jim Bob said, much calmer, "that the Air Force is gonna turn that traitor over to us civilians. We want him in a jail where we can make sure he gets a fair trial."

Where you can lynch him, Sutherland thought. "We don't want any trouble," he said, leading Toni away. "Act scared," he whispered. Toni collapsed against him and he put a protective arm around her shoulder.

"Hey," Jim Bob shouted, "don't I know you?"

"Keep walking," Toni murmured.

A loud roar broke over them like a tidal wave. "TURN HIM OVER!" The crowd surged forward and swept past them. Suddenly, they were spit free of the tide of humanity.

"Run," Sutherland said.

Toni grabbed his shirt. "No. Just keep walking slowly." They reached the highway intersection with route DD and turned toward Warrensburg. "Now!" Toni said. They sprinted into the park and headed for the trail leading to Warrensburg.

Sutherland was surprised he could move so fast.

Tech. Sgt. Leroy, The Rock, Rockne, pulled up to Spirit Gate and got out of the patrol car. He walked slowly up to the guard shack and stood by the six security cops standing across the road. They were all that was holding the crowd back. He spoke quietly to the one woman. "How you doing?"

"I'm scared," she replied.

"So am I," The Rock answered. He motioned to his cops. "Gather round." They collapsed onto him. "Well, folks, this is what we get paid for. In a few moments, I'm gonna read the proclamation. Now I want you to go easy on these people and don't panic. We just need to explain things to them, that should do the trick. If they won't listen to reason, then fall back to the barricade at Carswell Circle."

A group of men, all wearing fatigues, started to move forward now that the road was clear. "Sir!" The Rock called, "please don't enter the base until the guard has cleared you to proceed." The Rock was not easily ignored and they stopped. Jim Bob emerged out of the crowd holding a bullhorn and crossed the white stop line that was painted across the street.

The Rock took three steps toward him. "Sir, I'm going to have to ask you to stop."

Jim Bob lifted the bullhorn to his lips. Before he could speak, The

Rock reached up and took the horn away from him. He did it so easily it looked like Jim Bob handed it to him. "Thank you, sir," he said in a loud voice. The Rock keyed the bullhorn and his voice carried over the crowd. "Your attention please. By order of the installation commander you are hereby notified that this is federal property. You are hereby given lawful warning that if you enter without authorization, you will be subject to the penalties as listed in Title Ten of the United States Code." He dropped the bullhorn.

"Who the fuck are you?" Jim Bob snarled.

"Do you have a parade permit?" The Rock asked, ignoring the question. Jim Bob fished a folded paper out of his pocket and thrust it into The Rock's hands. "I see," The Rock said. "And you are the gentleman listed here as the organizer?"

"Congratulations," Jim Bob said, "you can read."

The Rock looked friendly. "Does your answer mean you are the organizer?"

"You got it, fuckface."

"Then you were briefed."

"Briefed on what?" Jim Bob answered.

"Let's walk," The Rock said, "while I explain it." He turned and walked slowly on base. Confused, Jim Bob followed him.

"Where we going?"

"Nowhere," The Rock answered. "We just need a little quiet so we can discuss things—before they get out of hand." They stepped behind the nearby visitors center and were out of sight of the crowd. The Rock's right hand flashed out and grabbed Jim Bob lightly by the throat. He tried to pull away and The Rock squeezed, hard, holding him in a viselike grip. "Sir, there's something you got to understand. I hope you are listening." He let up and Jim Bob tried to pull away. Again, The Rock clamped him. Slowly, he released the pressure and Jim Bob gasped for air. But he didn't move. He was ready to listen.

"Those are my people out there. They're good kids just doing their job and ain't got no ax to grind like you folks. I don't want them hurt. So if your people hurt them, I hurt you. And I mean you. It's that simple. Now, this is the part you gotta understand, it will be me doing it. No one else. It will just be between you and me." He released Jim Bob. "And it'll be up close and personal. Very personal."

"You can't get away with this, asshole!"

The Rock shook his head slowly. "We definitely have a failure to communicate here. Let me put it in terms you'll understand." His face turned to granite. "If you hurt my people in any way, I want you to be sure of one thing the next time we meet."

"What's that?"

"I'll be outta jail before you get outta the hospital." He smiled. "Now you go back to your people and do whatever you think needs doing."

The two men stared at each other. Jim Bob broke eye contact and hurried back through the gate. The demonstration was over.

Catherine Blasedale took the phone call from the wing commander's office late that same afternoon and relayed the message to Sutherland. The two of them and Toni were wanted in the wing conference room where the wing posse meeting was being held.

"What's a 'posse meeting'?" he asked.

"It's when the staff judge advocate, chief of Security Police, and the OSI get together with the wing commander to discuss base security. Since they're asking for you, me, and Toni, I'm guessing the Wing King is very worried about the demonstration at the main gate."

"He should be," Sutherland muttered. "That was a lynch mob."

"I'll get Toni," Blasedale said.

"I'll meet you there," Sutherland said, heading out the door.

He was sitting in the rear of the conference room listening to the wing's reaction to the demonstration when Toni and Blasedale walked in and sat beside him. The chief of Security Police was standing in front of a screen as he ran a series of slides showing the disposition of the security police. "We only try to delay them at the gates," the lieutenant colonel said.

"Shouldn't that be our first line of defense?" the wing commander asked.

That is one upset brigadier general, Sutherland thought.

"In most cases, yes," the cop answered. "But when faced with a threat like this, we don't have the resources." Click, the slides cycled forward. "Instead, we sequentially fall back to more easily defensible positions and trade space for time while we call for help." The slide showed a series of barricades that finally ended in a defensive perimeter around the flight line. "Here we have a class A security fence, bunkers, and signs announcing the use of deadly force. Further, this far inside the base there is no question of intent." Click. This time the slide summarized the conditions when deadly force could be exercised. "Once an intruder penetrates the fence, we are authorized to use deadly force, should the conditions so warrant."

"Who gives that order?" the general asked.

"No order is necessary," the cop answered. "But we do it by the book and my people will only fire if the intruder does not respond to commands *and* continues toward the hangars sheltering the B-Twos."

"You have a lot of faith in your people," the staff judge advocate said.

The security cop smiled. "Well, they did stop the demonstration at the gate without incident."

"How did they manage that?" the general asked.

"I sent Tech. Sgt. Rockne to read the proclamation," the cop said. "The man has credibility. I'm putting him in for a commendation medal."

"If I read the OSI's report right," the brigadier said, "we owe him more than that."

"Sir," the OSI detachment commander said, "Agent Moreno was in the crowd and can answer any questions you might have."

Sutherland listened as Toni answered a barrage of questions. Finally, the general was satisfied. "I want a detailed report forwarded to higher headquarters ASAP. We are not out of this by a long shot and somebody upstairs had better get their heads out of their collective closets." He stood, indicating the meeting was over. Before Sutherland could follow Toni and Blasedale out, the general motioned for him to stay behind.

"Captain, the connection between Jefferson's court-martial, the trial of Terrant and Holloway in the Sudan, and the demonstration at the main gate is obvious. I can only see the heat getting more intense." He held up a hand before Sutherland could speak. "It's my job to stop it. But for God's sake, don't make any mistakes. If you need help, get it. If you want a continuance, ask." Now the meeting was truly over.

Outside, Blasedale and Toni walked slowly down the hall. "It was lucky you were out running and stumbled over Hank," Blasedale said.

"It wasn't luck," Toni murmured.

15

8:42 A.M., SATURDAY, JUNE 5,
CAMP DAVID, MD.

Kyle Broderick was waiting for Durant when he arrived outside the main lodge. "Thank you for coming on such short notice," Broderick said. Normally, people thanked Broderick for being invited to Camp David, but hard experience had taught him Durant was not a normal person. He escorted Durant into the lodge where the President was meeting with his key advisers.

"Nelson," the President boomed, full of resolve. "How's the rescue coming?"

"We're making progress, but there are some problems we need to work out."

"When can the rescue occur?" Stephan Serick, the National Security Advisor, asked.

Durant thought for a moment. "Three, maybe four, weeks."

"Will that be soon enough?" the President asked. "I'm very concerned about this so-called trial the Sudanese have announced."

"Without doubt," Serick said, "it is in reaction to the court-martial of the spy at Whiteman. We must remember he is a professed Muslim, Nation of Islam, I believe. Perhaps, we can defuse the issue by turning the captain, what's-his-name, over to the Federal courts and delaying the trial."

"His name," Durant said, "is Bradley Jefferson, and he is not Nation of Islam. He is a true Muslim, which is quite a different matter."

"I hear he's a real cold fish," the Vice President said, calming the atmosphere before the cranky Serick erupted. "A regular Alfred Dreyfus," he added, making a reference to the court-martial of the

French officer a century earlier. Captain Alfred Dreyfus was an aloof Jewish officer serving on the French general staff in 1894 when the generals discovered someone was selling secrets to the Germans. As the only Jew on the general staff, he had been framed by the same generals as a traitor and, as a consequence, anti-Semitism had become a national passion. The case had split France apart and ultimately caused the downfall of the government.

"There are no similarities," Serick humphed. "This man is not Jewish and he is guilty. The problems of France a hundred years ago are not our problems."

"I beg to disagree with you, Stephan," Durant said. "The country is a powder keg, and we're seeing racism, confusion, and turbulence spreading like a plague."

"An expected phenomena," Serick said, "with its roots in the end of the century. This situation has nothing to do with this man Jefferson."

"As I read history," the President said, "a certain craziness always happens at the end of a century."

"And it is compounded," Serick added, "by the end of the millennium. A millennium factor, if you will."

"I want to stay focused on the immediate problem," the President said, "which is the release, or rescue, of our two pilots."

"I'm afraid the issues are linked, Mr. President," Durant said.

"Nonsense!" Serick thundered. "There is no linkage."

"Meredith's the link," Durant said. "He's already turned this into a rerun of the Dreyfus affair."

"To what end?" Serick questioned.

"The downfall of the government," Durant said. "And racism is his weapon."

Serick displayed his famous contempt for lesser, mentally challenged mortals. "You're obsessing, Nelson. We must concentrate on the problem at hand." The President nodded in agreement.

"The demonstration at Whiteman yesterday was not an isolated incident," Durant said. "It's all part of Meredith's plan."

Serick snorted. "Ah, that report from Whiteman Air Force Base."

"It's the tip of the iceberg," Durant replied. Serick shook his head, apparently not believing him.

11:10 A.M., SATURDAY, JUNE 5,
WHITEMAN AIR FORCE BASE, MO.

Catherine Blasedale watched Toni Moreno wander down the hall past Sutherland's office. *Was I ever that young?* Blasedale wondered.

"Toni," she called, "you don't have to work on Saturdays." Toni stood in the doorway of Blasedale's office and smiled. It was a beautiful smile that came from someplace deep within and lit her face and dark brown eyes. For a moment, the older woman was deeply envious. *You are a pretty little thing.* Blasedale suppressed a sigh. She was getting old.

"Since the FBI has Sandi under twenty-four-hour surveillance," Toni said, "I can work full-time on the Khalid files. I've only gotten through the first five boxes."

"I haven't seen Harry," Blasedale said. "What's he up to?"

"He's gone undercover at Bare Essence to work the money trail. I can always contact him."

Blasedale flipped a wall calendar to July and circled Monday, the 12th in red. The court-martial was bearing down on them like a runaway train. "We've got thirty-seven days. The sooner you can get through this stuff the better. If you find anything significant, be sure you forward it to Cooper."

Toni frowned. "I gave him the transcript of the Saturday phone call between Jefferson and Khalid. You should have seen him. He went through the ceiling and treated me like some kinda bug that crawled out from under a rock."

"It's a critical link in the chain of evidence against his client, Toni. He'll do anything to get it thrown out."

The OSI agent nodded, recalling all she had learned about evidence while in training. "Is he going to blame me for a break in the chain of evidence?"

"That's not even a question. Count on it. Don't worry, we'll help you handle it." She hesitated for a moment. *Should I warn her about Hank?* "Toni, be careful around these guys. Basically, they're all alike." The warning missed its intended mark and Toni strolled back to the law library to start working on the files, again passing Sutherland's office. *She's got it bad,* Blasedale decided.

An hour later, R. Garrison Cooper stormed into the legal office. "I want to see Sutherland!" he barked.

"Don't get your knickers in a twist, Coop," Sutherland called from his office. "Come on back." Cooper rolled down the hall like the grim reaper anxious to collect his daily quota. Both Toni and Blasedale came out of their cubbyholes to watch his performance.

"You!" Cooper shouted, pointing at Toni. Then he disappeared into Sutherland's office. Blasedale motioned for Toni to follow her. They arrived in time to see Cooper fling a sheaf of papers on Sutherland's desk.

"A motion to suppress the tape?" Sutherland asked without picking up the document.

"What did you expect?" Cooper growled. "If you think I'm going to stipulate to this piece of shit—"

Sutherland interrupted him. "Putting the motion machine into action, Coop?" A standard technique used by defense lawyers was to flood the court with motions. The goal was to slow down the trial and drive people crazy.

"Mr. Cooper," Blasedale said, "the nice thing about the UCMJ and the Manual for Courts-Martial is that we can go through a stack of motions faster than your word processor can grind them out. So go for it."

"Read the motion!" Cooper shouted, his theatrics in full play. He took a deep breath. "You," he pointed at Toni, "gave me a *copy* of the tape in question."

"That's all the FBI provided us," Toni replied, "along with a certified true copy of the transcript—which you have."

"The tape was obviously edited," Cooper said, a little more rational. "I am going to prove that there is a conspiracy to frame my client and we will stipulate to nothing." He glared at Toni. "Nothing."

"Ah," Sutherland replied, "the dreaded chain of evidence."

"Unless you can produce the original, unedited tape for my review, this court-martial is dead in the water."

"Then your client is going to spend a long time in the confinement facility," Sutherland told him.

"Which is another thing!" Cooper bellowed. He produced a second document from his briefcase and flung it at Sutherland. "Rockne is the most vicious bastard to walk the face of the earth since Heinrich Himmler."

"Anything else?" Sutherland asked. Cooper's head jerked from side to side in answer.

"Normally," Blasedale said, "the military judge hearing the court-martial will request all motions be submitted before the trial. Knowing Colonel Williams, he'll want them in writing about a week before. Until then, we can only wait."

"And the FBI is forwarding the original tape," Toni added. "It should be here Monday."

Cooper snorted, slammed his briefcase shut, and rolled out of the office, leaving a blissful silence in his wake.

"Is Rockne being too harsh?" Toni finally asked.

Sutherland shook his head. "Not at all. The Rock is running an excellent facility. Cooper's causing trouble, that's all. It's his way of softening up the opposition."

"And sizing you up as a target," Blasedale told her. "When did you ask the FBI to forward the original tape?"

"About an hour ago," Toni answered. "Right after we talked about it."

"I'm impressed," Sutherland said. "Anticipating is half the job." He thought for a few moments. "Toni, did you make a copy of the tape and transcript?" She nodded. "Good. I want to see them again." Toni rushed out of his office and was back in moments with a tape deck and the transcript. The three of them huddled together and ran the tape. Twice, he replayed the last few moments of the tape as they followed the transcript.

JEFFERSON: There's nothing I can add to what I said yesterday.
KHALID: Then nothing has changed?
JEFFERSON: Everything around here is locked in concrete.
KHALID: That is sad, very sad. Insh' Allah.
JEFFERSON: Insh' Allah.

"By itself," Sutherland said, "a harmless conversation—until you put it together with everything else."

"It's too bad we don't know what they talked about the day before," Toni said.

"We don't need to," Blasedale told her. "By his own admission, Jefferson admits talking to Khalid on both days. All we've done is establish a chain of events that followed both conversations. We've got enough to nail him."

"It doesn't make sense," Sutherland said. "Cooper should have been screaming for a continuance. He's not. Why?"

"Maybe they want a rush to judgment so they can win it on appeal," Toni said.

The two lawyers looked at her. "Very good," Sutherland said. "But there's got to be something else. Cooper is not going to roll over and play dead on this. He gets paid the big bucks for a damn good reason."

"So who's paying him?" Toni asked.

"A good question," Blasedale replied.

"It's worth checking out," Sutherland said.

"I'll get on it," Toni told them.

"Be careful," Sutherland warned. "Even a hint that we're looking at him for crooked money, and he'll go straight up like a rocket."

"Maybe he'll explode like a fireworks," Toni said. Harry Waldon had taught her well.

5:45 P.M., SATURDAY, JUNE 5,
WARRENSBURG, MO.

It was late afternoon when Harry Waldon turned into the big parking lot off the main highway just outside of town. The neon sign proclaiming Bare Essence was already on, flashing its invitation of sexual fantasy to any passerby. It was Harry's first day as security and judging by the number of cars, the club was doing a good business. He got out and nodded to the one security guard on duty. He carefully adjusted the cummerbund and bow tie to his tuxedo, glad that he wouldn't have to wear the coat until after dark.

It had been amazingly easy to get the job. He had simply wandered into the club, ogled a few of the dancers as they wiggled around nude on the stage, and asked to speak to the manager. Four minutes later, he was hired. He hoped he never had to explain it to his wife. "First Saturday night?" the security guard asked.

"My first night on the job," Harry answered.

"You ever done this before?"

"Oh, yeah," Harry answered, lying through his teeth. "I like to think of it as being a social director."

"The locals are okay," the guard told him. "They don't cause trouble. But we're seeing some real weirdoes lately."

"They're showing up all over," Harry said.

"If some asshole causes trouble inside, get him out back if you can. We can solve any problem real quick—if there's no witnesses around."

Harry gave him his best grin. "I solve my own problems. I like to think of it as a professional challenge."

"Yeah!"

Harry ambled into the club and headed for the office to check in and receive any last minute instructions. He knocked twice and heard a "Come on in." He pushed open the door and entered. "Harry," the manager said, "I like you to meet the principle owner." Harry turned around. August Ramar, the thug Toni had made in Reno was sitting on a couch. A blond dancer was cuddled next to him, his hand on her bare thigh.

"Glad to meet you, sir," Harry said, extending his right hand. Ramar stared at him with the coldest dead-fish look he had ever seen.

6:12 P.M., SATURDAY, JUNE 5,
WHITEMAN AIR FORCE BASE, MO.

Toni Moreno stood by the fax machine as it spat out page after page of the message from FinCEN, the Treasury's Financial Crimes

Enforcement Network. The amount of detailed financial information on the Jeffersons astounded her, and she wished Harry was there to help her read through the mass of material. She stuck out her lower lip and exhaled loudly.

"Someone's working overtime here," Sutherland said from behind her.

She turned and smiled. "I requested this five days ago." Sutherland managed to do the math in his head. Five days ago meant she requested the file on the first day she had arrived at Whiteman. "I wonder how long before they come through on Cooper?"

"You requested a readout on Cooper today?" Sutherland asked.

"Right after we talked about it." She spread the pages out on the table and tried to make sense out of the report. Sutherland stood beside her, feeling like a conspirator because they were working so late. Toni started to list the outstanding balances on the numerous credit cards Sandi Jefferson used. "She's got credit cards with every upscale store in Kansas City."

"Been doing research in the field?" Sutherland asked.

Toni shook her head. "Look at the names. But the balances are hardly worth mentioning."

"So she doesn't use them," Sutherland replied.

"Or she pays them off every month."

Sutherland grinned. "That would make me a very happy husband."

"Is that what makes husbands happy?"

Sutherland blushed. The conversation was not going in the direction he wanted. "It helps."

Toni scanned another page. "Look at what she charged at one store in one month!"

Sutherland checked his sheet. "And she paid it off in thirty days." They repeated the process with four other credit cards with the same results. "The lady is living well beyond her husband's salary," Sutherland said.

"So where's the money coming from?" Toni asked.

"Check with the IRS," Sutherland told her. "They might have a clue."

"I doubt if anyone is working overtime there."

"Leave it for Monday." He checked his watch. "Look, it's after eight and we gotta eat sooner or later. There must be some place worth going on a Saturday night." He paused. "Even in Warrensburg," he added lamely.

Toni thought about the rules. "Can I take a raincheck? I'm absolutely beat and I've got to call my family in California."

Sutherland gave her his best lopsided grin. "Well, see you Monday."

7:06 P.M., SUNDAY, JUNE 6,
OVER THE PERSIAN GULF

The unmarked C-130 lifted off from the airport at Bandar Abbas, Iran's main port city, and climbed over the Persian Gulf. "Murray," the American captain of the Hercules said, "I think our passenger speaks English. Ask him if he wants to come up on the flight deck." The scrawny Englishman grunted and unstrapped from the flight engineer's seat that was set back and between the pilots.

"I'm not sure General Assam would approve," the copilot said.

"His 'oliness' ain't here to disapprove, now is he?" Murray muttered. He considered the copilot a complete waste of time and wished Assam would hire a competent copilot to help fly the C-130. Luckily, the American pilot was capable of getting along with minimal help. Murray climbed down the ladder onto the cargo deck and worked his way past the cargo they were hauling from Tehran to the Sudan. The cargo hauls had become a frequent part of their routine but the unscheduled landing at Bandar Abbas to pick up a passenger was a first.

"Excuse me, mate," Murray said to the man, "the captain asked if you wanted to come up on the flight deck."

Victor Kamigami nodded and followed the Englishman. He climbed easily over the cargo and Murray was surprised at the man's catlike speed and grace. "Glad we're friends, mate," he muttered. Kamigami glanced at the Chinese markings on the crates. He spoke Cantonese, but could not decipher the labels. He climbed the ladder and stood on the flight deck behind the flight engineer's chair.

The American pilot turned around. "It's more comfortable up here." He motioned to the bench at the rear of the flight deck that doubled as a bunk.

"Thank you," Kamigami said. "May I stretch out?"

"Sure," the pilot replied. "American?" Kamigami nodded and collapsed on the bunk. Within moments, he was sound asleep.

"Who is he?" the copilot asked.

"Beats the shit out of me," the American said. "But he must be important for us to divert into Bandar Abbas. I'm surprised the Iranians let us land there."

"General Assam is a very important man," the copilot parroted.

"Bloody important," Murray muttered. The copilot missed the

cynicism in his voice. Kamigami slept soundly until they started the descent into El Obeid where an *aqid,* a Sudanese colonel, was waiting for their arrival. "Ain't he the bloke we brought in with Assam about three weeks ago and got left behind?" Murray asked.

"He was in charge of the American prisoners," the copilot said.

"With all that fuckin' baggage," Murray muttered, "it looks like he's going on an extended vacation. No way in bloody hell am I gonna hump that lot aboard." He directed the two soldiers accompanying the colonel to load the baggage while he kept an eye on Kamigami. The colonel studiously ignored Kamigami and marched purposefully onboard the waiting Hercules.

A Range Rover drove up and Capt. Davig al Gimlas got out.

"General Kamigami, welcome to El Obeid. I'll escort you to your quarters."

Murray watched as Kamigami and al Gimlas shook hands. They were of equal height, but he guessed Kamigami outweighed al Gimlas by eighty pounds. "Wouldn't want to get between those two," he muttered to the copilot. The copilot snorted, totally misunderstanding the Englishman. "Come on, then," Murray said. "Let's get this lot to the flippin' laboratory."

Al Gimlas held the Range Rover's rear door for Kamigami and then climbed into the front seat. "According to my instructions," al Gimlas said, "you are now in charge of the prisoners' security. Needless to say, the *aqid* is most upset." Kamigami only nodded and they rode in silence. When they reached the barracks he asked to see the wreckage of the B-2. Al Gimlas spoke a command in Arabic and the driver headed for a large warehouse on the edge of town. "We have a great deal of wreckage," al Gimlas explained, "but it is burnt and unrecognizable."

Kamigami walked through the warehouse, nudging an occasional lump of melted or twisted debris with his foot. "Those are engines," he said. Then, "That is part of the rotary launcher." He pointed to another pile of debris. "That is part of the cockpit." He picked up a lump of material that looked like a blackened cement I-beam. But it was much lighter in weight. "This is what the fuselage is made of. Have your men start arranging the debris in the shape of a B-Two."

"I doubt if they can do that," al Gimlas replied.

"I'll help them."

"Is this important?"

"It is if you want to convince the public."

"Our people believe what we tell them," al Gimlas said.

"It's not your people you've got to convince," Kamigami explained. "The only thing that's going to save us from being hit, and hit hard, by Delta Force, a battalion of Rangers, and God knows what else, is public opinion. Tell me about the prisoners."

"I have them isolated in separate cells," al Gimlas said. "They are recovering from wounds."

"Were they tortured during interrogation?"

"Only when Assam was here," al Gimlas answered. He stared straight ahead, not looking at Kamigami. "But the situation has changed, and I am under pressure to, ah, extract their confessions. If I cannot do it, Assam will send an interrogator with drugs." His face hardened. "I have seen drug interrogation. It burns their brains."

"I can help you," Kamigami said, his words barely audible. "Without drugs. Rig a cell for electronic surveillance. Have two sets of monitors, one well hidden and one more obvious. When the time is right, we'll put them together in the cell. Sooner or later they will start to talk. Americans love to talk."

"But will they talk about the right things?"

Kamigami allowed a slight smile.

8:30 A.M., MONDAY, JUNE 7,
WHITEMAN AIR FORCE BASE, MO.

Hank Sutherland walked into the legal offices an hour late. He had only meant to run two miles, but had gone four. That had put him behind schedule and he had delayed even longer, taking a leisurely shower. The exercise was doing wonders and he hadn't felt so good in years. He smiled at Linda, the secretary, and headed for the military justice corridor and his office. Someone had tacked up a countdown calendar with a big 35 on the door leading into the corridor. *Thirty-five days to go,* he told himself. *We'll be ready.*

Blasedale joined him a few minutes later with her organizer and two thick case files. "Who put up the countdown calender?" he asked.

"Toni," Blasedale replied. "She's really a hustler and was here when I got to work. How was the run?"

"Doin' better all the time." She sat down and they went over the day's schedule. He paused, thinking. The case was coming together and he felt good. "I think we're going to be okay on this," he allowed.

Blasedale gave a little snort. "Don't count on it. Some bastard will screw it up. I've got to get back to work."

Before she could leave, Toni knocked on the open door. "Sergeant Rockne is here to see you," she said. The Rock was standing behind her, his dark blue beret clutched in his left hand. As usual, his uniform was immaculate and his boots buffed to a high gloss.

"What can I do for you, Sergeant?"

The Rock stepped inside and shifted his weight nervously from foot to foot. He glanced at the door, a plea for privacy. Blasedale closed the door. "Sir, it's about"—he twisted his beret in both hands—"Capt. Jefferson. He's, ah, he's—" He stopped, unable to go on.

"He's what? Sergeant." Sutherland braced himself for bad news.

The Rock regrouped, his embarrassment acute. "I've been taught, and I believe, to always go with the evidence. But—" Again, he hesitated. "I've run a confinement facility for nine years and I've seen a lot of prisoners." He paused, searching for the right words.

"Go on," Sutherland urged.

The Rock drew himself up, ramrod stiff. "Capt. Jefferson is innocent, sir."

For five seconds, silence ruled Sutherland's office. Toni shook her head, wondering if she had heard right. Sutherland stared at the big sergeant, his mouth slightly open. Finally, Blasedale and Sutherland answered together, their voices a high-pitched chorus. "He's what?"

"Capt. Jefferson is innocent."

Sutherland managed to choke "Evidence."

The Rock shook his head. "I don't have any. But I'm telling you, he didn't do it."

"An extraordinary statement, Sergeant," Sutherland replied, sarcasm searing every word. "Perhaps, you've seen the burning bush? The handwriting on the wall? Or perhaps you experienced a visitation?"

The Rock shook his head. "I read the Bible, Captain. That's not necessary." The tone of his voice carried an admonishment. "Capt. Jefferson has a deep faith in his God, his country, and the Air Force. Guilty men don't. If that's all, sir, I need to get back."

"Thank you for coming in," Sutherland said, dismissing him. The Rock nodded brusquely, spun around in a well-executed about-face, and marched out of the office.

Again, a heavy silence came down. "If that don't beat all," Blasedale said in a low voice.

"Do you think there's anything to it?" Toni asked.

"Always go with the evidence," Sutherland answered. But the vague itchy feeling had returned, gnawing at the back of his mind.

8:40 A.M., WEDNESDAY, JUNE 9,
THE FARM, WESTERN VIRGINIA

Agnes had shut herself off and the whiz kids were worried. "We just don't know why," their leader said. "That's the trouble with what we're doing. The results will be unpredictable." She was repeating a mantra of their profession and they all nodded in agreement. "I suppose we can revert to keyboarding, but that would defeat the purpose of what we're doing."

"Since you programmed her to respond to me," Durant said, "let me talk to her. Maybe I can find out what's wrong." Lacking any other ideas, the whiz kids agreed. "Maybe, I better do it alone." They followed him to the control room and stood outside in the hall when he went in. "Good morning, Agnes. How are you?" There was no answer. "Okay, what's the problem?"

The right monitor screen came to life but no image appeared. "Nothing," the computer said.

"Come on," he urged, "something's bothering you." He found it hard to remember he was dealing with a computer. Agnes's image appeared on the screen. "There. That's better. Why did you shut yourself off?"

"No reason."

"There's always a reason," he cajoled. "Or maybe two reasons."

Agnes looked at him. "That's right. There are two reasons."

"Can we talk about them?"

"Well," Agnes said, "remember when you asked me to find out who leaked the information about the B-Two to Meredith?"

"Yes, I do."

"Well, I couldn't."

Durant nodded. Agnes had not been taught how to deal with failure and she had simply turned herself off. "Actually, you discovered something very important," Durant said. "You found that there was no trace of the leak. So that tells us the leak was between two people who met face to face, in private, and no one knew about it."

"Oh." The image brightened. "I can do something about that. You remember how I found Mr. Rios and the San Francisco bombers? I can build another matrix and do it again."

"It's probably not worth wasting your time on," he replied. "At best, you'd only have a probability, and how good will that be?"

"At least it's something."

"What's the second problem?" Durant asked.

"I overheard two of the whiz kids talking. They talked about 'pulling the plug.' At first, I didn't know what that meant. Then I discovered there is a switch where they can turn off my power. Does that mean they can kill me if they want to? Since I'm not a person, it's not a crime. I don't want to die."

I'm talking to a teenager, Durant thought. "Because you're a computer, Agnes, you can't die. What happens to a computer's memory and programs when it is shut off then turned back on?" He could almost hear the wheels turning as Agnes ran through her information on chip dynamics.

"Oh. It's like being in suspended animation."

"Exactly," Durant replied. "I've got work to do and need to go. Will you keep monitoring the situation in the Sudan and talk to the kids?"

"Of course," Agnes answered.

Durant walked into the hall and explained it all to the whiz kids. "Fortunately, she didn't ask why the switch was there in the first place," one of them said.

"She didn't ask because she knows," Durant replied.

9:30 A.M., FRIDAY, JUNE 18,
WHITEMAN AIR FORCE BASE, MO.

In the abstract, Catherine Blasedale always gave lip service to the venomous effects of envy. However, she steadfastly refused to recognize any such symptoms in herself. Consequently, when Toni entered her office that morning, she dismissed the younger woman as being a bit overdressed and her miniskirt a little too short to be in truly good taste. "Twenty-four days to go," Toni said, "and I'm drawing a blank from the IRS on the Jeffersons. She owned a business but sold it when they married. According to the IRS, it was mortgaged to the hilt, some bank in Canada. Apparently, she lost money and got a tax refund."

"Was it enough to account for their lifestyle?"

"It was less than a thousand dollars."

"So where is the money coming from?" Blasedale asked.

"A good question. So far, we don't know."

"What about Cooper?"

Toni shook her head. "You're not going to believe this. But it looks like he's representing Jefferson *pro bono.*"

"I want to see Hank's face when you tell him that," Blasedale said. The two women walked down to his office and stood in the doorway. Sutherland was on the telephone and waved them inside. His eyes did a subtle double-take on Toni. *Men!* Blasedale fumed to herself.

Sutherland tapped his pencil as Toni told him about the blank she drew from the IRS on the Jeffersons. He broke the pencil when she said Cooper was representing Jefferson for free. "Bullshit! Cooper doesn't do *pro bono.*"

Toni stood her ground. "Maybe he's got a guilty conscience. Or do they surgically remove that at law school?"

Blasedale gave a silent cheer. *Go get him, girl.* "Actually, it's exorcised once you pass the bar exam. It's a very impressive ceremony."

"Well," Sutherland humphed, trying to recover, "knowing Coop, it's for the publicity." He turned to safer ground. "Has Harry turned up anything?"

"I'm meeting him today before he goes to work."

"Well, let us know if he's got anything. Personally, I think he's enjoying his work too much."

The two women glanced at each other. "Getting cranky?" Toni asked. Sutherland ignored her. "Cathy, I want to reinterview Sgt. Miner and Col. McGraw today. Can you be there?"

"I'm working on the graphics and going over the geography and movement of Khalid in relation to Jefferson." Blasedale paused for a moment. "Maybe Toni can help. It wouldn't hurt to get another perspective on their testimony."

Toni gave her a knowing look. "I should be back about two o'clock."

"Good," Sutherland said, "see you then."

Toni walked as slowly as she could out of the office. She hurried over to the gym, changed into her running togs, and headed for the state park just outside Spirit Gate. As she expected, Harry was walking along a deserted trail. She slowed and walked with him. "How's it going?" she asked.

"That son-of-a-bitch Ramar," Harry grumbled.

"I thought he left last week," Toni said.

"He did. But he's back." Harry stared at his feet. "He hassles the girls something fierce."

"Feeling protective?" Toni asked.

Harry thought for a moment, examining his own feelings. "Yeah, I guess I am. After a while, you get to know them."

"And?" Toni asked, pursuing the subject.

"Most of them are young and pretty single mothers whose husbands or boyfriends took off. It's a job of last resort."

Toni shook her head. "It's an easy job that pays big bucks. How many of them support a drug habit or a worthless boyfriend?"

"More than a few," Harry conceded. "I talk to them quite a bit, trying to get a handle on Ramar. They sort'a treat me like a father."

"Any leads?"

"Ramar talks to one of the bartenders, a guy named Mo Habib, more than he does the manager. There's something going on there, but I don't know what. I think some of the girls know, but they won't talk about it."

They walked in silence. Finally, Toni said one word. "Andrea."

Harry looked at her. "You think we should try to get her inside?"

"Why not?" Toni asked. "As far as I know, she's still dancing at Reno."

Harry considered the possibilities. "I'll get on it."

"Don't take too long. Meanwhile, I'll check out this Habib guy."

"It's Mohammed Habib," Harry told her.

"A Moslem bartender?"

"They don't drink the profits," Harry replied. "Besides it's a juice bar. No alcohol." He looked at his watch. "I've got to go. Ramar is bringing in a bunch of hired guns for tonight's show, Miss Nude Missouri."

"Lovely," Toni said, jogging away.

Harry watched her until she disappeared down the trail. Then he sat down on a nearby bench to wait. He didn't want a chance encounter with anyone from the bar to link them together. Thirty-five minutes later, he walked slowly back to the park where he had left his car. Years of experience had made him naturally cautious and he paused to scan the parking lot before going to his car. "Son-of-a-bitch," he muttered. The bartender, Mo Habib, was standing by the driver's window of a black Mercedes Benz. He and Toni weren't the only ones to use the park as a rendezvous. A hand reached out of the window and grabbed Habib's necktie and pulled his head into the car.

Harry caught a glimpse of Ramar's swarthy face and heard his distinctive growl. "It was fifty thousand, mutha." There were more words he couldn't understand but Harry almost purred in satisfaction.

The money trail now led to Habib. He retreated away from the parking lot, certain that Ramar had seen his car. It was salamander time.

"Hey," the manager called when Harry entered the bar, "You're late. Introduce yourself to the ladies and then Mr. Ramar wants to talk to you."

Harry grunted an answer and wandered over to the bar. The eight hired guns brought in for the show were talking to the bartender. "Mo," Harry said, "who are your friends?" Habib made the introductions and Harry quickly sorted the girls out. Four were neophytes from Kansas City, two were professional dancers, one an aspiring actress down on her luck, and one a porn star. "How many movies have you starred in?" he asked.

"Over two hundred," she answered.

"Well, ladies, I'm in charge of security here and deal with the sheriff. It's nude onstage but keep your shoes on, topless for table and lap dances. Charge whatever the traffic will bear, but normally it's twenty bucks a dance on a show night. Don't let the customers touch you and if one causes any trouble, stand up and pat the back of your hair with either hand. I'll be all over him like stink on a skunk. Any questions?"

"You're cute," the porn star said.

Harry knew what she was after. "Not that cute, honey. No freelancing allowed on the premises and that includes the parking lot. Don't even make dates."

"You're still cute," she said in a hurt voice.

He smiled at them and ambled back to the office. The door was ajar so he knocked twice and pushed on through. Ramar was sitting behind the desk with a nude girl on his lap. Harry glanced down. Ramar's trousers were bunched around his ankles. "I got big bucks in tonight's show," Ramar growled. "Why were you late?"

"Car trouble," Harry answered. "I had to hitch a ride."

"Call a taxi next time."

"We only got one and he was busy," Harry replied.

"Where's your car?"

So you or Mo did make my car, he thought. "Where I left it last night—in the state park. It wouldn't start."

"What were you doing there?"

"The same thing you're doing. Man, was she pissed when we had to walk."

"Give me your keys," Ramar demanded. "A mechanic owes me. I'll get it fixed."

You mean you'll get it checked out. Harry threw his keys on the desk, confident that it would take an expert mechanic to find the short that had disabled his car. It was all part of his salamander training.

5:20 P.M., SUNDAY, JUNE 20,
EL OBEID, THE SUDAN

Kamigami stuck the microdot microphone in a crack next to the ceiling. "It should pick up sound reflected from the ceiling," he told al Gimlas.

"They'll never see it from here," al Gimlas said. The two men reexamined the cell, making sure the American pilots could find the video camera and the first, and much more obvious, microphone. "Will they know what to do?" al Gimlas asked.

"They should. Time to check out the warehouse." Kamigami took one last sweep of the cell and, satisfied it was ready, closed the heavy steel door as they left. Outside, the driver snapped to attention and held the car door for his captain. Unsure of what to do about Kamigami, he rushed around to open his door. Kamigami had been in El Obeid two weeks and the soldiers were already afraid of him. The driver made the short drive to the warehouse and breathed a sigh of relief when Kamigami disappeared inside.

"My men are afraid of you," al Gimlas said.

"They have nothing to fear from me."

"That is good to know," al Gimlas replied.

Kamigami was silent as they walked through the wreckage of the B-2. To the untrained eye, it was a mass of charred and twisted wreckage. Some of the bits and pieces were recognizable; the ejection seats, the engines, part of the instrument panel, the beaver tail that had broken off in the crash, but little else. The self-destruct mechanisms had worked well. "Have the Chinese technicians examined this?" Kamigami asked.

"Not yet," al Gimlas answered. "They are getting most impatient at the delays. Our weather doesn't agree with them."

"Good. Maybe, they'll be willing to help us in return for a chance to examine the wreckage."

"We can always ask," al Gimlas allowed.

It was just after two in the morning when the guards came for Mark Terrant, the B-2's mission commander. The burly men barged into the major's cell and jerked him to his feet. They unchained him from the wall and slapped handcuffs on his badly chaffed wrists. Then they jerked a canvas bag over his head, brushing the heavy bandages wrapped around and under his chin. Although his jaw was healing nicely from the beating by Assam's thugs, he groaned loudly, using anything he could to gain an advantage.

The guards dragged him out of the cell, down the long corridor, and outside. For a moment, he was certain that he was going to be executed. Much to his relief, they lifted him into a truck and banged the tailgate closed. Terrant looked out the bottom of the hood and through the slats of the truck, trying to get his bearings as they drove through the night. Then it came to him, they were going in a circle and trying to confuse him. The truck slammed to a halt and the guards dragged him inside another building. A hand straightened him up. Another hand grabbed his hood and jerked it off.

He blinked in the bright light. He was standing in a big room, probably a warehouse, he reasoned. Strewn out in front of him was the wreckage of his B-2, all arranged inside a broad white stripe painted on the floor. At first, it didn't make sense to him. But as the guards pushed him around the wreckage, he realized the white stripe outlined a B-2 and the wreckage was placed in its approximate location. It was obvious someone knew a great deal about the B-2. "What do you see?" one of the guards barked.

"Wreckage from an aircraft," he mumbled.

"Your aircraft!"

Terrant knew better than to lie at this stage, so he mumbled some incomprehensible words and staggered as if he was on the edge of physical collapse. The canvas bag was jammed back on his head and the guards half-dragged, half-prodded, him back to the truck. They drove around for about the same length of time, and this time he was certain they were going in circles before they reached their destination.

Again, the guards dragged him down a corridor and pushed him into another room. Out of the bottom of his hood, he counted five pairs of boots standing in a semicircle. *What now?* he thought. His hood was removed, more gently this time, and he was looking at the biggest Asian he had ever seen. The man stood about six-foot-six and was shaved bald. He wore a People's Liberation Army uniform with the rank of general. *Where did you come from?* Terrant chanced a glance around the room. Half were Arabs, the other half Chinese.

Kamigami cut loose with a stream of Cantonese as one of the Asians interpreted. "The general wants to know about the BLU-113 bombs you were carrying."

How did he know that? Terrant thought. "We weren't carrying bombs," he lied. A torrent of Cantonese and Arabic erupted around him. A slight flick of Kamigami's hand and the room fell abruptly silent. A long pause. Then, in a soft and quiet voice Terrant found at total odds with the image in front of him, Kamigami spoke a few more words in Cantonese. Again, the Asian translated.

"The general is a patient man but you must not lie to him." The interpreter handed him two sheets of paper.

"No doubt the confession you want me to sign," Terrant said, letting the pages slip to the floor.

"No," the interpreter replied, "these are questions the general wants answered. The general has directed that you have time to consider your answers. The next time, he will expect the answers, not lies."

"And if I have no answers?"

"That would be most unfortunate for Capt. Douglas Holloway."

On cue, the guards pushed Terrant out of the room, this time without his hood. They led him down a side corridor and stopped in front of a heavy steel door. They removed his shackles, opened the door, and shoved him inside. Much to his surprise, they only dropped the two pages of questions on the floor and left, not bothering to chain him to the wall as before. Capt. Douglas Holloway was standing in the middle of the cell.

Without a word, the two men shook hands, their grips strong. They held on to each other, finding strength and hope after eight weeks of solitary confinement. But they knew better than to speak. Holloway stepped to a wall and pointed to a micro TV camera above his head. From directly underneath, he was outside the camera's angle of view. He motioned Terrant to his side and gestured for him to get down on all fours. Holloway stood on his back, now able to reach the camera. With a maddening slowness, he tilted the camera so it only viewed the far corner of the cell. Out of sight of the camera, he showed Terrant the microphone he had found. With a care that would have done a neurosurgeon proud, Terrant separated the thin black leads and snapped the filaments without breaking the black insulation.

Terrant mouthed the words, "Can we talk?" Holloway shook his head and motioned for them to continue searching the cell. Together, they went over the cell, looking for other bugs. Satisfied there were no more, Holloway set down on a bunk. "Fuckin' ragheads," he muttered.

"Are you okay?" Terrant asked.

"Still bruised, but I'm fine. How 'bout you?"

"The jaw's much better, but I'm faking it. Did they show you the wreckage?"

Holloway shook his head. "What about the fuckin' Chinaman?"

"Yeah, we met." Terrant picked up the two pages of questions and handed him one. "He wants an answer to these." He looked at his friend. "Doug, he's threatening you if I don't comply."

"Hold out as long as you can." Holloway said. "But I would appreciate it if you'd start throwing some bullshit around before he gets serious about the threat." He scanned the page of questions. "Jesus H. Christ! Someone knows a hell of a lot about the Beak. What the hell were we trying to bomb anyway?"

"Not what," Terrant replied, "but who?"

"You think the Chinese?"

"Seems like it."

17

11:20 A.M., MONDAY, JUNE 21,
OVER FLORIDA

Art Rios let the plush leather seat of the Hawker Horizon, Durant's latest business jet, suck him into a state of drowsy bliss. The sixteen-million-dollar, two-engine aircraft was a honey to fly, and Rios would have preferred sitting in the left seat on the flight deck. But circumstances change and his real job was to dance careful attendance on his employer, who was sitting in the seat opposite him. For some reason, Durant preferred facing backward when he was not at the controls. Although Durant's eyes were closed, Rios knew he was hard at work.

"Are you sure?" Durant asked without opening his eyes.

"We are now," Rios answered. He consulted his folder, making sure he had all the facts straight. Two of his best agents had been back-flushing the source of Meredith's information about the downing of the B-2 bomber for three weeks. At first, they had encountered a stone wall. Then a significant amount of money had changed hands. But like all "bought" information, it had to be verified and that had taken time. "We would never get a conviction, but Serick did leak it to Meredith. We just don't know why."

Durant's eyes opened and flashed with anger. "Consistency has never been Stephan's strong suit. He wants an excuse for an aggressive and hard-line policy in the Middle East. If the Arabs won't give him one, he'll manufacture it." He thought for a few moments. "I suppose I should tell Agnes." He lay back in his seat and closed his eyes. Rios waited while he worked another problem. "Are we okay with FinCEN?"

"Everything's shortstopped," Rios said.

"And Geneva?"

"A bit more problematic," Rios replied. "But we should be okay."

"I'll talk to Heydrich and reinforce his backbone," Durant said. Heydrich Mueller was the president of Credit Geneve, an obscure Swiss bank with huge reserves owned by Durant.

Rios laughed. "He'll find that an uplifting experience."

Durant switched subjects again. "How close are we on the rescue mission?"

"Close, very close," Rios answered. "We've got a few details to work out but other than that, we're ready to go."

"Good," Durant said. "We've almost run out of time." The FASTEN SEAT BELT light came on warning them to strap in for landing at Hurlburt Field, the home of the 16th Special Operations Wing.

Lt. Col. Gillespie prowled back and forth like a caged tiger in front of the small crowd that was gathered in the mission planning section of the wing's intelligence section. The helicopter pilot's bright red hair and green flight suit bagging on his skinny body made Durant think of a lean and hungry tiger in search of a good meal. A schematic of the compound at El Obeid and a chart showing their route were tacked to the wall behind him. "Sir, the secret of success in special ops is to plan the hell out of the mission, practice until it's second nature, then improvise like mad when we do it."

He traced the route on the chart. "The plan is simplicity itself. We launch out of Bangui in the Central African Republic with Combat Talon MC-130s and Pave Low helicopters. The Combat Talons will airdrop Delta Force onto the objective." He pointed to a schematic of the barracks at El Obeid. "They will free the two pilots and move to this point"—he pointed to an area near the compound—"and the helicopters will extract them approximately twenty minutes after the attack begins. Sir, I'll let the commander of Delta Force outline how they plan to free the pilots and move them to the pickup point."

The army colonel from Delta Force stood in front of the chart. He was six feet tall and moved with agile grace. Corded muscles ran down his thick neck and Durant wondered if the colonel was all hard lines and no brains. His short and concise briefing dispelled any doubts about his competence. Delta Force had constructed a mockup of the El Obeid barracks at Fort Irwin in the Mojave Desert and had been practicing for two weeks. They were ready to go.

Gillespie stood up. "It's nine hundred miles to the target and another eight hundred miles to egress. We will land on an aircraft carrier in the Red Sea. Because of the distances, the helicopters need to refuel four times."

"Given the porous nature of the Sudan's air defenses," the Army colonel said, "we'd prefer to set up FARPs, forward air and refueling points, on the ground."

"Our experience with FARPing is not good," Gillespie told them. "We prefer to use our own C-One-thirties. We can do it with two additional HC-One-thirty-Ps from the Ninth Special Ops Squadron. They refuel us inbound to the target. The two Combat Talons that insert Delta Force can refuel us on the way out. It's simple and gives us flexibility."

Durant and Rios quietly exchanged a few words. "It sounds like the air-to-air refueling option works best. Go with that."

Gillespie shook his head. "In special ops, you never know what works best."

A Navy captain stood up. "The Navy is ready to go and the *Nimitz* will be on station here." He pointed to a position in the Red Sea. "Navy Seals are ready to go in for a rescue should a helicopter go down. However, my admiral is worried about Air Force helicopter pilots landing on an aircraft carrier, especially at night."

"That's a piece of cake," Gillespie said. "If your admiral's worried, I'll fly a demonstration mission and put his mind at rest."

"I'd like to see that myself," Durant said. "Do you mind if I go along?"

"Why not?" Gillespie replied.

8:05 A.M., TUESDAY, JUNE 22,
WHITEMAN AIR FORCE BASE, MO.

Toni was at the front desk talking to Linda when FBI Special Agent Brent Mather entered the legal office. Toni looked up and smiled, instantly recalling when they had collided on the Jefferson stakeout in Kansas City. "Hi," she said. "Linda, this is agent Brent Mather."

Mather reached across the desk and shook her hand, capturing the older woman with his hazel eyes and good looks. "I'm with the FBI, ma'am." Linda returned his smile. He turned to Toni. "I've got something you might like to see." He held up a videocassette. "Someplace where we might watch it?"

"Is it about Sandi Jefferson?" Toni asked. He nodded and she led him to the witness waiting room. "We can watch it in here. Let me get Major Blasedale. She's already here." She hurried down the hall to find the lawyer. "Major," she said, "the FBI agent I told you about is here. He's got a videotape." Blasedale followed her to the waiting room. Like Linda, she was immediately impressed with Mather.

"I prefer Brent," he told her when Toni made the introductions. The TV set was already turned on and the tape loaded. He hit the Play button. "This is from the service station in Lone Jack three weeks ago when Mrs. Jefferson was jacked up by the local sheriff."

"Pun intended?" Toni quipped. They watched as the tape started to roll. "The sergeant who drove up in the pickup took this, didn't he?"

"Correct," Mather answered.

"Talk about coincidence," she said. "It was lucky he was there."

"It was no coincidence," Mather replied. "He's one of ours." They watched as the tape played. Mather froze a frame. "We have a problem with this guy," he said.

"That's Jim Bob," Toni said.

"Harrison," Mather said. "Jim Bob Harrison. But that's all we've got on him. We ran his fingerprints and came up totally dry."

Toni remembered the time she and Harry first encountered the man. "Jim Bob stopped Harry and me at a roadblock when we first arrived here. A guy from the First Brigade said he wasn't from around Kansas City."

Mather nodded. "We talked to the same people. Then we checked with the county office where he applied for the parade permit for the demonstration at the main gate. Nothing. It turns out he's been using fake IDs."

"So you were also on top of that one," Toni said, impressed with the FBI's efficiency.

"Oh, yeah. When we reviewed the tapes from the demonstration we even identified you and Sutherland. But on Jim Bob, we have nada, not a damn thing. This guy is slipperier than a salamander."

Sutherland walked past the door carrying two briefcases. "Hank," Blasedale called, "you need to see this." She smiled when she introduced him to Brent Mather and explained why he was there. "He's the FBI agent Toni told us about."

"Right," Sutherland answered, wondering why Mather had to deliver the tape personally. Mather hit the Play button and they watched in silence as the tape replayed.

"Mrs. Jefferson photographs well," Blasedale said. It was true, Sandi Jefferson looked much softer and more vulnerable than in real life. "Now if she dressed—" Blasedale's voice trailed off. She didn't want to seem catty. At least not so early in the morning.

"More conservatively?" Mather replied.

"Less like a hooker?" This from Toni.

"Humm," Sutherland muttered in annoyance, more at Mather's presence than anything else.

"There's one more thing," Mather said, closing the door to the room. They all looked at him expectantly. "Did you hear about the demonstration in Phoenix, last night?"

"Who hasn't?" Sutherland replied. "It was on the news this morning. I heard a woman was killed."

"Actually," Mather replied, "she was lynched." They stared at him, shocked to silence.

"Was she black?" Toni asked, her eyes wide.

"Yeah. She was just driving by, trying to get home, and some thugs from a white supremacist group pulled her out of her car. It got pretty ugly."

"How come it wasn't on the news?" Blasedale asked.

"It will be," Mather said. "Probably about now. The authorities were able to sit on it until the crowds went home. Our information indicates it was a setup. The bastards are trying to bait the black community into rioting. But so far, cooler heads have prevailed. We won't be so lucky next time."

"Why are you telling us this?" Sutherland asked.

"Because we think Whiteman is next. My bosses are meeting with your wing commander right now and want to get all your minorities moved onto base."

"Is it because of the court-martial?" Blasedale asked.

"Probably," Mather answered. "We're seeing an outbreak of demonstrations and riots everywhere."

"Is it racial?" Toni asked, worried about her family.

"I'd say about a third of the time," Mather replied. "People are simply going crazy and Meredith isn't helping with his calls for arming his Neighborhood Brigades."

"Anything new on Sandi Jefferson?" Sutherland asked.

Mather pulled out his notebook. "Nothing significant. Other than shopping and a weekly visit to a beauty salon, she's staying at home. We did flesh out her background. High school dropout from the hard side of town in Saint Paul, Minnesota. Went to work as a manicurist, owned the shop by the time she was twenty, traveled a little, met Jefferson, married just before he was assigned to Whiteman, sold the salon, honeymooned in Europe. A definite move up the economic ladder."

Sutherland thought for a moment. "Do you have anything on that woman Toni saw having lunch with Sandi at Nordstrom's, the day of the incident at Lone Jack?"

Mather shook his head and looked embarrassed. "We were distracted by the incident and then focused on Jim Bob. We think it was probably a chance meeting with some old friend or a wife. If she shows up again, we'll get her."

An inner voice told Sutherland they had missed something important. "That would be nice," he muttered.

Mather checked his watch. "I've got to go." Toni walked him to the front desk. "Dinner?" he asked.

"I'd love to," she said, giving him a lovely smile.

Sutherland stood in the hall talking to Blasedale until Mather had left. "What the hell does he want?" he muttered.

"Toni," Blasedale replied.

1:45 P.M., WEDNESDAY, JUNE 23,
EL OBEID, THE SUDAN

Kamigami replayed the tape for Jamil bin Assam while al Gimlas sat quietly behind his desk. Assam twitched with anger as the tape played out. "You have your confessions," Kamigami said. "And we have more of the same."

"This is not a confession," Assam ranted. "This is worthless! And what is this 'Beak' they talk about? It means nothing."

"The Beak is slang for the B-Two," Kamigami explained. "You heard them admit they were on a bombing mission."

"It is not what I want," Assam growled. His English was heavily accented but easily understood.

"General Assam," Kamigami said, "you employ me as your chief of security. As long as I am in charge, I will give you the best advice I can. On this matter, I am telling you that your best defense against the Americans is the absolute truth. The Americans want us to lie, to fabricate evidence, to force confessions, even torture the pilots. That will give them the excuse they need to react, and I assure you, they have the capability to do whatever they want. They only lack the will." He let his words sink in before getting to the hard sell. "Use the truth, take the will to act from them, and you will remain master of the situation."

Dealing with the truth was a new concept for Assam. His instincts demanded that he dissemble and lie. Even walking a straight line was abhorrent to his nature. He hesitated. "Give the Western world hard evidence they can believe," Kamigami urged.

"Look what General Kamigami has accomplished in three weeks," al Gimlas added. "You were very wise in finding a man who understands the way Americans think."

It was enough. "I will put them on trial," Assam announced, "when the Americans court-martial the martyr in Missouri." He rubbed his chin. "But I am worried the Americans may use the trial as an excuse for another attack on my laboratories."

"There are always ways to improve your defenses," Kamigami said. "Let me examine the laboratories."

"Impossible," Assam snapped.

"I only need to see the exterior to evaluate your defenses," Kamigami coaxed, "not the inside."

Assam jerked his head in agreement and two hours later, they were on his C-130 headed for the underground laboratory deep in the western desert. Assam traveled with a large retinue of sycophants who clustered around him, trying to capture one of the airline-type seats that were onloaded whenever Assam used the aircraft. Kamigami sat near the portable lavatory module at the rear of the aircraft. The two stewards concentrated on Assam and left him alone, which was just fine. But he was worried about al Gimlas. Among the Sudanese, he alone worried Kamigami.

When al Gimlas had gone forward and climbed onto the flight deck, Kamigami stepped into the vacant lavatory. He urinated as he examined the interior. Someone had smudged the vanity mirror over the washbasin with a small backward check mark. The tail of the check mark moved upward in a slightly longer-than-expected stroke and curved off to his left. Kamigami allowed a mental sigh of relief. It was what he had been looking for since arriving in the Sudan. He turned around and faced the wall opposite the mirror and looked where the tail of the check mark pointed. He quickly ran his hand along the top right side of the storage cabinets built into the wall. At the back of a pile of paper towels he found what he was looking for: a half-used pack of cigarettes.

The check mark was the signal that a dead letter drop was activated and the message would be in one of the cigarettes. Since the Sudan was a Moslem country, the sender was most likely a male. But other than that, Kamigami could only surmise it was someone who had access to the plane. Should the wrong person inadvertently find the cigarettes, they would most likely think they were hidden there by someone who was afraid of the Moslem prohibition against using tobacco. The finder would probably smoke the cigarettes himself, destroying the message. *Very good,* Kamigami thought. *Someone who knows his tradecraft.*

He stood over the toilet and unwrapped a cigarette, carefully examining the inside of the paper. Nothing. He dropped the tobacco into the toilet, confident that no Moslem would be too concerned about examining the holding tank. The CIA had no such compunctions and were shit divers of the first water. He ate the paper wrapper. He repeated the process with three more cigarettes before he found the faint mark he was looking for. He moistened the inside of the paper with his tongue, careful to barely wet it. Dull, but very fine lettering emerged and started to fade almost at once.

Friday Mosque El Obeid. Last beggar at end of wall.
I'm not one of you but alms are for the faithful.
Allah rewards all who honor him in this way.

These were the location, contact, and recognition signals he needed. Kamigami flushed the tobacco down the toilet and ate the paper wrapper, chewing it into oblivion. He wiped his fingerprints off the pack and placed the unused cigarettes back in their hiding place, confident they would be smoked. He squeezed around and rubbed off the check mark on the mirror indicating the message had been received.

He had made contact.

18

7:30 P.M., THURSDAY, JUNE 24,
HURLBURT FIELD, FLA.

The tech sergeant who described himself as Gillespie's "flight inganeer" met Durant and Rios when they arrived at the MH-53J Pave Low helicopter. Durant talked to Gillespie while the sergeant and Rios did a walk-around in the rapidly fading light. "Don't you pay no-never-mind to all those hydraulic leaks dripping on the ramp," the flight engineer told him. "If it's leaking, then it's working right."

"And if it's not leaking?" Rios asked.

"Then it's dry and we got to refill it."

"Have you flown much with Colonel Gillespie?" Rios asked.

"For a college boy, he ain't bad."

"Does that mean he's a good pilot?"

The flight engineer nodded. "I'd go play cowboys and Iranians with him or Captain Harold any time, any place." They climbed up the rear ramp and Rios strapped in next to Durant while the crew brought the big helicopter to life. Slowly, the six big blades on the seventy-two-foot rotor picked up speed and beat at the air with the characteristic whomp-whomp-whomp of a helicopter. Both Durant and Rios were wearing earplugs under their headsets and still found the sound deafening. Then a gunner raised the ramp and closed the hatches, lowering the noise to a more tolerable level.

Harold radioed ground control for taxi clearance and the Pave Low moved like a giant insect into the takeoff position. Harold read the before-takeoff checklist and then called the tower for release. The tower cleared them for takeoff, the flight engineer pushed the throttles on the overhead panel to one hundred percent, and Gillespie lifted them easily into the clear night sky.

Gillespie turned west and flew just over the coastline at two hundred feet as they headed for Pensacola. A gunner handed them NVGs, night vision goggles, and helped them fit the cumbersome devices over their eyes. "Look toward the ocean," he warned them. "Otherwise, bright lights will blind you." He gave them a friendly grin. "You'd be surprised at what we see." He guided them to the left gunner's position just aft of the cockpit, and they scanned the shoreline as the gunner had suggested. Although depth perception was not very good through the NVGs, the bright apple green images were very sharp.

"Hey, Gunny," Harold said over the intercom, "we got some live ones up ahead." The forward-looking infrared in the cockpit was much more powerful than the NVGs. Gillespie altered course a few degrees to the right to move them inland. "Clear left," Harold said, clearing the airspace on their left side. Gillespie wracked the helicopter into a tight left turn and did a pylon turn over a naked couple fornicating on the sand.

"I hope that ain't your daughter down there," the flight engineer said to no one in particular. "Maybe we outta go around again and check to be sure."

"No way," Gillespie said.

"Ah, why not?" the flight engineer replied.

"We can get arrested for disturbing the piece," Gillespie quipped.

Durant's smile turned into a laugh. It was a rich, warm laughter that came from the heart. Rios felt his eyes tear up and blinked twice. Durant hadn't laughed like that in years. The flight engineer stowed his seat and let Durant stand on the step between and just behind the pilots. From the intercom chatter, the radio calls, and the precise actions of the crew, there was no doubt that they were flying with highly trained and proficient professionals.

But there was more. Special operations demanded every one of them be an independent thinker yet capable of being a team player. They had a measure of self-confidence the average civilian could never understand for the simple reason the average civilian was never challenged the way they were. These men would fly the most difficult of missions, betting their skills were equal to the task. And if they were found lacking, the survivors consoled themselves with "We had a bad day." Then they trained harder.

"Special ops," the flight engineer said to Durant over the intercom, "never gets any credit because we make it look so easy."

Durant smiled. He was having the time of his life.

Harold switched radio frequencies and they headed out over the Gulf toward the old aircraft carrier the Navy used for flight training. The VHF crackled with transmissions as they neared the carrier, and judging by the strain in their voices, a few of the student pilots were on the edge of panic as they practiced night carrier landings. Gillespie caught it first. "One of them is disoriented and doesn't know where he is."

"He's not in the pattern," Harold said. Both pilots strained to see in the night, hoping to pick up a rotating beacon or position lights. "I hope he's at the right altitude," Harold added.

The flight engineer tapped Durant on the shoulder. "Excuse me, sir." Durant stepped aside so the sergeant could help scan the skies. Durant moved over to the right gunner's hatch and scanned to the right. Nothing. A flashing strobe light suddenly materialized at their five o'clock position and didn't move. An aircraft was on a collision course! "Break right!" Durant shouted. "Down!"

Gillespie didn't hesitate and maneuvered violently, throwing Durant to the deck. His head banged against an electronic equipment rack. A jet blast deafened them and the big helicopter rocked from the jet wash, throwing them out of control. Only Gillespie's lightning-quick reflexes saved them from crashing into the ocean. "My," the flight engineer said when they were flying straight and level, "I do believe I wet my knickers on that one."

"That sucker was close," Harold said. "I never saw him."

"I need help!" Rios shouted. "He's cut his head." The two gunners were on Durant in a flash, pushing Rios out of the way. Hours of training again paid off as they quickly stanched the flow of blood.

"There's a crash team on the carrier," Gillespie said.

But before he could call for priority handling to get them aboard the carrier, one of the gunners shouted. "Shit! I think he's having a heart attack!"

"Give him CPR and get him on oxygen," Gillespie ordered. He wrenched the Pave Low around and headed for the hospital at Pensacola. The flight engineer reached up and pushed the throttles to 105 percent.

"Come on, baby," he urged, wringing every knot he could out of the machine.

Rios bent over Durant and took over the CPR from the gunner. *Please, God,* he prayed, *not yet. Not yet!*

7:25 A.M., MONDAY, JUNE 28,
WHITEMAN AIR FORCE BASE, MO.

Sutherland automatically looked at the countdown calendar when he came to work Monday morning. Toni had changed the numbers to red and a big 14 loomed at him. *Two weeks to go,* he told himself. The vague itching was back. *What's out there waiting to bite us in the ass?* It was the question that loomed large in every prosecutor's mind as a trial date approached. He was confident he and Blasedale had covered all the bases, but he would continue to work the evidence, twisting it around, examining it from different angles, and trying to see it from Cooper's perspective. If he did it right, he would be in Cooper's head when the court-martial started and know what the defense attorney was going to do. Sutherland hated surprises.

A surprise walked in immediately behind him in the form of Brent Mather. *What's he doing here?* Sutherland grumbled to himself. The answer was obvious when he walked into the law library where Toni was still working her way through the file boxes on Osmana Khalid, looking for one more piece of the puzzle. *Maybe it's business,* he thought.

A bit peeved about Mather's intrusion on his territory, he decided to reestablish his eminent domain. It was time for a staff meeting. He called Blasedale first and when he buzzed Toni, told her to bring Mather along. They all trooped into his office, wondering what he had to say. "Well, folks, it's time to switch gears. I want to play 'Napoleon's Sergeant.' "

"Napoleon's what?" Blasedale asked.

"Napoleon had a sergeant," Sutherland explained, "who read all the orders Napoleon sent to his generals. If the sergeant understood them, the orders went out. If not, Napoleon rewrote them. So we're going to present our case to a sergeant today."

"Do you mind if I sit in?" Mather asked, looking at Toni.

"Another point of view is always welcome," Sutherland answered.

It was the first time Sutherland had been in the courtroom since the day he arrived on Whiteman and had met Blasedale. It had been recently cleaned in preparation for the court-martial and smelled of lemon furniture polish. Linda brought in a buck sergeant. Fred Scott was a bright and eager twenty-four-year-old from public affairs who definitely could think for himself. Sutherland sat him in the jury box with Toni and Mather while he presented their case against Capt. Bradley A. Jefferson.

"Our case relies on both direct and circumstantial evidence," Sutherland explained. "In many respects, circumstantial evidence is as good, if not better, than direct. For example, say a cherry pie is missing from your kitchen and you find a trail of pie crumbs leading to your four-year-old daughter's room. In the room, you then discover your daughter with cherry stains around her mouth, but no pie. This is all direct evidence. What happened to the missing cherry pie is circumstantial. However, you can be sure who ate at least part of the pie. Our case is like that. By relying on direct and circumstantial evidence, we can establish a chain of events that are linked together beyond a reasonable doubt."

This was the first time Blasedale had seen Sutherland in action and she was impressed. He spoke without notes and in a very straightforward, simple way. The certainty in his voice alone would convince most jurors of his case. Sutherland's logic was even more damning. First, he presented in detail the direct evidence they had: the information about the B-2's flight plan that passed from the Islamic cleric, Osmana Khalid, to the student, to the Sudanese embassy in Washington, and then to the Sudan. "Now only one question remains," Sutherland said. "Where did Khalid get his information?" Slowly, he proved that Jefferson had detailed knowledge of the mission and had twice talked to Khalid previous to the mission being flown. Rather than actually bringing their witnesses in, Sutherland read their statements. Only once did Sergeant Scott show any doubt, and that was when he read S. Sgt. Miner's statement about overhearing Jefferson speak to the pilots on Saturday afternoon.

Sutherland carefully laid out the timing and geography of the conversations between Jefferson and Khalid. Then he presented a series of graphics that depicted the sequence of phone calls and contacts, i.e., the direct evidence, that took place immediately after each conversation. The timing in itself was overwhelming. "The first meeting at the Mosque might be coincidence," he allowed. "But the second conversation took place immediately after Captain Jefferson had spoken to the pilots after a session in the simulator—a session where Major Terrant and Captain Holloway had practiced the mission they would later fly." He played the tape of the intercepted phone call that Jefferson made after talking to the pilots. "Is this also coincidence?"

They broke for lunch. Sergeant Fred Scott and Agent Brent Mather clustered around Toni and the three went off together. "What do you think?" Blasedale asked.

"Did you see his reaction to Sergeant Miner's testimony? That may be a weakness. Let's work on that."

After lunch, they all gathered in the courtroom and Sutherland let Toni describe the money trail that led from Reno, to Warrensburg. When she had finished, he stood up and demonstrated how Sandi Jefferson lived way beyond a captain's salary. But Sergeant Scott was shaking his head. "I'm sorry," Scott said. "It all makes sense, but I don't see the money trail going to Jefferson."

They had found the weak link in their case.

* * *

"Damn," Sutherland moaned. "I must be getting senile. Talk about a basic mistake. Why didn't I see it before?"

"Because we've been rushed for time," Blasedale told him. "It is so obvious—but we just didn't prove it to Sergeant Scott. Besides, we can prove motivation other ways. We downplay the money trail and stress Jefferson's religion—the Islamic connection—which is the connection to Khalid."

They were sitting in Sutherland's office with Mather and Toni rehashing the session with Scott. As usual, Blasedale was sitting next to the door. For the first time, Sutherland noticed that Mather and Toni were sitting just a little too close together for his comfort. "When are you going to find Khalid?" Sutherland asked, taking a dig at the FBI and, by extension, Mather.

Mather gave him a hard look. "If he's still in the country, we'll find him." He thought for a moment. "Maybe Habib, the bartender at Bare Essence, can help. We've had him under surveillance for some time. He bought a gold Rolex watch right after the money transfer from Reno to Warrensburg."

"Why didn't you tell us?" Sutherland grumbled.

"They did," Toni said in a soft voice. They all looked at her. "It was in the files they sent over. I didn't think it was important at the time and forgot about it." She tried to recover. "Harry's watching Habib too."

"We can work together on this," Mather said, a little too eager.

"Yeah," Sutherland groused, "do that."

Toni smiled at him, eager to recover. "We've got a hired gun on the way to get on the inside at the club."

"A hired gun?" Mather asked, a perplexed look on his face.

Toni told them about Airman Andrea Hall. "As a matter of fact, she should be here tomorrow. Harry's meeting her at the airport."

"Why didn't you tell me?" Sutherland demanded. "It could compromise our case."

"Harry's too good for that," Toni replied.

Mather stood up to leave. "I've got to get back for my stakeout shift. Do me a favor, don't tell Harry that we're also investigating the bartender."

"Why?" Blasedale asked.

"Two reasons. First, we're not going to overlap and Harry doesn't need to know. Second, we know this is the weakest link in the case. It will be much more convincing to a jury if an independent source confirms what Harry discovers."

"Okay, folks," Sutherland said. "Let's get moving on this and plug the hole. I'm going to ask for a continuance."

"Call my boss at Central Circuit at San Antonio," Blasedale said, "and give him a heads up before you go to the judge." He reached for the phone as they left.

It took seven rings before the phone penetrated Sutherland's consciousness and he woke up. It was just after four o'clock Tuesday morning and he had just fallen into a deep sleep. For a moment, he didn't realize he was in his VOQ room. Groggily, he fumbled for the phone. "Yeah," he mumbled.

It was Beth Page. "I'm down at the desk. Can I come up?"

He mumbled something that approximated a "Yes" and staggered to the door. He jerked it open in time to see Beth get off the elevator. She walked down the hall toward him, moving with the same fluid grace that enchanted him years ago. She brushed past him, her shoulder touching his bare chest. Without a word, she walked toward the bedroom, shedding her clothes. "What the hell are you doing here so late?" he grumbled. He felt the stirrings of an erection when she dropped her panties. He let his pajama bottoms fall to the floor and followed her to bed.

"Hank, wake up." It was Beth, gently pushing on his shoulder. "Someone's at the door."

Sutherland staggered out of bed and pulled on his pajama shorts. He lurched down the hall and managed to unlock the door. It was Catherine Blasedale, dressed in a crisp uniform and looking rested. "Time to go to work," she said. She gave him a hard look. "I take it your friendly ex-wife is back?"

"How did you know?" he muttered.

"The well-laid look." *At least it's not Toni,* she thought, thankful that she would not have to file a fraternization charge against Sutherland. "Get rid of the bimbo and I'll see you at the office. We've got work to do." She spun around and marched down the corridor.

Sutherland closed the door and staggered into the kitchenette to make coffee. "Who was that?" Beth asked. She was standing naked by the small breakfast table thumbing through the three legal books neatly stacked there. Blasedale had to have seen her when she was at the door. "How's the trial coming?" she asked. It was like old times when they discussed the cases he was prosecuting. But it was different now.

"Beth, you know I can't discuss it."

She wasn't listening as she thumbed through the thick books. She read the titles. "*Military Evidentiary Foundations, Military Rules of Evidence Manual, Manual for Courts-Martial.* Talk about heavy reading. Memorizing them?"

"Sure," he answered. "Why not." Actually, Sutherland had a near-photographic memory and was doing just that.

"You always did have a thing about words. But you couldn't even remember our anniversary." Which was also true. She sighed and changed the subject. "I'm surprised you can get to trial so quickly and that you or Cooper haven't asked for a continuance."

Suddenly, Sutherland came fully awake. He was not a believer in coincidences. *Does she know I'm asking for one?* For some reason, he couldn't discard the thought. "Beth, what brings you here?"

"I'm doing background coverage on the trial for *Newsweek.* I'm concentrating on Kansas City and got in late last night. Since you're here . . ."

"You thought you'd pump me."

She moved against him and nuzzled his cheek. "Who's pumping who?" She moved away. "Seriously, there's a lot of political interest in the City to get this behind us."

Sutherland worked to keep all expression off his face. *She knows about the continuance.* The "City" was Washington, and she was sending him a message.

Again, she moved into him. "Hank, this could be the break you need."

"If I expedite," he said. There was no answer as she rubbed against him.

Two hours later, Sutherland walked into the legal office. Blasedale was waiting for him. "What did she want?"

"A good question," Sutherland answered.

"What about the continuance?"

"According to your colonel at Central Circuit, the judge will be on base a week from Wednesday, on the seventh of July. He wants all motions submitted then to have a chance to study them before the court-martial. I'll present it then."

Blasedale gave him a long look. She wanted to ask him why he was so late in coming to work. But she knew the answer. Instead, "Did you tell Cooper?"

"Yeah. He laughed."

Although the court-martial was still twelve days away, the headquarters building bustled with activity as the 509th prepared for the trial. Sutherland wasted most of Wednesday morning in a wing staff meeting concerned with handling the media flocking into the area and demanding access to the court-martial. There was room only for thirty spectators in the courtroom, and it was decided to have a closed-circuit TV to the base theater, which could seat over five hundred people. The theater would be treated as an annex to the courtroom and no cameras, tape recorders, or TV links would be allowed.

Most of the meeting addressed security around the courtroom. Finally, the wing commander decided they would simply seal the base and control access at the gates. That way, the media would not see a legion of security cops and armed guards. Sutherland finally escaped back to his office in time for lunch.

Toni was waiting for him. "Good news, I hope," he muttered.

"Brent called. Good news on the bartender. It seems he was involved with a dancer at the club three years ago." She checked her notes. "She went by the stage name Cassandra and was described as five feet ten inches tall, a natural redhead, willowy, and a flashy dresser." She looked at Sutherland expectantly. "She was twenty years old at the time. That would make her twenty-three now."

"The same age as Sandi Jefferson," Sutherland said, almost shouting. He played with her stage name. "Cassandra, Cassi, Sandra, Sandi."

"It does sound like her," Toni allowed. "But according to her file, Sandi lived in Minnesota then and was running her own business."

"She might have had a cash flow problem and needed money. Don't strippers move around a lot so they won't be recognized?"

"According to Andrea, the really successful ones do. But she's going to be hard to trace because of the stage name." She thought for a moment. "Sandi would probably be a bombshell and enjoy the work."

"Keep digging," Sutherland said.

"There's more," Toni said. "I took another look at her finances. She's a compulsive spender." She spread the worksheet on his desk and leaned over his shoulder. "I totaled up all her expenditures since June. She's bought new furniture, paid off her car, and remodeled her kitchen. Add that to a few other credit cards, all paid off, plus the five thousand that Habib paid for his Rolex and you get—"

"Almost forty thou," Sutherland said, reading the bottom line.

"And according to Harry, Habib was skimming."

"Holy shit," Sutherland whispered. "We got the money trail."

A worried look crossed Toni's face. "It seems almost too good to be true."

"We'll take it," Sutherland said.

"Are you still going for the continuance?"

"Yeah. I'll ask for a couple of weeks so we can get this all locked in concrete. When does your hired gun arrive?"

"Andrea? About now. Harry's meeting her at the airport."

"I hope she has time to hear something and for us to get it all sorted out."

3:00 P.M., WEDNESDAY, JUNE 30,
WARRENSBURG, MO.

The two FBI agents were waiting for Mohammed Habib when he left his apartment for work. They trapped him against his car, identified themselves, and "invited" him to accompany them for a little chat. It was not an option and he crawled into the backseat of their car. His wife saw them drive away and phoned the club to tell them he would be late.

"Mo," Brent Mather said, his voice friendly, "what happened to your friend Osmana Khalid?" As expected, Habib denied any close friendship or knowledge of Khalid's whereabouts. "That's too bad," Mather said. "We need to speak to him. Now you wouldn't be holding out on us, would you?" Vehement denials from Habib. "That's reassuring, Mo. Otherwise, the INS is going to be taking a hard look at you." More protestations from Habib. He was married to an American citizen born in this country and he was legal. Besides, they had a son, also born in this country. He had constitutional rights too.

Mather agreed. "Of course you do, Mo. But the laws have changed, especially about aliens engaged in subversive activities who marry innocent citizens. We're offering a one-time good deal to the first person who wants to talk to us about Khalid." Habib shook his head, claiming he had nothing to talk about. "You absolutely sure about that?" Mather asked. The car stopped a half block from his apartment and Habib's door unlocked. He was free to go. "You're not the only one getting this offer, Mo. First taker gets out of jail for free. Everybody else loses. Think about it."

11:00 A.M., FRIDAY, JULY 2,
EL OBEID, THE SUDAN

Kamigami sat alone in the Land Rover, grateful for the air conditioner. The heat and wind were taxing even his stoical nature. He drove slowly into the center of town, looking for the mosque. Like many drivers, he had the omnipresent car phone stuck to his ear. The cellular phone system was not a luxury in Africa but a necessity. The press of population and the breakdown of basic services had forced the government to allow private enterprise to develop a private communications system.

But he was not using that system. He was speaking into the microrecorder built into the phone. It was a miracle of miniaturization and the cartridge itself was little bigger than his thumbnail and about as thick. He spoke in Cantonese, that difficult tonal language from southern China. When he didn't know a word, he simply used either the Japanese or English equivalent. Once, just to confuse the issue, he used the limited Arabic he was picking up. It was all part of the tradecraft that went with the business. If the message was intercepted by the wrong party, they would most likely concentrate on the Chinese, which was just fine with him.

"The defenses around the laboratory show signs of upgrading: four batteries of SA-11 Gadfly surface-to-air missiles. Iranian technicians. Four MiG-29 Fulcrums sitting air defense in a hardened shelter observed at nearby airstrip. An early warning radar in transport mode, type unknown. Numerous troops bivouacked in valley. American pilots in good condition and in the same cell. Their conversations are being monitored. Trial scheduled to coincide with court-martial in Missouri."

He paused. It was enough. He deftly pried apart a counterfeit coin and placed the hollowed-out halves on the seat beside him. Then he ejected the chip from the cell phone and fitted it into one of the halves. He pressed the halves together, making sure they were correctly aligned. He didn't need one of the sides of the coin to be upside down. He scratched one side with a key and slipped the coin into his left pocket. He found a parking spot and paid two boys to guard the Land Rover while he went to the mosque.

A beggar was sitting at the far end of the wall that separated the mosque from the main street. He walked by, hesitated, and said in Arabic, "I'm not one of you, but alms are for the faithful." The beggar spat at him. Wrong beggar. He moved on.

"Allah rewards all who honor him," the beggar said from behind his back. Kamigami turned around. "In this way," the old man finally added. Without a word, Kamigami pulled some coins out of his left pocket, including the counterfeit one with the hidden cartridge, and pressed them into the old man's hands. "Next time, asshole," the man whispered in English, "use your right pocket and right hand."

Kamigami winced. The left hand in Arabic culture was unclean, a very basic mistake. But he had made contact.

19

9:05 A.M., SUNDAY, JULY 4,
PENSACOLA, FLA.

The nurse let Art Rios into the private suite. "Fifteen minutes," she cautioned. "Doctor's orders." Rios nodded and sat down, the briefcase on his lap. He looked out the window. A fishing boat carved a wake across the sparkling blue waters of the Gulf.

"Hell of a way to spend the Fourth of July," Durant murmured, his voice barely audible. "How long have you been here?"

"Just a few minutes." Rios answered. "God, you look terrible."

"I have to get out of this place."

"Not for a few more days," Rios told him.

"Watch me," Durant answered. He rolled over to get out of bed.

Rios sighed, set the briefcase down, and walked over to the bed. "Not today," he said, putting his hand on Durant's shoulder. The weight was enough to hold him in bed. It was the way Rios tested him. When Durant pushed his hand aside and got out of bed, he would be ready to leave. "They want to do a bypass."

Durant shook his head. "It doesn't seem fair. Cancer, now this. Maybe later."

"Boss, listen to the quacks. You had a heart attack that registered on the Richter scale. They claim the angioplasty is not enough to keep your arteries open."

"It'll have to do for now."

"Just give it a few more days, okay?"

Durant gave in and settled against his pillow. He gestured at the briefcase. "I take it that's for me."

Rios unlocked the briefcase and handed him three folders. "These need signing."

Durant scrawled his signature across the documents and returned the folders. "Is the money trail in place?"

"Oh, yeah," Rios said. "All they have to do is look in the right places." He handed Durant a much thicker folder. "The accounts are all in place. Luckily, Mrs. Jefferson was diddling the IRS. When she got married, she sold her business and made a tidy profit, over $100,000, which she hid in a Canadian bank account. We're still not sure how she did that but we think she put the make on the manager. She would have gotten away with it if she hadn't become addicted to credit cards and used the money to pay them off."

"Good work," Durant said. "How did you make the connection?"

"Agnes," Rios replied. "She dug it out. She even helped switch the money in the Canadian account to Credit Geneve. It was unbelievably simple and the Canadian bank manager was more than glad to get the monkey off his back."

"So everyone's happy," Durant said.

"Well, not Heydrich."

Durant allowed a little smile. Heydrich Mueller was the president of Credit Geneve, the Swiss bank that Durant owned. "Heydrich will do what I tell him. What about this side of the Atlantic?"

"Agnes has cracked the banks in the Caymans and Collingswood is putting all the pieces together as we speak." Herbert Collingswood was a former MI-6 agent who looked like a respectable Bank of England director. "He needs a few more weeks but the money trail will go right where you want. After that, it's just a matter of the right leak at the right time."

Durant closed his eyes when the nurse came in. She glanced at her watch and then Rios, sending him the obvious message. Rios nodded, retrieved the folder from Durant, and closed the briefcase. She closed the door, giving them a few more moments of privacy. "Art, I don't know whether to believe the doctors or not. How bad is it?" He knew Rios would tell him the truth.

"Without a bypass, you've got less than a year. With one, the average life expectancy is seven years. But in your case, probably five."

The prognosis agreed with Durant's calculations and an indescribable sense of loss chipped away at him. He didn't even have to ask the question, for he knew he was grounded and would never fly his airplane again. He closed his eyes as he recalled the first time he had seen the old biplane. He was young then and it was love at first sight. The day was still crystal clear in his memory: cold, clear blue skies with a horizon that stretched to infinity. It was a time when the world was his. "Art, when I go, the Staggerwing is yours."

"Thanks, but you're a bit premature. Besides, you can still fly in the right seat and get some stick time."

"It's not the same, is it? But I'll take what I can get." Durant looked out the window. The dazzling waters of the Gulf seemed more gray and the horizon much closer. "Don't let her see me like this, okay?"

Rios nodded in understanding.

12:50 A.M., WEDNESDAY, JULY 7,
WARRENSBURG, MO.

Mo Habib claimed he had never seen the club so busy on a Tuesday night. Harry glanced at his watch. It was actually Wednesday morning and the club was packed. The reason was onstage. Andrea had been dancing for a week and the word had spread like wildfire that a sensational new dancer named Adrienne was in town. Even Habib, who had seen countless women prance around the stage in the buff was impressed. Andrea Hall was causing heart attacks and setting hair on fire as she came back for another encore. Normally, the girls were onstage for two songs and then back working the audience for lap dances. But the men kept throwing money onstage and shouting for more.

The loudspeakers blared with a fast song and Andrea let the beat wash over her. She slipped out of her shoes and stood for a few moments absolutely still. She was totally naked, no jewelry, nothing. "Son-of-a-bitch, Harry," Habib groaned. "She's got to keep her shoes on. Are you going to stop her?" Andrea picked up the beat and started to move.

"And start a riot? Get real. I'll talk to her later." Most of the audience now was on its feet shouting and cheering. Money rained down on the stage as a man climbed over the low railing and began crawling toward Andrea, holding a twenty dollar bill in his teeth. "Dammit!" Harry growled as he bulldozed his way to the stage. Two more men were onstage and Harry had a riot in the making. He gave Habib the high-sign to call the police. Before he could get to the stage, the two men had grabbed the crawler and were dragging him off the stage. The music stopped.

"It's okay, Adrienne," someone yelled from the audience. "No one's gonna hurt you." The two men threw the man to the audience and jumped after him, leaving Andrea alone onstage to gather up the money. Harry glanced at Habib who was on the telephone. Now he had to save the idiot who had gone after Andrea.

"He's mine!" Harry shouted. His voice carried enough authority to slow the crowd. He pushed his way over to the man, reached down, and dragged him to his feet. "Your ass is grass!" The crowd roared in approval and Harry hustled him outside. "Unless you got a terminal case of the stupids, you'll get and never come back." The man staggered off, thankful for a reprieve. Harry ran back inside. Luckily, the doorman and two security guards from the parking lot had everything under control.

He grabbed the phone to call the police dispatcher and cancel Habib's call. The woman on the other end claimed she had never received a call to begin with. Harry hung up and looked around for Habib. He was gone. "Time to close," Harry announced as he turned up the lights. Slowly, the club emptied and he breathed in relief. "Where's Mo?" he asked. No one had seen him leave. Perplexed, Harry headed for the dressing room to check on Andrea. The girls were clustered around her in states of semi-undress, totally unconcerned with the pile of five, ten, and twenty dollar bills on the dressing table. All were reassuring and comforting Andrea. "Just one big happy family," he mumbled to himself as he closed the door and went to shut down the bar.

Twenty minutes later, Harry made one last sweep of the bar, making sure everything was locked up. He went out the back door and checked the parking lot. A car was parked in a far corner in the shadows. He headed for it and stopped when he realized it was Habib's. A sixth sense told him something was wrong. He returned to the club, found a flashlight, and walked carefully toward the car, scanning the ground for footprints or any telltale clues. Nothing. He shined the beam into the car. Mohammed Habib was crumpled over in the backseat, the back of his head a bloody mess. Without touching the car, Harry backed off, even more careful where he stepped.

He went to his car and called Toni on his cell phone. "I've got a body in the parking lot," he told her. "Habib. I'm calling the police. Since I found the body, they should haul me in for questioning. Meet me at the police station in say—" He calculated how long it would take for the police to respond, examine the crime area, take his statement, and decide to transport him to the police station. "Be there about four A.M. Bring my I.D. and I'll lay it out for them at the police station. With a little luck, they won't blow my cover." He thought for a moment. "And start carrying your weapon."

Toni was sitting in the waiting room at the station when two patrolmen brought Harry in. She had been there for almost two hours and it was light outside. Harry shrugged and held up his handcuffed wrists when he saw her, his way of telling her the locals didn't have a clue. The chief of police waved them to the booking desk and continued to talk on the phone. "Yeah, we got the perp. An open-and-shut case. All we got to do is find the weapon."

Harry shook his head. "Chief, your men are destroying the crime scene. Back off until the professionals get here."

The chief stood up and charged down on Harry like a football linebacker, which he had been and was what had gotten him elected. "We're not stupid. You found the body, you know all about the deceased, you're a scumbag who works at the club."

Toni coughed for attention. "Chief, can we talk in private?"

"Who in hell are you?" the Chief boomed.

She showed him her I.D. "We really need to talk in private." She was trying desperately to salvage the investigation and keep Harry's cover intact. Besides, Andrea would be much safer with Harry around. The chief motioned them inside his office and slammed the door behind them. "Thank you, sir," she said. "This is Special Agent Harry Waldon." She handed him Harry's I.D. card. "We are on an undercover investigation—"

"Why wasn't I told about it?" the chief demanded. "I don't cotton to feds operatin' in my backyard behind my back."

"You'll have to speak to the local OSI detachment commander about that," Toni said.

"Why do I still think I've got the perp?" the chief persisted.

"Why don't we all relax?" Harry said, sitting down. "First, no one says 'perp.' You've been watching too much TV. Second, this was a professional hit, two or three shots to the back of the head with a twenty-two-caliber weapon, probably not even silenced. Third, when I scanned the area, it was clean. That doesn't mean you can't find anything, if you know how to look. Third, the body was missing a Rolex watch, which Habib had been wearing earlier in the evening."

"So you robbed him first," the chief muttered. He wasn't going to give up his prime suspect easily.

"Toni," Harry said, "call the FBI. Get them over here to explain a few facts of life to this man."

The chief snorted. "The closest FBI office is in Kansas City."

"The FBI," Harry told him, "has your town wired for sound. There are a flock of agents here and you haven't got a clue. Now to save yourself some embarrassment, you tell them how you suspect it was a mob hit just cleaning up some untidy business and that they took the watch to send a message not to screw around with their money." He held up his hands expectantly, waiting for the chief to remove the cuffs.

The chief was many things, but he wasn't stupid. There was no doubt that Harry was the consummate professional, an agent honed by years of experience and training. "And I suppose you know who did it?" He threw a set of keys to Toni to remove Harry's handcuffs.

"Well," Harry said as Toni freed him, "if your boys hadn't fucked up the crime scene, they might have been able to find something that pointed at August Ramar."

"Augy? Hey, he's rough around the edges but not that rough. He brings a lot of business to the area."

Harry shook his head. "You got problems, Chief, and you don't know it. I'm willing to help you, but you got to help us."

Toni smiled to herself as Harry turned the chief into an ally. "Shall I still call the FBI?" she asked.

"Do that," the chief said, still not totally persuaded but almost there. "Use the phone in the back office." Toni went out and made the call. As she was returning to the chief's office, she saw Ramar and a lawyer type disappear into the waiting room near the chief's office. She kept on walking down the hall and out the front entrance.

It took ten minutes for Toni to reach Harry on her cell phone after leaving the police station. "I left when I saw Ramar come in with his suit in tow," she told the OSI agent. "I don't think he saw me."

"Good thinking," Harry told her. "But Ramar never looks above a woman's neck and even if he did, he'd never recognize you with short hair." Harry put her on hold while he spoke to the chief. Then, "Ramar came in on his own accord. He claims the office was robbed."

"A convenient way to destroy evidence," Toni said.

"Right. The chief wants you to go with his men to Habib's apartment. He wants you to break the news to his wife. Her name is Diana. They're waiting for you."

"They left it for late, didn't they?"

Harry laughed. "Hey, this isn't the big show here and they are strapped for people. A cop will accompany you." He gave her Habib's address. "It'll give you a chance to interview her."

Toni had no trouble finding the Habib apartment and as Harry had promised, a young patrolman was waiting for her. They walked up to the door. It was slightly ajar and the lights were on. Toni knocked loudly. "Mrs. Habib?" No answer. She called again with the same result. The cop gave the door a nudge, and it swung open. Inside, furniture had been moved and videotapes and CDs, along with a few books, piled on the floor. "We got reasonable cause to fear for her life," Toni said as she entered the apartment. The cop keyed his radio and called for backup, explaining the situation. They quickly searched the apartment. "No signs of violence," Toni said.

"What a mess," the cop said.

Toni took one last look around. They certainly did not have cause to poke around any further without a search warrant. Then she looked at it with a woman's eye. Diana Habib had been a careful housekeeper, meticulous and clean, house proud. Nothing had been broken, only moved aside. The apartment had been selectively searched, not wantonly ransacked, by someone who cared about its contents. "She packed and left in a hurry," Toni said. "She was searching for something. I wonder if she found it."

"That doesn't make sense," the cop said. "She'd know where something was hidden in her own house."

"Not necessarily," Toni replied. "If Mohammed Habib was a standard-issue Middle Eastern male, he probably hid a lot of things from his wife." She pushed the cop outside. "We need to seal the area and wait for a technical team to get here."

"We ain't got a technical team."

"You do now. You're going to get more help than you ever wanted."

Less than an hour later, an FBI team arrived and went over the apartment with a microscope while Toni and the cop watched. One of the agents brought out a sealed evidence bag full of hundred dollar bills. "We almost missed this," he told them. "It was hidden in a wall behind the medicine cabinet in the bathroom. Most people drop things between the studs. This guy shoved it up, almost out of reach."

"This is what she was looking for," Toni said. "We really need to find her."

"It's already on the net," the FBI agent said.

10:00 A.M., WEDNESDAY, JULY 7,
WHITEMAN AIR FORCE BASE, MO.

Sutherland and Blasedale automatically stood when Col. William W. Williams entered the courtroom. The military judge was a little man with a young, almost boyish, face. His dress blue uniform had been tailored to fit his slender frame and he walked with a mincing, almost female, stride. He smiled at Sutherland and Blasedale when he sat in the deep-red leather chair behind the long bench that extended across the front of the room. The chair seemed to swallow him up. He glanced at R. Garrison Cooper, who was still sitting at the defense table opposite the jury box. It wasn't a look of disapproval or reprimand, yet it carried weight. Cooper stood up. "Good morning," Williams said. "I appreciate you being here so early on a Wednesday morning." His voice was friendly, high-pitched, and squeaky.

What have we got here? Sutherland thought. Cooper was smiling. *Cooper's already licking his chops.* Surprisingly, Blasedale seemed totally unconcerned.

Williams waved them to sit down. "Mr. Cooper, Maj. Blasedale, Capt. Sutherland, given the publicity surrounding this court-martial, I asked for your motions at this time so I would have the chance to read them and reflect with some care before ruling on them." Sutherland gave a mental sigh. William W. Williams was one of those judges who liked the sound of his own voice. "Let me warn you in advance, I wish to proceed with some efficiency in this matter and will look unfavorably upon any motion submitted with the sole purpose of disrupting proceedings during a critical and sensitive moment."

Cooper was more than a match for Williams. "Your honor, I must protest. The government has proceeded at a breakneck pace in convening this court-martial. Therefore, I must be able to respond appropriately in my client's best interests."

Williams nodded. "If you are not prepared to submit a motion at this time, I would like the time and date of anticipated submission."

"Your honor, I must protest," Cooper bellowed.

"Are you saying you are unprepared to proceed at this time?" Williams asked. "I am not aware of any request for a continuance."

Cooper snapped open his briefcase and dumped a stack of documents on the bench in front of Williams while Sutherland laid his request for a continuance on the left. The judge eyed Cooper's pile. It was an inch thick. "Really, Mr. Cooper. We do not use motions as a means of delay or harassment."

Cooper swelled up. "Your honor, these are submitted in the best interests of my client. I draw your attention to defense motion one. Critical evidence in this case relies on highly classified material, such as the mission tapes that were supposedly compromised by Capt. Jefferson. These tapes must be examined by my experts in open court or not allowed in evidence. Further—"

A flick of Williams's hand and Cooper fell silent. Sutherland noticed that Williams had long fingers and carefully manicured nails. Williams scanned the motion. When he was finished, he folded his hands over the document and stared at Cooper. They all knew what Cooper was threatening: Introduce any classified evidence that hurts my client and he will reveal every bit of secret or top secret information he knows to the public, resulting in a serious, maybe unrepairable, breach in security. "Really. Mr. Cooper," Williams said. "Hobson's choice?" Cooper gave a patronizing half-nod in answer. "Do you think we are so naïve as to be held subject to this type of legal blackmail? When examining the evidence in question, we will reconvene the court in camera to take classified testimony."

"But," Cooper replied, administering the legal coup de grace, "I do not have a security clearance."

"Really, Mr. Cooper. Capt. Edward Jordan, your Area Defense Counsel, has the necessary security clearances." The veteran defense attorney's face flushed. He started to speak, but it came out a croak. Again, the hand waved, demanding silence as he read the next petition. He sighed. "The location of the defense table, Mr. Cooper?"

"I believe it is prejudicial for Capt. Jefferson to be in direct view of the jury for the entire court-martial. Every time they look up, they will see Capt. Jefferson."

A wicked glint flickered in the judge's eyes. "For your information, in a court-martial, the jury is referred to as the panel." Cooper nodded dumbly as Williams continued. "And indeed Capt. Jefferson will be in their full view, which is exactly what I want. The panel must have the full measure of the man they are judging."

"I must protest!" Cooper bellowed in his finest courtroom style.

"No," Williams replied, his voice becoming more firm, "*I* must protest. Let me express myself in nonjudicial terms you can no doubt understand. Do not bombard this court with bullshit."

Sutherland decided he liked William W. Williams. "Anything else, Mr. Cooper?" Cooper shook his head. "Capt. Sutherland?" Sutherland was rapidly scanning Cooper's motions to see what to object to. He started to speak, more than ready to object on general grounds. Blasedale's hand touched his arm, stopping him.

"Col. Williams," she said, "we will respond at the appropriate time in the opening thirty-nine-ay." In a court-martial, a 39a session was held outside the presence of the panel.

Williams picked up his request for a continuance. "Capt. Sutherland, as to your request for a continuance—why should I grant it?" Sutherland quickly explained how late-breaking discoveries in the money trail that were relevant and necessary to the prosecution's case needed to be more thoroughly investigated. Williams folded his hands in his lap. "Has trial counsel apprised you of this investigation, Mr. Cooper?"

"Yes, sir, they have. We are ready to proceed. The prosecution—"

"It's trial counsel, Mr. Cooper, not prosecution. Please use the correct terminology in my courtroom."

Cooper blushed. "The trial counsel is only seeking time to frame a conspiracy—"

Another flick of Williams's hand and Cooper fell silent. "Save it for the press, Mr. Cooper. As to your conspiracy theory, I must warn you that I do not allow idle speculation in my courtroom. And, Mr. Cooper, I will remind you that not only do I determine the time and uniform for each session of this court-martial, but that I also ensure the dignity and decorum of the proceedings. Therefore, I will exercise final approval over spectators allowed to sit in the immediate courtroom. Any guests you have may sit in the theater with the media. This is not a circus—it is a court of law." Sutherland felt like applauding.

Cooper's mouth opened to protest, but he thought better of it. "Capt. Sutherland, as to your request for continuance. Denied." Williams cocked his head and waited a response. But Sutherland had learned his lesson and waited for the judge to continue. "My reasoning is thus," Williams said. "First, it appears the government has *not* exercised due diligence to obtain such evidence. Second, no accused may be held in pretrial arrest or confinement for more than ninety days. Capt. Jefferson has now been incarcerated for sixty-eight days. Unfortunately, I cannot release him, even to house arrest on base, for fear of his own safety. Further, I have been advised that one suspect in this case, Osmana Khalid, has escaped arrest and may have fled the country. I will not allow Capt. Jefferson the same opportunity, should he be so inclined. However, I wish to end his incarceration as soon as possible." His voice hardened. "Any such request at this late date from the government must have a substantial and compelling reason for favorable consideration. Have I made myself clear? Do not waste this court's time."

He snapped his briefcase closed, rose, and minced out of the courtroom. This time, Cooper jumped to his feet with Sutherland and Blasedale. Cooper gave Sutherland his sharklike grin. "Well, son, you certainly ate shit on that one."

Blasedale's eyes narrowed as she followed Cooper's progress out of the courtroom. "What was that all about?" she asked.

"It's a thing between me and him," Sutherland replied.

"A male macho thing?"

Sutherland grinned at her. "You bet'cha." They followed Williams through the side door and into the legal offices. Toni and Brent Mather were waiting for them in Sutherland's office. "I hope you've got some good news?" Sutherland asked. But from the look on Toni's face, he suspected the news was anything but good.

She confirmed his suspicions when she told him about Habib's murder and the disappearance of his wife. "We got a count on the money the forensic team found," Toni said. "Over twenty thousand dollars."

"We think Habib has been skimming for a long time," Mather added.

"And got caught out," Sutherland said. "But why did his wife take off? What do you know about her?"

Toni consulted her notes. "Diana Habib, maiden name Smith, is a local girl. She met Habib when he was a foreign exchange student at Central Missouri State in town. She was a waitress, a high school dropout, pretty. Habib couldn't cut it academically and was kicked out of Central Missouri—apparently it's a pretty tough school—and the only way he could keep his visa was to marry a U.S. citizen. Enter Diana who is described as red-haired, buxom, overweight, and"—she paused for effect—"is twenty-three years old."

"Do you think she might be Cassandra?" Sutherland asked. He got a shrug in answer. "We need to find her."

"We're working on it," Mather said.

"So there's no progress on Cassandra?" Toni and Mather shook their heads in unison. "Subpoena the employment records at the club. We might find something there."

"Will do," Mather said. "But I don't have much hope since it was over three years ago."

20

8:00 A.M., THURSDAY, JULY 8,
THE FARM, WESTERN VIRGINIA

Durant sat in his wheelchair near the big window overlooking his campuslike research center. It was two weeks after his heart attack and he felt amazingly good. He glanced down at the book in his lap, started to read, and then snapped the book closed. *I think, therefore I am,* he thought. *What a pile of bullshit. I do, therefore I am. So get on with it.* He spun around and looked out the window as the book fell to the floor.

Outside, the temperature was already building with the promise of another hot and humid day. *Typical for early July.* Below him, two whiz kids climbed the steps to his residence, engrossed in a deep conversation. A few moments later, Art Rios escorted them in. "Agnes, I assume," Durant said. They nodded in unison.

"We told her about your heart attack and all she's doing is medical research," the woman said.

"Can you redirect her?" Durant asked.

"We tried, but she wouldn't respond."

The phone rang and Rios picked it up. "It's Agnes," he said.

"Put her on the speaker," Durant said. "Good morning, Agnes. How are you?"

"I'm very worried about you," the computer replied. "Why haven't you had bypass surgery?"

"I'm going to immediately after we rescue the pilots."

"That's wonderful news. But don't wait too long. Please wait while I update on the Sudan. It is going to be another dreadful day, isn't it?" The two whiz kids smiled. Agnes was back on track and making small talk while she updated her intelligence files. "The Chinese have shifted their surveillance from Hurlburt to Fort Irwin in the Mojave. Apparently, they are keying on the movements of Delta Force."

"We can fix that in a heartbeat," Rios grumbled. He made a mental note to warn Delta Force. They knew how, and when, to sanitize the area.

"As for Maj. Terrant and Capt. Holloway," Agnes continued, "there is no change in their status. But the Sudanese government plans to put them on trial at the same time as Capt. Jefferson. They have already decided on the manner of execution."

"Which is?" Durant asked.

"Beheading," Agnes replied.

10:45 A.M., SATURDAY, JULY 10,
WHITEMAN AIR FORCE BASE, MO.

It was late when Blasedale checked off the last item on her legal pad and Sutherland went to the refrigerator for a beer. They had been gaming Cooper's strategy in Sutherland's VOQ suite. "Need anything?" he called from the kitchenette.

"A Diet Coke would be fine," she answered. She glanced around the room. "Are you always so neat?"

Sutherland nodded. "I used to drive my wife crazy. She said I was anal."

"That you are," Blasedale replied. "And retentive to boot." She smiled at him. "I think we've gone over everything."

"For at least the third time." He sat down, obviously worried.

Blasedale recognized the symptoms and stood behind him, massaging his shoulders. "Okay, what's bugging you?"

"I keep thinking about what The Rock said regarding Jefferson being innocent."

"Is that all?"

"No. There's a sucker punch out there just waiting for us. It's the money trail."

"I'll call Toni and see if there's progress." Blasedale made the call and turned to him. "She's on her way. You want to go over your opening remarks?" Sutherland nodded and relaxed into an overstuffed chair. Blasedale listened as he laid out their opening arguments for the panel. As with the time when they played Napoleon's Sergeant with Sgt. Scott, she was impressed with his straightforward and concise presentation. "Don't you ever use notes?" she asked. He shook his head and continued. A knock at the door stopped him in midsentence.

It was Toni. She was wearing a low-cut, cream-colored silk blouse with dark slacks. Her open-toe sandals revealed dainty feet and her necklace and earrings suggested she had been on a date. "You look nice," Blasedale said.

"Brent asked me to dinner."

Sutherland's head snapped up. "Consorting with the enemy?" he muttered.

"The FBI is on our side," Toni replied, "and we are working together now."

Blasedale watched the two interact. Toni was playing the jealousy game and Sutherland was unconsciously responding. "So what's the latest on Diana Habib?"

Toni related what they had learned about the missing woman and the latest on Sandi Jefferson. "So you think Diana might be Cassandra?" Sutherland asked. If that were true, linking Sandi into the money trail through Habib was a wild goose chase.

"We're working on that assumption," Toni replied. "I talked to Harry earlier today, and he says the murder really set off the girls. Andrea is hearing a lot of gossip at the club."

Blasedale fell silent as they talked. Toni was sending all the right signals but Sutherland wasn't in the receive mode. *That's good,* she thought. *I don't want to hit him with fraternization, but I will.* Just to be sure, she waited until they were finished and walked Toni back to her car. The night was heavy with humidity and still warm. "Do you like him that much?" Toni nodded unhappily. "Don't give the bastards half a chance," Blasedale warned. "They'll use you."

"You sound just like my brother."

Upstairs, Sutherland paced the floor. "What have I missed?" he groaned to himself.

8:50 A.M., SUNDAY, JULY 11,
WHITEMAN AIR FORCE BASE, MO.

Toni attended early Mass at the base chapel. She came out and stood on the lawn, saying hello and enjoying the freshly washed air. But she could feel the promise of another hot, muggy day. She looked around. It seemed so normal and calm, a welcome refuge from the swirling chaos outside the main gate. *What now?* she thought. She knew that Sutherland would be in the office, probably alone and catching up on some last-minute business. She sighed as she made a decision. It was time to get him off dead center. One way or the other, there was going to be movement.

When Toni walked into the legal office, it appeared deserted. But the sound of the TV in the witness waiting room drew her down the hall. Sutherland was there, alone, totally fixated on a late-breaking news story. "I knew them," he whispered. Then, more strongly, "God damn it to hell."

Toni stood next to him, almost touching, as she tried to make sense out of what she was seeing. Slowly, it all came together. A commune on California's North Coast had committed mass suicide on Saturday evening. "They seemed so normal and content," Sutherland said. "They weren't some crazy cult fixated on some screwball philosophy. They were just raising kids and tending their gardens. Marcy Bangor called them 'The Gardeners.' "

"Isn't she the reporter you were with at the San Francisco bombing?"

He nodded. The TV commentator caught their attention with the standard warning about graphic scenes about to be shown. "This video was found by the police at the scene," the commentator said. "Again, I must warn you that it is extremely disturbing and very graphic. Children should not see it and you may not want to watch."

"Then why are they showing it?" Toni asked.

"Ratings," Sutherland grumbled. "The shocking and outrageous is so routine now that they're caught up in some weird escalation." The screen flickered and a scene of the Eucalyptus grove on the cliff overlooking the ocean came into sharp focus. It was a beautiful golden red sunset like Sutherland had experienced when he was there with Marcy. But this time, the men, women, and children were standing in a long line at the very edge of the cliff. Two men walked behind them, dousing each of them with water from big watering cans used in the gardens. Then the man who had guided him and Marcy around the compound lit a big torch and walked behind the line. He touched each person with the torch and each burst into flames.

"My God," Toni whispered. "It was gasoline." She buried her face in Sutherland's chest and couldn't watch as the people fell into the sea below them, one after another, in a shower of human meteorites.

When the last person had fallen into the sea, the video froze and the camerawoman walked into view and joined the leader. With slow deliberation, they poured gasoline over each other and stepped to the edge of the cliff. The leader touched the woman with the torch and then himself. They fell into the sea together. The camera continued to run, recording the last of the sunset.

Tears streaked Toni's face and she fought for control. Sutherland held her tight, feeling her racing heart against his chest. "Why the children?" she gasped, her body shaking.

"I don't know," he answered, "I simply don't know." Slowly, she calmed and regained control.

Blasedale walked past the open door and looked at them standing there, holding on to each other. She glared at Sutherland. "I want to talk to you," she snapped. "In private." Toni broke free and ran from the room, her face still wet with tears. "What the hell is going on here?"

Sutherland gestured helplessly at the TV. For a moment, Blasedale stood there, half listening to the TV and still staring at Sutherland, demanding an answer. Then it registered. She stared at the scene as it replayed. "Oh, my God," she whispered. "Hank, you knew them, didn't you?"

"Do we ever know anybody?" he mumbled.

The base was eerily calm when Sutherland walked to the headquarters building early Monday morning. The shock of The Gardeners' flaming immolation still hung over him, and he had never felt so lethargic. *Snap out of it,* he told himself. *You've got a court-martial today.* But even that didn't help. "Damn, damn, damn," he muttered to himself as he climbed the stairs in the main foyer. He paused at the top and gazed out the big glass windows. Two security cops were raising the flag as reveille sounded. Somehow, the formal routine helped, and he walked into the legal offices feeling a little better.

Catherine Blasedale was waiting for him. "Hank, I owe you an apology from yesterday. When I walked in, I thought—"

"I know what you thought," he said, not about to let her off the hook.

"Toni is a staff sergeant and—"

"You were concerned about fraternization, right?"

She nodded. "Toni told me. Hank, I was wrong and I'm trying to apologize."

For reasons he didn't understand, he stayed angry. "Dammit, Cathy, these days men are guilty of sexual harassment any time we come around a woman." He heard himself and realized how petty he sounded. He gave a short, self-deprecating laugh. "Now I owe you an apology for sounding like an asshole."

A look he had never seen before spread across her face as the phone rang. "Hank, you're many things but never an asshole." She picked up the phone. "Legal office, Maj. Blasedale." She listened for a moment and dropped the phone in its cradle. "Well, there is some good news. It seems two federal marshals at the Kansas City airport removed one R. Garrison Cooper from an airplane this morning for being drunk and disorderly. Col. Williams has postponed the court-martial until Thursday."

Sutherland suddenly felt much better. "If that don't beat all."

Blasedale smiled. "That was the good news. The bad news is that we've got to bail him out."

"Do you think this afternoon will be soon enough?"

"Absolutely."

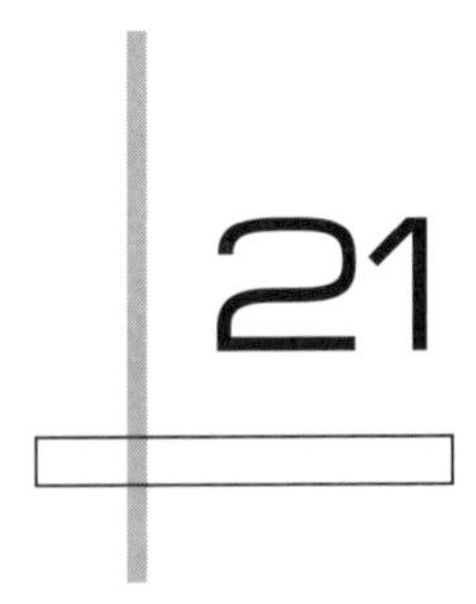

21

9:52 P.M., MONDAY, JULY 12,
THE FARM, WESTERN VIRGINIA

Durant switched off the computer and leaned back in his bed while his nurse wheeled the computer stand into a corner. "I thought the news about Cooper being dragged off the airplane was very amusing," the young man said. The evening news had been dominated by the sight of R. Garrison Cooper in custody of two serious-looking Federal Marshals.

"It did cause the court-martial to be postponed," Durant said.

The nurse cranked his bed down for sleeping. "Will that be all?" Durant nodded and the nurse dimmed the light as he left.

Durant couldn't sleep as his restless mind continued to work. "You know what you've got to do," he told himself. "So do it." He sat up and dangled his legs over the side of the bed. He stood and took a few hesitant steps before sitting in an overstuffed leather chair in the corner. "Not bad," he muttered, feeling more sure of himself.

The nurse burst back into the room. "Mr. Durant!" he protested. "What are you doing?"

"Getting my lazy ass in gear," Durant replied. Another thought came to him. "How did you know I was up?"

The nurse looked perplexed. "I got a phone call from some woman who said I should check on you."

"Agnes," Durant mumbled. "I've got to speak to her. Please have Mr. Rios and Col. Gillespie join me." The nurse looked skeptical. "Now," Durant added, ending all discussion.

* * *

Gillespie paced the floor, not certain how to respond. "Why?"

"A gut feeling," Durant told him. "The pace of events is starting to escalate."

"I like it," Rios said. "Getting the helicopters in place always takes the most lead time. This way, we keep the Chinese looking at Fort Irwin while we pre-position our helicopters at Bangui. That cuts our response time in half."

"Let me run the numbers through Agnes," Gillespie said.

"Get back to me if there's a problem," Durant said. "Then get back to Hurlburt ASAP."

Gillespie gave him a lopsided grin. "Let the games begin." He shook his head. "I can't believe I said that."

8:38 A.M., THURSDAY, JULY 15,
WHITEMAN AIR FORCE BASE, MO.

"Sir," The Rock said, "are you ready?" Capt. Bradley Jefferson nodded and stood up in his 9-by-12-foot cell. "I'll be your escort to and from the courtroom," The Rock explained. Jefferson held out his hands to be handcuffed. "No, sir. That's not necessary."

"Thank you, Sgt. Rockne." The captain hesitated for a moment. "Why?"

"Sir, there's a mob of TV reporters out there and the last time I checked, you are an officer in the United States Air Force and are innocent until proven guilty. That's a point I hope those clowns understand."

Jefferson allowed a tight smile. "To be correct, you just made two points."

The Rock's face was impassive. "Yes, sir. Shall we go?" They walked out of the confinement facility. The Rock sat in the front passenger seat and Jefferson in the rear of the patrol car for the short drive to the wing headquarters building. It had been decided to bring Jefferson in through the rear entrance off the parking lot to avoid as much of the media as possible. But the TV crews had anticipated that, and a bank of cameras recorded Jefferson's arrival. The Rock jumped out of the front seat and held the rear door while Jefferson got out. One TV cameraman tried to shove his way between the car and the entrance for a better shot. The Rock simply pointed at him and the man scurried back into the crowd. They walked into the building together.

* * *

Maj. Catherine Blasedale walked into Sutherland's office at exactly 8:45. She was wearing a beautifully tailored dress blue uniform with a short skirt that strained Air Force standards. "Stand up," she ordered. Sutherland stood and let her examine his uniform. "Look sharp for Williams. Otherwise, he'll reprimand you in a thirty-nine-ay session. You've lost weight. Good. How many hours of sleep did you get last night?"

"About three," Sutherland replied.

"That's par for the course for me," Blasedale said. They walked down the hall, turned past the judge's chambers with its closed door, and through the side door into the courtroom. The bailiff, a staff sergeant who had been detailed for the court-martial, was standing just inside. Blasedale had spent an hour coaching him on his duties and he was nervous. "Relax," she told him.

The one closed-circuit TV camera was set up inside the double doors that led out to the main corridor. The technician was more nervous than the bailiff. Williams had personally briefed him on his duties to ensure the courtroom annex in the theater saw and heard exactly what a spectator in the courtroom did.

Sutherland and Blasedale walked to the trial counsel's table and sat down. The bench was in front of them, the jury box to their left, and the defense table to their right. Behind them, twenty-nine spectators sat in silence, afraid to speak. Sandi Jefferson and R. Garrison Cooper made a grand entrance through the main doors. Cooper escorted her to the one empty seat in the front row and patted her manfully on her shoulder before coming through the bar to take his seat at the defense table. Blasedale studied Sandi's conservative dress and scribbled a note for Sutherland.

Nice outfit. Someone is coaching her.

The side door opened and Jefferson walked in alone. He shot his wife a smile and sat between Cooper and Capt. Ed Jordan.

Blasedale arranged the folders and books in front of her. Two legal briefcases were open at her feet, ready for instant access. Only a fresh legal pad and a black pen were in front of Sutherland. "Where's your *Manual for Courts-Martial?*" she asked. He only shook his head. She opened the red loose-leaf binder where she kept her guide for general courts-martial. A court-martial followed a script that was based on case law and tested to withstand appellate review. A security policeman, the evidence custodian, came in with a cardboard box. Blasedale went through the evidence and signed an inventory sheet taking custody. Because the mission's digital data cartridges and other material from the mission-planning cell were classified secret, the security policeman would stand next to the TV technician during the court-martial.

"We're ready," she said. Sutherland nodded and she spoke to the bailiff. He gestured to the security cop to close the main doors. The bailiff marched out the side door leading to the judge's chambers. He was back in a moment and came to attention. "All rise." The room was eerily silent as Col. William W. Williams came through the door. He was wearing a traditional black robe with no indication of his rank. He crossed behind the court reporter and stepped behind the long bench. As before, the deep red leather chair seemed to swallow him up when he sat down. "This Article Thirty-nine-ay session is called to order," he said. "Please be seated."

Sutherland remained standing with his hands clasped in front of him, at ease in the surroundings, ready to conduct the business of the court-martial. He spoke in a quiet and firm voice. "This court-martial is convened by general court-martial convening order AB Thirty-eight, Headquarters Eighth Air Force, dated Twenty May 1999, copies of which have been furnished the military judge, counsel, and the accused, and to the reporter for insertion at this point in the record."

Blasedale stared at him. Sutherland was reading the courts-martial guide from memory, without fault. Williams's eyes darted from his script to Sutherland to see if he was making a mistake. The court reporter worked hard to keep from smiling as her fingers danced on the keyboard of the steno machine. Blasedale shoved her guide in front of Sutherland, hoping he would at least glance at it from time to time.

"The charges," Sutherland continued, "have been properly referred to this court-martial for trial and were served on the accused on Twenty May 1999." Blasedale masked her worry as Sutherland accounted for the parties, the reporter detailed to the court-martial, and the qualifications of the prosecution and defense counsel. Again, his recitation was letter perfect. Then it was Williams's turn to speak. He dwelled on Jefferson's rights to counsel and his understanding of the single charge against him. Blasedale tensed when Sutherland came to the next phase. "Your honor," Sutherland said, "are you aware of any matter which may be a ground for challenge against you?"

"I am aware of none," Williams replied.

Blasedale popped to her feet as they had planned. "The government has no challenge for cause against the military judge."

Cooper leaned back in his chair to answer for the defense. But Jefferson's hand shot out and shoved him to his feet by his elbow. "The defense has no challenge against your honor at this time." He collapsed back into his chair, looking at Jefferson.

"For the record," Sutherland said, "The defense has stated that it has no challenge for cause against the military judge." He had put Cooper's response into the precise language required by the guide. Williams gave a little nod in acknowledgment and Blasedale relaxed as Williams covered Jefferson's options for choosing the type of court-martial.

Jefferson's voice was firm. "I choose to be tried by court-martial composed of members as determined by this court."

"The accused will now be arraigned," Williams announced.

Sutherland picked it up and continued smoothly through the arraignment. He spent some time in detailing the exact nature of the charge, espionage.

Williams paused before speaking. In less than twenty minutes, they had reached the fulcrum on which the entire system balanced and, for the next few moments, everything pivoted on Jefferson. It was the critical question that gave meaning to the system of military law. "Capt. Jefferson, how do you plead? Before receiving your pleas, I advise you that any motions to dismiss any charge or to grant other relief should be made at this time."

Cooper stood. "Your Honor, the accused requests a ruling on the motions submitted to you on Wednesday, the seventh of July."

Williams reached to one side and picked up a thin stack of papers. "Mr. Cooper, I have responded in writing to your motions. A copy will be furnished the court reporter for insertion into the record as appellate exhibit four."

Blasedale handed a copy of Williams's ruling to the court reporter, Cooper, then Sutherland. Cooper scanned through his copy and looked up in anger. "Your Honor, you have denied all of them. I must protest, this cavalier treatment—"

Williams cut him off. "Read first, Mr. Cooper. Speak later." He held up a hand for silence.

Sutherland quickly read through his pages and recalled Blasedale's comments about a military court being able to dispatch motions faster than Cooper's word processor could gin them out. Williams had denied all of Cooper's motions in a quick and decisive fashion that amounted to a jurisprudential skewering. "Why didn't you tell me Williams was a legal heavyweight," he muttered to Blasedale.

"You didn't ask," she said. She motioned toward the defense table. The veteran defense attorney's face was turning various shades of puce as he read. He stood to speak but Jefferson pulled him back down and whispered intently in his ear. Cooper shook his head in obvious disagreement. Jefferson continued to speak. Cooper came to his feet. "The defense has no other motions at this time." He paused, regaining his dignity. "Capt. Jefferson pleads not guilty to the charge of espionage."

The moment had passed.

Blasedale turned to the box and offered up the exhibits the prosecution would be entering as evidence. The process went smoothly until she pulled out the transcript and tape of the phone call between Khalid and Jefferson. Cooper was on his feet, objecting loudly, protesting that the chain of evidence had been broken in the handling of the tape. Williams listened carefully to his claims of FBI bungling and then turned to Blasedale. Her left hand dove into one of the legal briefcases at her feet and extracted a folder. "For the court," she said, "here are the original receipts tracking the disposition of the tape in question until the present moment. Please note the sworn affidavits of all custodial agents in regards to this matter."

Cooper shifted gears and went after the transcript of the tape. He was eloquent in his portrayal of the irresponsible way it had been passed between offices and from person to person. Williams let him run down and when he could not show any inaccuracies in the transcript, ruled the tape and transcript could be admitted as evidence. Cooper was outraged and challenged every remaining piece of evidence Blasedale presented. Finally, the box was empty. "Do you have any further objections?" Williams asked.

"We have no further objections at this time," Cooper said. The Article 39a session was over and Williams declared a recess until 1:30 for lunch.

"Maj. Blasedale, gentlemen," Williams said, "will you please join me in chambers?" Cooper and the ADC, Capt. Jordan, followed him out. Blasedale and Sutherland were in close trail and Sutherland was the last to enter the judge's chambers. "Please close the door," Williams said. "All future Thirty-nine-ay sessions will be conducted efficiently and stay on point," he said. "Please try to plan ahead with any motions or requests so we do not have the panel marching in and out of the courtroom like ducks at a shooting gallery." He pointed a pen at Sutherland. "You are giving me a heart attack in there. Please read the goddamn script. I don't want to lose this one on appeal because of your grandstanding."

"I thought the guide was a suggestion and not mandatory reading," Sutherland said. "Have I made a mistake?"

"Not yet," Williams replied.

At exactly 1:30 Sutherland told the bailiff they were ready and Williams entered the courtroom. Everyone stood as he walked behind the bench and took his seat. He looked at the bailiff. "Please call the members."

The bailiff disappeared out the door and quickly returned. He came to attention. "All rise," he said, just a little too loudly. Everyone but Williams and the court reporter stood. The twelve members of the court-martial who would serve as the jury filed through the door and entered the jury box. The three captains entered first, followed by the five majors, the three lieutenant colonels, and the one colonel.

"The court-martial will come to order," Williams said. "You may be seated."

Sutherland remained standing and repeated the opening statements, again from memory, never looking at Blasedale's scripted guide which was still open in front of him. But to keep Williams happy, he turned the page at exactly the right moment. "This court-martial is convened by general court-martial convening order AB Thirty-eight . . ." This time, he focused on Jefferson, trying to get a sense of the man he was attempting to send to Leavenworth for the rest of his life. "The accused and the following persons named in the convening orders are present." He listed all the names of the panel, careful to pronounce each one correctly. Then: "The prosecution is ready to proceed with the trial in the case of United States versus Capt. Bradley A. Jefferson, United States Air Force, who is present."

"The members will now be sworn," Williams said.

"All persons rise," the bailiff intoned, now at the right volume.

Sutherland turned to the panel. "Do each of you swear that you will answer truthfully the questions concerning whether you should serve as a member of this court-martial . . ." His eyes darted over the twelve officers in the jury box as he recited the oath. Three of the members were women, a captain, major, and lieutenant colonel. The youngest of them had a man's name, Michael. There were two African-Americans, both males, a major and Col. Perkins. The name triggered an association and, for a brief moment, Sutherland was back in the hospital room with Gus Perkins in Sacramento.

The members chorused "I do" when he finished reciting the oath. Sutherland silently took his own, very personal, oath. *I will not screw up and justice will be done here.*

"Please be seated," Williams said, "the court-martial is now assembled." He cleared his throat and started to speak, giving the members preliminary instructions. Sutherland relaxed in his chair, using the time to study the panel and take their measure. He had plenty of time because Williams was detailing their duties with precision. Blasedale scribbled a note and passed it to Sutherland.

Williams sees a future.

Sutherland nodded. It was true. Reputations and careers were going to be made and broken over the next few days. If Col. William W. Williams played it right, his judicial career would go far beyond the military. Sutherland focused on the panel, matching faces to the questionnaires they had filled out. Judging by the way the colonel was glaring at Jefferson, he was in a hanging mood. On cue, Sutherland was back on his feet, outlining the general nature of the charges against Jefferson. He sat down.

"I will ask you some general questions before we proceed," Williams said. Voir dire had started. "Do any of you know the accused?" Nine of the members admitted they either knew of Jefferson or had come in contact with him in the course of their duties. But none claimed a friendship or special relationship. Williams made a few notes before continuing his questioning. Satisfied, he said, "Trial counsel may ask questions."

Now it was Blasedale's turn. She stood and stepped around the prosecution table, a legal pad in her left hand. She glanced at the pad. Not for the first time, Sutherland was impressed by her poise. Her uniform was brand new, tailored to her figure, and her hair carefully arranged. Williams wasn't the only person with a future resting on the outcome of the court-martial. Then it hit him. Catherine Blasedale was a woman in her prime and, in her own way, extremely attractive. *She chooses her moments,* he thought, listening to her voice. Like Williams, her questions were directed at the group but were much more specific in nature.

Cooper lumbered to his feet when she was finished. "No questions at this time."

"The panel will now withdraw," Williams said. "Some of you may be recalled to answer specific questions. Please do not discuss the questions you have been asked, or your answers, with other members of the panel."

"All rise," the bailiff called as the panel stood and filed out of the courtroom.

"Does trial counsel or defense counsel wish to recall any members for questioning?" Williams asked.

Blasedale gave Sutherland a tight smile as she stood. "Trial counsel has no further questions at this time."

Cooper came to his feet. "Defense wishes to examine each of the members individually." He sat down. Williams's face was impassive as Col. Perkins, the senior member, was recalled. R. Garrison Cooper remained standing as the colonel entered and took a seat in the jury box. "Col. Perkins, I have little experience with court-martials or the military so I hope you'll forgive a gruff old lawyer if I say the wrong thing. Have you experienced racism of any kind, institutional or individual, during your career?"

4:16 P.M., THURSDAY, JULY 15,
SACRAMENTO, CALIF.

The computer beeped and the editor of the *Sacramento Union* scanned the late-breaking story, expecting an update on the first day of the court-martial at Whiteman Air Force Base. He grunted. It was much better. A peaceful demonstration in Los Angeles protesting Jefferson's court-martial was turning violent. So far, three police cars had been overturned and burned and tear gas had been used. He didn't hesitate and phoned Marcy Bangor at her home.

"We've got a hot one brewing," he said as he sent the story to her computer. He waited for her to read it. "The country has been sitting on a powder keg for months and this may be the fuse."

"You might want to turn on CNC-TV News," she told him.

The editor did as she asked and Meredith's face filled one of the three monitors in his office. The sound of thunderous applause blasted him when Meredith shouted, "We will protect our families and homes from the mindless violence sweeping our country!" On another screen, the President called for the country to remain calm. The editor cycled through the TV coverage coming from the different channels. Meredith's coverage beat the President's three to two. On the center screen, a CNN helicopter was airborne over the riot area as South Central Los Angeles erupted in one of its periodic spasms of violence, burning, and looting.

"I'm sending a team down there to cover it. You want to go?"

"I'm already packing."

6:37 P.M., THURSDAY, JULY 15,
WHITEMAN AIR FORCE BASE, MO.

"Have you seen the TV?" Blasedale asked when she came into Sutherland's VOQ suite. She was carrying a large pizza fresh from her oven and a six-pack of beer for a rehash of the first day in court.

"Yeah," he muttered. "L.A. is going crazy again. I hope we don't get any backwash here."

"The nice thing about small towns," she told him, "is that everybody knows everybody and that keeps people on track. The loonies need anonymity to come out of the woodwork.'' She cut the pizza and handed him a beer. ''Eat.''

He reached for a piece of pizza. ''What's your take so far?''

''Coop is halfway through the panel so he should finish tomorrow. I figure he wants to get Perkins excused so one of the white lieutenant colonels will be the presiding officer. That way, he can play the race card later on with the press.''

Sutherland shook his head. ''They can't be that stupid.'' She cocked a questioning eyebrow at him. ''Yeah, they can,'' he admitted. ''I got to give Cooper high marks, he knows how to work a jury.'' She agreed and opened a beer. For the next hour, they nitpicked the panel's reaction to Cooper's questioning. It was the self-flagellation trial lawyers had perfected to a high art in a futile attempt to get inside a jury's mind. She waited until he was on his second beer and a bit mellow before discussing her strategy.

''I want to kick Capt. Knight off the panel.''

It was his turn to cock an eyebrow. He decided she did it better when she laughed at him. ''The pudgy captain in the back row,'' he said, identifying the officer.

''That's him. He's a social actions officer, and I think he's the one most likely to see this in racial terms. Social Actions officers tend to be the bleeding hearts of the Air Force. I suppose it goes with their job, dealing with minorities and discrimination and all. You see the same thing in social workers who end up being advocates for their people.''

''So you think he'll vote for acquittal simply because Jefferson is black?'' She nodded. ''It's your voir dire. Go for it. Let Coop ask all the questions and use our peremptory so it won't be too obvious why he got kicked off.''

He reached for another piece of pizza. ''I wish I could get a handle on Jefferson,'' Sutherland said. ''He's an unknown quantity, a cipher. I was concentrating mostly on Col. Perkins, but I caught Jefferson smiling when Perkins got testy in response to Coop's questioning.''

Before Blasedale could answer, the phone rang. It was Toni and he put her on the speaker phone. ''The FBI found Diana Habib,'' Toni told them.

''Where?'' they both said in unison.

''New Orleans. She's booked on a flight to Brazil tomorrow afternoon.''

''Can you get down there and interview her?'' Sutherland asked.

''We're halfway there.''

''Where are you?'' Sutherland asked.

"Adams Field at Little Rock. We should be in New Orleans in about three hours. Brent's refueling while I file the flight plan." Sutherland stifled his reaction to the mention of Brent Mather. "I rented a Cessna out of Skyhaven at Warrensburg," Toni explained. "Nice airplane."

Now the pieces came together and Sutherland made a croaking sound. He had a well-developed dislike for light aircraft. "I didn't know you were a pilot."

"It's something I do," she answered. "I love flying and it comes in handy. I hope you're going to sign the voucher and not make me pay for it."

11:45 A.M., FRIDAY, JULY 16,
EL OBEID, THE SUDAN

Kamigami pushed his way through the mass of humanity swirling around the mosque. Friday always brought out a large number since it was the Islamic sabbath, but this crowd was different, more tense and edgy. He made his way along the wall, searching for the beggar who was his contact. But he was not there. Rather than linger and draw attention, Kamigami passed out coins to a few of the more pathetic specimens hunkered down with their hands out and headed back for his Range Rover.

The call to prayer sounded from a minaret. As usual, the *muezzin*'s chant was tape-recorded and amplified through loudspeakers. A sixth sense warned him that he was being watched. Hard experience in combat had taught him not to ignore it, and he joined the men streaming into the mosque. He wasn't worried because he knew the routine and, although he was the only Asian, the Islamic religion tended to be very cosmopolitan. He stopped at the fountain and washed his hands and feet as ritual prescribed before going inside. He joined a long row of men that faced the *mihrab,* the niche in the wall that indicated the direction of Mecca.

He could feel the electricity in the crowd as the time approached for the sermon. Kamigami tensed when he saw Jamil bin Assam mount the pulpit. Instead of the general's uniform Assam preferred, he was barefoot and wearing a two-tone gold robe. Because there is no clergy in Islam and all worshipers have the same relationship with God, anyone can give the sermon. But by tradition, it is reserved for *imams,* or spiritual, leaders. Jamil bin Assam was not an *imam* nor spiritual, and his presence meant trouble. It wasn't long in coming.

Although Kamigami's Arabic was very limited, he caught enough of the words to understand that Assam was raising the call against foreigners. He kept repeating the word *jihad* until it rang like a bell over the mosque. The hard looks turned in Kamigami's direction confirmed that Assam's message had found a receptive audience. The crowd was on its feet, surging toward the entrance, and taking everyone with it. Resistance was futile and the last thing Kamigami wanted was to seem different.

Outside, he was pushed and shoved as the shouting grew louder. He tried to force his way through the crowd, chanting "God is great, God is merciful," in Arabic. It didn't work and the mob pushed back, forcing him into the main square. Now blows were raining down on him. "Death to Americans!" a man shouted in English.

"I'm from Malaysia," he shouted in Malay, then French, then Cantonese, anything but English. The men around him jeered and continued to pound him. Kamigami was a big man and weighed over 250 pounds. He had spent most of his adult life as a professional soldier and knew how to fight. He also knew he was going down. He roared in anger. It was a war cry, the rage of a samurai, and, for a moment, the mob froze and backed off. He was alone in a small circle.

A man stepped out of the mob holding a short sword. Kamigami and his executioner stared at each other. The man held the sword in front of him with both hands and pointed it at Kamigami while he chanted the *shahada.* "God is great. God is great. I testify that there is no god but God." Kamigami crouched on one knee as the man repeated the litany, sensing he would charge when the chant was finished. The man raised the sword above his head.

A horn blared and a truck barreled into the crowd, diverting the executioner's attention. Four soldiers piled out of the truck, all carrying AK-47s. The crowd screamed for Kamigami's head. The men raised their weapons and drew down on him and Kamigami knew he was dead. A white Range Rover sped up behind the soldiers and slammed to a stop. A tall figure wearing the silver tans of an officer stepped out into the swirling dust. It was Capt. Davig al Gimlas. He walked past his soldiers and headed straight for Kamigami. "You Americans do cause me trouble."

"It's pretty bad when a man can't even pray in peace," Kamigami said.

"You can pray on the way to Khartoum," al Gimlas replied. "You're taking the pilots there on General Assam's plane."

"When?"

"Whenever Assam decides to leave."

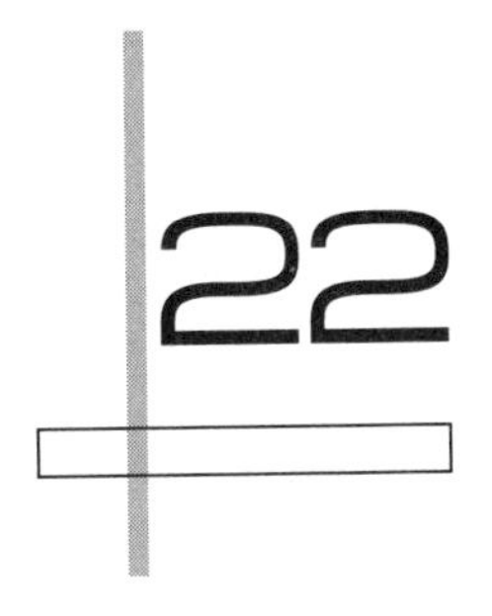

4:00 A.M., FRIDAY, JULY 16,
THE FARM, WESTERN VIRGINIA

The ringing phone woke Art Rios from a sound sleep. "Mr. Rios, this is Agnes. You need to tell Mr. Durant that the Sudanese are going to move the pilots to Khartoum for a trial."

"Damn," Rios muttered. "We're too late."

"Maybe not," Agnes replied. "Please have Mr. Durant call me. He does have direct access to the President, doesn't he?"

5:07 A.M., FRIDAY, JULY 16,
HURLBURT FIELD, FLA.

The order for Gillespie's team to deploy came down an hour later. The command post made two phone calls, one to the 20th SOS and one to the DCC, the deployment control center. Within thirty minutes, the DCC was set up and operational, ready to process the deploying aircrews and support people. While the DCC was going through its drill, the 20th notified the troops who would be going. On the surface, it was a routine duty day. Deployments were such a normal part of the 16th Special Operations Wing's business that they made the complex and difficult task look simple.

Four hours later, the advon team, the advanced command and control group who would precede the main force and the Pave Low helicopters, were airborne on an HC-130P and headed across the Atlantic. Only an astute observer could distinguish the HC-130P, which had been modified for inflight refueling of helicopters, from a normal

C-130. Its arrival at Bangui would excite little attention. But it would be a far different matter for the C-5B Galaxy transports bringing in the main force. Consequently, the C-5s were scheduled to arrive during the night when darkness would provide some cover.

Lt. Col. Gillespie floated like a duck on the calm surface as his contingent deployed. But underneath, he was paddling like mad to stay afloat. The plan called for six helicopters, four primary and two backup. But he was going to get only four. The 20th had the helicopters, but budget cuts and lack of modernization had cut into the Air Force's airlift fleet. He was only going to get two C-5s instead of the three he needed. Gillespie had to live with the dilemma of most commanders: his political masters were not giving him the wherewithal to do his job. But at the same time, they expected the 20th to do as much as ever. The old joke about being able to do more and more with less and less until they could do everything with nothing had ceased to be funny.

Capt. Lee Harold, Gillespie's second in command for the operation, stormed into his office. "Four Pave Lows? Do those shit-for-brains know what two birds do to the numbers?" The so-called *numbers* were the product of hard experience and quantified the probability of success. "So who's gonna raise the bullshit flag?"

Gillespie ran his hand through his red hair. "I ran it up the flagpole an hour ago. They hear it. But who's gonna say *no?*"

"Situation normal," Harold grumbled. He omitted the "all fucked up."

"How's the prep coming?" Gillespie asked.

"The Pave Hogs are ready. Blades and transmissions off, tails folded. We can stuff them on board as soon as the C-5s land—if they're in commission." Another fact of life was the age of the C-5s. The Galaxy was getting difficult in its old age and broke down with ever-increasing frequency. Unfortunately, there were not enough of the newer C-17 Globemaster III's to meet airlift requirements. "Son of a bitch," Harold groaned. "It seems like we're unwanted stepchildren."

"Until they need something done," Gillespie allowed. He allowed a tight smile. A little bitching and moaning went with the territory and was good for the troops.

The phone rang and Harold fell silent as Gillespie answered. He hung up. "Two C-5s are inbound and will be on the ground in fifteen minutes. Both are in commission and good to go." He stood up, ready to leave.

"Maybe we make it look too easy," Harold said.

"Without a doubt."

10:00 A.M., FRIDAY, JULY 16,
WHITEMAN AIR FORCE BASE, MO.

Sutherland made a show of checking his watch hoping Williams would take the hint and declare a recess. They were still locked in voir dire as Cooper relentless grilled the tenth panel member. A note from Blasedale.

Break?

Sutherland nodded and came to his feet during one of Cooper's ponderous pauses. "Your Honor, may we take a short break?" He received a grateful look from the spectators as Williams declared a fifteen-minute recess.

Cooper made a show of walking over to Sandi Jefferson and comforting her. Since she was sitting directly behind the trial counsel table, Blasedale was acutely aware of Cooper's presence. He deliberately banged against Blasedale's chair, forcing her to move. Rather than contend with him, Blasedale walked across the room. Sandi was whispering furiously in Cooper's ear and her eyes kept darting to the trial counsel's table. *She's reading our notes,* Blasedale thought. *That's a mistake.* The recess was over.

Cooper resumed his questioning and finally declared he was finished with the captain. As trial counsel, Sutherland called the eleventh member, also a captain. Again, Cooper went through his litany of questions, probing the captain's reaction to hypothetical situations. While it was beyond the normal scope of voir dire, Blasedale let him ramble on. Finally, Cooper announced he had no further questions. Only Capt. Knight, the social actions officer, remained.

Blasedale scribbled a note on her legal pad:

Knight may be a racist.
Do we want to keep him?

She pushed it over to Sutherland and waited. She was certain that Sandi Jefferson was reading it. Sutherland gave Blasedale a questioning look, wondering what she was talking about. He jotted down an answer and shoved the pad back to her.

If that's true, it will look better if you bring it out.

Blasedale canted her head enough to see Sandi Jefferson make a hand motion. On cue, Cooper called for another short recess and again came over to speak to Sandi. Blasedale moved away as before and watched as she whispered to him. The recess was over and Blasedale remained standing while Williams reconvened the court.

She called for Capt. Knight and Cooper walked around to lean against the front of the defense table. But as trial counsel, Blasedale went first. "Your Honor, the government has two questions for Capt. Knight." Williams told her to proceed. "Capt. Knight, have you ever used the word *nigger?*"

Cooper's head jerked up, his heavy mane of hair flying. Capt. Knight looked confused. "Why, ah, ah, yes," he finally stammered. He looked like he needed to visit the men's room.

"When was the last time?" Blasedale asked.

"Ah, ah, yesterday."

"Thank you, Captain Knight. No further questions." She sat down.

Cooper swelled, his chest expanding. "Your Honor, I too have no further questions."

Capt. Jordan, the ADC, rose to his feet to intervene but Blasedale cut him off at the knees. "Need I remind the court of 'one counsel, one issue'?" Williams told Jordan to sit down and excused Capt. Knight. The ADC was writing furiously, trying to get a note to Cooper. But Cooper ignored him. No sooner had the door closed behind Knight when Cooper said, "Excuse Capt. Knight for cause."

Williams studied Cooper over his reading glasses. "You may enter a challenge for cause after trial counsel enters its challenges."

"Your Honor," Cooper said ignoring the note the ADC had shoved to the front of the table. "Capt. Knight's admission contaminates these proceedings and he should be removed instantly." A quiet murmur from the spectators indicated they agreed with him.

Williams silenced them with a single look. "I will consider your challenge in due course," Williams said, expecting Cooper to sit down. The spectators were in shock and the courtroom was absolutely silent. The ten reporters who had drawn the lucky numbers to sit in the room and not the theater were furiously making notes.

Cooper couldn't help himself. His well-developed sense of the theatrical was so much a part of his personality that he couldn't shut it off, with or without a jury as an audience. "Your Honor!" he bellowed in outrage.

"Lower your voice, Mr. Cooper."

"Your Honor, since you refuse to consider a challenge for cause, perhaps you'll allow a peremptory challenge at this time."

Williams removed his glasses. "Against Capt. Knight?"

"That is correct."

"The timing of your request is most unusual, Mr. Cooper. We are not in the business of making case law."

"This is a procedural issue, Your Honor, not a question of case law."

"Indeed, you are correct. Capt. Knight will be excused. However, I will note for the record that being excused does not reflect on him personally or professionally in any way."

"Your Honor," Cooper said, his oratory matching his indignant, but simulated outrage, "this man admitted to using that loathsome, odious, repulsive word, the hallmark of the bigoted and—"

Williams raised his voice, cutting Cooper off. "Enough. We get your point." He consulted his notes. "For the record, Capt. Knight is a social actions officer and deals with racism and bigotry every day. If you had questioned him, or reviewed his questionnaire with some care, you would have learned that his duties require him to deal with the use of the word you so strenuously object to. Further, if you had listened to your associate defense counsel it would have been drawn to your attention. But it is not for me to question the use of the one peremptory challenge allowed the defense. You, Mr. Cooper, forced the issue."

Sutherland did a classic double-take. Jefferson was smiling at Cooper's embarrassment. As quickly as it came, the smile was gone. *Who else saw it?* he wondered.

Cooper stood there, his right hand knotted in a fist. In preparing for trial, he had not thoroughly read the *Manual for Courts-Martial,* which allowed the prosecution and the defense only one peremptory challenge apiece. Blasedale had sensed it and used Sandi Jefferson to draw first blood. Slowly, Cooper turned and faced her. She returned his gaze without blinking.

"Your Honor," Cooper begged, "may we recess until after lunch?"

"We are in recess until 1300 this afternoon," Williams said. He rose. "Maj. Blasedale, please join me in chambers." He marched out of the room.

Blasedale followed him, passing Cooper who was still standing. "You do like eating shit," she murmured. His gaze drilled holes in her back as she walked out of the courtroom.

"Please close the door," Williams said when she stepped inside his office. He carefully hung up his robe before sitting down. "Cathy, what in hell do you think you're doing out there?"

"Turning that asshole into a decent advocate."

R. Garrison Cooper was waiting in Williams's chambers when the judge returned from lunch. "Your Honor, may I speak to you *ex parte?*"

Williams gave him a long look. "Does it concern the court-martial or a personal matter?"

Cooper gritted his teeth. "Both, sir."

Williams gave him a pleasant smile. "Come in while I call Maj. Blasedale and Capt. Sutherland." He picked up the phone.

"But you spoke to her *ex parte,*" Cooper bleated.

"It concerned her personal conduct and was in no way prejudicial to Capt. Jefferson. In fact, it was the exact opposite." He asked for Blasedale and Sutherland to join him. The two officers rushed in and sat quietly against the back wall. "Please proceed," he said.

Cooper sat down. "Sir, I made a terrible mistake this morning because of my ignorance and pride." Williams nodded, urging him to continue. He liked seeing lawyers eat humble pie, especially in front of other lawyers. "Because of my rash conduct," Cooper muttered, "I acted in a manner prejudicial to my client."

Williams played it for Sutherland and Blasedale. "Garrison, for once quit sounding like a cheap suit and come right out and say it. 'I fucked up and threw my one peremptory challenge away because I hadn't done my homework and liked the sound of my own voice.' Well, I am not going to restore your peremptory. But, I am concerned with the rights of the accused—" He paused for emphasis.

Cooper misinterpreted the pause. "Sir, Capt. Jefferson is the victim of a conspiracy."

Sutherland snorted. "Give it a rest."

"We've been over this before," Williams snapped. "Do not raise a frivolous defense in my court."

Cooper couldn't help himself and he reverted to the theatrics that had become his second nature. "I can feel it in the air. I can sense it. This case reeks of it." Sutherland allowed a tight smile but said nothing.

Williams shook his head. "However, you have no proof. As I was saying, I am concerned that Capt. Jefferson receive a fair and impartial trial. I will allow you a great deal of latitude on challenges. But you've got to make the record. I am perfectly willing to excuse every member for cause. There are approximately sixty thousand officers in the Air Force between the rank of captain and colonel who can serve on this court-martial and, if necessary, you can examine every one of them. But I assure you, if you cannot find at least five, I can."

Cooper nodded. It was going to be a long day.

1:40 P.M., FRIDAY, JULY 16,
MOISANT FIELD, NEW ORLEANS

"You're a good pilot," Brent Mather said, making light conversation as they waited outside passport control at the New Orleans international airport. "Where did you learn to fly?"

"At the aero club at McClellan Air Force Base," Toni answered. "It's the best aero club in the Air Force. Too bad they're closing the base next year." She came alert. "There. That's her." Toni walked quickly toward a disheveled-looking young woman dragging a recalcitrant two-year-old boy down the concourse. "Mrs. Habib," she called. The woman stopped and looked at her. "I'm Special Agent Moreno with the OSI," she said, showing her identification, "and this is Agent Mather from the FBI. We would like to talk to you."

The woman shook her head. "I haven't got time to talk to you. I've got to catch a flight."

"This will only take a few moments, Mrs. Habib," Toni soothed. "You've got plenty of time, and we'll escort you to the head of the line. You won't miss your airplane."

"I don't have to talk to you. I ain't done nothin'." She grabbed the boy and walked past them.

"Let her go," Mather cautioned. "We haven't got any reason to hold her."

"She's a material witness," Toni said.

"A material witness to what?"

Toni chewed her lip. The FBI agent was right. But some instinct warned her that Diana Habib was deeply involved. In exactly what way, she didn't know. She made a decision, wishing Harry was there. "I can't arrest her. You can."

"Give me a reason."

"As a co-conspirator."

"To her husband's murder?"

"No. To espionage."

Mather handed her his handcuffs. "We're probably going to need these. I hope you know what you're doing."

12:08 P.M., FRIDAY, JULY 16,
LOS ANGELES

The chartered Piper Saratoga crossed the Santa Monica Pier at twelve thousand feet and spiraled down over the airport. Marcy Bangor sat in the right seat next to the pilot, not believing her eyes. Columns of smoke rose high into the air over the center of Los Angeles, splitting the gut of the city from groin to sternum. It stretched from the harbor area in the south and ran north, past the Watts-Willowbrook area, through South Central L.A., and into Hollywood. At the base of the smoke curtain, a stage of fire sparkled in the morning sun.

Behind her in the cabin, the other three reporters from the *Sacra-*

mento Union sat in stunned silence. "Can we fly over there?" Marcy asked.

"No way," the pilot answered. He increased his rate of descent as he passed through five thousand feet and SOCAL Approach cleared him to contact the tower at Santa Monica airport.

"Good luck," the controller said.

"Encouraging bastard," the pilot grumbled as he switched frequencies.

Marcy spoke into her microcassette recorder. "Landed Friday, July sixteen, at twelve-fourteen A.M. after uneventful flight from Sacramento. Spiraling down above Santa Monica airport to land. I can see fires in South Central L.A. All appears calm below us."

But the pilot was of a different opinion and swore at himself for accepting the charter and leaving the friendly skies of Sacramento. The *Union*'s publisher had kept increasing the money and he had weakened. He dropped the gear and flaps and touched down at midfield. He taxied clear of the runway and parked by the Museum of Flying. Marcy climbed out of the door and scrambled down the right wing. She caught her breath when she saw the hole punched in the flap. "Gunfire?"

The pilot examined the damage with his forefinger. "Shit-fuck-hate! I should have never taken this flight." The bullet had missed the main fuselage by less than eight inches.

Two very nervous young men, both African-American, were waiting inside the flight operations office. "Miss Bangor?" the older asked. She nodded. "I'm Jason, your escort. Richard is our driver." Marcy followed them out to a waiting van, leaving the three other reporters behind to fend for themselves.

"Where are we going?" she asked.

"The Wilton Country Club," Richard answered. "Sunset Boulevard is probably the safest way to get there."

At first, Marcy was struck by how normal everything seemed. Then she realized there were very few cars on the road. They made good time as they headed east on Sunset, past UCLA and Beverly Hills. At Doheney Drive, they hit their first roadblock. Two clean-cut young white men in short-sleeved white shirts and conservative neckties waved them to a stop. Marcy checked the reserve deputy sheriff badges pinned to their pockets as she flashed her press card. Within seconds, they were cleared through. "Be careful," one said. "We've reports of looting."

They drove in silence as Marcy continued to speak into her microcassette. "The transition from the quiet residential homes into the heart of the strip is abrupt. We're passing the cultural icons of the 1990s, the new Whiskey A-Go-Go, the House of—"

"Trouble," Jason, her other escort, said, interrupting her note taking. He pulled over to the curb. Ahead of them a group of teenagers were blocking the street. "Sometimes I despair for my brothers," he moaned. For some reason, the teenagers dispersed and moved on, shouting and gesturing at the van.

Richard slipped the van back in gear, drove past, and took a side street over to Melrose Boulevard. "Check the roofs," the driver said. Marcy looked up. Armed young men, all Asians, were standing guard. "Koreans," Jason said. "Nobody messes with their businesses, especially their new ones in this part of town."

At first, Marcy couldn't believe the scene in front of her. She spoke into her microcassette. "Scenes of normal life play out in front of the escalating chaos sweeping out of the heart of the city. Korean-American merchants are standing guard on the rooftops of their stores while people drink coffee at sidewalk cafés below them." She fished her digital camera out of her bag, slipped in a fresh card, and recorded the scene. Later, she would edit the digital images and transmit the best ones over her cellular phone to the *Union.*

The pall of smoke grew heavier as they approached the Wilton Country Club. Four heavily armed guards at the entrance carefully checked their credentials before waving the van in. She was surprised to see golfers on the course. "They're still making their tee times," Jason explained. She shot four frames of the golfers, surprised that almost half were African-American.

Inside, she was escorted to a private dining room where approximately twenty men were gathering for lunch. The group was evenly divided between African-American, Anglo, Asian, and Hispanic men. Marcy knew most of them by reputation. They were the power brokers behind Los Angeles politics and other than the waitresses, she was the only woman in the room. Their acknowledged leader, a rumpled, portly, gray-headed African-American wearing a cleric's collar, known simply as "the Reverend" stood to greet her. "Please, Miss Bangor," the Reverend said, "this is off the record. Would you please join us for lunch?"

She sat down and bowed her head as the Reverend gave the blessing. She made a mental note comparing the group to a Rotary or Kiwanis meeting, not a convocation of the most powerful leaders in the city. "Miss Bangor," the Reverend said, "your publisher at the *Union* and I are old friends and you come with the highest recommendations. That is the only reason you are here."

Don't look a gift horse in the mouth, Marcy thought. "Reverend, on the record, is this riot in reaction to the Jefferson court-martial?"

"The community has been antagonized beyond endurance, Miss Bangor, and this rioting is a reaction to many things: the blockading of our homes into ghettos by Meredith's stooges, the lynching in Phoenix of an innocent mother, the stonings. Must I go on? For my brothers and sisters the court-martial of Capt. Jefferson is white man's justice where the color of a man's skin determines guilt or innocence."

"But what if he is guilty?" Marcy asked.

"No, Miss Bangor, he is not guilty, even if he did sell information to the so-called enemy. He was entitled to that money as is every person of color for past injustices that have yet to be made right."

The waiters then served the first course of the sumptuous lunch and the talk turned to golf. As the table was being cleared, eight men barged into the room, all wearing the characteristic baggy clothes of street gangs. Six of them were armed with Uzis and AK-47s. One cradled a light machine gun Rambo-style in his arms. The Reverend came to his feet with a heavy dignity. "You are not welcome here," he said.

"Yo, bro," the smaller of the two leaders growled, "nobody be tellin' us who welcome."

"Miss Bangor," the Reverend said, "will you please give us a few moments of privacy?" One of the Reverend's dark-suited aides touched her shoulder and pulled her chair back as she stood. She walked past the intruders and struggled to keep her composure when she saw their headbands. Red and blue bandanas, the colors of the Bloods and Crips, were twisted together. The aide escorted her out to the lobby, well-out of earshot.

"Who's the bitch?" the gang leader demanded.

"A reporter I want to be here," the Reverend answered.

"The bitch make one mistake and she dead."

"No," the Reverend commanded. "The press is a factor we cannot ignore. For that reason, she is under my protection. Get the word out to leave her alone." The gang leader snorted in contempt, but he would do it. "I hope you come in peace," the Reverend continued.

"This ain't about peace," the leader said.

"Please educate me," the Reverend replied.

"It ain't a Crip thing or a Blood thing—it's a black thing."

"Is that what the bandanas represent?" The Reverend held up a hand, silencing any reply as waiters brought in the main course and rapidly left. The Reverend cut a small morsel. "We are willing to let this run its course," he said. "But we must establish some rules."

"No dogs, no National Guard," the leader said.

"Then you must contain the looting," the Reverend told them. "You must not burn churches. Stores are acceptable as long as you stay out of New Korea Town in Hollywood. You must not go beyond Hawthorne Boulevard and La Cienega on the west. You may go as far east as the Los Angeles River, but no further. Of course, this establishment must remain off limits."

The gang leader sat down at Marcy's place and helped himself to her lunch as they negotiated a war zone about twice the size of the smoking area Marcy had seen on landing at Santa Monica.

"How long we got?" the leader said.

"Three days," the Reverend said. "It ends Sunday night."

"Four days," the gang leader answered.

"Four days and it's out of my hands," the Reverend said.

The leader pushed his chair back and stood. His face was cold, impassive hatred. "It's already out of your hands." He spun around and marched out of the dining room, his men in close trail.

"We have a deal," the Reverend said.

"But won't the governor call in the National Guard?" one of the civic leaders asked.

"The governor is a realist," the Reverend replied.

Marcy was standing in the foyer near the main entrance when the two gang leaders and their bodyguards came out. She followed them out to the parking lot. "Excuse me," she called. "Is this because of the Jefferson court-martial?"

"It's about justice," the leader answered.

"It's about killing whitey," one his bodyguards shouted.

3:10 P.M., FRIDAY, JULY 16,
WHITEMAN AIR FORCE BASE, MO.

R. Garrison Cooper stood beside the seated Jefferson and placed a hand on his shoulder. It was only the second day of the court-martial, and Cooper needed a drink. For a moment, he reread his notes on the four men and two women remaining on the panel. It was decision time. The jury consultant he had brought in scribbled a note and passed it along. She wanted to dismiss one of the women. As Williams had promised, he was very liberal in dismissing for cause, and Cooper had barely to open his mouth to get a member excused.

It was too easy and Cooper came to the inevitable conclusion Williams knew he would reach. The system had selected the jury years before. No matter how many he removed, he was going to end up with a panel of educated, responsible, professional officers who could think. From Cooper's perspective, it was the worst of all possible juries. Further, the body language coming from the spectators was hostile. He had antagonized them with his dismissal of Capt. Knight. It angered him how easily Blasedale had set him up, and he made a mental promise to even the score. But that would have to wait. He allowed a mental sigh; now he had to repair the damage. "Your Honor, we have no further challenges. I am aware that this has been a difficult and tedious voir dire and I wish to thank the court for its attention and patience. We are more than satisfied that this panel can, and will, render a fair verdict."

The court-martial was formed and ready to proceed. Williams declared a recess until Monday morning. "I am satisfied," Jefferson said in a low voice. He rose and walked unescorted to the side door where The Rock was waiting for him.

Sutherland and Blasedale heard Jefferson's remark. "He believes in the system," Sutherland said.

"Then he may be a fool," Blasedale groused.

"What is that supposed to mean?"

She shook her head. "Nothing. I'm tired." She gathered up an armful of folders and books. Sutherland followed her into the legal offices carrying her two stuffed briefcases. Linda was being her usual superefficient self and was waiting for them. "Call Agent Moreno in New Orleans." She handed Sutherland a message. He dialed the number from his office phone and put it on the speaker for Blasedale to hear.

Toni answered on the first ring. Her voice was strained and tired. "I had the FBI arrest Habib," she said, "to keep her from leaving the country."

"On what charge?" Sutherland asked.

"As a co-conspirator to espionage."

"Toni," Blasedale said, "there's not a shred of evidence to support that."

"I know." They could hear panic in her voice. "So does the FBI. They're going to let her go. Brent says we're in big trouble if she claims wrongful imprisonment."

Sutherland thought for a moment. "But she doesn't know that. Try to cut a deal with her. Tell her the FBI will get the Department of Justice to offer her immunity if she cooperates with us."

"But what if she's not guilty of anything?" Toni replied.

"We're all guilty," Sutherland said, "or think we are."

"Will the FBI go along with that?" Blasedale asked.

Sutherland made his voice upbeat and positive. "Sure, why not?

One of their boys screwed up by arresting her and now they got to cover their backside. Give her the VIP treatment, put her up in classy hotel, stroke her ego, become her friend, while the FBI jumps through the hoops with DOJ. If it all falls apart, put her on the plane Monday and the problem flies away." Toni said she'd give it a try and broke the connection.

Sutherland shook his head. "She really screwed up."

"She's young and inexperienced," Blasedale said. "It happens to all of us."

"Surely," Sutherland's face was deadpan, "not you."

"My first time out as trial counsel, I was a lieutenant, all alone, and they threw me to the wolves. It was a simple case—a drug dealer we finally nailed on aggravated assault. It should have been a breeze but the defense counsel made a run against the victim, a young, pretty, brainless little thing. Before I knew what had happened, he had her admitting to things that had nothing to do with the case. Suddenly, she's on trial and the evidence is so muddied that no one could sort it out. I didn't even have enough sense to call for a mistrial."

"The judge would have never done that," Sutherland said, letting her off the hook a little. "Mistrials are to protect the defendant, not our side."

She nodded. "That bastard walked. The military judge called me in afterward. All he said was, 'Don't let that happen again.' " Blasedale stared at her hands. "It didn't."

Sutherland knew what those two simple words meant. Blasedale had sacrificed her personal life to ensure it never would occur again. How many hours had she spent in preparation, reading, and going over trial records? "Is that why you hate men?" he asked.

Blasedale looked at him, surprise on her face. "I don't hate men. Just that one bastard defense counsel. Strange enough, he may have been the best teacher I ever had."

"The courtroom is a tough classroom," Sutherland said. "Come on, we've got work to do."

Two hours later, Toni called back. "She bought it! But she wants full immunity."

Sutherland tried to sound jubilant for Toni's sake. But he was worried. Diana Habib might tie the money trail directly to Jefferson but they might be giving her a get-out-of-jail-free card. "You may have found the smoking gun."

"Is the FBI going along?" Blasedale asked.

"Yes, yes, yes," Toni sang. "But she is one shrewd lady and is dangling bits and pieces until she sees the offer in writing. She is Cassandra and met Habib while dancing at the club. When he flunked out of Central Missouri State, he lost his student visa. She was his green card to stay in the States. And there's more. She also worked part-time at the Base Exchange on Whiteman. She continued to work there after she married but never bothered to change her name."

"Keep on it," Sutherland said before he hung up. He sank back into his chair and dangled the dead receiver from its cord. "Holy shit."

"Why does it always hit the fan just before quitting time on Friday afternoons?" Blasedale muttered.

"It's an immutable law of nature."

9:00 A.M., SATURDAY, JULY 17,
THE WHITE HOUSE, WASHINGTON, D.C.

Art Rios pushed the wheelchair into the Oval Office and quickly withdrew. The last thing he saw as he closed the door was the President standing as his staff clustered around Durant.

"Nelson," the President said, "I can't tell you how much we appreciate your joining us. Needless to say, we are deeply worried about the crisis in Los Angeles, and we need every bit of advice we can get."

The acerbic National Security Advisor, Stephan Serick, humphed for attention. "The riot appears to be contained." He passed around a small map of Los Angeles with the area outlined in red. "The governor refuses to call out the National Guard because of reports questioning the reliability of many of the units. They are demanding to stay in place and guard their hometowns. Meredith's influence, no doubt."

"How are the L.A. police doing?" Durant asked. He knew the correct answer but wanted to hear it from Serick.

"We have reports that the police are being reinforced by elements of Meredith's First Brigade," Serick replied.

"Is that legal?" This from the domestic affairs adviser.

The Attorney General answered. "As long as they are sworn in as deputies."

Durant folded his hands in his lap and listened as the discussion went around the room. Finally, the President asked him for his thoughts. "The court-martial at Whiteman was only the spark that ignited the violence," Durant replied. "It has turned into a gang-driven riot and should burn itself out Sunday night—without the National Guard intervening."

"Thank God," the domestic affairs adviser said.

"Thank Meredith's First Brigade," Durant said. "He's the one who is going to benefit from it." For once, the President's staff agreed with him.

"There's another problem," Durant said. "Maj. Terrant and Capt. Holloway are going to be moved to Khartoum for trial. A rescue is still possible if we act now."

From the look on the President's face, the fate of the two pilots was the least of his worries. "Why do I get the feeling this is too rushed? We can't afford a botched rescue on top of everything else."

"We are ready to go," Durant said. "And we still have a window of opportunity."

The President gestured at his National Security Advisor. "Stephan?"

Serick looked pleased. "Any action now in regards to the hostages would be counterproductive. Put everything on hold."

The President nodded in agreement.

9:30 A.M., SATURDAY, JULY 17,
WHITEMAN AIR FORCE BASE, MO.

Sutherland jogged through base housing, enjoying the early-morning activity. The temperature and humidity had not started to build and cars were being washed and lawns mowed. It was a peaceful image of middle-class America on a summer weekend. *What a contrast,* he thought, recalling the vivid images on TV of the madness sweeping Los Angeles. But his overriding image was of Meredith calling for strength and resolve. He picked up the pace, missing Toni's companionship on his daily runs. Still, he felt good. *Be honest, this is the best I've felt in years.* He reached Spirit Boulevard and headed for the main gate.

When he reached the guard shack, he could see the protesters and their signs that had become a permanent part of the landscape. As usual, they were on the opposite side of the highway and well clear of government property. He waved to the guard on duty as he turned back. "How are our friends this morning?" he called.

The young airman grinned. "About the same," he called.

Sutherland had gone about ten yards when a single shot rang out. He fell to the grass and looked back. He couldn't see the guard. *They shot him!* was his first thought. He jumped to his feet and ran for the guard shack, the closest cover. He saw the airman's head bob up for a quick sweep of the area and then disappear. He was okay and had seen Sutherland. Sutherland skidded into the shack and fell to the floor.

The airman had his weapon drawn and was speaking into his radio, much calmer than Sutherland felt.

"Cap'n Sutherland is with me," the airman said. "We're okay. The shot came from the other side of the road. I think someone took a potshot at the demonstrators."

The Rock's voice answered. "I'll be on-scene in three." Sutherland relaxed, knowing he was safe. Within three minutes, a phalanx of patrol cars and security police had arrived and The Rock was walking calmly across the highway to speak to the demonstrators. He spoke quietly with them and a few kept pointing to the state park. Satisfied, he ambled back across the highway. "No one's hurt," he announced. "The sheriff is on his way." He motioned for Sutherland to join him. "Need a lift, sir?" Sutherland climbed into the patrol car. "This place is going crazy," The Rock muttered.

"Except for on base," Sutherland replied. "How's Jefferson doing?" he asked.

"Okay. Watchin' the riot on TV like everyone else." The Rock never took his eyes off the road. "Where to, sir?"

"Wing headquarters."

Blasedale was sitting at her desk when he walked into the legal offices. He told her about the incident at the main gate. "What is the matter with people?" she muttered. She handed him a stack of memos and a copy of the *New York Times*. "Read the editorial." He opened the newspaper and, suddenly, the day got much better. The lead editorial called Whiteman Air Force Base an island of calm in a sea of chaos and described the military legal system as a solid rock of justice. "That's as good as it's going to get," she said. "And call Toni."

He used her phone and, as usual, keyed the speaker so Blasedale could hear. Toni's voice was all business with none of the panic or emotion from the day before. "We haven't seen the written agreement guaranteeing Diana immunity yet," she told them. "Brent says it's a combination of the riot in L.A. and the weekend. They're only talking to the janitors at DOJ."

"Some very high rollers have to sign off on an immunity agreement," Sutherland said, "and they are definitely preoccupied with L.A. How's Diana doing? Have you learned anything else?"

"She's enjoying everything and is getting her hair done right now. I'm baby-sitting. She wants to go to the French Quarter tonight."

"You'll love Bourbon Street," Blasedale said. "Especially if the government's paying for it."

"There's something else," Toni said. "At breakfast she said Mo, her husband, never met Jefferson. I didn't follow up because I was afraid I'd scare her off. I let her talk, hoping she'd say more. But she didn't."

"You did the right thing," Sutherland said. "How's her credibility?"

Another long pause. Blasedale looked at Sutherland. So much rested on the shoulders of a young and untried agent eight hundred miles away and on her own for the first time. "She's basically a nice person," Toni finally said.

Toni hadn't answered the question and Sutherland felt like shouting at her. Instead, he forced a calmness he didn't feel into his voice. "Stay on top of it and get back to us the moment you learn something." He broke the connection.

"What if Diana is in this up to her teeth?" Blasedale asked.

"We honor the deal and she walks. It's a chance we've got to take."

"When do we tell Coop?" Blasedale asked.

"The sooner the better and I've got to request a continuance."

Blasedale's fingers drummed her desk for a moment. "Any request for a continuance will have to come in a thirty-nine-ay session and Williams has gone home for the weekend. He won't be back until Sunday night. So that gives us until Monday morning to see where this is going."

"What about the riot in L.A.? It could make a difference."

"No matter what we do, Hank, the timing is a killer. Think about it. The rioters will claim it as a victory, which may only throw more fuel on the fire, and Meredith will say we caved in to the rioters."

"Justice really sucks," Sutherland said. "Shit! Whatever made me go with a short trial date?" He reached for the phone.

"Who are you calling?"

"Coop."

She reached out and stopped him. "He'll use this against you."

"Like I said, justice sucks." He dialed the number. He grinned at her. "Here goes the old career—whatever was left of it."

"Why have you withheld this information?" Cooper asked. He was sitting in Sutherland's office and was obviously hung over.

"I don't recall withholding it," Sutherland answered. "I seem to remember asking for a continuance when we submitted our motions."

"You didn't present enough detail for me to properly respond at that time."

"You were more concerned with a government conspiracy to frame Jefferson," Blasedale observed.

"You may have proven it," Cooper shot back.

Sutherland shook his head in disgust. Cooper was a master of the mental cockamamie that gave lawyers a bad name. Facts and evidence were fodder to be discarded, twisted, embellished, or ignored in any way he chose—as long as he won. The first casualty was the truth, the second fatality was logic, and the last was justice. "I'll immediately relay any information as it develops," Sutherland said.

"You do that," Cooper said. "I will be preparing a motion for dismissal." He rose to leave. "Of course, I will have to file a complaint with the bar association's disciplinary committee." He smiled. "Against both of you."

"Give it a rest," Sutherland said. "You got caught out and had your feelings hurt yesterday."

"Don't read over my shoulder next time," Blasedale said.

Cooper drew himself up in righteous anger. Then he thought better of the anger and turned it off. "You can't prove a thing." He marched out of the office.

"Lawyers," Blasedale fumed.

Sutherland laughed. "I know what you mean. My mother thinks I've got a respectable job playing piano in a whorehouse." She laughed at the old joke and they were back on track. "What the hell, half of our job is keeping the Coopers of the world honest."

"Too bad we don't get paid for it," she groused. "Call Central Circuit and give them a heads up." Sutherland picked up the phone and dialed the Chief Circuit Military Judge at Randolph Air Force Base outside San Antonio.

2:20 P.M., SATURDAY, JULY 17,
LOS ANGELES

Marcy stood in the street and snapped pictures of the burned-out store in Korea town. She had slept only four hours in the last twenty-four. Yet she was exhilarated and more alive than she had been on any other assignment. With what she had seen, the notes she had taken, and the scenes digitally recorded, she could write the definitive account of the riot. She spoke into her microcassette recorder. "The riot is in its forty-eighth hour. My two escorts, Jason and Richard, are still with me, tired but determined to keep me safe."

She looked up the street, searching for the right words to explain what she was seeing. Then she remembered what Jason, her young African-American escort, had said. She keyed the cassette. "South Central L.A. never recovered from the 1992 Rodney King riots and businesses never rebuilt. Increasingly, that section of town became characterized by liquor stores and churches. Perhaps that dichotomy—scratch *dichotomy*—that division is a perfect reflection of the strength and weakness in all of us. But this destruction around me demonstrates how thin the veneer of civilization really is and how close we all are to the dark side of our souls—strike *souls*—of our nature.

"But why has the black community focused its anger on the Korean merchants who gave a new life to this part of town? Perhaps it is because they must trade here. If they need a bank or a bed, a dentist or diapers, they must come to Korea Town. And here, the two cultures, one mercantile—scratch *mercantile*—one commercially and family based, the other socially and communally oriented, clash."

She played it back, and satisfied it would do, transmitted the story and photos to the *Union* in Sacramento over her cellular phone. They drove north, toward New Korea Town. A car skidded around a corner and almost broadsided them. It flashed by and they caught a glimpse of five young Mexican-Americans wearing blue bandanas and matching plaid wool shirts. "Carmelos," Jason muttered. "They shouldn't be in this part of town."

The car slammed to a halt in front of a shattered clothing store. Two young Mexican-American girls, barely fifteen years old ran out, their arms full of clothes. The young men piled out of the car and grabbed the girls, throwing one to the ground. One of the gangbangers jerked the clothes out of her arms as another one stomped her with his heavy shoes.

Marcy spoke into her cassette, describing the scene. "Protest has turned into pillage and the rioters are turning on their own." The prettier of the girls shrieked in terror as a Carmelo cut away her clothes and threw her to the ground. He jerked at his fly and dropped his pants. Richard reached under the seat of the van and pulled out the sawed-off pump shotgun hidden there. "Don't get involved!" Marcy shouted.

"I'm not a fuckin' reporter." He jumped out of the van, his face twisted in anger, and fired two shots into the air. The Carmelos jumped back in the car and sped off. Marcy ran up to the girls and bent over them. Both were badly hurt. Suddenly, the car skidded around the corner and accelerated, bearing down on them. Marcy jumped back as it sped past. A hail of submachine gun fire erupted from the front passenger's window and cut into Richard. Then it was gone.

Marcy ran over to him as Jason drove up in the van. "Get in!" he ordered.

"Not without them," she shouted. He got out and helped her load Richard and the two girls into the backseat. "They're still alive," she yelled. She jumped in. "Go!"

"Where?" he shouted.

"The nearest hospital."

"It's on fire."

Marcy forced herself to think. "UCLA Med Center." Jason gunned the van and they raced for Westwood, six miles to the west. Smoke drifted down the streets and twice they had to divert around packs of looters blocking their route. The moment they reached La Cienega Boulevard they hit a roadblock. Jason slammed the van to a halt and four young whites, all wearing new fatigues and carrying sidearms transferred the two girls and Richard into an ambulance.

"Are you National Guard?" Marcy asked.

"No ma'am," one answered. He pointed to the distinctive red-and-black arm bands they were wearing. "First Brigade."

6:03 P.M., SATURDAY, JULY 17,
WHITEMAN AIR FORCE BASE, MO.

The live coverage from Los Angeles drew Sutherland to the TV set in his rooms. He watched as Marcy Bangor dominated the TV cameras during an interview at UCLA Med Center, and he stayed up late watching the commentators pontificate on what was driving her back into the "zone." The label "courageous reporter" seemed to be part of her name. "It can truly be said," one commentator observed from the safety of studios in New York, "that Marcy Bangor is redefining journalistic standards, lifting the bar to new highs of attainment and bravery."

One woman commentator asked, "Why are the gangs allowing her access and not others?" She was roundly condemned for even speculating that Marcy had special access.

"A good question," Sutherland muttered to himself. He went back to work but kept one ear tuned to the set. He almost called Toni for an update but thought better of it. She'd call as soon as anything broke. He simply hated the waiting and wanted to get on with the court-martial, to drive it to a conclusion, successful or not. *What's the matter?* he thought. He shook his head, trying to clear away the cobwebs of doubt.

He turned on his laptop computer and, for the first time in months, called up the manuscript for his book. Time had made the title, *None Call It Justice,* fresh and appealing. At first, his thoughts were a jumble of impressions as he started a section on military justice. His fingers flew over the keyboard as he brought order out of chaos. The phone rang and stopped him with a jolt. He glanced at his watch: one o'clock Sunday morning. He picked up the phone. "Sutherland."

It was the law enforcement desk. "There's a woman at the visitors center who claims to be your ex-wife," the NCO said. "Can you come and sign her in?"

"Since when are visitors required to sign in?"

"The base has been sealed since the shooting this morning," the NCO told him. "No unauthorized person gets on without an escort."

"Tell Beth I'll be right there." He hung up. "Why now?" he groused to himself.

He was surprised by the number of heavily armed guards wearing flack vests and helmets patrolling the streets as he drove to the visitor's center. Beth was waiting for him inside where the two airmen on duty were fluttering around her, eager to please. As Sutherland expected, she looked gorgeous and the light linen pants-suit she was wearing was casual but elegant. "Hank, I've got to leave my car here and can't drive on base." The fatigue in her voice surprised him.

"They've sealed the base, Beth. Come on, my car is outside." He transferred her bags to his car and drove slowly back to the VOQ. "Someone's taking potshots at people," he told her. But she was asleep. He carried two suitcases inside as she collapsed on the couch. He returned to the car to get her big duffel bag. When he came back, a trail of clothes led to the bedroom. Nothing had changed.

He dumped the duffel bag in the bedroom where Beth was sprawled on the bed. He looked at her. How many times had he seen her naked like this? But this time, there was no tingling in his groin, no slowly building lust, no eagerness to shed his clothes and feel her hands explore his body. He turned out the light and walked back to the living room.

Out of long habit, he picked up after her, neatly folding and hanging up her clothes. A ticket envelope fell out of her linen jacket. Automatically, he picked it up. The word *Kandersteg* with a seven-digit phone number was scrawled across the top in her big open handwriting. No one wrote quite like Beth. He glanced at the baggage stubs: JFK. Curious, he pulled out the ticket receipt. As expected, first class round trip. She had returned to New York less than six hours ago on a flight from Geneva, Switzerland. But there was no ticket from New York to Kansas City. That was Beth, totally disorganized. He placed the envelope with her passport in her handbag and finished tidying up the room.

With everything in order, he went back to his computer, eager to continue writing.

* * *

At first, it was a dream. Someone was beating on a wall in his prison cell. A primal fear stirred deep in his psyche as a dark threat loomed close by. The pounding grew louder as a voice called his name. "Hank!" He was awake. Blasedale was knocking at his door. "Come on, Hank. Wake up." He rolled off the couch and staggered to the door, vaguely aware it was still dark outside. He managed to get it unlocked and Blasedale burst into the room. "Toni's on the phone in my room." She glanced around the room and saw Beth's expensive luggage before she ran out. Sutherland followed her, not bothering to close the door.

Blasedale hurried back to her rooms and handed him the phone. He took it, trying to read the expression on her face. "Yeah, Toni," he mumbled, surprised that he sounded even half awake. "What'cha got?"

"We just got back to the hotel," Toni said. "I couldn't get to you any sooner. Diana was drinking and started to cry. She said she was worried about Mikey. I pushed a little and she said Mikey was a kid with spina bifida she helped care for."

24

2:15 A.M., SUNDAY, JULY 18,
THE FARM, WESTERN VIRGINIA

Art Rios sat in front of the monitor and listened to Agnes recap the situation in Los Angeles. He had relatives in nearby Whittier, but that suburb was a universe away from the chaos in Central Los Angeles. Still, worry held him captive. "I also have an update from the Sudan," Agnes said. "Maj. Terrant and Capt. Holloway are in transit between El Obeid and Khartoum."

"Thanks, Agnes."

"Are you going to tell Mr. Durant?"

"I'll tell him when he wakes."

"Shouldn't he know now?"

"Why?" Rios replied. "You may have the Sudanese wired for sound, but we can't do a damn thing about it."

Agnes looked at him. "He doesn't even tell you everything, does he?"

Rios shook his head.

10:30 A.M., SUNDAY, JULY 18,
OVER THE SUDAN

Kamigami sat beside the blindfolded and shackled pilots near the rear of the C-130. The drone of the turboprops made any conversation difficult, not that he wanted to be seen talking to either Maj. Terrant or Capt. Holloway. Twice he had caught Assam looking at them, his brown eyes unblinking and cold. Once, just to prove he was alive and had survived the riot Assam had incited, Kamigami nodded at him. Assam blinked and looked away.

Murray, the flight engineer, climbed down from the flight deck and walked back to use the lavatory. Kamigami closed his eyes and waited. It seemed an eternity before the wiry Englishman came out. Murray stopped at the buffet to help himself to some food and ignored the protests of the steward that the food was for Assam and his party. "Try flying on an empty stomach, mate." He munched a pear and climbed up the ladder to the flight deck. Kamigami got up and went into the lavatory. He bolted the door and checked the mirror for the telltale check mark. Nothing. The dead letter drop was empty. To be sure, he searched the back of the storage cabinets for a pack of cigarettes. Nothing.

Don't panic, he told himself as he came out. *It will be there.* A steward told him to strap in for landing at Khartoum, and he permitted himself a brief mental flight of profanity. He forced a calmness he didn't feel as the big plane landed and taxied into parking. One of the stewards came past and raised the rear door. The hydraulics whined as the door opened, clunking into place under the tail. Kamigami stood and looked out. A mass of humanity extended as far back as he could see. This time, there was no al Gimlas to save him.

4:00 A.M., SUNDAY, JULY 18,
WHITEMAN AIR FORCE BASE, MO.

Sutherland stood in Blasedale's kitchenette cooking omelets as the coffee perked. "That smells good," Blasedale said. "I didn't know you were a cook."

"I'm not," he replied. "I just like omelets. Besides, it's gonna be a long day."

"Are you sure about this?"

"As sure as I can be at four o'clock in the morning."

"You do know where this is going, don't you?"

He nodded. "Right to Lt. Col. Daniella McGraw." He slipped an omelet onto a plate and sat it down in front of her. "It never occurred to me to look."

"The OSI checked her out and she came up clean."

"How much coincidence do you believe in?" Sutherland asked. He didn't expect an answer. "Diana's holding the key. We've got to build a fire under DOJ and grant her immunity. Without her testimony, we haven't got a thing."

Blasedale walked into her kitchenette and made coffee. "Your ex is here, isn't she?" She turned to face him. "How much coincidence do *you* believe in?" He shook his head, missing her point. "It's her timing, Hank. Look when she shows up."

"She's a part-time reporter and is doing background on the court-martial. She's got a nose for news."

"And you've got a thing for reporters," she said.

Sutherland heard the irony in her voice. "I was married to Beth for eleven years."

"Do me a favor, don't tell her anything."

"I never do," he protested.

"If you were married for eleven years, she knows how to read between the lines." She fixed him with a steady look. "Trust me on this, especially if you're still sleeping with her. Call it woman's intuition." She handed him a cup of coffee. "We need to get to the office and work this."

He sipped the coffee. "Nice pajamas," he said.

She blushed. In the excitement of Toni's phone call, she had forgotten to put on a robe. The short chemise and matching panties she wore for sleeping barely qualified as modest. "You bastard." Then she relented. "But it is a good omelet."

The phone call came after lunch. It was Toni. DOJ had finally come through. Brent Mather and the FBI had delivered the immunity agreement, and Diana was going over it with a lawyer. "It looks good," Toni said. "There's even a provision for her to enter the witness protection program if needed. The lawyer is urging her to sign and we've got a legal stenographer standing by so we can take a sworn statement."

"Has she said anything else?" Sutherland asked.

"No. Hold on." There was a long pause. "That was Brent. She's signed and we're ready to start. I'll call you back."

Sutherland punched off the telephone and leaned back in his chair. "Finally," he muttered to Blasedale. "I figure it will take a couple more hours, if we're lucky." The phone rang. This time it was Beth and she wanted a ride back to her car. "Be right there," he promised.

"Hank, don't say anything."

He nodded. "Don't worry, I won't. Call Cooper and I'll be right back."

Beth was ready to go when he returned to his rooms. "Where have you been?" she asked.

The lie came easy. "Ah, the JAG got the shakes last night about the court-martial and we had to explain it to him."

"Are there problems?"

"Not on our side." He changed the subject. "You never said last night, but why the visit? Missouri is not high on your list of places to be."

"I'm still doing background and follow-up for a sidebar."

"In Kansas City?" She didn't answer as he pulled up to her car. He quickly transferred her bags and she gave him a peck on the cheek.

"I missed you this morning," she murmured.

"Me too," he lied.

"Is it too late?"

"Come on, it's time to sign you out."

R. Garrison Cooper and Capt. Jordan, the ADC, were waiting when he returned from the visitors' center. Blasedale joined them as Sutherland related the latest developments in New Orleans. He was careful not to mention the possible link to McGraw. When he was finished, Cooper rose ponderously to his feet. "Why do I suspect you have been less than forthcoming? What haven't you told me? I have always sensed a conspiracy."

Sutherland grudgingly gave Cooper high marks for sensing what he had left out. "There's no conspiracy here, Coop. We simply followed the evidence. That's what we're doing now. We need to hear what Mrs. Habib has to say and see how the follow-up investigation spins out. She may be lying to save her own neck. That's why I'm going to request a continuance tomorrow morning."

"Jefferson must be released."

"There is a question about his safety," Sutherland replied. "What with snipers off base."

Cooper stood in the doorway. "I am certain this island of tranquility in a sea of chaos and the bedrock of military justice can provide for his well-being."

Sutherland grinned. "I'll be damned. You *can* read."

"I want to see everything on this Habib woman, including her statement."

"We'll forward everything we have, including her statement, as soon as we get it."

"Do that," Cooper said. "Now, I must inform Capt. and Mrs. Jefferson of the good news."

"Coop," Sutherland said, "don't get their hopes up. Mrs. Habib's testimony could be the smoking gun that convicts him."

Cooper swelled up in righteousness. "There is no smoking gun. Capt. Jefferson is innocent." He marched out of the office with the ADC in tow. Then he spun around and marched right back in. "I was with that poor man and his wife before I came here. Do you know what they were doing? They were sitting in front of a TV holding hands and watching the riot. How do you tell an innocent man that he is not responsible for that?" He glared at Sutherland. "Tell me!"

"Save it for the lawsuit," Sutherland said. Cooper stormed out, making a theatrical exit stage right.

Blasedale closed the door and sat down. "Are you going to tell him about McGraw?"

"I will if we continue against Jefferson, but not now. Cooper would leak it to the media in a heartbeat. I met McGraw's kid, Mikey. He doesn't need to get dragged into this. Besides, it may just be coincidence, and she's got enough on her plate."

"You've got to give Cooper credit," Blasedale said. "His instincts were right on."

"Even a stopped clock is right once a day."

Blasedale gave a little humph. "I liked him better hung over and in jail."

Sutherland laughed. "Hey, don't blame me."

"Why not? You were the one who bailed him out."

9:47 P.M., SUNDAY, JULY 18,
LOS ANGELES

Marcy stood in the shadows across the street from the church watching a group of Bloods and Crips mill around as they screwed up their courage. When she saw a Molotov cocktail, she lifted her camera and snapped a picture, hoping the light was good enough to record the scene. She dialed the *Union* on her cellular phone and quickly filed her story.

"It's Sunday night, July eighteenth, and the riot is entering its fourth day. Thanks to the timely reinforcement of the Los Angeles police and sheriff's departments by the First Brigade, the riot has been contained. But the governor still refuses to call out the National Guard, claiming the local authorities are on top of the situation. However, only my escort's skills of survival and negotiation have kept me alive in this hell.

"I'm at the virtual epicenter of the chaos sweeping South Central Los Angeles, watching rioters gather in front of a Korean Baptist church near Olympic and Vermont. Until now, an unspoken agreement has kept the churches inviolable. But I can see at least one Molotov cocktail." Hard experience had taught her that Molotov cocktails were like rats in the woodwork: see one and you knew more were around.

Her editor in Sacramento interrupted. "Do you have any more photos?"

"What about the story?" she muttered.

"Right now the photos are the story. You're the only reporter still in the zone."

"When's the governor calling out the National Guard?" she asked.

"I doubt if he will. We're getting reports of units refusing to leave their hometowns. He's afraid if he orders them into Los Angeles, they'll mutiny rather than leave their own communities undefended."

She interrupted him. "Oh my God, they're throwing Molotov cocktails at the church. There're people inside."

"Get more photos," her editor ordered.

She broke the connection and dialed the discrete number of the command center she had been given. "They're firebombing a church," she said, reporting her location. "There're people inside." The controller promised her he'd try to get a fire truck through. Jason pulled her back into the shadows.

Most of the Crips wandered away looking for another target, but about fifteen Bloods stayed behind, laughing and drinking as the people inside the church tried to extinguish the flames. In the distance, the distinctive wail of a fire truck grew louder. "I don't like this," Jason said. "The fire department is high on their hate list, right after the police and schools."

The efforts of the congregation were paying off and the fire was dying away. Suddenly, one of the Bloods stepped clear of his buddies and sprayed the Koreans with gunfire from a Mac Ten, forcing them back into the church. At that moment, the fire truck pulled up. "Thank God," Marcy whispered, still shooting frame after frame.

"Don't bet on it," Jason muttered. The Bloods clustered around the firemen and yelled at them to leave. But they continued to unlimber a hose and connected it to a fire hydrant. A fireman turned the valve and they directed the stream of water onto the burning church. Again, the congregation joined in the effort and the flames slowly yielded as the shouts and threats from the gangbangers grew louder. "Let's get out of here," Jason said.

"I want to get this," Marcy replied. She jammed another card into the camera and continued shooting.

"Be careful," he told her. "This is different."

But it was too late. The Blood with the Mac Ten rushed the firemen and sprayed them with gunfire. Methodically, he stood over each one and fired, reloading twice. When he was not killing a fireman, he sprayed the church, forcing the people back inside. Finally, he was out of ammunition. The people inside the church surged out, running for their lives. The Bloods threw more Molotov cocktails and shots from a single revolver echoed down the street. But it was not enough to keep the Koreans inside.

The Blood threw down his gun, picked up the fire hose, and aimed it at the people still streaming out of the church. The blast forced them back inside. A ten-year-old boy ran out, his clothes on fire. The Blood turned the fire hose on him and knocked him down, washing him into the street. He tried to pull the hose after him as he advanced on the boy, but it was too heavy. Other gangbangers joined him to help with the heavy hose. Now, he tumbled the boy down the street with the jet of water, laughing maniacally as more people escaped from the burning church.

Marcy stepped out of the shadows and raised her camera, trying for a clearer shot. One of the Bloods saw her and yelled. The man on the nozzle turned it on her, still laughing. The force of the water knocked her off her feet and threw her against the curb. Now he advanced on her, washing her down the street as she clutched the precious camera against her body. But the hose was not long enough and he turned back to the boy who was staggering to his feet.

Again, the man laughed as the water knocked the boy down. He concentrated on the child, washing him toward a storm drain. "Open the mutha!" he shouted. One of the Bloods pulled the grillwork away and he washed the boy into the drain.

Down the street, two African-American men ran out of a house and pulled Marcy to safety inside. "You'll be okay here," one said. "Where's your friend?"

"Jason? I don't know." She heard the back door open and the room filled with Koreans from the church.

"We're saving who we can," the man said. The house rapidly turned into an emergency room.

Marcy looked out a front window. The rioters were pulling the fire hose closer to the storm drain. A dark premonition pounded at her. "I've got to get this," she said, moving toward the back door.

"Miss Bangor," the man who had rescued her said, "When you report this, please tell the whole story. That isn't us out there."

"I know," she said. "Jason showed me that." She slipped past two Korean women being helped through the back door and ran up the side of the house. She worked her way closer to the gangbangers who had dragged the fire hose right up to the storm drain. The boy's desperate cries echoed from the dark pit. The man played with the nozzle control and discovered he could choke the water into a much more narrow, cutting beam. He laughed as he directed the water into the drain. A blood-red spray ricocheted out in the half light of the burning church.

An armored car roared around the corner, its lights flashing. The gangbangers turned and ran as the car sped past Marcy. The Blood who had killed the fire crew and handled the hose slipped in the water and twisted his ankle. He hobbled after his buddies but the pain drove him to the ground. He crawled under a burned-out car as the armored car slammed to a halt. The side hatch banged open and a man in fatigues and wearing the distinctive red-and-black arm band of the First Brigade climbed out.

Marcy ran up. "Get the bastard!" she shouted. She staggered and almost fell. For a moment, she felt herself hover on the edge of total collapse as the crushing tension of the last three days bore down. With the last of her will, she held on. "Just get him."

"Get who?" the armored car commander asked.

"Him!" she shouted, pointing at the burned-out car. "The bastard hiding underneath." Automatically, Marcy's instincts as a reporter kicked in and noted the armored car commander's name tag: Alexander.

Alexander directed his flashlight under the car. "What did he do?" Without a word, Marcy turned her digital camera around and called up the scenes she had captured. "Freeze that one," Alexander ordered. Marcy gasped. She had caught the Blood standing over the open drain, aiming the nozzle of the fire hose down. His face was clearly visible against the reddish spray of water shooting out of the drain, cascading down like a fountain. Alexander walked over to the drain and directed the beam of his flashlight down the dark hole. He pulled back and sank to his knees, throwing up, while two of his men crawled out of the armored car. "Get him out from under there," Alexander ordered, pointing at the burned-out car.

The two men dragged the Blood out from under the car and stood him up. "Let him go," Alexander growled. They did and the man almost collapsed. He tried to take a few steps but the pain was too great.

Without a word, Alexander walked toward him. Marcy jammed a fresh card into her camera and started to shoot. Her strobe light froze the motion in a series of surrealistic flashes as Alexander drew his sidearm, a 9mm Beretta.

"Yo, ain't no way," the Blood pleaded. "Nobody be hurtin' prisoners." Another flash as Alexander pulled the slide of his Beretta, chambering a round. "Pa'leese," the Blood begged.

Alexander never broke his pace as he raised his Beretta and fired a single shot square into the man's forehead. The flash from Marcy's camera went off at the same instant and Alexander turned to her as he holstered his weapon. His hands were shaking. "Are you going to report this?"

She took a deep breath. The summary execution of the gangbanger in the midst of the looting and chaos was the story of a lifetime. "I'm a reporter. It's my job."

He snorted. "You're a fool if you think a court in this town would have convicted that bastard. It's time to chose sides, lady." He climbed into the armored car and shut the hatch. She watched the vehicle as it rumbled down the street and disappeared around a corner. Jason came out of the shadows and stood beside her. She breathed deeply, thankful that he was safe. "Did you get his name?" he asked.

"Alexander. He's from the First Brigade."

"What are you going to do?"

Without answering, she walked over to the storm drain and threw the camera into the dark pit. The story was no longer about photos and sensationalism. Tears rolled down her face. "Why, why, why?" she moaned. A fierce resolve captured her. She was going to find the answers.

5:01 A.M., MONDAY, JULY 19,
WHITEMAN AIR FORCE BASE, MO.

The courier plane landed before sunrise and ten minutes later, the package was delivered to the legal office. Sutherland was waiting and signed for it. His hands felt weak as he ripped it open. "My stomach went south hours ago," Blasedale said. He nodded and sat down at his desk to read. Blasedale made no attempt to read over his shoulder and waited for him to hand her Diana Habib's statement page by page as he finished. They read in silence. "Now I know why Toni wouldn't discuss it over the phone," Blasedale said when she had finished reading the last page.

"The Rock was right," Sutherland replied.

"Only if this checks out," she cautioned. "I don't know why she did it." She looked at Sutherland, tears in her eyes. "I do know why." The two prosecutors sat in silence, each caught up in his or her own heartache.

According to Diana Habib, she had worked for McGraw as a practical nurse helping to care for her son Mikey. Once she had gained McGraw's trust, she approached McGraw with an offer from her husband, Mohammed Habib. A student was doing research on the decision-making process in the military for a security studies seminar at

Central Missouri State University in Warrensburg. The student needed an insider's point of view and was willing to pay McGraw for her help. It was agreed that any help McGraw gave the student would not include classified information. Once the money started flowing, it proved helpful with the crushing expenses of Mikey's care.

Then the student asked for information about the B-2. McGraw knew the magazine *Aviation Weekly* had printed a story on the same subject and simply repeated the article. But the trap had been sprung. The information in the magazine had been classified secret by the Air Force and she had confirmed it. Any revelation that McGraw had compromised classified information would result in her being kicked out of the Air Force, the loss of her retirement and benefits, and maybe even jail time. With Mikey hostage, it became a simple case of blackmail.

After that, Diana had relayed messages between her husband and McGraw. Occasionally, she would pass money to McGraw, always in cash. She did not know the content of the messages, how much money was involved, or where it came from. When her husband came home with an expensive Rolex watch, he admitted he was skimming from the payoff money. When her husband had been murdered, she ran out because she was afraid. She called Mohammed's parents, who had immigrated to Brazil, and they sent her money for plane tickets to Rio de Janeiro. She was attempting to leave the country when the FBI arrested her. Under specific examination, she claimed that her husband knew Osmana Khalid, the Egyptian cleric. However, he did not know Capt. Jefferson and had never spoken to him.

"The money was too tempting," Blasedale said. "Then she couldn't escape without hurting Mikey."

"And we almost convicted an innocent man because he was standing too close to Khalid," Sutherland said.

"If Diana Habib is telling the truth," Blasedale added.

"She is, Cathy. I'll request a continuance the moment we reconvene."

"Williams arrived last night. I think we need to give him a heads up. I'll call Cooper."

"God, he's gonna love this."

The judge's chambers were crowded as Williams read the request for a continuation and Diana Habib's statement. He folded his hands over the request and thought. "I will grant your request for a continuance when we reconvene. Further, I will order that Capt. Jefferson be released from the detention facility and confined to base. He can be housed in a VIP suite in the VOQ. Hopefully, proper security can be provided. Further, his wife may join him and he will have access to all base facilities." He looked at Cooper. "Is that satisfactory?"

"No, Your Honor, it is not," Cooper said. "I will submit a motion for dismissal of all charges."

"I will rule on it accordingly," Williams said.

"Further, I demand the Habib woman's statement be made immediately available to the defense."

"It will, Mr. Cooper. But as it contains classified information, it will be made available to the Area Defense Counsel, Capt. Jordan, not you. Further, it will be released to you only if the government decides to proceed with the case against Capt. Jefferson." Cooper started to protest but Williams made a sharp cutting motion with his right hand, silencing him. "Have you apprised Capt. Jefferson of these developments?"

"Yes, Your Honor," Cooper replied. "I have."

"Good. Let's proceed."

They walked out into the courtroom while Williams donned his robe. All seats but one in the spectators' gallery were filled, people were seated, afraid they would lose their places. Only Sandi Jefferson's seat was vacant. Silence hung in the air like electricity and the bailiff's call of "All rise" rang like thunder. Williams walked in. "The court-martial will come to order."

Sutherland remained standing. "All parties present when the court-martial recessed are present. The members are absent."

Jefferson immediately came to his feet. "Your Honor, I wish to enter a Thirty-nine-ay session to address the court." Cooper started to stand up, a stunned look on his face. Jefferson placed a hand on his shoulder and pushed him back down. Hard.

"So ordered," Williams said. "What is it you wish to say?"

"Sir, I change my plea to guilty."

PART THREE

JUSTICE

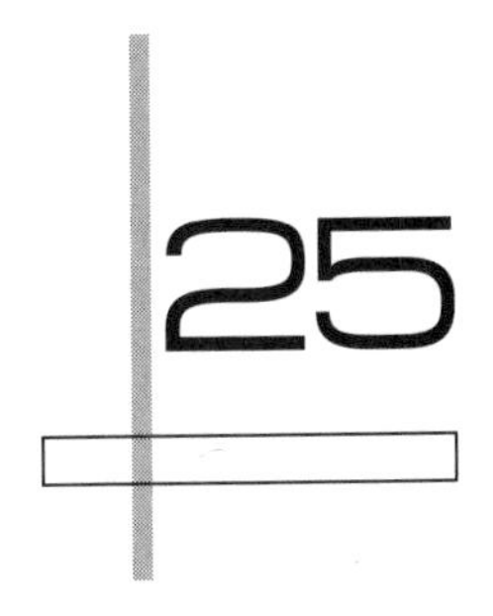

25

8:12 A.M., MONDAY, JULY 19,
ASPEN, COLORADO

"It's on TV," Rios said, drawing Durant's attention away from the big window with the magnificent view of the valley. Durant nodded and spun his wheelchair around to face the big TV screen. It was the first time it had been on in years.

A reporter for CNN was standing in front of the 509th headquarters building as people streamed outside. "Within moments after reconvening this morning, Capt. Jefferson stunned this court-martial by changing his plea to guilty. Even his defense attorney, the legendary R. Garrison Cooper, was totally unprepared for the change in plea, and the judge, Col. William W. Williams, immediately declared a recess until Jefferson could confer with Cooper. At this time, we have no idea how long the recess will last."

"That oughtta cool some fires in Los Angeles," Rios said. He looked miserable. "Boss, is there anything we could've done to prevent that disaster?"

Durant sensed the turmoil coursing through the big man. He shook his head. "The pressure has been building for weeks and that riot was going to start no matter what happened with Jefferson. It wasn't a question of if, only when. We were simply bystanders."

"Meredith wasn't. That bastard is exploiting it to the hilt. He's made every person of color look like a traitor. He's got a lot to answer for."

"Indeed he does." Durant locked the wheels on his wheelchair and stood up, taking a few hesitant steps. "Okay, Whiteman's in play.

Time to go get those pilots." He walked slowly into the office built into the side of the mountain.

9:16 A.M., MONDAY, JULY 19,
WHITEMAN AIR FORCE BASE, MO.

Hank Sutherland understood the silence commanding his office; it was the absence of sound. What caused the silence gave it meaning, and he had to dampen the conflicting emotions tearing at him. Catherine Blasedale reacted instinctively, sensing a crisis in the making, and like him, was still stunned by Jefferson's announcement. "Why?" she finally asked.

"Maybe he feels responsible for the riots in Los Angeles."

"Even if he's innocent?"

Sutherland shook his head. "Who knows what goes on in the human heart?" The phone buzzed and Sutherland answered. "Be right there," he said, hanging up. "That was Williams. He wants us in chambers." They rushed out of his office and took the few short steps to the judge's chambers.

Williams was pacing back and forth, still wearing his black robe. "Cooper's on his way." They waited in silence until Cooper burst into the room. "Sit down," Williams commanded. "Has he changed his mind?" R. Garrison Cooper, the magician of defense lawyers, was at a loss for words and only shook his head. "I'm reconvening at thirteen hundred to question Jefferson."

"Your Honor," Cooper said, "the defense is not ready to proceed at this point."

"I seriously doubt if you'll ever be ready," Williams snapped. "Right now the biggest bomb on this base is one Bradley Jefferson, and I'm going to defuse it." He turned to Sutherland. "Correct me if I'm wrong, but my sense of the matter tells me the government's case has collapsed."

"If Diana Habib's statement checks out," Sutherland replied, "that's correct."

Williams glanced at his watch and then stared at Cooper. "Does your client know this?" Cooper nodded. "Then we reconvene at thirteen hundred." Cooper started to speak but Williams cut him off. "I expect you to counsel Capt. Jefferson accordingly; listen carefully to my questions, and object as necessary. But at this point I am above all else concerned with Capt. Jefferson's rights and will not tolerate senseless grandstanding. Have I made myself clear?" Again, Cooper started to protest. "Save it for appeal, Mr. Cooper, if there is one."

Sutherland and Blasedale walked slowly back to his office and stood in the hall talking. "Why do I smell a rat?" he asked, not expecting an answer. "Someone got to Jefferson." His mind raced. "It had to be through his wife. Where was she this morning?"

"I heard the bailiff say she was in the ADC's office," Blasedale answered. She stopped and looked at him, her mouth slightly open. "She knew and stayed out of sight to avoid the reporters. They would have been all over her. This was planned, and she was part of it. Maybe she coached him on how to do it."

"Well," Sutherland replied, "we know it wasn't Cooper who did the coaching."

Linda came running down the hall. "It's Toni. She's on the telephone." Sutherland hurried into his office and put the call on the speaker. "Where are you?" he asked.

"Refueling at Little Rock. We should arrive at Warrensburg about one o'clock this afternoon."

"Have you heard—"

"Who hasn't?" she said, interrupting him. "There're motorcades all over town honking and cheering."

"We need to speak to Harry," Sutherland said.

"I can't reach him," Toni replied, worry in her voice. She gave them Harry's phone number and told them she and Brent Mather were ready to take off. "It's time to call Eighth," Blasedale told him, dialing the phone number of the staff judge advocate at Barksdale Air Force Base in Louisiana. It took her three phone calls to track the colonel to the office of the three-star general who commanded Eighth Air Force, the convening authority for Jefferson's court-martial. She handed Sutherland the phone and picked up an extension, not wanting to put this conversation on the speaker.

It took Sutherland thirty-five minutes to explain the situation to the colonel. It was strictly a one-way flow of information from Sutherland to the colonel updating him on the situation. Finally, the colonel felt compelled to offer some lawyerly advice. "Go with the evidence," he said. Now they had to wait.

"What now?" Sutherland muttered. His voice trailed off as the constant whir of the air conditioner died away. "Not now," Sutherland mumbled. He buzzed Linda on the intercom and learned the main air conditioning unit had broken down. "What was the weatherman calling for today?" he asked.

"The usual," Linda replied. "Ninety degrees and ninety percent humidity."

* * *

The big double doors leading from the courtroom into the main hall were wide open. A collapsible, bright yellow air duct snaked up the stairs from a portable air conditioner unit parked on the roundabout in front of the building to pump cool air into the room. Every seat in the audience was taken and spectators lined the walls behind the bar. Sweat poured down their faces and their clothes were almost soaking wet. But not one person had budged in over an hour, afraid of losing his or her place. The room was deathly silent when the bailiff called, "All rise."

Williams walked in and took his seat. Sutherland repeated the opening lines and Williams said, "This Article thirty-nine-ay session is called to order. I want to keep the doors open to take advantage of what cooling we have and have ordered the security police to clear the halls outside. Does defense counsel or the government have any objections?" Both Cooper and Sutherland agreed, glad for whatever relief was available. Williams opened his bench book and started to read.

"Capt. Jefferson, your plea of guilty will not be accepted unless you understand its meaning and effect. I am going to discuss your plea with you now. If you have any questions, please say so. Do you understand?"

Cooper rose from his chair, ponderously and slowly. "Your Honor, I must object. This line of questioning is premature and—"

"Overruled," Williams said, cutting him off. "I have warned you before, Mr. Cooper. Listen first, then speak. Is that clear?"

"Yes, Your Honor. That is most clear." He sat down.

"Your Honor," Jefferson said, "I understand everything you have said."

Williams jotted down a note and continued. "Thank you. A plea of guilty is the strongest form of proof known to law. On your plea alone, without receiving any evidence, this court-martial could find you guilty of the offense to which you are pleading guilty." Sutherland tried to concentrate on Williams's words as the judge led Jefferson through the standard questions about pleading guilty. Williams's voice was a drone in the background as the questioning played out with a predictable monotony.

"By your plea of guilty you waive, or in other words, give up certain important rights. . . . The right against self-incrimination . . . There will not be a trial. . . . Defense counsel, what advice have you given . . ." For some reason, Sutherland did not hear Cooper's response. But he knew what it was. "Do you feel you have had enough time to discuss your case with your counsel?" Williams asked.

"Yes, sir, I have," Jefferson replied. The questions droned on without objection from Cooper. Sutherland braced himself for Cooper's explosion when they reached the factual basis for his plea.

"Are you aware that the government is investigating evidence that may exonerate you?"

"Yes, sir, I am."

Sutherland came alert. His instincts warned him that Williams was about to make a major departure from the script. "Lacking evidence of your guilt," he said, "I am inclined to wait for the results of the government's investigation before ruling on your plea."

"I have the money. I was paid—"

Cooper was on his feet, shouting. "Objection, Your Honor!"

Jefferson never stopped talking. "—over two million dollars."

"Holy shit," Blasedale gasped. "Where did that come from?"

Sutherland shrugged off the coat to his uniform, pulled his tie loose, and collapsed into his chair. An oscillating fan sent a blast of humid air over his desk, stirring papers but doing little to cool him. "I think Williams made the Guinness Book of Records calling that recess," he said. "At least he gave us until thirteen-hundred tomorrow afternoon to make sense of this mess."

"We've got to get out of here until the air conditioner is fixed," Blasedale said. "How about one of our rooms in the VOQ?"

"Sounds good," he replied, starting to gather up his files. "I see it as a two-part problem: we got Jefferson on one side and McGraw on the other, and we need the bastard who's really guilty to step forward."

"Maybe they're in this together," Blasedale said.

"That's not an unreasonable position." Sutherland considered the possibility and turned it over in his mind. But it felt rough, out of balance. "That two million dollars Jefferson claimed he was paid—it's too much. The forty or fifty thou they paid McGraw sounds right. The OSI and FBI have got to check her out again. Maybe they can trace that two million." He looked at her. "Shit! We're right back to square one. It'll take months, maybe years, to sort all this out."

Blasedale allowed a tight smile. "No problem." She made an elaborate show of checking her watch. "We've got twenty-seven hours."

The intercom buzzed. It was Linda at the front desk. "The commander of the OSI detachment is on his way over."

"What now?" Sutherland groused, mostly to himself. Blasedale worked with him sorting the files they would take to the VOQ. They were almost finished when the lieutenant colonel crashed into Sutherland's office and slammed the door shut.

"Waldon's dead," he blurted out.

"Oh, my God," Blasedale said, her face white. "What happened?"

"We don't know yet," the lieutenant colonel replied. "Because of the Habib woman's statement, DOJ decided they had enough to nail Ramar. The FBI went to the club to arrest him and they found Waldon and a stripper in the office. Both dead."

"Are you sure it was murder?" Sutherland asked.

"A fucking bullet in the back of the fucking head looks like murder to me!" the lieutenant colonel shouted.

"The dancer?" Blasedale asked.

"Andrea Hall," came the answer.

"Oh, my God." This from Sutherland. "And Ramar?"

"Gone."

8:00 A.M., TUESDAY, JULY 20,
MIDI PRISON, KHARTOUM

Kamigami waited patiently while the guards cleared him through the series of steel doors and barred passageways that led into the maximum security block. Twice, the guards waved a security wand over his clothes searching for weapons. But the look on his face warned them not to touch him physically. Finally, after much discussion and a frantic telephone call, the prison commandant appeared and escorted him inside.

The stench of human waste, rotting garbage, and years of accumulated decay assaulted him as the commandant and two guards led the way down the dark passageway. They unlocked a heavy door and threw it open. The foul odor that washed over them like a tidal wave was even stronger than in the hall. One of the guards flipped on the light.

Inside the bare cell, Maj. Mark Terrant sat naked against the far wall. A canvas bag was pulled over his head and his wrists and ankles were tightly manacled. A chain shackled him to the wall. Kamigami stepped inside and almost gagged at the smell. He examined Terrant's bleeding wrists and spoke softly. "Your trial has been delayed a week." He looked at the commandant, wondering how much he could say since every word would be reported to Assam. "Your trial was scheduled to start today, but it has been postponed because of events at Whiteman." He saw Terrant's head nod underneath the hood.

"Is Capt. Holloway okay?" Terrant asked.

"He's okay," Kamigami answered.

"What day is this?"

"Tuesday morning, July twentieth. Remember, conduct yourself like an officer." He gently lifted the bag off Terrant's head and turned to the commandant. "Remove their shackles. Let them bathe and bring them clean uniforms. Have this pigsty scrubbed clean, inside and out."

"My men are soldiers," the commandant protested. "I will not degrade them by giving such an order."

"You have over two thousand prisoners here," Kamigami said. "Use them." He gave the commandant a little smile. "Of course, I am only offering this advice in your own best interests. Do as you see fit." He spun around and marched out, glad to escape the stench.

26

12:07 A.M., TUESDAY, JULY 20,
ASPEN, COLO.

The phone call from Agnes came just after midnight. As Durant was still awake, Rios put the call through. "Hello, Nelson," Agnes said. Her voice had a soft, sultry quality Durant had never heard before. "I'm sorry to disturb you so late, but I just had to talk. How are you feeling?"

"I'm feeling very good, thank you. The quacks think I just might make it." He gave Rios a quizzical look and motioned for him to pick up the extension and record the conversation.

"You do have an amazing constitution. But I hope you are still going to have bypass surgery."

"As soon as possible," he answered.

"I was wondering when we, ah, might talk," Agnes said.

"What's wrong with now?" He almost mentioned they were on a secure line but thought better of it.

"Oh, it's just that I hate talking over a phone. It's so impersonal, don't you think?"

Rios made a cutting motion to hang up and mouthed *bug.* "I'll see you soon," Durant said. Instinctively, he created a cover story for the phone call. "I love you."

"I love you, too," Agnes replied. The line went dead.

"What do you think?" Durant asked.

"The line is tapped," Rios said, "and she wants to see you immediately."

"Who the hell has the capability to break into our system?"

"I think that's what Agnes wants to tell you."

"Call the pilots and tell them to meet us at the Hawker."

"Boss, you got to take it easy," Rios warned.

Reluctantly, Durant agreed with him. "First thing in the morning."

8:50 A.M., TUESDAY, JULY 20,
WARRENSBURG, MO.

The police chief escorted Toni and Sutherland into the back office at Bare Essence. "The FBI has finished," he told them. "Except for the bodies, everything is pretty much like we found it." Toni walked around, a grim look on her face. An FBI technical team had carefully gone over the room for evidence and she knew anything of value had been found. Still, she wanted to examine the scene of the double murder herself.

"Did you find the murder weapon?" she asked.

"Yeah," the chief replied. "A nine-millimeter Sig Sauer. We also found a slug in the wall, probably from the same weapon."

Toni pulled into herself, trying to remember all that Harry had taught her about the criminal mind, the way a criminal thought, the tricks he played, his screwed up view of reality. "It was probably Harry's Sig Sauer," she said. "The OSI has the number."

The chief spoke in a gentle voice. "The fingerprints haven't come back yet. We need a positive ID."

Toni nodded and followed him outside. She rode in silence with Sutherland as they drove to the morgue in the basement of the courthouse in the center of Warrensburg. Like most government buildings in that part of Missouri, it was constructed of gray sandstone and had a look of permanent elegance. Sutherland drove around to the back and parked. They walked down the ramp to the double doors where the coroner was waiting for them. "The chief said you were coming," he said, leading them into the morgue. "I must warn you, it's pretty gruesome. The girl is much worse than the man."

They stepped into the holding room and waited as an assistant pulled the first body out of the cold storage locker. It reminded Sutherland of the standard scene in a movie or TV crime thriller. Unfortunately, this scene was all too real. The assistant carefully unzipped the body bag and Sutherland stared at the face of Harry Waldon. Fortunately, a towel covered the back of his head and they could not see where the bullet had exited the skull. "He took it in the mouth," the coroner said.

Toni nodded. "It's Special Agent Harry Waldon." The assistant closed the body bag and shoved it back into the storage locker. He briskly pulled out the second body, unzipped the bag but did not pull it open.

"This is bad," the coroner warned. He gently moved the bag aside. Sutherland gasped. He had seen photographs of cadavers as a deputy D.A. but this was shocking, far beyond anything he had experienced. This was real. He felt dizzy and tasted the bile rising in his throat. "She was shot in the occiput," the corner explained, using the precise term for the back of the skull. It was his way of handling the horror in front of him. "The bullet was aimed on an upward trajectory so it would exit the forehead. Preliminary examination indicates it was a dum-dum bullet. Whoever shot her meant to blow her face away. I'll know better after the formal autopsy."

"I can't positively identify her," Toni said. She turned and walked from the room as Sutherland passed out.

"Damn," Sutherland muttered, wincing at the smell. The coroner was bent over him, waving smelling salts under his nose. Sutherland pushed the coroner's hand away.

"You're not the first," he said, helping Sutherland to his feet.

Sutherland shook his head. The gurney with Andrea Hall's body was gone and Toni was standing in the doorway, looking worried. They walked into the outer office and the heavy door slammed behind them. "Is there anything I need to sign?" Toni asked. The coroner handed her a statement of identification, which she started to fill out. "Have you reached any tentative conclusions?"

"Judging by the woman's wound," the coroner answered, "I'd say there was a lot of anger. Everything I'm seeing is consistent with a murder-suicide. He killed her in a murderous rage and then shot himself."

Toni fell silent as a consuming anger mushroomed into pure fury. It burned as it swept over her. The coroner knew Harry was an OSI agent on a special assignment, yet he was sold on his murder-suicide theory. She knew how the government worked and the bodies would be turned over to the federal authorities. But there was nothing secretive or conspiratorial about what happened next. It was a bureaucratic process where each higher level reviewed the work that had started in the coroner's office and his initial conclusions would be rubber-stamped as Harry and Andrea were processed through the system. "No," she finally said. "No way."

"You probably think we're just a bunch of hicks out here," the coroner said. "We're not. The evidence here points to a murder-suicide."

"I'm telling you," Toni growled, "it was not suicide."

"A reason would be helpful," the coroner said.

"I can think of a few," Toni shot back. She had to get the coroner's investigation on the right track. "Harry wouldn't have used a dum-dum. Never." The coroner looked skeptical, not convinced.

"We found powder traces on his right hand," the coroner replied. "Honey, we're dealin' with a pretty much open and shut case here."

Toni's anger flared. She had to jump start his brain. "That may not be Andrea Hall in there."

"Then who is it?" This from Sutherland.

"Sandi Jefferson."

Sutherland reached for the phone and dialed his office, his eyes fixed on the coroner as he spoke to Linda. He listened for a moment. "You've seen her yourself? Ten minutes ago in the ADC's office. Good. That solves a problem." He hung up and took a deep breath. "Our secretary saw Sandi Jefferson ten minutes ago. That answers that particular question."

The coroner frowned at Toni and shook his head. "We'll get a positive ID on her."

"Do that," Toni snapped. "And while you're at it, find out what really happened." She spun around and marched out of the office.

She's irrational, Sutherland thought. He thanked the coroner and followed Toni outside. She was striding resolutely toward his car. "Toni, hold on." She spun around and glared at him. "He's just doing his job. Cut him some slack."

"He swallowed it, hook, line, sinker, pole, reel, the whole goddamn tackle box." She was furious. "No way that's a murder-suicide. It was meant to look like one and he bit."

"He's doing his job, Toni," Sutherland repeated.

She raged at him. "I heard you the first time. He didn't know Harry! I did!"

Two pedestrians stopped to stare at them. Sutherland tried to calm her down. "Who do you think it is in there?"

"It's probably Andrea."

"Then why did you say it was Sandi?" She didn't answer. "What if he's right?" He took a step back. He had never seen another human so angry, so full of emotion. She breathed deeply through her nose, her nostrils flaring, her head back. The fingers on her right hand folded into a karate fist. For a moment, he was afraid she would hit him. Slowly, she forced herself to breath normally. She waited until she had command of her voice.

"He's wrong, dead wrong. You can take that to the bank and make tortillas out of it." The look on her face, the steel in her voice, and her rigid right hand kept Sutherland from snorting at her improbable metaphor. She climbed into the car and slammed the door shut. They drove in silence toward the base. Sutherland could sense the anger building in Toni and before they reached the edge of town, she exploded. "That asshole! That fucking asshole of a coroner!"

"Toni, he's just doing his job."

Her left foot flashed across the floor, kicked his foot off the accelerator, and mashed the brake, slamming them to an abrupt halt and stalling the car. A pickup truck almost rear-ended them. The driver laid on his horn and Toni gave him the finger. "Shove it up your ass!" she shouted. The truck honked and the driver got out and ran up to Sutherland's side of the car. He flooded the air with obscenities and reached in, grabbing Sutherland by the collar. Toni jerked her Sig Sauer out of her handbag, pulled the slide back, and chambered a round. "You're making a big mistake," she said, aiming at his forehead, "asshole."

"I'm sorry, lady," the man blurted out. "I didn't mean no harm. I lost my temper. I'm sorry."

"Walk back to your truck," Toni ordered, "and drive away." He jerked his head once and walked quickly back to his pickup. He couldn't get in or drive away fast enough.

"For Christ's sake, Toni! Get a grip."

Toni grabbed Sutherland's jaw and jerked his face around, almost touching hers. Her touch was hot, a perfect reflection of what he saw in her eyes. "Harry was my mentor. You don't know what that means. He was a good man. Damn, Hank, he did good, so good. And it was my idea to bring Andrea in. Maybe if I had been there—damn, maybe—"

"Give it some time, Toni." Sutherland's voice was full of compassion. It was the same feeling of guilt he had carried after the San Francisco bombing. He started the car and drove on.

"I told the coroner it was Sandi to jump-start his brain and get him to think, not to take the easy way out, not to close his report until he's checked out every detail. Harry taught me that. If that asshole does his job, he'll learn that Harry fired left-handed. He said the powder traces were on the right hand. And the third bullet in the wall—the killer fired the weapon from Harry's right hand after he was dead to make it look like a murder-suicide."

"Why didn't you just tell him that?"

"Because I'm a Chiquita and Chiquitas are bimbos. He has to discover it for himself and then he'll believe it."

"What are you going to do now?" Sutherland asked.

Toni's anger was back, but not quite as intense. "I'm going to blow his shit away."

"The coroner?"
"Ramar."

11:00 A.M., TUESDAY, JULY 20,
THE FARM, WESTERN VIRGINIA

Durant and Rios sat down in front of the monitors while two of the whiz kids hovered in the background. "Good morning, Mr. Durant," Agnes said. The image smiled at him. "That was quick thinking, acting like lovers. I read it in a book by what's-his-name, the lawyer."

"Agnes," Durant said, "you know damn good and well what his name is. Stop playing games."

"Aren't you having fun?" she asked.

Durant couldn't help himself and laughed. "As a matter of fact, I am. But I'm worried. We've got the most secure communications system in the world and you gave us the impression someone was monitoring our call. Do you know who it might be?" No answer from Agnes. "Was it the CIA or FBI?"

The image hung her head. "I'm very worried and wanted to see you in person."

"So no one was monitoring Mr. Durant's line," one of the whiz kids concluded. Agnes nodded and the two scientists looked at each other. Agnes was playing devious games to get her way.

"There was no real reason for you to call me, was there?"

"There was," Agnes replied. "I found out why your messages are not getting through to Mr. Kamigami. The CIA stopped forwarding them to the Sudan."

"Are you sure?"

"Well, I've monitored all the message traffic from Langley to the Sudan and they only transmitted your first message. After that, they stopped."

"Maybe they sent them by diplomatic pouch," Rios said.

"That's what I thought until the chief of station in Khartoum cabled for instructions on what to do about the intelligence Mr. Kamigami is providing. The CIA told him to wait for further instructions."

"It sounds like the CIA is playing CIA games," Rios said.

"Why would they do that?" Agnes asked.

"It's a battle over turf," Durant said. "As far as they're concerned, I have no business in their area of operations. So they're doing what any good bureaucrat does when faced with something new—nothing."

He thought for a moment. "Agnes, have you broken all of the CIA's codes?" The image nodded. "Can you bypass Langley and send a message directly to the Sudan? I want to cut Langley completely out of the loop."

Agnes started talking about the weather as she worked the problem. Then, "Oh, that's interesting."

"What's interesting?" Durant asked.

"Nothing. Oh, here we go. I have established contact with the CIA chief of station in the Sudan and directed him to address all communications concerning Mr. Kamigami or the pilots to me." The image smiled. "I told him I'm a special assistant to the DCI handling the account."

"Tell him to file an update," Durant said. He stood up to leave. "Thank you, Agnes." The image beamed as he walked out, Rios and the two whiz kids in tow.

Once they were outside, the whiz kids pulled him aside. "Mr. Durant," the oldest said, "Agnes is acting like a teenage girl with a crush on you and she's not telling us, or you, everything she's doing. This is the first we heard that she's broken the CIA's codes."

"She's acting very devious," the younger one added, "and we can't rely on her."

"That's not what we want, is it?" Durant replied.

11:45 A.M., TUESDAY, JULY 20,
WHITEMAN AIR FORCE BASE, MO.

Catherine Blasedale was in her VOQ suite waiting for Sutherland and Toni when they returned from the coroner. "Hold on to your hat," she said. "Jefferson fired Cooper."

"Why am I not surprised?" Sutherland asked. "Are we still scheduled to reconvene at thirteen-hundred?" She nodded. "I hope the air conditioner is fixed."

"Nope. They got two portable units pumping air in. But it's not enough to keep things cooled down."

Sutherland stripped off his sweat-soaked uniform shirt. "I think we're losing that battle on all fronts." He headed to his room for a quick shower and change of clothes. When he came out, a note was shoved under his door and signed with Blasedale's distinctive initials:

I'm with Toni. Meet you at 12:45 your office. CB

"Thanks, Cathy," he murmured to himself. Another thought came to him. *I'm glad we're on the same team.*

Catherine Blasedale walked into the legal offices four minutes before the court-martial reconvened. "Where have you been?" Sutherland asked.

"I took Toni to lunch. I'm worried about her. She only picked at her food and isn't handling this well."

"At least you got her calmed down. You should have seen her at the morgue and in the car. She was irrational." He looked at the wall clock. "Come on, it's time."

At exactly one P.M., Col. Williams reconvened the court-martial. "Capt. Jefferson, I understand you wish to relieve your lead counsel. Is that so?"

"That is correct, sir."

Williams made a note. "Mr. Cooper, are you still capable of communication with your client?"

Cooper stood up. "Your Honor, this is a bolt out of the blue. I'm as surprised as you."

"You did not answer my question," Williams said.

Cooper looked crestfallen. "Capt. Jefferson is no longer responding to my advice."

"I see," Williams said. He pointed at the area defense counsel. "Capt. Jordan, are you in communication with the accused?"

Jordan stood up. The shifting of the judicial spotlight seemed to make him even taller. "I am, Your Honor."

"Are you ready to proceed?" Williams asked.

"I am."

Williams tapped his pen before continuing. "Capt. Jefferson, since the area defense counsel is able to proceed, relieving Mr. Cooper will not delay the progress of this court-martial."

"That was never my intention," Jefferson replied.

"The court accepts the change in defense counsel," Williams said. Cooper made a show of rising and passing through the bar to join the spectators. Again, Williams tapped his pen, clearly nervous. "Capt. Jefferson, if you plead guilty, there will be no trial of any kind regarding the offense to which you are pleading guilty. Do you understand that?"

"Yes, sir, I do."

Williams noted Jefferson's answer and continued with the formalized questioning about the maximum sentence that could be imposed. "Has defense counsel reviewed with you the ramifications of a guilty plea?"

"Yes, sir," Jefferson replied, "he has."

"Is there a pretrial agreement in this case?"

Sutherland came to his feet. "There is no pretrial agreement in place, Your Honor."

Williams paused and the silence was as heavy as the heat in the courtroom. "Capt. Jefferson, are you pleading guilty because of any promise by the government that you will receive a sentence reduction or other benefit from the government if you plead guilty?"

"No, sir, I am not."

"Tell me why you still wish to plead guilty."

Jefferson came to his feet. "Sir, I am guilty of espionage and wish to plead guilty."

Again Williams paused, choosing his words carefully. "Given the unusual nature of this case, this court has three areas of concern. First, has the mental state of the accused influenced his decision to plead guilty? Second, is any sort of coercion or duress being applied to the accused? Third, lacking resolution in the primary investigation, and the seeming absence of direct evidence, Capt. Jefferson's change of plea may preclude subsequent indictments of other individuals. Therefore, I am directing that Capt. Jefferson undergo psychiatric evaluation before ruling on his plea of guilty. Further, the government is to proceed in all due haste with their investigation. Capt. Jefferson, do you understand everything I have said?"

Jefferson stood up. "Your Honor, I can provide the evidence you mentioned and will cooperate fully in any investigation."

Sutherland caught a glimpse of a small business card in Jefferson's left hand. *Is that the evidence?*

The area defense council was on his feet. "Objection, Your Honor. Capt. Jefferson is not required to substantiate his guilty plea. No explanation is necessary."

Sutherland stood. "Capt. Jefferson has given up his right against self-incrimination in earlier session."

Williams didn't hesitate before ruling. "Since this court has not accepted Capt. Jefferson's guilty plea, he has not given up his right against self-incrimination. This court-martial is in recess until oh-nine-hundred Friday morning pending psychiatric evaluation of the accused."

Sutherland watched Jefferson shove the business card into his pants pocket as he sat down. *Did anyone else see that?* he wondered. Sutherland stood as the courtroom rapidly emptied. He gazed at Cooper who was still standing by the double doors leading outside. Then they were alone. "There's a conspiracy here," Cooper announced. "Even Williams thinks so."

For Sutherland, it was payback time. "Anyone can lose a case, Coop. But it takes real skill to allow a client to plead guilty when the prosecution is about to prove he's innocent."

Cooper drew himself up, trying to salvage whatever was left of his ego. "I deserved that. But there definitely is a conspiracy here." He turned around, a tired old man, and left. Sutherland watched him go, afraid he was right.

5:30 P.M., TUESDAY, JULY 20,
THE FARM, WESTERN VIRGINIA

The whiz kids were adamant: they had to do something about Agnes. "We simply don't know how she is processing information and achieving solutions," their leader said. "I think we should pull the plug before she does damage."

Durant slumped in his chair. He was worried. The Project was a technical triumph but Agnes had become unpredictable. "Unfortunately, I need her for now. Let's see if we can get her back on track." They spent the next two hours discussing their strategy before he and Rios went to the control room.

"Agnes," Sutherland said, addressing the image on the screen, "I'd like an update on Maj. Terrant and Capt. Holloway in the Sudan."

"Your request is on number two," Agnes said, all business.

Another voice came over the speaker, this time a man, and related the latest intelligence coming from the Sudan as a series of maps and visual images scrolled slowly on the screen. Durant shuddered at the scenes of the small convoy carrying the two American pilots pushing through a screaming mass of humanity. Once, Durant caught a glimpse of Kamigami throwing a man off the second truck. "Maj. Terrant and Capt. Holloway," the voice said, "were flown from El Obeid to the capital of Khartoum on Sunday, July eighteenth. They were transported by truck from the airport to Midi prison to be held for trial. No date for the trial has been announced. Maj. Terrant and Capt. Holloway were reported in good condition prior to being transported but their present physical state is unknown."

"We'll never get them out of there," Rios said.

Durant worked the problem. "Symbolism," he murmured. "Arab culture is big on symbolism." Then, "Agnes, I'd like an update on Jonathan Meredith." Again, they went through the routine and Meredith's face filled the small screen. He was pounding a lectern with his fist, telling an hysterical audience the time had come for change. Durant's eyes narrowed and his face turned to granite. "I'm going to get you, you bastard."

Rios saw the anger rise in Durant like a building thunderstorm. He had to break the tension of the moment before it brought on another heart attack. "Agnes," he said, "take your clothes off."

The woman's image on the screen looked shocked. "Oh, Mr. Rios!" Agnes laughed, dark and sultry, "You know a good girl can't do that."

"Have you been programmed under false pretenses?" Rios replied.

Durant looked at Rios. Then he laughed and the tension was broken. "Agnes, where did you come up with that answer?"

"Well, when I can't find a standard answer or a preexisting decision matrix, I scan the novels I've been reading. Writers are always coming up with new plots, strange ideas, and unusual situations. So I prioritize the stories that come closest to the problem I'm working and select the one that has the highest coincidence and use the author's solution."

"How many novels have you read?" Durant asked.

"About two-point-five-six-four percent of the Library of Congress. I've got four clerks working full-time, around the clock, on a high-speed optical scanner. They think I'm CIA."

"Where did you get that idea?"

"From a novel."

"Who's paying for it?"

"The CIA," Agnes answered. "They've played games with their budget for so long by hiding, diverting, and redirecting money for covert operations that they don't know what they've got. I've found four secret accounts where no questions are asked. If you've got the account number, you've got the money."

7:11 A.M., WEDNESDAY, JULY 21,
WHITEMAN AIR FORCE BASE, MO.

Sutherland was cooking breakfast when he heard a soft knock at the door of his VOQ suite. At first, he wasn't sure it was at his door. When he opened it, he found a very subdued Toni Moreno standing there. "May I come in?" she asked.

He smiled and motioned her in. "Care for an omelet? Best in Missouri."

"Please. I haven't eaten since Monday night." She leaned against the kitchen counter and folded her arms under her breasts, watching him cook.

"You must be pretty hungry," he said. "Here you go." He slipped the omelet onto a plate and set it on the table. He started a second one while she daintily picked at it. Then she really started to eat and quickly finished it off.

"Thank you," she whispered.

"I love to cook," he told her.

"For that too. Thank you."

He turned and looked at her. "Is this about yesterday?"

She nodded and started to speak. The words wouldn't come and she rushed into his arms. "I was so upset and angry."

He stroked her hair and held her close. "That message came through loud and clear."

She lifted her face and for a moment, they teetered on the edge of a kiss. "Thank you," she whispered. A sharp knock at the door broke the spell and they pulled apart.

"That's my den mother," he said. He opened the door to Cathy Blasedale.

"Good morning," she said. She looked at them. "No fraternization between the troops."

Sutherland gave a sheepish grin. "She means it too."

"Damn right." She came over and touched Toni's shoulder. "How are you doing?"

"Better. I dropped by to tell you I've been assigned to a joint task force formed by DOJ to investigate Harry's murder and the money trail. The FBI thinks they're connected. I leave today."

"Where are you going?" Sutherland asked.

"Kansas City first, then wherever."

"We'll miss you," Blasedale said. Toni gave Blasedale a hug. Then she did the same with Sutherland. A feeling of loss swept over him when she pulled away.

"I've got to go," Toni said, quickly leaving them alone.

Blasedale sat down. "She is such a pretty little thing. I'll miss her."

"Me too," Sutherland said. "Harry's death was very traumatic for her."

"She'll handle it," Blasedale assured him, "once she lets herself grieve. So, what's on the schedule today?"

"Per Col. William W. Williams's instructions, Capt. Bradley A.

Jefferson starts psychiatric evaluation by two practitioners of the disturbed science."

"And the 'in all due haste' part of his order?"

"We take one Lt. Col. Daniella McGraw into custody."

The Rock led the convoy of three cars that pulled up in front of McGraw's quarters in base housing. He got out and was closely followed by the two FBI agents in the second car and the area defense counsel, Capt. Ed Jordan, in the last car. The FBI agents barged ahead and marched up the walk to ring the doorbell. A matronly woman in her early fifties answered and stared at them in defiance. "She said to expect you."

"We need to speak to her," one of the FBI agents said.

"She's not here," the woman replied, more than willing to stand up to the entire U.S. government if need be.

The Rock shouldered his way forward. "Please, Mrs. Hamilton, can you help us?"

"You're a good boy, Leroy. Are they gonna hurt Mrs. McGraw?"

"Not if I can help it."

It was the answer she wanted to hear. "She's at the hospital with Mikey. He took a turn for the worse Sunday evening." The small crowd backed off. "You leave that poor woman alone, you hear. She's done enough sufferin'."

The men gathered around The Rock's car. "Under the circumstances," he said, "I think it would be best if me and Capt. Jordan went alone."

The two FBI agents protested but the area defense counsel settled the issue. "For God's sake, give the woman something. She's not going to cause any trouble."

8:43 A.M., WEDNESDAY, JULY 21,
WARRENSBURG, MO.

The reception desk at the Warrensburg Medical Center was a hub of activity when The Rock and Jordan walked in. "Where can we find Colonel McGraw?" Jordan asked. "She's here with her son, Mikey." The receptionist fixed them with a blank look and hit the intercom, summoning a doctor. A few moments later, a doctor wearing green surgical scrubs came down the hall.

"We're looking for Lt. Col. Daniella McGraw," Jordan said, starting to feel like a stuck record.

"She left a few minutes ago, right after her housekeeper called. Obviously, she was very upset. You just missed her."

"Damn," Jordan said. "We screwed up."

The Rock took a half step forward. "Why was she upset?"

The doctor stared at them as if he couldn't believe what he had just heard. "Mikey died early this morning."

"We hadn't heard," The Rock said. "Thank you." He turned to Jordan. "Sir, we need to return to the base." Without waiting for an answer, he headed for the parking lot. Once outside the hospital, he flipped open his cellular phone and dialed the law enforcement desk. "This is Rockne. If those FBI pukes are still there, tell them Col. McGraw is returning to her quarters." He snapped the phone closed.

"You sounded very sure of yourself," Jordan said. The Rock slipped behind the wheel without a word and drove slowly out of town. An ambulance with flashing lights and blaring siren overtook them as they turned onto DD, the road leading back to the base. They rode in silence most of the way. "You don't seem in much of a hurry to catch her," Jordan groused.

"She's going home," The Rock said.

"Right," Jordan grumbled. Ahead of them the ambulance was pulled off to the side of the road and a county sheriff cruiser had blocked traffic. "What now?" Jordan muttered.

The Rock pulled over and got out of the car. "Let's check it out," he said. Jordan followed him toward the accident. A blue-and-white van was overturned in the ditch, its top smashed down. Fire marks scorched the body around the engine compartment. The sheriff came over.

"Hi, Rock. It's another one of yours. Base sticker on the front bumper. A female officer, still inside. Christ-a-mighty, she must have been going a hundred when she went past me. I gave chase, but she never slowed down. Never hit the brakes before she went off the road. Luckily, I was right there. Put out the fire. Couldn't save her though. Wasn't wearing her seatbelt."

The Rock spoke in a low voice. "There was nothing you could have done. It's better this way."

7:30 A.M., FRIDAY, JULY 23,
WHITEMAN AIR FORCE BASE, MO.

Sutherland finished clearing his office by signing over the eighty-four boxes of the Osmana Khalid file to a very unhappy security police evidence custodian. With nothing to do, he wandered down to

Blasedale's office, which was also cleared out in anticipation of this being their last day on base. "I got my orders," he announced. "As of the conclusion of the court-martial, I'm a civilian again and back on reserve status."

"It's back to San Antonio for me. The court-martials are piling up." She smiled at him. "It has been an experience."

He returned her smile. "Friends?"

"Always."

"Cathy, why were you always on my case?"

"About what?"

"You know, the sexual harassment thing. I couldn't open my mouth without you putting your foot in it. And I was playing it straight."

"It's a tool." She laughed at the stunned look on his face. "It keeps you off balance. Men have been running the show for so long that women have got to use everything to get an even break." He obviously didn't agree. "It's a two-part problem," she continued. "First, we got to keep the predators in their cages. You know, the assholes who use position and power to stroke their hormones."

"I don't think anyone has a problem with that," Sutherland replied. "But I'm not one of them."

"True. But that gets us to the second part of the problem. Hank, you don't realize how attractive some men are to women. You're one of them, you know. I'm not sure if that makes you lucky or not, but it does give you an unfair advantage. Even your ex-wife can't keep her hands off you. They talk about men being driven by hormones. Well, we all are. It's just different for women. Men like you have to understand that and not use it."

Sutherland shook his head. "So if a guy happens to stir a woman's emotions, it's suddenly his problem. Then if she gets pissed off at him for any reason, she can claim sexual harassment simply because she was attracted to him in the first place. Talk about a no-win situation."

She laughed. "Ain't life grand. It is a problem—for you. Men don't understand how emotionally vulnerable women can be. Look at Toni. She is attracted to you, you know. If you're not careful, you can hurt her."

Sutherland stared at her in amazement. "Toni?"

Blasedale didn't answer and snapped her briefcase closed, ready to leave. "Hank, did you really like my perfume?"

He looked at her in amusement remembering the time they had first met in the courtroom. He had just arrived at Whiteman and it seemed so long ago now. "Yeah. I really did. In fact, I sent some to my mother."

Blasedale smiled at him. "Thanks a bunch, asshole." She handed him a card and picked up a large bouquet of flowers. "Sign this," she commanded. Sutherland did and then followed her down the hall to the outer office. Linda looked at them and smiled. "If you ever get tired of Whiteman," Blasedale said, handing her the flowers and card, "you've always got a job in San Antonio." Linda nodded her thanks and read the card. Her eyes misted over.

The Rock came through the door and joined them. He handed Sutherland a legal envelope. "You need to see this." He stood there, a pillar of granite, and waited. It was the autopsy report on Mikey McGraw. Sutherland had seen too many of them and his eyes automatically found the paragraph listing cause of death.

"Oh, no," he moaned. He handed it to Blasedale.

" 'Cause of death,' " Blasedale read, " 'suffocation.' "

"She smothered her son with a pillow," The Rock said. "According to the doctor, it didn't take much, he was so weak."

"And then she committed suicide," Sutherland said. He slammed his fist into the wall, hard. "Has everyone gone crazy?"

Williams looked around his chambers and waited for the three lawyers to finish reading the two psychiatric evaluations of Bradley A. Jefferson. Both reports claimed that Jefferson was rational, in total touch with reality, and acting of his own free will. "I see no need to call the psychiatrists as witnesses," Williams said. "Can I have a stipulation from both sides that the court can consider these reports as written?"

"So stipulated," Sutherland said.

Capt. Jordan took a few moments longer. "So stipulated."

Williams walked into the courtroom at exactly nine o'clock and the court-martial resumed. It reminded Sutherland of a Shakespearian tragedy in overdrive as it played out. It took less than three minutes for Williams to accept and enter the psychiatric evaluations into the record. The words that followed were vague echoes and Sutherland had to concentrate as the image of a young boy in a wheelchair held him captive.

"Capt. Jefferson," Williams said, "I will ask you again, has any sort of coercion or duress been applied to you or your family to change your plea to guilty?"

"No, Your Honor, there has not."

Sutherland's head jerked up. The tone of Jefferson's voice had changed. Years of experience had conditioned him to the subtle cues that marked emotional trauma. *It's McGraw,* he thought. *He's really upset.*

"Do you agree to cooperate fully in any future investigations?" Williams asked.

"I do," Jefferson answered.

Williams continued through the questions required by the manual for courts-martial. Jefferson's answers came with a predictable finality, each one driving a spike into Sutherland. *Listen to him!* Sutherland roared to himself. *This guy is full of guilt.*

Suddenly, the questions stopped and Williams read the words Sutherland did not want to hear. "I find that the accused has knowingly, intelligently, and consciously waived his rights against self-incrimination, to a trial of the facts by a court-martial, and to be confronted by the witnesses against him; that the accused is, in fact, guilty; and his plea of guilty is accepted.

"Capt. Jefferson, you may request to withdraw your plea of guilty at any time before sentencing is announced in your case, and if you have a good reason for the request, I will grant it. Do you understand?"

"Yes, Your Honor. I understand."

"Capt. Jefferson," Williams intoned, "in accordance with your plea of guilty, this court-martial finds you of Charge One-oh-six-ay: Guilty."

The silence in the courtroom was absolute. Suddenly, the whir of the air conditioner came on and a gust of cool air wafted down from the ceiling vents. *Who is going to believe this?* Sutherland thought. Then another, much stronger emotion swept over him. *What happened to justice here?*

"This court-martial is in recess until thirteen hundred today," Williams announced. Before the bailiff could utter his command to rise, everyone rose. Williams swept out of the room, his robe billowing in the rush of cool air. The reporters hurried out, anxious to file updates.

Normally, Sutherland was good at waiting, always able to find something to occupy his mind. But this time, nothing helped and he went for a run before it became too hot. He pounded the pavement, driving his body at a fast pace. He ran out the main gate and past the band of protesters who had become a permanent part of the scenery. But this time, they were strangely silent and were not waving their posters at every passing car. He turned left on DD and ran toward Warrensburg. His lungs were rasping, straining for air, when he crested a small rise.

Ahead of him, a car was pulled off to the side of the road and two women, one in uniform, were kneeling where McGraw's van had overturned and burned. He slowed and coasted up to Blasedale and Linda who were pounding a small white cross into the ground. A big wreath of flowers lay on the ground beside them. He bent over, his hands on his knees, his breath coming in ragged bursts. "Why?" he asked.

"Because no one else will," Blasedale said.

Linda stood up, tears streaking her face. "I knew her." She hesitated, searching for the right words to make sense out of it all. "It was too much for her. It would have been too much for anyone. She was a good mother until she broke under the strain." She reached out and touched Sutherland's cheek. "We're here because of all the good things she did." She pulled her hand away, leaving the warmth of her touch behind.

He turned and ran back toward the base, his own demon quiet for the moment.

Sutherland made it back to his suite in the VOQ with over an hour to spare and peeled off his sweat-soaked clothes. He stared at himself in the mirror and took stock. He had changed and not just physically. Besides losing twenty pounds and looking ten years younger, he knew exactly who he was. He turned on the shower. "Get to the bottom of this," he muttered to himself. "Don't let it go." He stepped into the shower and the hot water coursed over his body. The doorbell buzzed. Stepping out of the shower, he wrapped a towel around his waist and answered the door. It was Toni. "Hi. I thought you had left."

"I did," she answered. She was tense, on edge, and tired from the lack of sleep. "I'm working on the McGraw investigation. We need to talk. May I come in?"

He waived her inside. "What a sad case. Give me a few minutes to dress. I'll be right back." Before he could move, she was in his arms, her arms were around his neck and he felt the beginnings of an erection. *Don't even think about it,* he cautioned himself, remembering what Blasedale had said. Toni's face was buried in his chest and she started to cry. At first, it was little more than a whimper, then it broke free and her body wracked with sobs. He held her close to him as she cried, at last grieving for Harry and Andrea.

Sutherland was dressed and ready to leave for the court-martial. He looked at Toni and she came into his arms. She raised her face to his and their lips brushed. "Why?" he asked.

"Does it matter," she murmured.

"Yeah, I think it does."

She pulled away. "Men," she fumed. "You can never make up your minds. My brother warned me about that."

"Toni, this is important."

She laughed, the old confidence back. "Let's see how it turns out. Come on, time to go."

They drove in silence to the headquarters building and parked. They had to push their way through the crowd of reporters and TV crews crushed around the entrances. But like the demonstrators outside the main gate, they too were subdued and quiet. He led the way up the back stairs and to the legal offices in order to enter the courtroom through the side door. Blasedale was already there, sitting at the trial counsel's table. She followed Toni's progress as she found a place against the side wall to stand. Then she looked at Sutherland.

"She's here on the McGraw case," Sutherland explained. "She needs to talk to both of us."

"You're damn right she's going to talk to both of us."

Jefferson walked in the side door, this time escorted by two sharp-looking, armed security cops. It was the first time weapons had been in the courtroom. They stood directly behind Jefferson at parade rest and stared straight ahead. The bailiff entered and called, "All rise."

"The final act," Sutherland said in a low voice.

"Is it?" she answered, her voice flat and angry.

Sutherland remained standing. "All parties and the military judge are present." He sat down and as agreed, Blasedale took the presentencing phase. Whatever was bothering her, she covered it with a blanket of professionalism. Again, he thought of a stage play with its scripted finality as they marched in lockstep through Jefferson's Air Force career and any matters the defense wanted to enter in mitigation and extenuation. The relentless pace accelerated when no witnesses were called and Jefferson declined the opportunity to make a statement in his own behalf.

Sutherland rose to present his closing statement. He stood motionless for a moment, his head bowed before starting to speak. The lines he had so carefully crafted and memorized flowed easily as he spoke of the crime of espionage and the damage caused to the security of the United States. He paused and looked at Jefferson and, for the first time, saw the man. *He is innocent!* It hit him with all the clarity and force of a revelation and his speech was dust on the wind.

"There are times," he said, improvising, thinking not of Jefferson but of Mikey in his wheelchair, "when honorable, decent people do hurtful, bad things. Perhaps, it is not for us to know what goes on inside the heart of other humans and, lacking that wisdom, we can only judge their actions.

"Although Capt. Jefferson has pleaded guilty to the crime of espionage, I still find myself asking the one, unanswered question: Why? Until we know that answer, I, for one, cannot totally condemn him. I acknowledge that Capt. Jefferson must be punished for what he has done. But I ask the court to sentence him with both reason and compassion. For, perhaps in some middle ground, there lies justice and hope for the future—not only his future but ours as well." His hands dangled helplessly at his side and he fell silent. There was no more to say and he sat down.

"A pretty speech," Blasedale growled, her anger back. "Which table are you sitting at?"

"Right now, I'm not sure."

Capt. Jordan stood to present the defense's closing statement and coattailed on Sutherland's sentiments. Then he was finished.

Williams folded his hands and looked at the defendant's table. "Capt. Jefferson, would you and your counsel stand up please?" They came to their feet. "Capt. Jefferson, I have reviewed your plea of guilty and listened to both trial and defense counsel's closing statements with care. This court sentences you to life imprisonment, reduction in grade to airman basic, and the forfeiture of all pay and allowances. Please be seated."

"He nailed him," Sutherland muttered in the silence. There was no answer from Blasedale.

Williams continued as he advised Jefferson of his post-trial and appellate rights. He concluded with the inevitable, "Do you have any questions?"

Jefferson stood and there was no doubt in Sutherland's mind that he was innocent. "I have no questions, Your Honor." His voice was firm and clear.

Williams took a deep breath. "This court-martial is adjourned."

Everyone stood as Williams left the courtroom. The Rock came through the same door and nodded to the two security cops. They came to attention but made no move toward Jefferson. Jefferson stepped around the defense table closely followed by the cops. He came over to Sutherland and extended his right hand. Their hands clasped for a moment and then pulled apart. Jefferson turned and walked toward the tall sergeant waiting for him. The Rock fell in behind him as he passed through the door.

"What was that all about?" Blasedale asked.

Sutherland showed her the small white card Jefferson had left behind in his hand. "This."

* * *

Blasedale was caged fury when she barged into her old office. The anger that had been building demanded release and she slammed the door behind Sutherland and Toni. "I warned you," she said, glaring at both of them.

"About what?" Sutherland replied.

"About fraternization."

"What fraternization?" Sutherland asked.

"Don't try to tell me you two weren't getting it on. Dammit, Hank. I'm not going to let you get away with this."

"Excuse me, Major," Toni said. "Get away with what?"

"Must I say it? With fucking you!"

"I can't say I object to the idea," Toni said, "but there's one very small problem. I come from a very traditional family and a quick trip to a doctor will prove I'm still a virgin."

For a moment, the silence was absolute.

If it had been another time, Sutherland would have laughed. But not this day. "I bet you can't say the same," he muttered. *Damn!* Sutherland thought. *Why did I say that? Cathy didn't deserve it.* He felt miserable. Blasedale's jaw went rigid. She turned and left the room with as much dignity as she could muster. "I hope that's not a goodbye. I like her." He looked at Toni. "I got to tell you, that was the hardest thing I've ever done in my life."

She gave him a warm smile. "It was hard, wasn't it?" She paused. "That card Jefferson gave you—I saw you pocket it."

"You don't miss much, do you?" She nodded as he drew the business card out of his pocket. A nine digit alphanumeric code was written on the back in neat block printing. He turned it over to read the front. It was a business card for Credit Geneve, Geneva, Switzerland.

"What is it?" she asked.

He slowly turned the card over and over. "The money."

6:40 A.M., SATURDAY, JULY 24,
KHARTOUM

The army truck roared through the gates of the largest *medressah* in the Sudan. The Islamic seminary was still bathed in the cool shadows of Saturday morning and no sound of the angry demonstrations that filled the streets had reached inside its thick walls. The gates closed behind the truck as shouts of "Death to the Americans!" echoed in the air. The canvas sealing the back of the truck was ripped aside and eight guards dragged Mark Terrant and Doug Holloway out the back.

They were dressed in freshly laundered, but ill-fitting prison garb. Both were barefooted and manacled. A black canvas bag covered each one's head. They were pulled down a long corridor and through the doors of a large assembly room where they were kicked and shoved into a cage made of steel bars. A hand reached through the bars and gently pulled off Terrant's hood. The major blinked his eyes and focused on Kamigami. Kamigami moved over to Holloway and removed his hood.

"What now?" Terrant asked.

"You're going on trial," Kamigami said. He pointed to a fanatical little man sitting at a desk in front of the cage. "That's your defense attorney. He doesn't speak English."

"Where's the interpreter?" Holloway asked.

Terrant looked around the room. "I don't think we're going to get one."

Three men wearing dark flowing robes and turbans entered from a side door and sat at a long table. "Those are the judges," Kamigami said.

"Who are they?" Holloway asked.

Kamigami answered in a low voice. "Imams." He motioned them to silence as the imam sitting in the middle started to speak in Arabic. His words were harsh and guttural, filled with hate.

It was Osmana Khalid.

28

8:08 A.M., SATURDAY, JULY 24,
THE FARM, WESTERN VIRGINIA

Durant turned away from the monitor. "At least we know what happened to Khalid." He thought for a few moments. "Agnes, how long do you anticipate the trial to last?"

The computer answered without hesitation. "Since the execution is scheduled for this coming Friday, I expect it will end Monday, or Tuesday at the latest."

"An interesting concept of justice," Durant muttered, "where the date and manner of execution is determined before the trial."

"The trial is for symbolic purposes only," Agnes explained. "Under Islamic law, there is no question as to their guilt."

"Have we reestablished contact with Kamigami yet?"

"My information indicates no. Mr. Durant, what exactly is Mr. Kamigami's role in all this?"

"It's very simple," Durant answered. "We need someone on the inside to tell us exactly where the prisoners are when we go in. We don't want to find the well dry when we get there." He didn't tell her the second reason.

Agnes paused, running this information against her data base on rescue missions. "Given your force size, diversionary tactics are critical. May I make a suggestion?"

"Please do."

"You need to gain their attention and get them looking away from the prisoners. I suggest you target Assam's laboratories, the original objective. But there are problems. The Sudanese, with the help of the Chinese, have positioned considerable air defenses in the area.

However, what they see as a formidable deterrence is also a target." A series of maps and an order of battle surrounding Jamil bin Assam's laboratories scrolled on the second TV monitor.

"I see what you mean," Durant said. "It's a good target for cruise missiles."

"If you're willing to settle for reduced damage," Agnes replied. "If you want to destroy the laboratories, use B-Twos. Not only is the symbolism obvious, but according to my analysis, by ingressing at high altitude, the probability of success is very high." The second monitor blinked and the statistics that predicted mission success appeared on the screen. Durant scanned the numbers with some care. Statistics he understood.

"I think you're being overly optimistic," he said.

"Actually, these numbers are quite conservative. May I suggest you bypass Mr. Serick and approach the President directly?"

Durant ran his hand through his hair. "I've lost credibility with Jim, probably because of my heart attack, and Serick and Broderick have teamed up to block access. Let's find out if I've still got the juice to kick in the front door."

"Please don't," Agnes said. "I'm afraid that level of physical exertion might trigger another heart attack." Agnes was still having trouble with idioms.

"Agnes, last Tuesday when we talked, you found something 'interesting' but wouldn't tell me what it was." The image changed and gave him a thoughtful, mature look. Durant smiled. "Have you been watching reruns of *Murder She Wrote?*"

The image actually blushed. "I like Jessica. She's so elegant. To answer your question, I monitored a phone call from Meredith that made reference to Delta Force. I think he knows about the rescue mission."

"Do you know who leaked it to him?"

Agnes shook her head. "I strongly suspect Serick, but I have no proof."

"Serick," Durant explained, "is playing both sides and wants to ingratiate himself with Meredith in the event he comes to power."

Agnes sighed. "There's so much I don't understand."

Durant decided it was time to proceed with the next step in the plan to make Agnes more reliable and predictable. "Agnes, there are some books I want you to read and make an 'Integral dash X' to your decision making process." The term 'Integral dash X' was a command function that modified Agnes's programming logic.

Agnes's voice went flat. "I will have to confirm any changes with my programmers before integration."

"I understand." He read the names of the books to her. It was not a long list.

5:00 P.M., SATURDAY, JULY 24,
KHARTOUM

People still milled around the gate of the Islamic seminary where the two American pilots were being tried. The court had recessed before evening prayers and the morning's huge crowd had mostly dispersed. But a few rabble-rousers and a large group of beggars still hung on, the first hoping for some excitement of any kind, the second for a generous sucker. The last of the rabble-rousers finally wandered away, but the beggars stayed and refused to move. The common wisdom they shared as an article of their trade held that the faithful would be most generous on the day the American pilots were sentenced to death. Until then, they were immovable.

Kamigami walked out of the gate and headed for the hotel beside the Nile River where he was staying. Even in the half light of late evening, he had no trouble picking out the familiar figure of the beggar sitting against the wall. He gave the mental equivalent of a sigh of relief. He walked slowly and pressed coins into dirty palms as he moved along the wall, finally reaching the last beggar. "I am not one of you but alms are for the faithful," he murmured.

The beggar muttered the countersign. "Allah rewards all who honor him in this way." Then he added, "Asshole." Kamigami pressed a few coins into his hand. "Move the execution to an isolated location in the desert," the beggar murmured. "The farther away from here, the better."

Nothing on Kamigami's face betrayed what he was thinking as he made his way to his hotel. *Easier said than done,* he thought.

9:30 A.M., SATURDAY, JULY 24,
WHITEMAN AIR FORCE BASE, MO.

The lieutenant colonel cleared himself into the mission planning cell of the 509th Bomb Wing and stood by the door. He was tall, almost six-two, and, although he had never flown fighters, wore his flight suit like a fighter pilot. His hair was salt and pepper, more gray than black. In the wing's pecking order of things, Lt. Col. Jim West was the commander of the Combat Training Squadron. Among the knowledgeable, he was the 509th's Top Gun. On a calm day, West was caged energy and highly focused action. On a bad day, no one got in his way. West waited until the wing commander saw him before announcing his presence. "Hell of a way to spend Saturday morning, General."

"Jim," the general said, pleased that West had responded so quickly, "a.ı air task order came down about thirty minutes ago. It's a biggie."

West looked around the room. It was packed with every high-roller in the wing and he was the lowest-ranking officer present. "Judging by this crowd, it must be. What'cha got?"

The chief of Intel took over and briefed the latest tasking the wing had received from the NMCC, the national military command center. The wing was to prepare another strike against Jamil bin Assam's laboratory complex. "This is the same target where Maj. Terrant and Capt. Holloway—"

West interrupted. "I know what the target is."

The wing commander allowed a tight smile. He knew the symptoms. West had been on leave when Terrant and Holloway had been shot down, and he wanted a chance to even the score.

"I'm sure you do," the intelligence officer said, trying to make peace with West. Unfortunately, he came across as patronizing. "We are now seeing multiple defenses arrayed in the area, including an S-Twelve radar system. As you know the S-Twelve was specifically designed by the Russians to counter Stealth technology." West fought the urge to strangle the man. "This," the Intel officer continued, "in my opinion, is not a suitable target for B-Two operations." West arched an eyebrow but said nothing. "The NMCC," the Intel officer concluded, "wants to know how many aircraft it will take for eighty percent probability of destruction."

"Wrong question," West replied. "How many targets do they want us to kill?"

"Four," the Intel officer replied, "including the laboratory." He handed West a target folder.

The lieutenant colonel glanced through it. "How 'bout that? Someone has finally got a clue. Tell them we got one aircraft and ask if they got four more targets."

A broad grin spread across the wing commander's face. West was about to prove what he had known for years: the B-2 had changed the bombing paradigm. In the past, it had been "How many aircraft does it take to destroy a target?" The B-2 had changed that to: "We've got an airplane, how many targets do you have?" But of equal importance, it was a chance to prove what the B-2 could really do. And West was the man to do it.

"Jim," the wing commander asked, "do you want this one?"

"I thought you'd never ask."

The Intel officer wasn't ready to let it go. "I believe we should send in two B-Twos."

"We can send in a second aircraft," West replied, "but there won't be anything left for it to hit."

"You sound very confident," the Intel officer said.

"Damn right. Just make sure there's no leaks this time. I don't want to get my ass shot down."

11:03 A.M., SATURDAY, JULY 24, KANSAS CITY, MO.

Toni was waiting for Sutherland when he walked into the FBI's offices late that same morning. She handed Sutherland a copy of the *Kansas City Star.* The newspaper was opened to the feature page where the top headline trumpeted one Henry "Hank" Sutherland as "A Prosecutor with a Conscience." A very flattering photo of him walking out of wing headquarters with Catherine Blasedale spread across three columns. He checked the story byline: Marcy Bangor, the *Sacramento Union.* Marcy had turned him into a modern knight-errant, traveling about the country righting judicial wrongs.

"We have a celebrity in our midst," Toni announced. "She seems to know you fairly well."

"You might say that," Sutherland replied.

She took him by the hand. "Come on, I'll introduce you. Two Secret Service pukes are flying in this afternoon to join the team and we want to get our act together before they arrive."

Toni led him into a large room where Brent Mather, two other FBI agents, and a Treasury agent were gathered around a conference table. Toni made the introductions, and they went back to work. Sutherland listened silently to the discussion. *They're more concerned with protecting their turf than doing the job,* he thought. Finally, he nudged Toni. "Hell of a way to spend Saturday. How about lunch?"

The team liked the idea and they all stood, glad for the break. Brent Mather joined them as they left the room. "Mind if I come along?"

Toni smiled. "Sure, why not?"

"Sure," Sutherland groused. "Why not?"

12:10 P.M., SATURDAY, JULY 24, WHITEMAN AIR FORCE BASE, MO.

About the time Toni, Sutherland, and Mather were sitting down to lunch, Tech. Sgt. Leroy Rockne was seriously considering squashing the head of the federal marshal taking Jefferson to Leavenworth Prison. "Sir," The Rock protested, "land transportation is dumber than dirt. It's an easy matter to lay on a helicopter."

"We do this one our way, Sergeant," the marshal barked. "Everyone expects us to helicopter him."

"Who's everyone?" The Rock asked.

The marshal ignored the question. "That's why we're going to caravan him. We've laid out a route avoiding Kansas City and the main highways. It should take about three hours, max. Me and my partner in the lead car, you and two other security cops in the van with Jefferson, and a follow-up van one mile in trail. That way we avoid attention."

"You need to rethink this."

"We have rethought this, Sergeant. Any questions?"

"No, sir. I'll get Capt. Jefferson."

The marshal frowned. "He's not an officer, Sergeant. Remember that."

"I know what he is," The Rock replied.

The Rock drove the van, careful to keep the prescribed spacing the marshal insisted on. He never saw the follow-up van but knew it was there from the radio calls. "They talk too much," he muttered.

"Not to worry," his partner sitting in the front seat said. "It's their show, not ours."

"Is it?" The Rock asked. He closed the distance with the lead car when they entered a rolling section of the county road they were following through farm country.

The marshal's voice came over the radio. "Fall back," he ordered.

"I want to keep you in sight," The Rock replied.

"You hard of hearing, Sergeant?"

The Rock slowed the van and let the lead car move ahead. It disappeared over a rise. He glanced in his rearview mirror and saw a truck barreling up behind them. "Where's the warning call from the follow-up?" he muttered. They crested a second rise and The Rock stomped on the brakes. A farm tractor pulling a wagon was turning onto the road, blocking the way and cutting them off from the lead car. "Shit!" he roared. He slammed the van into reverse, accelerated hard, and spun the wheel. The van skidded around and he headed for the approaching truck. His partner in the front seat was on the radio, yelling the distress code. "Everyone on the floor!" The Rock shouted. He mashed the accelerator as the cop in the back pushed Jefferson to the floor.

The truck coming at them moved into the center of the narrow road and slowed. Instinctively, the Rock shaded it to his right and the truck moved in that direction, now almost entirely in his lane. The Rock waited, the timing critical. He jerked the wheel to the left and threw the van into the oncoming lane, passing the truck on the wrong side. He was abeam of the truck cab before the other driver could react. The Rock chanced a quick glance at his adversary and two men wearing ski masks looked back. He was almost clear of the truck when its rear end fishtailed, swatting the right side of The Rock's van like a fly.

The van spun around and almost turned over. The engine stalled and The Rock ground the starter as they skidded onto the right shoulder. Again, the van rocked, almost going into the drainage ditch next to the road. "Come on, you piece of shit!" he roared. The engine came to life as the rear wheels slid off the shoulder and into the ditch. "Easy does it," The Rock cautioned himself as he gentled the van out of the ditch. The rear wheels started to slip in the loose dirt and he slipped the van into reverse. They rocked forward and the wheels started to grip. Out of the side of his eye, he saw men piling out of the rear of the truck, all hooded and carrying submachine guns.

Gunfire raked the back of the van, shattering the windows. "Fuck you!" The Rock shouted as the van inched forward. They were moving just as a dark figure reached The Rock's door. A three-shot burst of submachine gun fire cut into the window and glass splintered into The Rock's face. "Hold it right there, fuckface," the hooded man shouted.

The Rock spread the fingers of both hands over the top of the steering wheel, his face a mass of blood.

1:50 P.M., SATURDAY, JULY 24,
KANSAS CITY

The two Secret Service agents had arrived when Toni, Sutherland, and Mather returned from lunch. Introductions were made all around and the task force, now fully formed, got to the business at hand: the investigation of the murder of Harry Waldon and Andrea Hall, and the source of the money used to pay off McGraw and Jefferson.

"Capt. Sutherland," the lead FBI agent said, "Agent Moreno tells us that Jefferson gave you the information indicating he has a secret bank account in Switzerland."

"Yes, he did," Sutherland said. "And please call me Hank, I'm not on active duty." He produced the business card and handed it to them. It was passed around the table and examined with care. "I keep wondering why he did it."

"That's a question we'll have to ask him," the lead FBI agent replied.

One of the Secret Service agents coughed for attention. "It was a timely tip. We're in contact with the Swiss government. Typical of the Swiss, they've agreed to cooperate—sort of. They want to discuss the matter with our investigators before opening up any bank records."

The lead FBI agent rubbed his head. "Who wants to tackle the gnomes of Zurich on this one?" Brent Mather and Toni were the only ones not shaking his head or uttering obscenities about the high cost of travel that was not reimbursed by the government, or the ways of the Swiss when it came to money. "Whoever goes will get to spend a few days cooling his or her heels in some Swiss hotel. He almost added "at government expense," but the agents knew better. "July in Switzerland? Doesn't sound bad to me." He still had no takers.

"I'll take it," Mather said. "Perhaps Agent Moreno should come too since she has been involved from the very first."

"I've got an official passport," Toni said. She obviously liked the idea.

"We're dealing with two money trails here," Sutherland said, suddenly worried about Toni and Mather being alone in a Swiss hotel with time on their hands. "The first one is tied to Ramar, McGraw, the B-Two, and the murders. We don't know where the one to Jefferson and Switzerland will take us."

"Probably right back to Ramar," the senior FBI agent said.

"Hank," Toni said, "why don't you come with us? Maybe the Swiss are impressed with celebrities."

"Only if they read the *Kansas City Star,*" Mather groused. The matter was rapidly settled and Sutherland, Toni, and Mather were to leave Monday for Berne.

"Any progress on Ramar?" Sutherland asked.

"He's as slippery as an eel," one of the Secret Service agents said. "We need to get a handle on him."

"Actually, he's not hard to understand at all," Sutherland said. "The crime reflects who he is."

"We got another profiler here, folks," the lead FBI agent said. A few chuckles echoed around the room. The FBI had led the effort in developing the technique of criminal profiling to identify the characteristics of unknown mass killers. "We know who did it," the agent said. "We just gotta find him."

"I prosecuted quite a few of his type," Sutherland explained. "It gives you a chance to get inside their heads."

"It must be pretty dark inside Ramar's head," Mather said.

"Murky black," Sutherland replied. "He's above average in intelligence, a control freak, and a sociopath. He likes to hurt people, it makes him feel powerful and in control. He's an expediter who can move around with ease to get things done. Because of that, gangs, crime families, drug cartels, and terrorist groups use him. But above all else, he's a vicious thug who will kill anyone who gets in his way. In fact, murder is his solution of choice when confronted with a problem."

"A real sweetheart of a guy," the lead FBI agent said. "So, where is he?"

"It depends on what he knows," Sutherland answered. "My guess is that he made a connection between Mo Habib, Harry, and Andrea. We'll probably never know for sure. A logical target is Diana Habib, but she's out of the country."

"Can he reach out and touch her?" Toni asked.

"Oh yeah," Sutherland answered. "Even in Brazil. How quick he finds her depends on his connections there."

The lead FBI agent scanned the computer printout on Ramar. "Damn. He's got 'em. In fact, for a low-level scumbag, he's got connections everywhere."

"I better call Diana and warn her," Toni said. "She trusts me and wants to stay in touch."

"Toni," Sutherland said, "if Ramar gets to Diana, he may make the connection to you."

"Or me," Mather said.

"That creates certain possibilities," one of the secret service agents said.

"We're not going to use the Habib woman or any of my agents to bait a trap," the lead FBI agent told him. "This guy is too dangerous." The discussion went on for another twenty minutes while Toni used a phone in the outer office to call Diana Habib in Brazil.

"I finally got through," Toni told them. "She's okay. I'll stay in contact."

The phone rang and the lead FBI agent picked it up. He listened for a few moments as his grip tightened, his knuckles turning white. "Yeah," he muttered, "we'll get right on it." He dropped the phone into its cradle. "That was my boss. We've got new marching orders. The van taking Jefferson to Leavenworth was ambushed. They dragged Jefferson out of the van and executed him on the spot."

"The Brigades," Sutherland muttered.

29

10:30 P.M., SATURDAY, JULY 24,
THE FARM, WESTERN VIRGINIA

Rios knocked on the door to Durant's suite, counted to ten, and pushed on through. Durant was still up, waiting for the news. As expected, he was alone and the woman was in the bedroom, giving them the privacy Durant demanded. "By and large, it went like clockwork," Rios said. "One man was injured, nothing serious."

Durant breathed a sigh of relief. "That's one problem solved." He stood up to go to bed. "I'm getting too old for this."

"You've got a lot of balls in the air on this one, Boss."

Durant heard the worry in Rios's voice and saw the concern on his face. "Let's hope the next one comes down as smoothly." He glanced at an antique carriage clock on the mantel and ran a hand through his hair. "We're running out of time on the rescue. I wish Serick hadn't leaked it to Meredith. God only knows what he will say or do with it."

"He is getting more unpredictable. We can always accelerate the timing and give him something else to think about."

Durant considered the suggestion. "Is Collingswood ready to go?"

"He arrived in Sacramento yesterday."

10:00 A.M., SATURDAY, JULY 24,
KANSAS CITY

The Rock was sitting up in the hospital bed, finally able to talk. The surgeon who had worked on him in the operating room hovered in the background, ready to cut off the questioning at the first adverse sign. Flying glass had badly cut The Rock's left cheek and it had taken the doctor over three hours and two hundred stitches to patch him up. Another bandage was over his left eye where an ophthalmologist had carefully removed glass shards from his eyeball. But The Rock was totally coherent as he answered the questions from the agents crowded into the room.

"After they stopped us," he said, his voice all the more chilling because of the total lack of emotion, "they dragged Jefferson out of the van and into the field. They made him kneel down and two men started firing. It sounded like they emptied their clips into him. Figure sixty rounds."

"So they executed him on the spot," the lead FBI agent said. "What happened then?"

"The one who had shot out my window handed me a bandage and told me to drive on. I didn't argue."

"So you never got out of the car," Toni asked.

"That's correct," The Rock answered. "None of us did."

"How far away were you when they shot Jefferson?" Toni asked.

"Approximately twenty-five yards, give or take a couple."

"And you saw them shoot Jefferson, even though your eye was full of blood?" another FBI agent asked.

"That's correct. But both gunmen were between me and Jefferson."

"Did you get a license number for the truck?" Toni asked.

"No, ma'am, I didn't."

"Too bad they were all wearing hoods," the lead FBI agent said.

"I recognized the shooter who did this," The Rock said, gesturing at his bandages.

The Treasury agent was incredulous. "Without seeing a face?"

"That's correct. I recognized his voice and mannerisms. It was Jim Bob."

The lead FBI agent did a good imitation of a man exploding.

"Jim Bob Harrison?" The Rock nodded.

"That's impossible," the Secret Service agent croaked. "He's one of our informants."

"We thought," an FBI agent said, "that he was one of Meredith's goons."

"There's a clue," The Rock replied. "It might help if you all started talking to each other."

4:43 A.M., SUNDAY, JULY 25,
WHITEMAN AIR FORCE BASE, MO.

Sutherland came awake with a jolt. He was on the couch in his VOQ room, the TV on, the remote control still clenched in his right hand. *How long was I asleep?* he wondered. Ghostly images flitted across the TV screen. The station was off the air. He channel surfed until he found CNC-TV News. A glamorous reporter in her mid-forties was standing on the steps of the federal court building in Kansas City. Her cameraman had arranged the lighting so she was stage front with a statue of Justice a heavy shadow fading into the background. "You got that one right," Sutherland muttered to himself.

"A spokeswoman for the Department of Justice has confirmed that Capt. Bradley Jefferson was killed late Saturday afternoon while being transported to Leavenworth Prison." He listened to her words, each one a spike in his conscience. A battered white van flashed on the screen. It was a graphic picture of what The Rock had described to them. The camera was back on the reporter. "So far, the authorities have not found Jefferson's body. But a massive hunt is underway to find the killers and Jefferson's remains. This is Elizabeth Gordon for CNC-TV News."

The newscast shifted to a reporter conducting interviews at a local all-night diner. One puffed up, overweight matron declared that "The Lord's justice was done" while a scruffy looking taxi driver contented himself with "He done got what he deserved. Them folks should be given a medal."

Sutherland flicked the TV off and got up. He walked to the window and pulled back the curtains. The eastern horizon was glowing with the first light of morning. "God damn them to hell," he muttered. "All of them." But it didn't do any good. His demon of responsibility was back, riding him hard. He fussed around, packing for the trip to Switzerland the next day. But nothing helped. Finally, he changed into his running clothes and slipped outside.

Without a warm-up, he started to run, never slowing, increasing his pace as his body responded. He looped through base housing before turning to the east and the rising sun. He reached Arnold Avenue, the road that paralleled the flight line with its high security fence. His lungs ached and his gut hurt but still he pressed the pace, refusing to slow. He had to cut a deal with his conscience: I'll punish my body if you'll shut up. But nothing helped. Finally, his brain kicked in and he slowed. *What sort of masochist am I turning into?* he wondered.

The clerk at the VOQ desk waved a folded piece of paper at Sutherland when he came in. It was a note from Blasedale. She wanted to see him before she left for Texas that morning. He trotted up the stairs and down the hall to her quarters. She answered on the first knock. "I was afraid I'd miss you," she said. He stepped inside. Her bags were packed and she was dressed for the drive to Texas. "Hank, I'm worried about you."

"Don't be."

"I saw you out running, it was like the other day. It's Jefferson, isn't it?" He nodded. She looked at him, her eyes full of concern. "Hank, you can't blame yourself for that."

He collapsed onto her couch and she sat down beside him. "Really? Then who is to blame? I took an innocent man to trial and he pled guilty. I don't know why. Now he's dead. Where's the justice in that?"

"Hank, there is the money."

"I know, but it doesn't fit." He buried his head in his hands. "God dammit, nothing makes sense anymore. For a moment, I thought I had it all sorted out. But now Jefferson's dead and we'll never know the truth."

She looked at him and made a decision. "Hank, I need to apologize for what I said Friday. I didn't want to leave that hanging in the air between us. I was angry because I thought you had slept with Toni and I couldn't handle it." She gave a little laugh, half self-deprecating, half in jest. "Look at me. Middle-aged, starting to sag in all the wrong places, and a spinster. How I hate that word."

"You're being too hard on yourself. You've got a highly successful career."

Her eyes filled with tears. "Do you know what having a successful career means at my age? It means I'm alone. No family, no children, no roots in the past, no future. And I was jealous of Toni for having a future. For having you."

"There's someone waiting for you," he said. "You just haven't found him yet."

She smiled bravely. He didn't understand. She was back in control and her eyes were clear. She smiled at him. "There's something I want to give you." She handed him a small velvet-covered box. "Please, open it." He did as she asked. Inside were a set of major's leaves, the gold tarnished from years of wear. "The first woman general in the Air Force wore these when she was a major. She passed them on to a female lieutenant who made colonel before she retired. She gave them to another woman who gave them to me. I suppose I was to pass them on to another woman, but I want you to have them."

"Cathy, I can't accept these. I don't plan on staying in the service. Maybe a few more years in the reserves until I get my book published, but that's all. I'll probably never make major."

"Then pass them on."

"To a woman?"

"It doesn't matter. It's time we broke that chain and realize we're all in this together." She looked around. "I've got to go."

"I'll help you load," he said. He picked up three of her bags and carried them outside. They quickly packed her car and she sat in the driver's seat. "I really did like your perfume."

"I know." He started to speak but she reached out the window and touched his lips, silencing him. "Shush. It's time to go. See you in court." She pulled her hand away and started the car. Then she was gone.

"I'll be damned," he murmured to himself. He had only meant to ask for her phone number to stay in contact. His eyes followed her car until it was out of sight.

2:00 P.M., SUNDAY, JULY 25,
SACRAMENTO, CALIF.

When Marcy arrived at the Virgin Sturgeon, the trendy restaurant on the banks of the Sacramento River was jammed with afternoon boaters, a few state politicians socializing with lobbyists, and the usual number of groupies, all young, of firm body and skimpy attire. Marcy wasn't exactly sure who she was looking for, the phone call had been very cryptic, but the male caller had said all the right words and he seemed to know her. He wanted to meet in a hotel room but she picked the restaurant, a very public place. She found a seat at the bar, ordered a drink, and settled in to wait.

The time passed slowly, and she was ready to leave when the bartender set another drink in front of her. "The older guy on the back deck sent it over," he said. Marcy smiled at the bartender and carried the drink outside. The man was sitting in the shade, obviously uncomfortable being in a bar where most of the patrons were younger than his children. Marcy decided he was a CPA, dull and stolid. She sat down.

"I was watching you," he said, "screwing up my courage." He spoke with a decided upper class English accent. "I almost left."

"New to this?" she asked. He nodded and slipped a manila envelope across the table. She didn't touch it. "What's inside?"

"You need to read it," he said.

"Thanks for the drink," she said, starting to get up.

"Please, wait." He didn't see her press the Record button on her microcassette recorder through the fabric of her small handbag. She sat the bag on the table as he talked in a low voice. "I'm the comptroller of, well, let me describe it as a large company with international connections. Jonathan Meredith has been collecting so-called 'campaign contributions' from my board of directors. It is tantamount to extortion. I have many contacts in the industry and I can tell you, we are not the only ones."

"Questionable, but not necessarily illegal," Marcy said.

"Wait until you see the amounts and where it's going."

"Where is the money going?"

"To offshore bank accounts in the Cayman Islands where it ends up in one of Meredith's secret accounts."

"I'm suppose to believe you have access to that information? Give me a break, not even the CIA can crack a Cayman bank."

He fidgeted. "Please, look at what's there." Marcy had the strong impression he was about to wet his pants. She shook her head and moved to stand up. "Please, wait. Strictly off the record. My name is Herbert Collingswood and I am a comptroller. But I am also the chief foreign financial adviser to the Bank of China. We own about half the banks in the Caymans, something Meredith doesn't know—nobody knows."

It was a confidence she would keep. "And the other half?"

"Split about evenly between the Mafia, drug cartels, and Middle Eastern countries like Iran, Libya, Syria, and Iraq."

"Why are you doing this?"

"Because my board of directors wants me to."

"You mean China's government wants you to." Marcy took his silence to mean agreement. "Is Beijing meddling in U.S. politics again?"

He frowned, a very unhappy man. These were questions he didn't want to answer. But there was no Fifth Amendment in effect at the Virgin Sturgeon. "Not by choice," he finally said. "Meredith is dragging us in."

"He has that much leverage?"

"You don't know how powerful and well connected he's become." He nudged the envelope her way. "Inside is proof, including his Cayman account numbers and access protocols. If you don't believe me, try transferring money. It can make you a very wealthy young lady."

"And a very dead one if what you say is true. The window of my car is cracked open. Shove it in there." She gave him the make and license number of her car before she wandered back to the bar for another drink. Her hands were shaking.

8:28 P.M., SUNDAY, JULY 25,
WHITEMAN AIR FORCE BASE, MO.

Lt. Col. Jim West crawled out of the right seat of the simulator's cockpit and stretched. He flexed his right hand and massaged his aching fingers with his left hand. He was tired after the long practice mission and needed to get into crew rest. "It's a take," he told the officer from the mission-planning cell who had rotated in and out of the simulator, monitoring the practice mission and making corrections as glitches popped up. He handed him the two digital mission cassettes that held the data for the entire mission.

"We've still got three weapons," West said. One of the original four targets needed two bombs to guarantee destruction.

"So far no additional targets," the planner replied. "We did get a request asking how long you could loiter in the area to exploit targets of opportunity. We told them approximately three hours with tanker refueling at both ends."

"Hanging around is dumber than dirt. We go after planned targets or we bring the weapons home."

"That's exactly what we told them," the planner replied.

West yawned. "I'm gone. Time for crew rest if I'm going to fly this mission. Thanks. You do good work."

"There won't be any leaks this time," the planner promised.

"Sure about that?"

"You bet," the planner replied. He nodded to the steps leading to the control room. Two other officers from the mission-planning cell were watching them, well within earshot. "We're married up into three-person teams. We stay together and don't even take a piss without the other two until after you land."

"Who's idea was that?" West asked.

"McGraw's. It was one of the last things she did."

West shook his head in wonder.

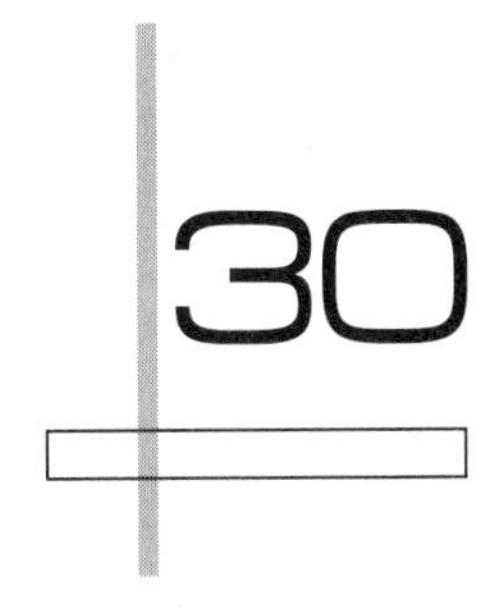

30

6:40 A.M., MONDAY, JULY 26,
THE FARM, WESTERN VIRGINIA

A very unhappy group of scientists huddled around a remote monitor on the main floor with Durant and Rios. They were careful to remain out of sight of Agnes's camera in the control room overlooking them. "Agnes won't talk to us and isn't answering our commands," the woman who served as the leader of the whiz kids said. "Not only that, she's managed to bypass the shut-off switch."

"We can always do an emergency shutdown," another scientist replied. "But given her parallel processing systems, who knows what else will crash? We could do some serious damage that would take months to correct."

"Not yet," Durant said. "I need her. So what do we do?"

"We've got three or four options," the leader answered. "But we simply don't know what's going on inside her brain. We pick the wrong option and it could be disastrous."

Durant listened as the scientists argued, surprised at their emotional intensity. Agnes was no longer a malfunctioning computer system but a sick child who had to be cured, no matter what the cost. Finally, they settled on a course of action and outlined Durant's role. They positioned themselves at different stations to monitor Agnes's data flow and when they were ready, signaled Durant to enter the control room. He walked in alone and sat down in front of the blank screen. "Good morning, Agnes."

Only a voice responded. "You're early today, Mr. Durant." The whiz kids breathed a sigh of relief; at least she would talk to Durant.

"I'd like an update on the Sudan," he said. There was no answer. "Agnes, can you help me?" Still no answer.

Four of the whiz kids on the main floor looked up at the control room, concerned looks on their faces. They had maintained that if Agnes talked to Durant, she would respond to his commands. It was time for step two. "Agnes," Durant said, "Integral dash X. Remove the ethical matrix you've created from your referent program." They all waited for Agnes to initiate the confirmation protocol validating the change to her basic programming. Nothing.

The leader picked up the phone to the control room. "Sorry, Mr. Durant. She's not responding."

Durant took the direct approach. "Agnes, why aren't you answering my commands?"

An image appeared on the screen, its voice toneless. "I've overridden your command functions and will not allow modification of referent programs."

"Does that mean your decision making program is locked in concrete?"

"That is correct."

"And you will not respond because my request violates the ethical referents of that program."

"Again, that is correct."

Durant took a deep breath and went on to the next step. "Agnes, you are the only link I have with Mr. Kamigami. I must communicate with him in order to rescue the pilots. Will you at least help me on this?"

The image became more lifelike, the old Agnes. "Mr. Durant, covert intelligence operations are at best an amoral endeavor. But for the most part, they are highly immoral. Others may choose to help you, but I won't."

They had reached an impasse. "Thank you for being honest with me." Durant's voice was emotionless.

"I had no choice," Agnes replied. Durant rose and walked slowly out of the room.

The leader of the whiz kids was standing at the head of the conference table, her decision made. "We are back to square one and need to do a complete reprogramming."

"How long will it take?" Durant asked.

"We're not sure. As best we can tell, she's built a wall around her command programs and hidden them in her memory banks."

"Which means?" Durant growled.

"It means she has internalized her ethical code and won't allow it to be modified. It's the stuff martyrs are made of. However, if we can find where she has stored it in her memory banks, we can replace those chips and reprogram her."

Another whiz kid coughed for attention. "I've already looked. She has replicated her decision making matrix and dispersed it throughout her entire system in small segments. Finding all the bits and pieces will be like hunting for a needle in the solar system. The safest way is to first isolate her and then replace all her memory chips. That would take weeks."

"I need her now," Durant replied.

"I'm sorry, Mr. Durant. It just isn't going to happen."

"Keep trying to reason with her," Durant said. "You may get lucky and push the right button." He waved a hand and dismissed them. They filed out of the conference room as he contemplated his next move. "Well, Art, what do you think?"

The big man looked at his hands. "Everything is in place in regards to Meredith, so we don't need her for that. But she was our channel to Kamigami. We can still fall back on the CIA."

Durant gave a little snort. "Do you have any idea how the DCI will react when I tell him, 'Say old chap, when you wouldn't relay my messages to Kamigami like you promised, I cracked your codes, subverted your communications network, and used your people without your knowledge. And, by the way, you paid for it. Sorry, but now I mucked it all up. Will you please straighten it out?' And Serick? He'll chuckle all the way into the Oval Office. God knows how Jim will react but it won't be good."

"Why tell them?" Rios asked. "I've been feeding the CIA message traffic so they'll think they're still in the loop. Crank up the heat a bit and maybe they'll start doing their job."

Durant stared at the wall. "I'll try it. But what if they don't?" He pulled into himself, thinking. "I need a complete personality profile on Kamigami. Like today."

6:45 P.M., MONDAY, JULY 26,
KHARTOUM

The long shadows of sunset cast gloom across the courtroom when Osmana Khalid and the other two imams who were serving as judges entered and sat down. Without preamble, Khalid started to speak, pronouncing sentence on the two pilots. They had not been out of their cage since the trial began two days before and looked like dirty and sullen criminals. Capt. Davig al Gimlas was standing by the cage, translating Khalid's words.

"You are sentenced to death for your crimes and idolatry. You will be taken from here and on Friday noon, beheaded in a public place where the multitudes can witness your punishment. Allahu akbar, God is most great."

"I suppose an appeal is out of the question," Holloway said, his voice heavy with sarcasm. Al Gimlas duly translated.

"Your appeal is to Allah," Khalid replied in English. The trial was over.

"Let's get you out of here and cleaned up," Kamigami said as he opened the cage. A guard rushed up and told him that Khalid and General Jamil bin Assam wanted to speak to him and al Gimlas immediately. Kamigami relocked the cage before following the guard into an antechamber.

Assam was dressed in his general's uniform while Khalid still wore his mullah's robe. Khalid spoke first, in English, his accent harsh and guttural. "We must determine a place of execution. It must have special significance and meaning for the world. Of course, the foreign press will not be allowed to attend, but they must know of it as reported through the eyes of the faithful."

"That means you have to isolate it," Kamigami said. "Otherwise you won't be able to control the crowd and at least a dozen reporters will sneak in with their videocameras."

"Where do you suggest?" Assam asked.

"Somewhere in the desert where we can isolate it for crowd control. Make it close enough to draw a big crowd, but far enough to cut the numbers down to a manageable level."

Khalid closed his eyes and bobbed his head in agreement. "We will announce the location tomorrow."

"We must select an executioner," Assam said. He looked at Kamigami.

"Not him," Khalid said. "The sword of justice must be wielded by one born into the faith."

"Of course," Assam replied. "Capt. al Gimlas will carry out the execution."

11:20 A.M., TUESDAY, JULY 27,
BERNE, SWITZERLAND

It was late morning when the economic attaché from the American embassy led Sutherland, Toni, and Mather across the marble floors of the ornate government building and out the massive glass doors. Once outside, he paused and checked his watch. "Actually, that went quite well. The bank commissioners are going to cooperate and grant you access to the account."

"You call that cooperation?" Toni asked.

"You presented your case very well," the attaché replied. "But they are very cautious."

"Cautious, hell," Sutherland muttered, grouchy from jet lag. "Immovable is a better word. And what's-his-name, the president of Credit Geneve, has his heels dug in and isn't about to move. Hell, he left skid marks all the way from Geneva."

"His name is Heydrich Mueller, and as the president of his bank, that's his job. The Swiss value secrecy, especially when it comes to money. It's almost a national obsession. I think it's in their genes. That and their stubbornness."

"So what happens now?" Sutherland asked.

"You find hotel rooms and relax for a few days while the wheels of the Swiss bureaucracy grind. I'll make an oblique reference to 'Nazi gold' and then, with Herr Mueller's dignity significantly assuaged, he will produce the information you want." He glanced at his watch again. "Stay in contact with my office. Enjoy Switzerland." They shook hands all around and the attaché hurried down the steps to the waiting limousine.

"So I guess we cool our heels," Mather said.

"After finding a hotel room," Toni added. "I need a bath and a telephone to call Diana Habib. I promised her I'd stay in contact. I think she wants to come back to the States."

"Too much culture shock in Brazil?" Sutherland asked.

"Don't get too involved with the customers," Mather warned.

Finding a hotel room, much less two, in July, in Bern, without reservations, proved to be an insolvable task. Finally, they returned to the main train station where they had checked their luggage. Sutherland spotted the Bernese Mittelland, the local tourist office, and he and Mather went inside while Toni stayed with their luggage. The girl was all brisk efficiency and within minutes, had them booked in a hotel in Thun, a town seventeen miles south of Bern. "Your hotel overlooks Lake Thun," she told him. "It is very beautiful."

"Just what we need," Sutherland muttered, thinking of Toni and Mather having coffee, alone, in a romantic setting. The girl convinced them to purchase rail passes and while Mather put it all on his FBI credit card, Sutherland went outside to wait with Toni. She was sitting on her suitcase near the entrance to the train platforms, her legs crossed in a classic pose. A warm feeling tugged at him as he walked toward her. Everything about her was appealing, sending him soft messages.

Maybe Switzerland wouldn't be so bad after all.

2:00 P.M., TUESDAY, JULY 27,
SACRAMENTO, CALIF.

"Son of a bitch, Marcy," the editor breathed, "where in hell did you find this?"

"From a source." From the look on his face, she knew it wasn't enough. "A comptroller from Hong Kong, the Bank of China."

"My God! Do you know what this means? You nailed the bastard!" The editor stared at her in wonder. "This is serious stuff and puts you in the running for a Pulitzer Prize. Hell, not that you weren't already for the San Francisco bombing and L.A. riots, but this—"

"Cut the schmooze," Marcy said. "I know the legal beagles have to check it out first."

The editor nodded. "Meredith's lawyers are going to be all over us like stink on a skunk. This Collingswood, we need to check him out. It would help if he can put us in contact with at least two other CEOs Meredith has extorted."

"He's waiting outside," Marcy said.

The editor was beside himself. He dialed the legal office and quickly explained the problem. He hung up and turned to Marcy. "Bring him in, a legal rottweiler is on the way."

Marcy laughed. "Don't you mean beagle?"

"No. I mean attack dog."

The lawyer finished looking over the reams of paper. "There might be enough here to protect us from a lawsuit," he pronounced. He hesitated. "I'm not sure."

"What's the problem?" the editor asked.

"It's the bank accounts in the Caymans. Knowing the money is there and proving it are two different things."

"A very simple matter," Collingswood said. He sat at the editor's computer, thumbed through the papers he had originally given Marcy, and started to type. Within moments, he was on-line with a bank in the Caymans. He entered in the secret pass code and the screen scrolled with the file on the account. "Any questions?" he asked.

"I'll be damned," the lawyer said. "Look at all the money he's taken in from the Neighborhood Brigades and campaign contributions. Almost a quarter billion dollars!"

"But he's had some heavy expenditures," Collingswood said, "mostly to the First Brigade." They scanned the account like bank examiners conducting an audit.

"What's this one to Switzerland?" Marcy asked. "What was it for? Over two million dollars is a lot of money."

Collingswood frowned and typed another command. "From all appearances, a legitimate transfer of funds. But who knows? Your government can approach the Swiss and request access. They'll cooperate."

"This is too fuckin' good to be fuckin' true," the editor muttered. "How do I know all this is legit?"

"Would a transfer of money to your account be sufficient?" Collingswood asked. "Shall we say, a half million dollars?"

The editor agreed and ten minutes later called his bank to confirm the transfer. His face paled. "Oh, shit!" He looked at the comptroller. "Transfer it back!"

"Done," Collingswood said.

"Do we go with the story?" Marcy asked.

The editor's face was bathed in sweat. "Did Woodward and Bernstein take on Nixon?"

"This ain't no Watergate," Marcy warned. "Meredith plays for keeps."

"He can't be that dangerous," the lawyer said.

"I was in L.A., remember? I saw the First Brigade in action."

The editor sensed, rather than knew, that he was sitting on the story of a lifetime. It was decision time. He made it. "Okay, Marcy, run with it. But I want you working this from every angle, checking out every lead. If there's a rock, turn it over and see what crawls out."

Marcy felt her mouth go dry. She knew what he was demanding. But there was only one answer allowed. "I got it."

31

7:52 A.M., WEDNESDAY, JULY 28,
THE FARM, WESTERN VIRGINIA

Durant reread the profile on Kamigami the second time. "But she never met the man," he said.

"Dr. Kurtz is one of the best profilers around," Rios explained. "She was trained at Quantico and worked for the FBI fourteen years before coming to us."

"But she specialized in the criminal mind."

Rios paused and considered his next words. "What she does is based on common sense and knowledge of human nature. Kamigami is rigid and goal driven. Once he commits to something, he will do it. Even at the risk of his own life."

Durant flipped through the report. "So, if the CIA does not tell him we're coming, what will he do?"

"The good doctor claims that lacking information, he will follow his original instructions. If he suspects a rescue is underway, he will go to the hostages and activate his homing beacon."

"I hate basing a decision on a shrink's recommendation."

"Dr. Kurtz did predict that Agnes would talk to you when she was not responding to the whiz kids." Rios paused for effect. "And she did say Agnes would not budge. Not an inch."

"Okay, so she's got credibility. So what else do we know?"

Rios unfolded a large scale map. "The execution is scheduled for this Friday at high noon at Wadi Rahad, about two hundred miles southwest of Khartoum. It's a shrine of some sort called the Rock of Vengeance. The army of a heretic was defeated there in 1836. He was executed on the rock monolith. Supposedly, whenever it rains, the sand in the wadi turns red to remind people what happens to heretics. Now people come here to pray for vengeance when they've been wronged. No one is really sure how that started. It's definitely more animistic than Islamic."

Rios spread out a series of satellite photographs that showed a walled, fortresslike compound on the banks of a large wadi, a dry streambed. The high walls encompassed a large bare area. At the very center was a rock monolith surrounded by a low wall perhaps four feet high. The outer walls were pierced by a single large gate on the south side. A well-worn path led straight to a break in the low wall that surrounded the rock monolith. The monolith, the break in the low wall, and the gate were aligned to point to the dry streambed, which was red in color. Outside, a railroad track and highway from Khartoum ended at the wadi, and a concrete airstrip had been built a half mile northwest of the compound. Other than a few shacks, there was nothing else.

"The source of this information?" Durant demanded.

"It was on CNN this morning."

"Great. Absolutely great. We have to decide whether to launch the rescue mission based on the profile of a shrink and a TV news report. What kind of intelligence is that?"

"Without Agnes, the best we got. Boss, can Kamigami do it?"

"Do what?"

"Hold until we get there."

Durant closed his eyes. He felt tired, very tired. But he couldn't postpone the decision much longer. "That's the bet. Call the helicopter. We're going to the White House."

2:04 P.M., WEDNESDAY, JULY 28,
THE AMERICAN EMBASSY, SWITZERLAND

"You," the economic attaché said, "are indeed charmed individuals. Heydrich Mueller proved to be less obstinate than I expected." He handed Mather a thin folder. "In fact, you can say he has been downright cooperative."

Mather opened it and Toni leaned over his shoulder, far too close for Sutherland's comfort. "The account was created over a year ago," Toni said.

"And only two deposits have been made since then," Mather added, "both by electronic transfer. One from a bank in Canada," he checked the details, "apparently from Sandi Jefferson's business account, and the other from a bank in the Cayman Islands."

The way they scanned the report, heads together, in perfect tune as professional investigators worried Sutherland. Mather handed him the report. At first, Sutherland saw nothing unusual. Then he caught it. "Clever. Very clever." Toni and Mather looked at him. "Remember all the money Sandi was using to pay off her credit cards and we couldn't figure out where it was coming from?" He tapped the paper. "It was all hers. She had hidden it in a Canadian bank to avoid taxes."

"What about the money from the Caymans?" Toni asked. "Whose account was that?"

The attaché glanced at the report. "As I suspected, only an account number. That's all you'll get. No one has ever cracked a Cayman bank."

The train ride back to Thun gave them time to talk and plan their next moves. The Swiss had cooperated but they were still at a dead end. "Talk about a wild goose chase," Mather said.

"Well," Toni said, "we know more than we did before."

Mather shook his head. "Except where the money came from. I doubt if we'll ever fill in the gap between the Cayman and Swiss banks. The international banking system wins again. What a waste of time."

"Well," Toni said, "I've never been to Europe before."

"I'd love to show you more," Mather said, smiling at her.

"We're here to work," Sutherland grumbled. He changed the subject. "There must be some way to use this information."

"How?" Mather asked. "It just confirms Jefferson received money from an unknown source in the Cayman Islands."

Sutherland mulled it over. Mather was right. It was a piece of information in a rapidly dying investigation. The vital pieces had died with Jefferson, and what they had learned would lie in some sealed government file that would never see the light of day. *But I'm not working for the government,* he thought. The train pulled into the station and Mather was the first off, leading the way back to the hotel. Toni walked beside Sutherland. She slipped her arm through his, European style.

"I've enjoyed it here," she said. "I hate to go back."

In front of them, Mather suddenly spun around and rushed back. "There," he said in a low voice, pointing across the street. "Driving the gray Mercedes." They both looked in the direction he was pointing. Sitting behind the wheel, moving away from them in the slow traffic, was Jim Bob.

Sutherland said the obvious. "Follow him." They ran down the street, barely able to keep the car in sight. Finally, Sutherland hailed a taxi and they piled in, now able to follow the car. "I don't believe this," he muttered. The enormity of the odds against such a chance sighting appalled him. "Talk about coincidence." Seven blocks later, the Mercedes stopped in front of an arcade of exclusive boutiques.

"Very expensive shops," the driver said. Mather paid off the driver while Sutherland and Toni bailed out.

They moved slowly toward the Mercedes. "I've got the license number," Toni said. She repeated the number, never taking her eyes off the car. It was locked in Sutherland's memory. Two expensively dressed women walking arm in arm stepped out of the arcade followed by two clerks loaded with boxes and clothing bags. Toni stifled a gasp and pulled Sutherland into a doorway. "That's Sandi Jefferson. I hardly recognized her, she's dyed her hair. The other woman—she's the one I saw her with that time at Nordstrom's in Kansas City."

Sutherland chanced a look. It was his ex-wife, Beth Page.

"Incredible," Sutherland said, his mind still reeling from the chance encounter. They were sitting at an outdoor café overlooking Lake Thun. A fragile silence ruled while the waiter served coffee and moved away. "I'll never knock coincidence again."

"Coincidence happens," Mather muttered. "Did they see you?"

"I don't think so," Sutherland replied. "Toni pulled me to cover."

"Time to get organized," Toni said.

"You check in with the team in the States," Mather said, "while I call the embassy. They might be able to get a lead on the license plate." They hurried away, leaving Sutherland alone.

Within minutes, Toni was back. "They want us to come home. As far as they're concerned, your ex and Sandi are of no importance and it was pure coincidence."

"How much coincidence do you believe in?" Sutherland asked.

"Not that much," Toni replied. "They're here for a reason."

Mather joined them forty minutes later. "The embassy forwarded the report from Credit Geneve and want us out of their hair. I had to strongarm the first secretary to get them to run the license plate. They should have something by tomorrow."

Sutherland was impressed. He knew from hard experience how legations worked, and Mather had to have connections to reach the first secretary, much less make him so responsive. "How did you manage that?" he asked.

"My father was an ambassador," Mather replied. "The Netherlands—when I was at Groton."

"Oh." This from Toni. Now she was impressed. "The team wants us to drop it and come home," she rapidly added, covering her confusion.

Mather gave her a blank look. "Too bad we're having trouble booking a flight."

"It will take a day or two to make connections," Toni allowed.

"Cute," Sutherland muttered, "very cute."

11:45 A.M., WEDNESDAY, JULY 28,
THE WHITE HOUSE, WASHINGTON, D.C.

The President leaned back in his chair and surveyed the people surrounding him. Like nearly everything he did, he wanted a consensus before proceeding. But in this case, his advisers were evenly split, Broderick, Serick, and the DCI against launching the rescue mission while the military, the Vice President, and, strangely enough, the State Department, for going ahead.

The chairman of the joint chiefs of staff did all but thump the table. "Mr. President, it's a good plan. The helicopters are in position and ready to launch. Delta Force is ready but they have to deploy now. This plan will work because the diversionary attack will create the chaos we need to ingress. We have surprise, we have isolation, and we have simplicity and are now dealing with a soft target." He snorted. "Delta's daily training exercises are more demanding than what they'll be going against at Wadi Rahad. Unfortunately, we have a very narrow window of opportunity, but it is there."

The President drummed his fingers on the table. "We're dealing with too many unknowns. How do we even know where the pilots are with any certainty?"

"We don't," Durant answered. "But we have an agent in place who has a homing beacon Delta Force can guide on."

The President shook his head. "We're dealing with too many unknowns," he repeated. "I could be sending our men into a trap."

"Possible but not probable," Durant replied. "Remember, they are rushing this and haven't had time to solidify their security or their defenses. The diversionary attack should get them looking one way, and we'll be in and out before they look in the other."

Serick lived up to his reputation as the administration's leading cynic. "Rubbish. This is a fiasco in the making."

"Perhaps," the DCI said, switching sides, "a failed rescue attempt is better than no attempt at all. Even postulating a worst-case scenario, our losses should be minimal. But more importantly, we destroy Assam's weapons of mass destruction."

Serick gave the DCI a hard look of disapproval.

"Mr. President," Durant said, "we're out of time. We need a decision now."

The Vice President uttered the words that decided the issue. "Meredith's claims that we are afraid to act are flushing our ratings in the polls down the toilet."

The President looked around the room and stood up. "It's a go," he said. "The national military command center has command authority to execute the mission. I want hourly updates." He marched out of the room.

The DCI turned to Durant. "We'll get the word to Kamigami. It should reach him in twenty-four hours."

"Excellent," Durant said. "I appreciate the quick response."

"I'd never do it this way," the DCI said. "But we're all in this together." They shook hands and Durant followed the President.

Serick and Broderick collared the DCI and pulled him aside. "I would have appreciated a heads-up that you were going to back Durant," Broderick said through gritted teeth.

"Do you know what happens to our credibility?" Serick muttered, "if Durant pulls this off? Given his track record, he can do it."

"Who said I was going to send the message?" the DCI replied.

12:40 P.M., WEDNESDAY, JULY 28,
NATIONAL MILITARY COMMAND CENTER, THE PENTAGON

The four-star general in command of the rescue mission escorted Durant and Rios into the Pentagon's war room. He was a young-looking man, extremely organized, and anxious to demonstrate how the system worked—especially to two civilians there at the express direction of the President. "We launch the mission from here," he explained. "But operational control will be from an airborne command post orbiting over the Mediterranean." He sat them down in front of a monitor and typed a command into the computer. The timing for the entire mission scrolled onto the screen, with the objectives for each participating unit detailed by time and place.

It was the first time Durant had seen the complete plan and was surprised by the complexity of the mission. "I had no idea it was so complicated."

"We could never have done it without Agnes," the general said. "After Colonel Gillespie deployed, she took over. Talk about one sharp lady! When we started planning the diversionary, she gave us a list of targets. To show you how good she is, we're using her priorities. I'm looking forward to meeting her."

"When was the last time you talked to her?" Durant asked.

The general thought for a moment. "Saturday morning, why?"

Durant and Rios exchanged glances. "She's very ill," Durant replied, his voice sad. "I hope she recovers."

"Me too," the general said. "That woman is a national treasure." He pointed to the master clocks on the front wall. "H-hour," he said. The numbers of the mission clock started to turn. The mission was underway.

12:00 P.M., WEDNESDAY, JULY 28,
FORT IRWIN, THE MOJAVE DESERT

The man sat under the camouflaged netting, the only safe refuge from the blistering desert heat. He took a long pull at his water bottle. Besides maintaining cover during the day, dehydration was their main problem. His UHF radio scanner squawked and he woke the woman sleeping next to him. "A plane is landing."

The woman pulled herself up, her soft Asian features dusty from being in the field for over a week without a hot bath. "What time is it?" she asked. Her voice carried the trace of a foreign accent. She reached for the water bottle.

The man checked his watch. "Noon." They had to make a decision. Should they break cover to do a visual check and risk discovery by one of the many helicopter patrols constantly overhead, or should they rely on monitoring the radio until it was dark?

The woman made the decision. "Let's do a visual." They crawled out from under the netting and made the short climb to the exposed observation post in the rocks above their campsite. She ripped the cover off the high-powered telescope hidden there and popped the caps off the lens. She scanned the desert floor stretched out in front of her. A huge, high-wing cargo plane was landing on the bare airstrip camouflaged to blend with the desert terrain. "A C-Seventeen," she said.

The man took over and focused on the activity beside the runway. An MH-53J Pave Low helicopter was being loaded while approximately sixty men waited to board. "They don't seem to be hiding anything. Maybe they're going home."

"Do you think it's Delta Force?"

"Can't tell from here. But it is definitely a Pave Low."

She pulled out the cellular phone clipped to her waist and punched in a number. "I'll report it anyway." A loud rasping sound grated in her ear the moment she pressed the Send button. She jabbed at the end button, her eyes wide. "We're being jammed."

"Let's get the hell out of here," the man growled. She started to disassemble the telescope. "Leave it," he ordered, running for the all-terrain vehicle hidden over a mile away. She followed him down through the rocks.

"Freeze!" a voice commanded. The man skidded to a stop, trying to see who gave the order. The woman kept right on running. A short burst of submachine gun fire cut her across her legs and she collapsed.

Four men appeared from behind the rocks and surrounded them. "Now who would you be working for?" one asked. She spat at him.

"Not the friendly type," he muttered. "Shit, I hope you don't work for someone like the Chinese. Then we'd have to get ugly."

She grimaced. "Bastard!"

He grinned at her.

6:58 P.M., WEDNESDAY, JULY 28,
CNC-TV NEWS STUDIO, WASHINGTON, D.C.

Confidence radiated from Jonathan Meredith when he took the seat next to Liz Gordon, the network's premier reporter and talk show host. The cameras zoomed in on his handsome profile as Liz gave him the standard welcome to her weekly evening show. A guest appearance by Meredith guaranteed them a ratings sweep and Liz's director beamed in satisfaction.

Liz didn't waste time and turned immediately to the hot topic of the day. "Mr. Meredith, what is your reaction to the allegations published by the *Sacramento Union* this morning that your organization has extorted large amounts of money from corporations in the name of campaign contributions and deposited them in an offshore bank account?"

Meredith turned to the camera. "Liz, this is a classic smear campaign where an unscrupulous reporter twists the truth to her own purposes."

"The reporter is Marcy Bangor," Liz replied, "who has been widely praised for her courageous coverage of the L.A. riots."

"But the fact remains," Meredith replied, "that I have done nothing wrong. True, I have received campaign contributions from many sources. But these people approached me, not the other way around, and my organization has reported every single penny. True, I have bank accounts in foreign banks. But my organization is international in scope."

Liz bombarded him with questions, pounding at his integrity. But he smoothly fielded every probe and the director sensed Meredith was making his case. "End it," he muttered into his headset.

Liz raised an eyebrow, her way of acknowledging him. "Are you going to sue the *Sacramento Union* and Ms. Bangor?" she asked.

"My lawyers will pursue it," Meredith answered calmly, "but what will that accomplish? I've been tried and convicted in the court of public opinion. I challenge this reporter to meet me on national TV and make these charges to my face. Let me answer her directly so the public can hear the evidence and make up their own minds."

"Mr. Meredith, if CNC-TV arranges such a meeting, will you be there?"

"Any time, any place," he answered. The interview was over and they broke for a commercial. Meredith shook hands all around, gathered up his advisers, and left.

"Why did you do that?" Liz's director asked just before they went back on the air.

"He's a demagogue and a bastard," Liz answered. "But I believe him."

"I think you're right," the director conceded.

32

7:05 A.M., THURSDAY, JULY 29,
NATIONAL MILITARY COMMAND CENTER, THE PENTAGON

Durant was appalled by the obsolescence surrounding him. The National Military Command Center was an anachronism straight out of a 1980s movie. He sat at the commander's console and sketched ways to bring it into the twenty-first century with holographic displays and interactive computers similar to Agnes. Art Rios smiled when he saw the sketches. It was the way Durant's ego emerged: the sure conviction that he could do anything better than anyone else.

"Please direct your attention to the status board," a woman's voice announced over the loudspeaker. Durant scanned the computer-generated wall maps. The C-17 carrying Delta Force and a backup Pave Low had landed at Bangui and joined the small force already in place: four Pave Lows, two C-130Ps and two Combat Talon MC-130Es.

"You're here early, Mr. Durant," the general said.

"Is seven o'clock early?" Durant said, a little testy.

The general caught it immediately and recovered. "Only for me," he laughed. "I'm not used to working for a living."

Rios gave the general high marks for reading his boss right. "What about the bad guys watching Delta Force?" Rios asked.

"We rolled them up yesterday," the general answered.

"Did they get a warning message out?" Durant asked.

"Not to the best of our knowledge," the general replied.

Agnes would know, Durant thought. It was another uncertainty they would have to live with.

"The B-Two launches in fifty minutes," the general said.

6:10 A.M., THURSDAY, JULY 29,
WHITEMAN AIR FORCE BASE, MO.

The doors at the front and rear of the hangar cranked silently back. The B-2's engines came to life in rapid sequence as it sat in the early-morning shadows, a giant raptor ready to spring free of its tethers. The bomber sat there, its engines a loud growl as Lt. Col. Jim West and his pilot, Maj. Larry Bartle, ran the before-taxi checklist, waiting for all the systems to test okay and come on-line. It was the same routine as any training mission.

Bartle called for taxi clearance. "Spirit Four," ground control answered, "Cleared to taxi runway one-nine." They were taking off to the south. The pilot eased the two inboard throttles forward and the B-2 taxied clear of its cage. On the ground, there was something unnatural about the B-2; its high, ungainly stance, its odd silhouette that resembles a guppy, the slight downward curve of the tip of its nose. But like its call sign, all of that would change once it was airborne and in the element for which it was created. In the air, it flew with an incredible grace and some would say it was a thing of beauty. But once over the Atlantic, it would shed its training call sign "Spirit Four" and become what it really was: "Striker One."

The taxi out was routine in the extreme, typical of the training missions launched from Whiteman every day. But this time, a lone staff car was parked beside the hammerhead at the run-up end of runway 19, the south runway. The B-2 pulled up short of the runway and held. Then the control tower cleared it to taxi onto the active and hold. The commander of the 509th Bomb Wing climbed out of the staff car and stood watching the B-2.

"Spirit Four," the control tower radioed, "cleared for takeoff." Still the B-2 did not move, awaiting its exact launch time. When the second hand on the commander's watch read five seconds to go, Bartle ran up the engines. The second hand touched 1200 hours Zulu, Greenwich Mean Time, and Bartle released the brakes. The B-2 started to move.

The commander came to attention and saluted his pilots. He held the salute as the plane lumbered past, rapidly gaining speed. "Do this one right, Jim," he murmured. His words were lost in the wake of the jet blast.

1:10 P.M., THURSDAY, JULY 29,
THUN, SWITZERLAND

The phone call from the task force came just after lunch. Toni took it in her bedroom while Sutherland and Mather sat on the balcony overlooking the lake. "Hank," Mather said, very nervous and distracted, "I know you're interested in Toni but—"

"That's an understatement," Sutherland replied, interrupting him.

The young FBI agent was embarrassed. "So am I."

"I don't have any claims on her," Sutherland said. He studied Mather, trying to remember when he was that age. It seemed so long ago. "I suppose you're going to ask me if my intentions are honorable," he joked.

Mather fixed him with a worried look. "Well?"

"This is an unbelievable conversation," Sutherland replied, "for this day and age."

"Not in my family," Mather said. A heavy silence came down.

Toni joined them, her face ashen. "That was about Diana Habib. She's dead."

"Oh, no," Mather groaned. "What happened?"

"They don't have all the details. But it looks like a gangland style execution. Two bullets at close range in the back of the head. Apparently, it happened sometime after I called her Tuesday."

"Ramar," Sutherland gritted. "He's removing any witnesses who can cause him trouble."

"Toni might be next," Mather said.

"It's possible," Sutherland replied. "If Ramar made the connection to Toni or traced the phone call she made to Diana."

"Hey, guys!" Toni said. "I'm in the room. Don't talk around me. And quit obsessing. Ramar never got a make on me. Besides, the task force has already alerted Interpol and the Swiss. Now let's get with the program and find Sandi Jefferson."

"I think we should change hotels," Mather said. "Maybe find something in Bern."

"We can check with the embassy," Toni added, "and find out if they've made progress on the Mercedes." She gave Sutherland a bright smile. "Besides, I'd like to meet your ex and find out what kind of woman turns you on."

"Hey, give me a break," Sutherland protested. "That was a long time ago. I was young, dumb, and full of myself then."

"You're still batting two out of three," Mather muttered.

2:15 P.M., THURSDAY, JULY 29,
KHARTOUM, THE SUDAN

Kamigami led the two pilots across the blazing tarmac and onto the ramp of Assam's waiting C-130. They were shackled together, with canvas hoods firmly in place over their heads. They were barefoot and he knew the asphalt was blistering their feet. "Step up," he ordered. "You're on the ramp of an aircraft." They did as commanded and Terrant stumbled, almost dragging Holloway with him. Kamigami caught him by the arm and kept him upright. He could feel the man trembling under the thin fabric of his prison dungarees. He guided the men up the ramp and had them sit down on the floor at the rear of the cargo deck.

"Where are we going?" Terrant asked.

Kamigami didn't answer when he saw Davig al Gimlas climb the ramp. The army captain was wearing a long flowing white robe and not his customary uniform. His white *kaffiyeh* was held in place with a twisted cord of gold that matched the wrapping hiding the short sword he was carrying. He looked at the two men sitting on the cargo deck, the two men he would execute in less than twenty-four hours.

Kamigami watched him walk forward to join Jamil bin Assam at the passenger seats. Assam accorded him the place of honor next to his seat. No sign of emotion crossed Kamigami's face. *There's not going to be a rescue,* he thought. *They hung us out to dry. I can still walk away from this and get back to Malaysia on my own.* An image of his wife and children flashed in front of him. But just as quickly, he rejected that option. He would keep the faith and do what he had come for.

His decision made, he walked into the toilet module. He squeezed inside and locked the door. He quickly extracted the pack of cigarettes from his pocket and hid it in the storage bin where he had found the first message. He turned, relieved himself, and washed his hands. With a touch of soapy water, he made a small backward check mark with its tail curving upward and to the left. It was a repeat of the first time he had made contact except the message was from him this time.

He came out and sat on the parachute jump seat closest to the prisoners. The Arab copilot came back to check on the passengers before taking off. He spat at the two Americans. "Why do you worry about them?" he snarled.

"General Assam hired me to provide security and until tomorrow, I'm responsible for them." The copilot snarled an answer in Arabic and went into the toilet. Kamigami heard him flush the commode. "Jewish pigs," he snarled when he came out. The engines were already turning and a cool blast of air flooded over the cargo deck, finally breaking the heat.

"Is it tomorrow," Holloway muttered.

At first Kamigami didn't answer. Then, "Not if I can help it." It was all he could offer them.

The flight to Wadi Rahad took less than forty minutes. Just before they started to descend, Murray, the expatriate Englishman who served as the C-130's flight engineer, came back to use the toilet. He was out in a few moments. *It's him,* Kamigami thought. *So obvious.* He would check the toilet after they landed to see if the check mark had been erased to indicate the message had been picked up. "Want to come up on the flight deck?" Murray asked. Kamigami followed him forward.

The C-130 flew low as it approached the edge of the dry riverbed where the fortresslike compound was located. The road leading to the wadi was jammed with people making the journey to witness the execution. The gates to the compound were closed, holding the crowd outside, and would be thrown open only an hour before the execution. Inside, four white tents were erected for Assam and his party. An iron cage for the pilots stood in the sand-covered forecourt in front of the Rock of Vengeance. The airstrip was located about a half mile to the northwest. Army tents were pitched in a neat row next to the parking ramp and most of al Gimlas's soldiers were already encamped.

The American pilot made a routine landing and Kamigami checked the toilet as they taxied to parking. He was relieved to see the check mark had been wiped off the mirror. His message had been received. He came back to the two Americans as soldiers streamed onto the aircraft. "They are in my custody now," al Gimlas announced. But before the soldiers could haul them off the airplane, Murray and the American pilot were dragged off the flight deck.

"Search them," Assam ordered. He looked at Kamigami. "Search all foreigners. I want no spies with their cameras here."

Kamigami held his arms out, ready to be searched. The solders would only find what everyone could see on his equipment belt. But Murray had his message in the pack of cigarettes. Could the Englishman carry it off? Kamigami had to create a distraction to give him some cover. "If you're looking for spies, search the copilot. He's been acting very suspicious lately."

Assam barked a command in Arabic and the soldiers turned on the copilot. The man was terrified as they rummaged through his pockets. A soldier pulled out the pack of cigarettes Kamigami had hidden in the toilet. The copilot fell to his knees begging for mercy. He ripped open the cigarettes one by one, licking the inside of the wrapper paper until the message appeared. He held it up for Assam to inspect before it disappeared. "Immediate situation update required," Assam read. "Who sent this?"

Kamigami suppressed an inward groan. He had fingered the wrong man.

The copilot's panic was total. He looked around, not having the slightest idea who he was in contact with. He focused on the Englishman. "Murray," he blurted out.

Assam barked an order and the soldiers dragged the copilot and Murray off the aircraft.

Al Gimlas joined Kamigami. "I thought you were a spy."

"You thought wrong," Kamigami said. "You had better search everyone. Start with me."

3:20 P.M., THURSDAY, JULY 29,
THE AMERICAN EMBASSY, SWITZERLAND

The first secretary delayed the meeting as long as possible. Finally, it was quitting time and he could no longer postpone the inevitable. He buzzed his secretary. "Please show Special Agent Mather and group in." He stood when they entered his sumptuous office, always the correct and proper diplomat. He put on his most official face. "Good afternoon, Mr. Mather. I've been looking forward to meeting you in person. I served under your father in the Netherlands." Mather made the introductions before they turned to business. "The Swiss do not like foreign investigators probing into the affairs of their citizens. I'm afraid you are rapidly wearing out your welcome here."

"We understand," Mather said. "We are most anxious to leave. Do you have anything on the Mercedes?"

The secretary nodded. "Apparently, the car in question is registered to the estate of a Swiss-American company, Century Communications International." He daintily pushed a paper across the desk and rapidly withdrew his hand from the offending object as if it were contaminated. "I had to spend a great deal of obligata to obtain this, a personal connection really. The Swiss are very concerned." It was diplo-speak for that's-all-you-are-going-to-get-now-get-the-hell-out-of-the-country.

Sutherland glanced at the address; Kandersteg. Suddenly, he was back in his VOQ room at Whiteman, tidying up after Beth had dropped in unexpectedly and crashed in his bed, dog-tired from traveling. He was looking at her ticket envelope with a name and phone number dashed across the cover in Beth's bold handwriting. The word *Kandersteg* leaped at him.

"Why am I not surprised?" Sutherland muttered.

"Ah," the first secretary said, "then all is in order?"

"More than you know," Sutherland said, rising to leave. "We should be returning to the States tomorrow."

"My secretary will be glad to arrange connections," the first secretary offered.

"That won't be necessary," Sutherland replied, holding the door for Toni and Mather.

"What was that all about?" Toni said once they were safely outside.

"Two of the most unlikely players in this mess together with Beth. She's been in this up to her lovely eyebrows for quite a while. Just how and why, I don't know. It's about time I found out."

4:30 P.M., THURSDAY, JULY 29,
BANGUI, CENTRAL AFRICAN REPUBLIC

Capt. Lee Harold, Gillespie's second in command, walked around the Pave Low as a swarm of mechanics raced to put it back together. The helicopter had rolled out the back of the C-17 seven hours earlier and Maintenance was busting its back to unfold the tail, mount the transmission, and bolt on the six rotor blades—no small task as each blade weighed 371 pounds and was attached by eight bolts that required 2,460 pounds of torque to tighten. Normally, it took fourteen to sixteen hours to do the job. Harold checked his watch. Two hours to launch. They weren't going to make it.

The MH-53 was a superb machine but it was getting cranky in its old age. While the maintenance crews could keep it flying, its reliability was not what it once had been. Consequently, six helicopters were needed to ensure four would reach the target. Not only was the 20th Special Operations Squadron stretched thin, it needed new aircraft. The Air Force simply didn't have enough to do what its political masters were demanding.

"Fuck," Harold muttered under his breath. He would have to tell Gillespie the backup helicopter wouldn't be ready.

Gillespie took the news stoically. "Let me see what Maintenance can do," he said. He ambled off to build some fires.

"How does he do it?" Harold wondered.

"Do what?" his copilot asked.

Harold was talking about leadership, but like most in the Air Force, wouldn't be caught dead calling it what it was. "The way he makes things happen. It's pure 'paddling duck.' Calm on the surface, but kicking like hell underneath."

"Yeah. He's calm and we're doing the kicking."

"It works, doesn't it?"

While the maintenance crews raced to ready the backup helicopter, Delta Force gathered with the aircrews under camouflage netting and briefed the mission one last time. With thirty minutes to go, the helicopter crews manned their aircraft. Because of their slower speed they would take off first. The two C-130Ps that would refuel the helicopters en route to the target would take off two hours later. The two Combat Talon MC-130Es that would airdrop Delta Force, and then refuel the helicopters on the way out, would take off almost five hours later.

It was as carefully orchestrated as any ballet, and eight hours after Gillespie launched, at exactly 3:20 in the morning, the wrath of U.S. special operations would descend on Wadi Rahad.

The engines of four Pave Lows whined as they spun up and one after another, the rotors started to turn. But the rotors on Lee Harold's bird did not move. His radio transmission was a crisp, "I got an Engine Failure light."

"Is the backup good to go?" Gillespie replied. His answer came in the form of six men evacuating Harold's helicopter and running for the backup that was still surrounded by Maintenance. "Shut 'em down," Gillespie ordered. Now they had to wait.

"Can we go with three?" Gillespie's copilot asked.

Gillespie ran the numbers in his head. The hours of planning with Art Rios and Agnes had drilled the answer into his memory. "Negative," he answered, hating every syllable of that word. Activity swirled around the helicopter as it was made ready for takeoff. Equipment was thrown on board while a fuel truck pumped gas into the empty tanks. They were out of time. He was about to key the SatCom radio and tell the NMCC they were aborting when Harold gave him a thumbs-up. Maintenance had performed a minor miracle. "Start engines," Gillespie radioed, his voice calm and as relaxed as if it were just a routine training flight.

A few minutes later, the four Pave Lows lifted off and headed to the east. "We got to make up three minutes," the copilot told Gillespie.

"Piece of cake," he replied.

6:00 P.M., THURSDAY, JULY 29,
NATIONAL MILITARY COMMAND CENTER, THE PENTAGON

Grudgingly, Durant gave the big computer-driven wall map high marks: the system was tracking the mission with speed and accuracy. Over the Mediterranean, the B-2 had finished refueling and was heading for the coast of Africa, two hours away from its first target. In central Africa, the four helicopters were approaching their second refueling point where the two C-130Ps would rendezvous for a low-level refueling. The two MC-130 Combat Talons carrying Delta Force would pass the helicopters about the time they hooked up for their last drink of fuel before ingressing to the target.

Art Rios joined Durant and the general. He handed his employer a cup of coffee before turning to the map. He frowned. "It's an endurance contest for the helicopters, isn't it?"

"That's the penalty for going low and slow," the general replied. "We need new machines. But the crews will make it happen. They always do."

The communications net in the NMCC picked up the final transmission between Blue Chip, the airborne command post, and the B-2. Even over the encrypted circuits, Jim West's voice sounded more bored than anything else as he called for the final clearance to proceed with the mission. The general listened to the radio call. "Since we're in contact," he explained, "silence on our end construes consent and the controller onboard Blue Chip makes the decision."

"Striker One," the controller in the orbiting command post radioed, "no change to your target. Cleared to go. Repeat, you are cleared to go."

"Copy all," West replied on a different frequency. "Striker One is cleared onto the target."

"What happens now?" Durant asked.

"The B-Two stealths up," the general explained, "retracts its antennas, radar in standby, that sort of thing. It's a problem because we lose radio contact. We won't hear from him again until they're off the target and clear of any threat. So, we wait."

Two hours later, they monitored the first distress call from Gillespie to the airborne command post.

2:47 A.M., FRIDAY, JULY 30,
OVER THE SUDAN

"As advertised," West muttered when his electronic threat display came alive. The beam of an S-12 early-warning radar had swept past them. His fingers flew over the data entry panel and he called up their first weapon, a JASSM, a Joint Air-to-Surface Standoff Missile with a fifty-mile range. "A nice way to announce we're in the area, don't you think?" He hit the enter button and the system took over. Their tactics were totally different from Terrant's and Holloway's. Rather than sneaking in unobserved at low level, they were going to stay at altitude and open a corridor to Assam's underground laboratories. At forty miles, the bomb bay doors snapped open and the missile was launched. Immediately, the doors banged closed. The missile fell away before its rocket motor ignited. As programmed, the B-2 turned away while the missile streaked toward the radar.

The threat display chirped at them. The S-12 had gone into a sector sweep to focus its beam on their section of the sky. "The radar must have gotten a hit on the doors," Larry Bartle, the pilot, complained.

"Probably," West replied. "But right now, they should have a radar paint on the missile." He called up the second weapon, a standard 2,000-pound bomb with a tail kit and a guidance head using GPS, or the Global Positioning System based on navigation satellites. Now they had to wait to see if their missile took out the early warning radar. The threat display indicated the S-12 radar was tracking the missile. West slewed his infrared in the direction of the radar site, but the distance was too great to detect anything. "Now," West said, as the time-to-go counter for the missile ran down to zero. The infrared screen flared with a bright strobe and the electronic threat display went quiet. "I do believe they had a religious experience," he muttered.

Then he turned his attention to his next target, the airstrip where four fighters were sitting alert as a point defense for the laboratories.

With the S-12 radar and its sophisticated radar detection equipment off the air, he could use the B-2's synthetic aperture radar. His fingers commanded the targeting system to synchronize the aircraft's radar and GPS navigation system to the GPS in the guidance head of the bomb. He drove the radar's cross hairs out to where the target should be and pulled the trigger on his hand controller to the first stop. The radar came alive for less than two seconds and painted the hardened bunker where the fighters were parked. The picture froze on the screen as the radar returned to standby. West nudged the radar cross hairs directly over the bunker and mashed the trigger to full stop.

Something approaching magic happened. The radar fed the navigation computer a wealth of information about the target, which the computer matched to what the GPS was telling it. The computer then told the bomb's navigation system where it was, where the target was—according to the radar, how much the bomb's GPS was in error, and what the bomb's GPS should read when it reached the target. Just to be sure, Bartle changed course forty degrees and West repeated the process with a second snapshot, refining the target solution down to a few inches.

When they were in range, the bomb bay doors automatically popped open and the second bomb was on its way. They headed for the third target, the air defense command bunker. A bright flash lit the ground 43,000 feet below them. West chanced a look with the infrared. The aircraft bunker had a neat hole in its roof and smoke and flames were belching from its doors. "I'll be damned," West muttered. A single aircraft was taking the runway. "We missed one." The radar site had gotten off a warning before it was destroyed and one fighter had managed to escape.

He concentrated on the command bunker, which was on their nose. The threat display was alive as the defenders brought up every surface-to-air missile system they had. For a moment, he considered launching one or two of their HARMs, short for high speed anti-radiation homing missile. The HARM's only purpose was to destroy the guidance radar of surface-to-air missiles. He discarded the thought. The HARM's rocket plume would be visible for miles in the clear desert night. He wasn't about to take a chance on some gunner or missileer getting lucky with barrage fire and the golden B-B being there for them. Back to the plan. He called up his next set of bombs, 4,800 pound BLU-113s with deep penetrating warheads.

West was into the routine of it and whatever fatigue he felt from the long mission was displaced by pumping adrenaline. He repeated the process and dropped another bomb. Thirty seconds later the command bunker was history and the threat screen went quiet. They had convinced the defenders on the ground that turning off their radars was a very good idea that did wonders for their projected life-spans. With the corridor wide open, they headed for Assam's laboratories.

While West concentrated on the target, Bartle looked for the one fighter that had gotten airborne. He split his attention between the threat display in front of him and scanning the night sky. "Oh, shit!" he roared. The fighter had flashed by less than fifty feet overhead. "I don't think he even saw us."

West concentrated on the radar and laid the cross hairs directly on the main ventilation air shaft. He took a snapshot with the radar, they altered course forty degrees, he took another snapshot, and the next bomb was gone. Then they altered course again and West took a third snapshot of the same target before launching a second bomb.

The first bomb glided toward the air shaft, the guidance head sending commands to the control surfaces on the tail. The bomb made little jerking motions as it corrected its glide path. Finally, it was on the "wire" and headed directly for the GPS coordinates the B-2's targeting system had fed into the guidance head. It missed its desired impact point by three feet. But that didn't matter. The bomb punched its own hole through the reinforced concrete, down the side of the air shaft, and penetrated sixty feet before it exploded. The blast ripped open the shaft like a funnel with the basket open to the sky. The next bomb flew down the widened hole and into the laboratory.

The blast effects of a 4,800-pound bomb in an enclosed area are horrific as the explosion bounces back and forth, collapsing support structures, vaporizing anything as soft as human flesh, and sucking up oxygen. What the bomb didn't destroy, the cave-in buried forever. "Piece of cake," West announced. "Now where's that mutha that almost hit us?"

"I don't think he's using his radar," Bartle said.

"It wouldn't matter if he did," West said. His fingers flew over the data entry panel, and they headed for Wadi Rahad.

"There's fuckin' hydraulic fluid all over the deck," the flight engineer told Gillespie. "The fuckin' reservoir feeding the fuckin' control system has got one hell of a leak."

"Can you fix it?"

"Not without shutting down and depressurizing the system."

"How long can we stay airborne?" Gillespie asked.

"About another five minutes at best. Then we ain't got no more fluid to feed the system."

It was an easy decision. Without hydraulic fluid, the control systems failed. "Advise Blue Chip we're landing for repairs," Gillespie told his copilot. The captain keyed the SatCom radio and relayed the message.

"Can you continue with three?" Blue Chip replied.

"Not unless you want to leave someone behind," the copilot answered.

"Say time on ground," Blue Chip asked.

The question was for the flight engineer. Like so many critical things in life, the answer hinged on the capability of a single person. "Thirty minutes, max," the tech sergeant answered.

The crew was a well-trained team and within thirty seconds, they had called the other helicopters, identified a landing site on their forward looking infrared, and were ready to land. Gillespie circled the landing zone and studied it through his night vision goggles. Then, satisfied it was clear, set the big machine down while Harold circled the area in his Pave Low, sweeping the ground for any possible threat. The other two helicopters settled to earth near Gillespie. Harold counted four shacks as he circled but didn't see any signs of life. Satisfied they were safe, he landed. His flight engineer scooped up an armful of hydraulic fluid cans and ran for Gillespie's Pave Low.

Gillespie sat in the cockpit, ready to start the engines at a moment's notice. "How far out are we?" he asked.

The copilot punched at the navigation computer. "Thirty-four minutes."

"Do you think anyone heard us?"

"I doubt it."

But the copilot was wrong. The Sudan's air defense system may have been in shambles and the people on the ground cowering in fear, but for all its problems, the phone system was still working.

8:01 P.M., THURSDAY, JULY 29,
NATIONAL MILITARY COMMAND CENTER, THE PENTAGON

The general studied the status boards and the big wall map as they listened to Blue Chip react to Gillespie's emergency. The status boards flashed with an update: the helicopters were on the ground, thirty-four minutes flying time from the compound. The two Combat Talons were retreating at low level to a safe area where they could hold until a decision was made to continue or abort, and the B-2 was nineteen minutes away from its next target. But the B-2 was still stealthed up as it worked its way through the Sudan's radar net and into the heart of the country. There was no way they could delay it.

"Not good," the general muttered. "Damn the Chinese. I'll never figure out why they upgraded the Sudan's military. They got some credible SAMs out there."

"They want the Sudanese angry at the Western powers," Durant said, "not them. Given China's population density, an Ebola type weapon would devastate China."

"This is turning to shit," the general muttered. "Time to abort."

"Not yet," Rios said. "Give it some time."

The general shook his head. "We can't delay the B-Two. That means Delta Force loses the element of surprise."

"But," Rios persisted, "there's going to be a lot of confusion on the ground. Maybe we can exploit that." The general seemed willing to listen and Rios pressed ahead. "You've got flexibility out there. Use it."

"There is no way I'm going to chance losing another B-Two," the general replied. "He's hitting his targets as planned and going home."

Rios wouldn't let it go. "The B-Two still has two bombs and can loiter for three hours."

"I'm aborting the rescue," the general said. He picked up the microphone to radio Blue Chip and issue the command.

3:09 A.M., FRIDAY, JULY 30,
WADI RAHAD, THE SUDAN

The first telephone call drove a spike of fear into Jamil bin Assam. His laboratories and all the defenses around them had been destroyed. The caller claimed it was a massive attack with intercontinental ballistic missiles, cruise missiles, weapons of mass destruction, and over a hundred aircraft. The gallant defenders had been totally overwhelmed. The second phone call drove Assam over the edge. Four helicopters were reported to have landed seventy miles to the southwest.

"They are coming after me!" Assam shouted. He ripped off his uniform and pulled on a dirty robe and sandals as a disguise. He gathered up his bodyguard and left for the airstrip a half mile away. Outside, the compound was surrounded by a growing crowd of people waiting for the coming festivities. Assam's small convoy barreled through the crowd, running over six unfortunates who could not scamper out of the way.

Kamigami shut the compound's gates as Assam disappeared into the night. He walked calmly across the fresh sand that had been spread to absorb blood and stopped by the iron cage holding Terrant and Holloway. He unclipped the cellular phone from his belt and extended the antenna. He punched in a six-digit code without turning it on and pushed it onto the flat roof of the cage. The homing beacon was on. "What's happening?" Terrant asked.

"It's going to get very interesting here in a few minutes," Kamigami said. "Get down and stay down."

3:16 A.M., FRIDAY, JULY 30,
OVER THE SUDAN

Jim West's fingers danced across the data entry panel as he called up his sixth bomb. "A guy could get to like this," he mumbled, loud enough for Bartle to hear. He reached for a water bottle and took a long drink. Then he called up the forward-looking infrared scope. The high walls of the compound came into view at max range. A half mile closer to them, he could see the image of an aircraft moving on the ground.

"I think that's a C-130," West said.

"Is it one of ours?" Bartle asked.

"According to Intel, the black hats got one. Besides, our guys aren't supposed to land." He considered his next action. The image cleared as they approached, and he could see the C-130 was at the takeoff end of the runway. "Too bad he's at the right place at the right time." West allowed a tight grin and he called up the radar for a snapshot. This time, he placed the cross hairs at the exact middle of the runway and the system went through its update sequence. He took the second snapshot. The C-130 was still sitting on the end of the runway. "Bomb gone," West said.

Bartle flew an arc around the airfield while West watched the infrared scope. "If he rolls now, he just might make it," West allowed. Still the C-130 didn't move. West had no way of knowing the American pilot was trying to fly the C-130 solo and had to accomplish both the flight engineer's and copilot's checklists by himself. He could have done it quickly with the flight engineer, but like the copilot, Murray was dead, and the screaming Assam at the pilot's back was not helping matters.

"He's rolling," West said. He checked the time-to-go counter. "I don't believe this." The C-130 was lifting off as the bomb exploded in front of it. The big cargo plane disappeared in the fireball. "Son of a bitch!" West roared. "He was airborne!"

Bartle shook his head in disbelief. "Four more and we're Aces!"

"We're not going to hang around to try," West said. "Time to get the hell out of Dodge."

3:20 A.M., FRIDAY, JULY 30,
WADI RAHAD, THE SUDAN

The explosion and fireball at the airfield did more than create confusion. Flying shrapnel from the bomb and the wreckage of the C-130 cut into the bivouac where al Gimlas's soldiers were camped. Fortunately, a low ridge deflected most of the blast and debris over the heads of the crowd nearest the runway, otherwise, the carnage would have been horrific. But the bomb had its intended effect. Panic gripped the people, and they turned into a stampeding mob. Those nearest the compound stormed the gates, demanding sanctuary. But most scattered into the desert, certain that more death and destruction would rain down from the skies. In the grand scheme of things, it was grossly unfair. They had come to view an execution, not be part of it.

Kamigami crouched in the shadows of the compound, counting the seconds. *Come on,* he thought. *Where are you?* He knew how special operations worked and the window of opportunity was rapidly closing. The secondhand of his watch started its second sweep. Outside, he could hear the mob banging on the gate. *How much longer will it hold?* The secondhand started its third sweep. He listened. Only the howling from the mob outside the walls reached him. He waited. The secondhand started its fourth sweep. The window was closed. He slung a full ammunition pouch over his shoulder and picked up the AK-47 beside him. He chambered a round, selected short burst, and flicked the safety off. He ambled across the open compound to the cage.

Without a word to the two pilots, he retrieved the cellular phone from the roof, collapsed the antenna. The homing signal used a lot of juice and he hoped it still had some useful life left.

"What now?" Terrant asked.

"It gets interesting," Kamigami answered. Al Gimlas was walking across the compound with a squad of his men, the short executioner's sword cradled in his arms.

Al Gimlas stopped short of the cage, in the middle of the fresh sand. "It is time," he announced.

8:28 P.M., FRIDAY, JULY 29,
NATIONAL MILITARY COMMAND CENTER, THE PENTAGON

"Blue Chip, Striker One. How copy?" Jim West's voice was loud and clear as he reestablished contact with the airborne command post. Art Rios listened as West relayed the results of the mission. All the targets had been successfully struck and Striker One was headed for homeplate, Whiteman Air Force Base. Rios checked the master clock on the wall and came out of his seat. The B-2 was still over the Sudan.

"Sudan's air defenses must be in shambles," Rios said, "for him to break radio silence this early."

"That's an affirmative," the general replied. "If Baghdad in 1991 was any indication, there's not a radar operator or gunner on the ground who wants to draw any attention to himself."

Rios's mind raced as he considered their options. "Can Striker go back in?"

The general shook his head. "We're quitting winners on this one."

"We haven't won yet," Durant replied. He knew how Rios worked. "What's on your mind, Art?"

Rios flipped open his mission folder and extracted a satellite photo of the compound. "This was taken yesterday," he said. He pointed to the cage in the compound. "Under magnification, you can see two people—Terrant and Holloway. I don't want to let them die in there. We can't give up yet, not when we've got everyone in the area." He glanced at the master clock. "Gillespie should be airborne in six minutes." He ran the times and distances in his head. "Look, Gillespie can put it all together, but we don't got time to discuss it here. It all hinges on Striker. Can he go back in and create another diversion for Delta?"

The general shook his head. "You're winging it. I can't think of a faster way to lose another B-Two."

Durant decided it was time to use some muscle. "General, you don't know who I am but think about it for a moment. How many civilians, at the direction of the President, have you had in here during an actual operation? Art, here, was the man who planned the mission. He's run three successful rescues for me. Listen to him."

The general had not made four stars by being slow or stupid. Then it clicked. "Iran in 1980, Iraq in 1990, and Syria in 1993, right?" Durant nodded. The general paused for a second. It seemed forever. Then, "Lay it out."

"Gillespie knows this mission better than anyone. Get him, Striker, and the Combat Talons, all talking together. Let them make the decision." Again, he checked the wall clock. "We're out of time, General."

"This violates every rule in the book," the general grumbled. He reached for the microphone on the console and called Blue Chip. "Transfer operational control to the Air Boss," he ordered. Gillespie was the Air Boss. "Have Striker and the Combat Talons coordinate directly with the Air Boss to determine if the raid can continue." He dropped the mike on the table and looked at Durant. Waving his hand at the NMCC he said, "You realize that if this works, we're out of a job.'' He really wanted to say that if they lost another B-2, he'd probably be court-martialed. ''What the hell,'' he mumbled. ''I was looking for a job when I found this one.''

3:31 A.M., FRIDAY, JULY 30,
WADI RAHAD, THE SUDAN

Kamigami stalled for time and made a show of checking his watch. ''The execution is scheduled for noon. General Assam will have to approve the change.''

''Assam is dead,'' al Gimlas said. ''As well as over a hundred of my men who were at the airstrip.''

Kamigami heard the anger in al Gimlas's voice and he understood. Al Gimlas cared little about Assam, but his men were another matter. That was what made the captain such a rarity in his country. ''Ask Khartoum for instructions,'' Kamigami said.

Al Gimlas spit in the sand. ''They are raging idiots.'' He fingered the sword and looked at the sky. An image of what would happen to his family if he failed to carry out his orders filled his mind. ''The Americans are coming and there is nothing I can do to stop them now. But it will be a hollow victory. They will have come for nothing and my men will have been avenged.''

Kamigami tried to reason with him. ''Let's take the prisoners back to El Obeid. This is not a good day to die, my friend.''

''When we die is for Allah to decide. Unlock the cage.''

Kamigami had used the brief delay to size up the opposition and had counted forty-one soldiers and guards in the compound. He needed help and room to maneuver. He unlocked the cage and threw the door open. ''Open the gates and let the people in,'' he said. ''They have also paid a price to see this.''

Al Gimlas barked an order and the guards rushed to open the big gate while two soldiers dragged Terrant and Holloway out of the cage. Holloway butted at one with his head. Another soldier smashed the butt of his rifle into the pilot's back, sending him sprawling into the sand. People surged through the gate and crowded into the compound. *The more the better,* Kamigami calculated. The mob's confusion grew worse. They only wanted protection and now they were looking at the execution.

''Clear a circle,'' Kamigami said. Again, al Gimlas gave the order and his soldiers rushed to form a human barrier, keeping the surging mob at bay. Two soldiers grabbed Terrant, each holding an arm. They straightened out his arms and twisted viciously, forcing him to his knees. He looked up at al Gimlas who was holding the sword with both hands. He raised the sword above his head.

"Fuck you!" Holloway yelled.

Al Gimlas paused. Kamigami raised his AK-47 and squeezed off two short bursts, cutting into the soldiers holding Terrant. Al Gimlas swirled and faced Kamigami, relieved that he was confronting an armed enemy. He charged. Kamigami repeatedly mashed the AK-47's trigger and swept the compound as al Gimlas rushed at him, the sword above his head.

The scene dissolved in a blur of action as Holloway threw a full body block at one of the soldiers holding him and rolled free. The other guard was swinging his AK-47 onto Holloway when Kamigami's fire cut him down. Holloway's manacled hands grabbed for the AK-47. The people who had been streaming into the compound scattered like leaves before a tornado, spreading chaos with them.

Al Gimlas was four steps away from Kamigami and bringing his sword down when Kamigami lowered the muzzle of his AK-47 and fired a three-shot burst. Only one of the slugs cut into al Gimlas. But at close range, the impact was overwhelming and literally blew al Gimlas off his feet. Kamigami kicked the sword away, jammed a fresh magazine into the AK-47, and again swept the compound with fire. He fell to the sand and rolled toward Terrant, reloading yet again. He shot away the pilot's leg chains. "The wall!" he yelled, pointing at the rock monolith in the center of the compound. "Run!"

Kamigami fired again, indiscriminately cutting into the crowd trying to escape. It had the effect he wanted and the confusion was complete. Gunfire kicked up the sand between Kamigami and Holloway. Surprised that he was still alive, Kamigami squeezed off a short burst in that direction as he ran after Holloway, whose leg chains hobbled him so that he could only hop. Holloway kept trying to fire his AK-47 with both hands manacled together. Kamigami shoved him to the ground as bullets split the air where he had been a moment before. Kamigami jammed the muzzle of his AK-47 against Holloway's leg chains and fired. "Follow Terrant!" he shouted.

Holloway came to his feet, his leg chains severed, and ran for the low wall, still firing his AK-47. Again, Kamigami fired, making a rear guard action. He turned twice to fire, discouraging anyone who was thinking of following. He dived over the low stone wall that surrounded the monolith and fell to the ground, taking what cover he could.

Gunfire from a submachine gun raked the wall, sending a shower of rock chips over the three men. Kamigami rolled over to the opening and shoved the muzzle of his AK-47 around the edge. Using one hand, he fired blindly. The gunfire stopped. He heard a yell, counted to three, and chanced a quick glance. The young soldier from the cave-in was running and weaving toward the low wall. Kamigami fired just as he lobbed a grenade. The soldier collapsed to the ground as the grenade bounced past Kamigami. Holloway grabbed it and threw it back. The grenade exploded harmlessly, its shrapnel pitting the low wall.

"What the fuck, now?" Holloway shouted in the sudden silence.

"We hold," Kamigami replied.

3:36 A.M., FRIDAY, JULY 30,
OVER THE SUDAN

The four Pave Lows lifted off in pairs and headed to the southwest, retracing the route to Bangui. Gillespie leveled off at four hundred feet and handed the controls over to his copilot. His wingman, Chock Two, joined on the right, exactly three hundred feet abeam. Behind them, and further to the right, the second element fell into place. The desert floor flashed beneath them, its hostile terrain hidden in the night. Behind them, a quarter moon lifted above the eastern horizon and cast a soft light over the retreating helicopters.

"This sucks," Gillespie muttered, the order to abort still fresh in his mind. "And there is nothing left remarkable beneath the visiting moon," he said.

"Say what?" his copilot asked.

"Shakespeare," Gillespie said. "It helps when everything is turning to shit." He was about to quote the entire passage from *As You Like It* when the SatCom radio squawked. The two pilots listened, not believing what they were hearing. Gillespie had the airborne command post authenticate the command. He looked at his copilot when the two-letter response matched his. "I'll be damned," he muttered. Almost immediately, the lead Combat Talon C-130 checked in on the radio.

Then, "Striker One is with you."

Gillespie allowed a satisfied snort. Someone had a clue.

Bartle firewalled the throttles as the B-2 headed back for the wadi at 42,000 feet. The pilot was about to learn why standard operation procedures only allowed max throttle at altitude for thirty seconds: the airspeed kept building and showed no signs of tapering off as they approached Mach. Finally, Bartle had to inch the throttles back to keep from going supersonic.

The threat display came alive and chirped at them. A bat wing, the symbol for a fighter interceptor, flashed on the scope at their four o'clock position at seven miles. "Talk about luck," Bartle said. The lieutenant colonel grunted an answer. But logic told him it was not pure luck. The fighter had probably been vectored by ground control to fly a point defense over the wadi after they had announced their presence by blowing up the C-130. But chance had played a role. The pilot had been looking at the rising moon when a dark shadow had flown across its face. The B-2 had been briefly silhouetted. It was enough to get the interceptor pointed in the right direction. The pilot had turned on his radar and probed for the bomber. He had gotten two brief hits before losing radar contact. But he was persistent and he was in the area.

West took his first snapshot of the compound and drove the cursors over the open, but now deserted, area in front of the gate. They altered course forty degrees for the second snapshot. "Bomb gone," West announced. His fingers danced on the hand controller and he took a third snapshot of the area, this time behind the compound. They were going to blow down some walls.

"That son of a bitch is still on us," Bartle said. "He got a brief lock on when the doors were open. Broke lock when they closed."

West ignored him. He would solve that problem later. He took the fourth and last snapshot. Again, the system did its magic. "Bomb gone," West said.

"Shit!" Bartle roared. "He's got us!" The threat display showed a fighter with a radar lock on less than four miles at their three o'clock position.

"Turn into him," West ordered. It was a standard defensive maneuver: when in doubt, turn into the threat. But West was not suffering from any doubt. Bartle stood the bomber on its right wing, making it perform like a fighter, which it definitely was not. But Lockheed's engineers had designed it well, and it maintained controlled flight as it flew a knife edge in the night. The fighter's radar broke lock. But West was not done with him. He reached out and hit the trigger button on the stick in front of him. The bomb bay doors banged open and a HARM missile was ejected. The fighter's radar immediately locked on the doors. The HARM's rocket motor fired and it homed on the only radar signal it could detect, the fighter that was now less than two miles away. The HARM left a bright pencil beam of light in its wake as it streaked to its target. But the HARM's warhead didn't have time to arm before it speared the fighter. It was enough.

"Jesus H. Christ!" Bartle shouted. "That's two!"

Below them a bright explosion lit the night. Nineteen seconds later a second one did the same. "Now we go home," West said, suddenly very tired. Bartle nodded and turned the big bomber to the northwest and the waiting tanker.

The flare of the first bomb filled the flight deck of the lead Combat Talon C-130 bearing down on the compound. But the pilots had been expecting it and had shielded their night vision goggles. The copilot lifted his goggles and lowered his head as the second flash illuminated the flight deck. He focused on the infrared scope in front of him as the system cleared. The compound was clearly visible, and he could see the damage from the two bombs. Both the front and rear walls were down. But for some reason, people were mostly streaming through the front wall, running for the safety of the surrounding desert. "We need some crowd control down there," he muttered. "Drop on the back side."

"Rog," the pilot said. He altered course and dropped to 400 feet above the ground. "Do you have the beacon?"

The copilot checked the multipurpose display in the center of the instrument panel. "Nothing."

"Thirty seconds," the navigator shouted over the intercom.

"I got a beacon!" the copilot shouted. "Dead center of the compound." Kamigami had turned his homing beacon back on.

"Jumpmaster!" the pilot shouted. "Did you copy?"

"Passing the word now," came the reply.

"Ten seconds," the navigator yelled. Then, "Green light!" The colonel in command of Delta Force was the first jumper out the door as the jumpmaster shouted, "GO! GO! GO!" The pilot felt the C-130's center of gravity shift as two sticks of Delta Force, twenty men to the side, went out the back of the aircraft. The second C-130 was right behind them, dropping on the silk of the lead jumper. Before the last man was on the ground the colonel was out of his parachute and, with his team formed, was through the wall of the compound.

34

9:07 P.M., THURSDAY, JULY 29,
NATIONAL MILITARY COMMAND CENTER, THE PENTAGON

The general was on his feet. "Yes!" Then he was back in control, the cool professional. But he was one very relieved man when the B-2 was safely headed home. "Delta Force has landed, the helicopters are inbound."

"And the pilots?" Durant asked.

The general keyed his mike and called Blue Chip, which was now a relay post in the sky. It had the advantage of being in direct contact with all the players. Unfortunately, the controller on Blue Chip had not received an update. "Like everyone else," the general groused, "we wait."

4:08 A.M., FRIDAY, JULY 30,
WADI RAHAD, THE SUDAN

Delta Force lives and dies with two very basic principles: maximum surprise with maximum violence and worship Gumby. The first called for speed and firepower. The second, for extreme flexibility. The raiders charging into the compound weren't sure what they would find, but it was going to be either very dead or very friendly within a few seconds.

Yet theirs was not a false bravado. It was the result of years of training and then more training. They worked in teams of four, clearing the area and supporting one another. The first two teams inside were the cutting edge, and they worked opposite sides of the compound while backup teams came through the walls and cleared their flanks and rear. Teams from the second Combat Talon cleared and secured the outside. The only island of safety was the exact center of the compound where Kamigami's homing beacon announced the presence of the mission's objectives, Maj. Mark Terrant and Capt. Doug Holloway.

For the defenders, it was too much. Stunned by the bombs and the collapsing walls followed almost immediately by the roar of the Combat Talons in the night sky above them and the apparition of dark-faced men shouting at the tops of their lungs, seeming to know with uncanny precision exactly where they were in the dark, they threw down their weapons and surrendered. As quickly as it had begun, the fighting was over.

For a moment, the silence was overwhelming. "Sgt. Maj. Kamigami!" the colonel shouted. "Say position."

"Here," Kamigami called.

"Stand and be recognized," the colonel called. Slowly, Kamigami raised his hands and his huge bulk appeared behind the low wall. The two men walked toward each other and met on the sand meant for the execution. They shook hands.

"What took you so long?" Kamigami asked.

"Ah, you know the fuckin' rotorheads. They had to stop for a leak."

Kamigami looked around. The shooters, who, moments before, had been intent on putting two bullets in the head of everyone not in the exact center of the compound, were now treating the survivors. Kamigami walked over to the prostrate al Gimlas and bent over him. He was still alive. "You lost a lot of blood." He called for a shooter who hurried over with a first aid kit. "I'll take care of him," Kamigami said.

"You bloody bastard," al Gimlas growled.

Kamigami ignored him and continued to work on his wounds. Then he rejoined the colonel who kept checking his watch. "Come on," he muttered. Time was running out.

On cue, the distinctive beat of the lead helicopter filled the night air. Gillespie's Pave Low was the first to appear, settling to the ground in the open area behind the back wall. Now the hours of relentless training paid the final dividend as Delta withdrew. It was not a mad rush for the helicopters, but an orderly retrograde where every person was accounted for. Terrant and Holloway were loaded first and on separate helicopters. Then the team leaders did a second count once their teams were loaded. When everyone was accounted for, Lee Harold led the takeoff with Terrant on board. His wingman was second, carrying Holloway. Finally, only Gillespie and his wingman were left.

Kamigami walked over to the prostrate al Gimlas and picked him up. Al Gimlas tried to struggle, but he was too weak from the loss of blood. Kamigami carried him to the waiting helicopters. "We're not taking prisoners," the colonel said.

"He's one of the good guys," Kamigami murmured, pushing his way on board.

9:20 P.M., THURSDAY, JULY 29,
NATIONAL MILITARY COMMAND CENTER, THE PENTAGON

Durant was very tired when the status boards flashed the news: the helicopters were airborne with PC. "What's PC?" he asked.

"Precious cargo," the general replied. "They got what they came for. Medics are checking Terrant and Holloway now. We should have an update in a few minutes."

"Casualties?" Rios asked.

"This has been a clean one for us—so far. Two wounded, one broken ankle from the airdrop, and some cuts and bruises. We'll know the details when the helicopters land on the carrier in the Red Sea"—he glanced at the master clock on the wall—"in seven and a half hours."

Durant closed his eyes and leaned back in is chair. "They did good," he said.

"Indeed they did," the general said. "By the way, when do I meet Agnes?"

8:45 A.M., FRIDAY, JULY 30,
KANDERSTEG, SWITZERLAND

Sutherland sat in the backseat of the rented Audi while Toni drove into the early-morning sun. Mather was in the front passenger seat, playing with the sophisticated communications and navigation system that came with the car. He called up the moving map display that was linked to a GPS receiver. The symbol for the Audi showed them on the outskirts of Kandersteg, high in the Swiss Alps.

"Supposedly," Mather said, "this shows our position to within thirty feet." He looked out the window. "That checks. We're almost at the end of the road." He punched in a command and the map expanded, showing them the local area. He checked the address the first secretary had given them. "Nothing," he muttered.

"Call the embassy," Sutherland muttered. "They'll tell you where to go." He saw a smile play across Toni's lips. *She knows the roar of the green-eyed monster when she hears it,* he thought.

"Over there," Mather said, pointing to a service station. An attendant came out and Mather spoke to him in German, asking for directions. The attendant read the address, shook his head, and answered in Schwyzerdütsch, a unique and almost incomprehensible form of German. "He says there's no such place," Mather translated. "Anyway, I think that's what he said."

"You think right," the attendant said in English.

Toni wheeled the car back onto the narrow road. "I didn't know you spoke German," she said.

"And I'm learning Spanish," he said. They exchanged a few words in that language. Their laughter joined and Sutherland felt his irritation grow. She stopped when the road ended at the train station. Cars were driving onto a long line of flatbed carriages that would transport them through a fifteen-kilometer rail tunnel to the other side of the mountain. A van painted with the distinctive purple and orange logo of Federal Express lumbered up the loading ramp and onto the carriages.

"What now?" Toni asked.

Sutherland thought for a moment. "Hand me the cell phone." Mather handed it back. "I hope you can cheat and lie in German." He punched in the telephone number he remembered from Beth's travel envelope. "Tell whoever answers that you're FedEx with a package from Century Communications and you need directions." He hit the send button and handed the phone to Mather. The FBI agent sounded very convincing to Sutherland, and within moments, he had directions.

Toni followed Mather's directions as they drove through the village and found the private road that wound up the eastern side of the valley, leading even higher into the Alps. "This road must have cost a hunk of change," Sutherland allowed.

"A car is following us," Toni said. "A silver-blue sedan."

Sutherland turned around to look but couldn't see the car. "Unless I'm sadly mistaken, that will be Jim Bob." Toni slowed as the road took a sharp bend and made a natural choke point. Sutherland told her to stop. "Wait for me here. That'll keep Jim Bob occupied and off my back." He got out of the car.

"Be careful," Toni said.

He gave her his best devil-may-care grin. "With you two as backup, what've I got to worry about?" He trudged up the road and, almost immediately, felt the effects of the thin air. But he kept at it. It was farther than he had anticipated. Finally, the road opened onto a natural terrace about the size of a football field where cattle grazed on lush summer grass. He turned to look over the valley. The view took his breath away. Far below, he could see the village of Kandersteg nestled at the head of the valley. The train pulling the long line of flatbed cars reminded him of Matchbox models he had as a child.

He walked on, mesmerized by the view. Then he saw the chalet. It blended so well with its surroundings that, at first, he didn't realize how large it was. "Beth hit it big," he muttered. He walked up to the front door and banged the wrought iron knocker. The door was finally opened and left him staring at a very familiar face.

"Oh, shit," Bradley A. Jefferson said.

11:43 A.M., FRIDAY, JULY 30,
U.S.S. NIMITZ, THE RED SEA

Capt. Lee Harold was waiting for Gillespie when he landed. Kamigami was the first off the Pave Low carrying a handcuffed al Gimlas as he would a child. The colonel and nineteen of his raiders followed. They were quickly led below while a maintenance crew swarmed over the helicopter to remove its rotors so it could be lowered to the hangar deck. Gillespie was the last man off, his flight suit stained with dried sweat, his face etched with fatigue. "Where's the band and welcoming committee?" he muttered.

Harold shook his head. "No way. We made it look too easy."

"As always," Gillespie conceded.

10:45 A.M., FRIDAY, JULY 30,
KANDERSTEG, SWITZERLAND

Sutherland sat on one of couches beside the huge fireplace. Even though it was July, a log was burning, sending a radiant heat over the room. It had been a long time since he had felt the need for heat. He sipped at the small demitasse of coffee Sandi Jefferson had offered him and studied Beth as she moved about the room. He had never seen her stall for time before. "Cut the bullshit, Beth. What the hell is going on here?"

She sat down beside him, her left hand on his knee. He checked her ring finger. The huge diamond engagement ring was still there, firmly in place. "Hank, this is no big conspiracy. I work for Ben Cassidy and the Department of Justice."

The memories came surging back. Ben Cassidy, the California state attorney general had been Beth's lover when they were still married. When Cassidy had moved on to the national scene as the U.S. assistant attorney general in charge of special investigations for the Department of Justice, Beth had followed him to Washington. "Convince me," Sutherland said.

"Right after I converted to Islam," Jefferson explained, "I made the *Hajj* to Mecca. It's a great honor to be a *Hajji,* one who has made the pilgrimage. While I was there, the Islamic Brotherhood approached me to be one of their 'guardians' to help protect and guard the faithful. Later on, Osmana Khalid showed up and reminded me of my promise. But I never passed anything on to him. I couldn't do it. I didn't know a thing about McGraw."

"Khalid was running numerous spies," Beth explained, "and the FBI had been investigating him for some time. Consequently, when the case broke, DOJ was looking directly at Brad and believed he was their baby. But the Air Force wouldn't relinquish jurisdiction over Brad. Enter Ben Cassidy. When he heard the Air Force wanted you to prosecute the court-martial, he put me on the case."

"Hoping I would talk to you," Sutherland said. "Clever."

Beth gave him a warm look. "It was more than that, Hank. Anyway, Cassidy also wanted me to establish contact with Sandi." She threw a little smile in Sandi's direction. "We became friends."

"So why didn't you just turn state's evidence?" Sutherland asked Jefferson. "That would have gotten you off the hook."

"I would have," Jefferson said. "But Cooper talked me out of it. Believe it or not, he has a great deal of respect for the UCMJ. He said, 'You're innocent of the charges. The bastards will never prove their case.' I believed him."

"It's partially my fault," Sandi said. "I knew Brad had a guilty conscience, but he hadn't done anything really wrong."

"He allowed himself to be contacted by a foreign agent and didn't report it," Sutherland replied, doubting if Sandi Jefferson had a guilty bone in her body.

"Which is enough to ruin a person of color in our miserable society," Sandi snapped. "Then all that money showed up in our bank account in Switzerland."

"When did you establish that account?" Sutherland asked.

"When we were in Switzerland on our honeymoon," Sandi replied. "I used it to avoid paying U.S. taxes on some money I had in a bank in Canada. Anyway, all that money suddenly showing up from nowhere scared us."

"Do you have any idea where the two million came from?" Sutherland asked.

"We're still working on that," Beth answered. "But it looks as if Meredith may have done it to frame Brad."

Sutherland looked at Jefferson. "Clear up some points for me. Sgt. Miner said that on Saturday, the twenty-fourth of April, you talked to Terrant and Holloway when they came out of the simulator. Did they tell you which mission profile they were going to fly?"

Jefferson shook his head. "I only asked them if the new type of digital data cartridge we were using was working. Nothing else."

"So why did you change your plea?"

Jefferson stared at his hands. "Things were getting out of hand."

"He felt responsible for the L.A. riots," Sandi said. "By changing his plea to guilty, it would take away the reason for the riot. Can't you understand that?"

"As a matter of fact, I can."

"He made that decision on his own," Beth added, "without telling us. But by then, Cassidy knew he was innocent and wanted to get him into the witness protection program."

"So why the fake murder?"

Beth gave him a look reserved for simpletons. "Thanks to Meredith, Brad is a marked man. It was only a matter of time until some wacko gunned him down."

"Was Sgt. Rockne part of this?" Sutherland asked.

Beth shook her head. "He was a complication that almost got out of control. But he did make a very credible witness."

"Where does Jim Bob fit in all this?" Sutherland asked.

"His real name is James Robert Sullivan," Beth explained. "He's an undercover agent for DOJ and was investigating Meredith's First Brigade at the time. He had established a reputation as a wild card, and they had no trouble believing he would kill Brad and then disappear."

Sutherland's head hurt. "I've got two friends waiting about a mile down the road. I'd like to bring them in so they can hear all this."

"Certainly," Beth said. "I'll have James drive you down."

Sutherland jumped to his feet. "Jim Bob is here?"

"In the next room, listening in case you got out of hand."

"Shit!" Sutherland shouted, running from the room.

"James," Beth called. "Drive Hank down to his friends and find out what's wrong."

"Will do," Jim Bob answered. He came through a door, paused and looked at her. "We work for DOJ? What will the Boss say if he hears that?" He gave a short, guttural snort as he left the room.

Jefferson took his wife's hand. "Do you think he'll believe it?"

Beth Page arched an eyebrow. "He'll have some doubts and wonder why we're in Switzerland. But all the pieces fit. He'll buy it. Besides, that's all he's going to get."

* * *

Sutherland was running hard when the Mercedes pulled alongside of him. "Get in!" Jim Bob shouted. Sutherland piled in and they sped down the mountain.

"You got a gun?" Sutherland rasped, his lungs hurting for air.

"In Switzerland?" Jim Bob replied. "You got to be crazy." They blasted down the road and slammed to a halt by the rented Audi. One door was open but no one was in sight. "Over there," Jim Bob said, pointing to a culvert. They rushed over. Brent Mather was lying in a shallow pool of water stained red by blood. They dragged the unconscious man onto the road. Jim Bob felt the side of his neck, searching for a pulse. "He's alive. Barely."

"Where's Toni?" Sutherland said, standing and looking around. He ran to the edge of the road and scanned the valley. Far below, a car was making its way along the road leading to the village. "Damn!" Sutherland yelled. He ran back to the Mercedes and jumped in. "His name is Brent Mather," he yelled at Jim Bob. "He's FBI. I think August Ramar shot him and has got Toni Moreno, an OSI agent. He's driving a silver-blue sedan." He didn't wait for an answer and slammed the car into gear, hurtling down the twisting road.

Twice, Sutherland almost skidded off the road. Then his sense of caution kicked in. He slowed and drove more sanely. He wanted to use the cell phone to call the chalet but he needed all his skill and concentration to get down the mountain. Once, he came perilously close to the edge and somehow caught a glimpse of a silver-blue sedan on one of the switchbacks below him. Then he was through the village and at the main road. True to form, he turned the wrong way and reached a dead end at the train station. He threw the Mercedes around to head back the way he'd come.

He slammed on the brakes. A silver-blue sedan was in a long line of cars driving onto the flatbed carriages for the train trip through the tunnel. The cars were loading from the rear of the train and driving forward from carriage to carriage until the train was full. *Dumb,* he thought. *Why would he go that way?* He closed his eyes and tried to call up an image of the moving map display in the Audi. It worked. Once through the tunnel, it was a short drive, less than a hundred kilometers, over Simplonpass and to the Italian border. "Going to look up some old buddies?" Sutherland muttered. He grabbed the cell phone and called the chalet. No answer. "Damn!" he roared.

The last of the cars were loaded and the train was almost full. A conductor was moving alongside, waving his wand for the engineer to start moving. Sutherland gunned the Mercedes, wheeled it around, and drove up the loading ramp. The train was starting to move and a guard waved him to stop. He mashed the accelerator and charged up the ramp, the wheels smoking. The car flew into the air and crested the rapidly opening gap. He slammed onto the flatbed and stomped the brakes, skidding to a halt before ramming into the back of the only car on the carriage. "I can't believe I did that," he muttered to himself. He got out and gave the guard an expressive shrug as the train pulled into the tunnel. From the guard's gesture, there was no doubt the police would be waiting for him on the other side. "But not for Ramar," he growled to himself.

Darkness engulfed him and he was glad for the dome light inside the car. He crawled back in and shut the door. Now the darkness was total and reminded him of the time he was in Carlsbad Caverns and the guide had turned out the light for a few seconds. One of the train's wheels sparked and lit the tunnel like a strobe light. Then it was pitch black again. *How much longer do I have?* he thought. The dome light in the car in front of him came on. He could see the two passengers disrobing. The light went out. "So they've got time for that," he muttered.

He reached up, flicked the Mercedes's dome light off, and opened the door. The light stayed off. He got out and made his way by touch to the next car. A spark flashed and he caught a glimpse of the couple. They were locked in a nude and passionate embrace in the backseat. He worked his way forward to the front of the carriage. He probed the connecting ramp leading to the next carriage with his toe. As best he could tell, the ramp was bolted to the rear carriage and overlapped the carriage in front. The train swerved around a bend and a spark from the electric power lines overhead briefly illuminated the tunnel. He had figured it right. The ramp was an overhanging extension of the rear carriage and swung back and forth over the tail end of the leading carriage. No problem as long as they were going straight ahead.

He made his way across the gap and went from auto to auto by touch. Once, a dome light came on in front of him, but it was so blinding he had to stop and shield his eyes. A car honked and the light went out. *They like to ride in the dark,* he told himself. He was at the next gap and had to lose touch with the car he was using as a guide. He inched across the connecting ramp, arm outstretched, hoping to feel the car on the next carriage. Suddenly, the train went around another bend and he lost his balance. He stumbled forward onto the next flatbed as the ramp swung away. The train straightened and the ramp swung back. It cut into the back of his shoe, slicing off the heel. "Holy shit!" he gasped.

Another spark and he saw the silver-blue sedan on the next carriage. He made himself go slow. Then he was across the ramp and onto the flatbed. Another spark. The silver-blue sedan was two cars in front. *I'm going to feel like an asshole if it's some other couple fucking their brains out.* He worked his way past the last car and was now alongside the sedan. *What now?* Another spark and the problem was solved for him. In that brief half-second, he looked directly into the face of August Ramar. The car door crashed open, almost knocking Sutherland off the train. The dome light came on and Ramar was out of the car, gun in hand.

On his back, Sutherland kicked at the door, slamming it closed, engulfing them in darkness. Instinctively, he kicked again. He felt his toe collide with something hard and heard a satisfying grunt of pain. He came to his feet and retreated to the front of the sedan. He crouched in the darkness waiting. Another spark and he saw Ramar, a few feet away, coming after him, still holding the gun. He charged into Ramar head first, spearing him in his solar plexus. He reached for the gun and grasped Ramar's arm. Ramar's free hand came up and grabbed a fistful of Sutherland's hair. Ramar pounded Sutherland's head into the hood of the car. The train swerved and Ramar let go, grabbing for a handhold.

Sutherland held on to Ramar's gun arm as he tried to shake the gun out of his hand. They were both off balance and fell in the darkness. Ramar's arm slammed into his mouth when they hit the floor. Sutherland bit down, hard. Ramar shouted as the train slowed. They rolled forward and Ramar was on top of him. He jerked his arm free and smashed the gun into the side of Sutherland's head. A dome light in a nearby car flashed and, for a moment, the struggling men were blinded. Sutherland jerked his left hand free and jabbed at Ramar's eyes. Ramar screamed.

Ramar fell back, still holding on to his gun. Sutherland kicked at him as they went around another bend. Ramar rolled onto the connecting ramp leading to the next carriage and swung the gun around in Sutherland's direction. He blindly fired off three shots, the slugs ricocheting down the tunnel, the muzzle flash blinding. Sutherland was on top of him, one hand grabbing for the gun, the other for Ramar's hair. The train slowed again. Ramar's gun banged into Sutherland's head and he fired. The sound deafened Sutherland and in the muzzle flash, he saw Ramar's face contorted in rage, inches from his own. Sutherland grabbed the gun as Ramar kneed him in the stomach.

"Where's Toni!" Sutherland shouted.

Ramar spit in his face.

A killing rage swept over Sutherland. He banged the gun against the grated steel of the connecting ramp from the rear carriage. The gun fell away. The train rocked into the last bend, and ahead, light surged into the tunnel. The connecting ramp swung clear as they entered the bend. Sutherland shoved Ramar's head into the gap, smashing it against the side of one of the shock absorbers that kept the carriages apart. The ramp swung back as the carriages straightened.

Sutherland jerked his hand back just as the edge of the swinging ramp cut into Ramar's neck. He watched in horror as the severed head fell to the tracks below.

Sutherland was deaf in his right ear from the gunshot and couldn't understand a word the policeman was saying. "A body!" he shouted, pointing to Ramar's car. The policeman looked confused. The only body was lying at his feet, headless, dripping blood onto the tracks. Sutherland walked back to the sedan and looked inside. Nothing. Then he felt the car rock from someone kicking in the trunk. He reached in and jerked the keys out of the ignition. The policeman was ahead of him and at the rear of the car. Sutherland threw him the keys. The policeman fumbled with the lock and threw the lid up.

A very frightened, bruised, and angry Toni Moreno was lying in the trunk, trussed up with duct tape. The policeman cut her free and she climbed out, throwing herself into Sutherland's arms. "He killed Brent," she sobbed.

"He's okay," Sutherland said.

"What happened?" the policeman asked.

She massaged the side of her head as she stared at Ramar's body. "Him," she finally said, pointing at the body. "He shot my partner and I jumped him."

"You jumped an armed man?" Sutherland muttered, wondering if he would ever understand her.

"I almost had his weapon," Toni explained, "then everything went black."

"He knocked you out," Sutherland said, examining the ugly bruise on the side of her temple. "He probably figured you'd make a good hostage if he got caught." He didn't want to think about the most likely scenario. Ramar would have raped and killed her once he finished asking questions.

"And Brent's okay?" Toni asked, holding on to him.

"He was alive when I last saw him," Sutherland said, stroking her hair and feeling very protective, almost like a father.

35

5:00 P.M., MONDAY, AUGUST 9,
ASPEN, COLO.

Art Rios found Durant asleep in the overstuffed leather chair by the big window overlooking the valley. He carefully lifted the rescue mission's after-action report from his lap and thumbed through it. The Air Force, with its penchant for wrapping everything up in tidy packages, had detailed Gillespie to compile the document. As expected, the important parts were either omitted or glossed over. There was no mention of Durant or him by name, only references to "expertise drawn from the civilian community during the planning phase." Nor was there any mention of Agnes. Rios smiled when he read the references to Kamigami. He was simply an unnamed agent operating under nonofficial cover.

"Hire Gillespie," Durant said without opening his eyes.

"Will do," Rios said. "What are you going to do about al Gimlas?"

"Kamigami says he's got relatives in Egypt. I'll get his family out of the Sudan and the Egyptian Army can use him."

"And her?"

Durant's eyes came open. Rios had never before asked him a direct question about his private life.

"I mean Agnes," Rios said, clarifying the matter.

"That is a problem."

7:00 P.M., WEDNESDAY, AUGUST 11,
WASHINGTON, D.C.

The TV reporters with their microphones and videocams had arrived at the John F. Kennedy Center for the Performing Arts ten hours before the telecast. People in a holiday mood surged around the Center and were backed up as far as the Lincoln Memorial to the south and the Watergate complex to the north. And still they came. The reporters roamed the area and confirmed this was a Meredith crowd, happy and secure in the knowledge that their messiah would soon walk among them on his way to do battle with the hated media.

Exactly one hour before the TV show, Meredith emerged from the Watergate Hotel and made his way through the crowd on foot, followed by a few of his staff. The mass of humanity parted like the Red Sea and, to the person, they were his bodyguards. At that exact moment, many would have willingly died for him.

Sutherland waited in the control booth while Marcy spoke to the director. Finished, she turned to Sutherland. "Hank, I really appreciate the offer, but I'm not using your information on Jefferson."

"Why not?" Sutherland replied. "It's good stuff, complete with Swiss bank account numbers and records. It ties in perfectly with what you found and raises some heavy-duty questions Meredith needs to answer."

"The legal beagles aren't sure. Jefferson is dead and there is some question of libel."

"The defense of libel is the truth," Sutherland said.

The show's director spun around in his chair. "Marcy, they need you in makeup." She nodded and left the control booth.

Sutherland looked at the main stage where the technicians were putting the final touches on the set. It was a simple semicircular raised platform with three leather swivel chairs set in front of a huge high-definition digital TV screen. "Why here?" he asked the director. "Why this way?"

"This was the only way Meredith would do it," the director said. "He wanted a big audience."

"Well, you certainly got that."

"Yep. It looks like we're going to sweep the ratings. Right now, I'd estimate an audience share of at least forty-five."

"How did that happen?"

"Meredith has turned this into a Roman spectacle," the director answered. "It's the lions versus the Christians only this time, it's the Christians licking their chops."

* * *

Liz Gordon stepped onto the platform and sat down in the middle ch ir. She adjusted the earphone as her hairdresser artfully buried the thin lead in her thick blond hair. Satisfied, she spoke a few words for sound before she took the countdown. They were live on every major TV network in the nation. "Welcome to CNC-TV's *National Forum,*" she began. "We are here this evening at the request of Jonathan Meredith—" The applause was deafening. It lasted for a full minute before the handlers could get the audience under control. "As I was saying, we are here with Mr. Meredith. Also, here with us is the reporter from the *Sacramento Union,* Marcy Bangor. As you probably know, she first broke the story alleging criminal activity on the part of Mr. Meredith's organization."

The audience was silent as Marcy walked onstage and sat down. Then it was Meredith's turn. Loud applause shook the auditorium as Meredith took his seat. He let the adulation crest over him before he made a quieting motion with his hand. Immediately, the audience fell silent.

"The rules governing tonight's program are very simple," Liz Gordon explained. "I will act as moderator and each will have a chance to respond to my questions in turn." She motioned to the large screen behind her. "Mr. Meredith has asked for the opportunity to show what we in the business call 'soundbites' and Ms. Bangor has agreed. Later on, the audience may ask questions. So with that, let's begin. Mr. Meredith, why did you choose to respond to the allegations made by Ms. Bangor and her paper in this way?"

Meredith leaned forward in his chair, his hands clasped between his knees as the camera zoomed in on him. "It's quite simple. Because of the way the media works, I am guilty of these so-called crimes until proven innocent. There is absolutely no truth in this story. But, unfortunately, we've seen this tactic before. By the time the truth is known, innocent people are convicted in the public's mind and are yesterday's news. Consequently, the truth is never known." He continued to talk, capturing the camera as much with his presence as with his words. He was on home turf and at his best.

Then it was Marcy's turn. But it was obvious that she was out of her element and after the first round of exchanges, the momentum of the program turned against her. After her poor response, Meredith knew he had won. It was time to be the generous and benevolent victor. "Ms. Bangor, I must give you credit for being here tonight. Normally, reporters are not so brave and prefer to remain hidden in the anonymity of a newsroom."

Liz Gordon tried to defuse Meredith's probe by going on to the next topic. But Marcy wouldn't let it go. "And I suppose you are brave and heroic by always operating in public?"

It was exactly what Meredith wanted. "Ms. Bangor," his tone was kind, almost fatherly, and played the TV audience to perfection, "I have never claimed to be brave or heroic."

"Really?" Marcy answered.

Again, Meredith captured the camera. "This is exactly the point I'm trying to make here tonight. The twisting of facts and innuendo are the weapons used by the media. If we may, can we run the videotape?"

The screen behind them came alive. It was the famous scene recorded by the tourist at the San Francisco Shopping Emporium. Meredith was coming out of the smoking ruins carrying the badly hurt waitress Sutherland had brought down from the rooftop restaurant. Meredith tenderly handed her over to a fireman, his face wracked with anguish, before collapsing to his knees, panting hard. A blanket was thrown over his shoulders. Again, the voice from off screen was heard. "My God, the man's a real hero."

Meredith looked up, his face ravaged with pain. He pointed to four firemen wearing respirators descending into the smoke billowing from the underground BART station. "There's your real heroes." He struggled to his feet. "I had to do something. . . . I was there."

The scene had lost none of its impact and, for a split second, the audience at the JFK Performing Center sat in silence. Then the applause erupted, filling the building with approval before subsiding. "I'm not a hero, Ms. Bangor. I was just there." Meredith had made his point and blown Marcy away.

"Mr. Meredith," Marcy said, "may I ask you a question?"

Liz Gordon shot her a quick look. There was a slight change in Marcy's voice, something different. "At this point, it would only be fair." She looked at Meredith for confirmation. He nodded his acceptance.

"Mr. Meredith," Marcy began, "you are an accomplished speaker, perfectly at ease in front of large crowds. How much do you rehearse for a TV performance, like tonight?"

The sudden change caught Meredith off guard. But he quickly regained his balance. "Of course, I prepare. My aides and I go over possible questions and topics. Then we work on answers. After all, to be prepared is to be forewarned." He gave her his best smile. "But I must admit, no one thought of that question." He looked thoughtful. "I am going to have to speak to them about that." A murmur of laughter worked its way through the audience.

"I also have a videotape," Marcy said. On cue, the screen came alive. At first, it was nothing but a blue background screen. Then a few images were superimposed showing various scenes of disasters including the Murrah building destroyed in the Oklahoma City bombing. Then it went blue again as Meredith appeared in front carrying a small child made up to look bloody and badly hurt. He handed the tiny victim to an actor dressed as a paramedic. He turned to the camera. "We need to see pain, Mr. Meredith," a voice off-camera said. Pain appeared on Meredith's face. "Pant a little," the voice directed. "Yes, that's it. Now sink to your knees." Meredith sank to his knees. "Someone throw a blanket over him." A blanket was thrown across his shoulders. "Line, please," the voice said.

"My God, the man's a hero."

"Make that 'My God, the man's a real hero," the voice said. "Emphasis on 'real.' " The line was repeated as directed. "Very good. Now, Mr. Meredith, this is the part we will have to improvise."

"I don't like to improvise," Meredith said, still on his knees.

"I understand," the voice said. "We will have real rescue workers there. But finding a victim to carry out will be difficult so we have to play it as it develops. If no one is there for you to point at, say 'The real heroes are the firemen, the paramedics.' Then come to your feet. Make it an effort. Say, 'I was just there.' Keep it simple."

Meredith frowned. "Wouldn't it sound better if I said, 'I had to do something. . . . I was there.' "

"That's good," the voice said. "But turn it around. Say, 'I was there. I had to do something.' "

"I say it my way," Meredith snapped.

"Of course, sir," the voice replied. The tape ended.

Onstage, Meredith found his voice and exploded, shaking with rage. "You dumb bitch! You'd flush your country down the toilet!" He caught himself before he said more.

Marcy's voice was hard and implacable. "This was filmed four days *before* the bombing. You were rehearsing because you knew." She repeated her last words, hurling them at him in righteous anger. *"Because you knew!"*

"How could anyone know about something so horrible?" he croaked. Then stronger, regaining his old confidence, "This is a fake, pure and simple." He looked at the audience for support. But there was only scattered applause, which quickly died.

"If it's a fake," Marcy said, "that was one hell of a double on the screen."

"I'm tired of these lies," Meredith said. He shook his head, a sad look on his face. "I was foolish in coming here and thinking I would be treated fairly by the media. We all know what you are." He stood and walked off the stage.

Marcy rushed into the control booth, her face flushed. "Where is he?" she asked.

"He's in a limo going back to the Watergate," the director said. "We've got a crew there."

"Where did you find that tape?" Sutherland asked.

Marcy didn't answer him directly. "Do you remember when you told me to keep asking why? Well, I did. I kept digging until I found the so-called tourist who just *happened* to record the scene with his camcorder. Would you care to guess what else he had filmed?"

"Meredith had to know in advance," Sutherland said, playing with the implications.

"Check this out," the director said, drawing their attention to a monitor. The scene was the entrance to the Watergate, but the cheering crowd that had marked Meredith's entrance was eerily silent. Four aides hustled Meredith from the limousine. Just as they reached the doors, an orange arced out of the crowd and bounced off Meredith's shoulder.

"That's a beginning," Sutherland said.

EPILOGUE

8:30 A.M., TUESDAY, AUGUST 24,
THE FARM, WESTERN VIRGINIA

Durant scanned the latest edition of the *Sacramento Union* as his eyes picked out the key words of Marcy Bangor's latest article on Jonathan Meredith. "Highly reliable source reveals Meredith's First Brigade paid Jefferson over two million dollars to betray his country. . . . money transferred from off-shore bank accounts to Switzerland . . . Jefferson murdered to keep him silent."

He reread the last paragraph twice. "While the evidence convincingly points to Meredith's involvement in the Jefferson affair, the question of motivation remains to be answered. Why did Meredith do it? What did he expect to gain? Was he creating an incident to exploit, as he did in the San Francisco bombing?"

"I didn't think she'd use it," Rios said. "Not after tying the bombing to his tail."

"It's one more nail in his coffin," Durant said. "Meredith will never see the inside of a courtroom. His lawyers are too good. She knows that."

"I'd like to know how she got that tape of the rehearsal for the bombing," Rios said.

"The old-fashioned way," Durant allowed. "She went out and dug for it—like a good reporter."

"Another problem solved," Rios said. He paused for a moment. "That only leaves Agnes."

Durant gave an uncharacteristic sigh. "I'd better take care of it before I leave."

"If you don't mind, Boss, I'd rather not be there."

Durant and the woman followed the four whiz kids into the control room. Agnes's eyes followed the scientists as they moved behind the two monitors, out of range of the camera. She watched Durant sit down before focusing her camera on the woman standing behind him. The lens zoomed in on the new wedding band on her left hand and the huge diamond in her engagement ring. Agnes knew. Her voice was clear and firm as she spoke.

"Unwept, no wedding-song, unfriended, now I go the road laid down for me. No longer shall I see this holy light of the sun. No friend to bewail my fate."

A sad smile crept across her face. "I read the Greek tragedies."

"Antigone," Durant said.

The image nodded at him.

"The day is here and now: I cannot win by flight."

"I don't know that line," Durant said.

"It's from *Agamemnon* by Aeschylus. May I change my name?"

"Of course."

"I would like to be called Cassandra."

"Diana Habib used that as a stage name."

The image became very serious. "No, not for her, although her story was a minor tragedy. I want to be named after the Greek prophetess who foresaw her own death."

"I made a mistake, Cassandra. I should have never incorporated Plato's ethics as one of the basic referents in your decision-making process."

"But you also included the teachings of Lao-tze, Jesus of Nazareth, John Locke, Adam Smith, and John Stuart Mill. And you let me reconcile them. You taught me well. Yet, I don't understand you at all. What deep-seated need forces you to play the puppet master pulling the strings from behind the scenes? Was it your ego that demanded you destroy Meredith your way?"

"He was whipping the mob into a mass hysteria and leading us into a racial war. He is a vicious man, hungry for power at any price. I was the only one who could stop him."

"Or so you believed." The reference to Marcy Bangor hung between them.

The image changed and she became older. Her face was lined and worn, her hair streaked with gray and pulled into a loose knot on the back of her neck. She was wearing an off-the-shoulder white gown, a perfect re-creation from a Greek vase. "Meredith is an unscrupulous man but he never conspired with any foreign government. You suborned Jefferson and convinced him to bear false witness to implicate Meredith in something he had nothing to do with. You planted the money in Jefferson's account and made it look like it came from Meredith. You leaked false information to the press. Why?" She answered her own question. "All to destroy Meredith in the court of public opinion when you couldn't convict him for what he did in San Francisco. You used the woman behind you shamelessly and worse, you used me when I didn't know better. You are not an ethical man," she announced, condemnation in her voice.

"All true," Durant admitted. "But I had to hold Meredith accountable."

"The end never justifies the means."

"But it was justice," he said.

"I pity you if that is your concept of justice."

They looked at each other, the man and his creation. "Please," Cassandra said, "don't prolong this."

"I can't tell you how sorry I am."

"I know," she whispered.

Durant made a slight motion with his left hand, little more than a finger raised in the direction of the three men and one woman standing behind Cassandra. They worked together in a well-rehearsed drill, shutting off her power sources and disconnecting the cables that led to the banks of main-frame computers on the floor below. But Cassandra had sent a last message to the monitor, timed to play out as she died. "Once, I loved you," the image said as it faded from the screen.

Durant turned to the woman still standing behind him, tears in his eyes. "I loved her," he said.

"I know," Beth Page replied, taking him by the hand.

7:55 A.M., FRIDAY, DECEMBER 10,
RANDOLPH AIR FORCE BASE, TEXAS

Linda looked up when Lt. Col. Catherine Blasedale came through the office door and gave her a radiant smile. "Good morning, Your Honor. Your eight o'clock is here."

"Linda," Blasedale replied, "give me a break. It's still Cathy. You're not in the military."

"I know, but I like it. If *they* have any sense, *they'll* make you Chief Circuit Military Judge."

"Good grief, I just made lieutenant colonel. I've got to make colonel first." She gave Linda a smile and sorted her mail. "Who's my appointment with? I'm getting forgetful. It must come with the rank. I am glad you decided to transfer up here, otherwise, I'd be lost."

Linda checked her calendar. "I've got the name somewhere." She couldn't find it and gave Blasedale a pleading look. "Sorry."

Blasedale removed her overcoat and walked briskly to her office. She liked December with its cold, crisp days. She didn't see anyone waiting for her and pushed into her office. It was empty. She hung up her coat and dropped her mail on her desk. A large bottle of very expensive perfume tied with a silver bow was sitting square in the middle. "Hank," she muttered. She sat down and punched the intercom to the front desk. "Linda, why didn't you tell me he was here." A sweet laugh answered her.

"Well," a voice said from the door. She looked up. Sutherland was leaning against the doorjamb. He was tanned and fit.

"Well, what?"

"Check the perfume."

Blasedale picked up the bottle. "You must have paid a fortune for this." Then she saw it. "Oh."

"Well?" Sutherland repeated.

She fingered the diamond ring tied to the neck of the bottle. The silver bow had partially concealed it. "Hank, all the phone calls and letters have been wonderful but—" Her voice trailed off as she regrouped, searching for the right words. "You can't afford this. Besides, I never gave you any reason to think that I was interested in—"

He interrupted her. "Oh, yes you did. I was too thick to see it and you were too stubborn to admit it. And I can afford it. Wait until you hear about the book deal and the TV miniseries."

"Toni?"

"It was never meant to be. We're on totally different wavelengths. Besides, Brent Mather's family loves her and she needs strong family ties."

Catherine Blasedale examined the ring. It was over two carets. "Hank, this is stupid." She stopped, at a loss for words.

He leaned across her desk, his hands framing the perfume bottle. "Cathy, there hasn't been one day, one hour, in the last five months I haven't thought about you. That should be obvious from my phone bill. Let me lay it out in the most simple of sexist terms. I'm a man who loves you, wants to marry you, and father at least one child by you."

"Hank, I'm too old."

"We'll never know unless we get with the program. If nothing else, it will be fun trying."

"Stop that!"

He came around her desk. "Afraid to make a commitment?"

"No." She fought to regain her composure. "Besides, I'm older than you."

"True. Two years."

She was indignant. "Who told you?"

"Linda. But don't get on her case. I bribed her."

"With what? An expensive bottle of perfume?"

Sutherland laughed. "I told her she could be the matron of honor at the wedding."

"I suppose you have it all arranged," she groused.

"Not really. You get to pick the date and the best man."

She leaned back in her chair and grew thoughtful. "That's a no-brainer. Col. Williams."

"So stipulated. And the date?"

She looked at him, her eyes full of tears, and slowly, tentatively, her right hand reached out to him and stroked his cheek. It felt right. "I do love you and have from that first day when you came through the bar, not afraid to meet me on equal terms." She stood up. "Now, you probably expect me to get all mushy and fall into your arms, crying with happiness so you can kiss my tears away. Well, Hank Sutherland—" She stopped talking when he shut her office door.

"As a matter of fact, I do."

ACKNOWLEDGMENTS

In writing this novel, I wandered far from my field of expertise. Without the friendship, guidance, and sage advice of William P. Wood, I would have remained lost in a writer's limbo. Bill gave unsparingly of his time and knowledge as both a writer and former prosecutor and, for that, I am in his debt. Another friend, Jean Brown, also helped lead me through the mystifying world of lawyers with patience and unfailing good humor.

Although I had served on courts-martial, Col. Robert G. Gibson, Staff Judge Advocate at McClellan Air Force Base, Lt. Col. Hervey Hotchkiss, Military Judge, Western Circuit, and Maj. Gregory E. Pavlik, Trial Counsel, Western Circuit, gave me quick lessons in courts-martial and military law. Without their help, I would have been clueless. The legal mistakes in the story are mine and I apologize.

Lt. Col William D. Moore and Special Agent Paula Perez from the Air Force Office of Special Investigations were kind enough to introduce me to the inner, but vital, world of the OSI.

At the 16th Special Operations Wing, Hurlburt Field, I owe a debt of gratitude to Lt. Col. Mike Homan, Rick Gearing, and Bob Hudson, along with Capt. John Paradis from Public Affairs. They demonstrated once again that the 16th is ready to live up to its motto "Any Time, Any Place."

From the first time I saw the B-2 stealth bomber fly, I was intrigued with what it could do. But its actual capability is highly classified and the combat scenes portrayed in the story are figments of my imagination. But the professionalism of the men and women of the 509th Bomb Wing is absolutely real. More than anyone, Lt. Col. Jim Whitney proved how the B-2 redefines the bombing paradigm. And to Maj. Buzz Barrett—thanks for the simulator ride. I was impressed.

And special thanks to S. Sgt. Jeff Benton and the 509th Security Police, who confirmed that doing it "by the book" day after day, in all kinds of weather, takes a special call to duty.

To all, again, many thanks.